P9-CRP-936

SANDRA BROWN

THE SILKEN WEB

WARNER BOOKS

A Time Warner Company

WARNER BOOKS EDITION

Cover design and illustration by Andrew Newman

Warner Books, Inc.
1271 Avenue of the Americas
New York, NY 10020

Ⓦ A Time Warner Company

Printed in the United States of America

Originally published in hardcover by Warner Books.
First Printed in Paperback: October, 1993
Reissued: July, 1995

10 9

Dear Reader,

THE SILKEN WEB was one of my first expanded romances, which I wrote under the pseudonym Laura Jordan in 1981. At that point in my career, this book represented a challenge because up to that time I had only written shorter romances under stricter guidelines. I therefore became very involved with the characters, delving deeper into their pasts and personalities, and found their story compelling.

Unfortunately, within a month of the book's publication, the publisher suspended operation, and the initial distribution of THE SILKEN WEB was limited. Only my most faithful fans knew of it.

I'm so pleased that I now have an opportunity to share this special story with readers who have since acquired a taste for my work. The book has been slightly revised for today's market, but none of the romance and sensuality that characterized my earlier work has been sacrificed.

Given the opportunity to reenter Kathleen and Erik's world ten years later, I found their love story as engaging and powerful as ever.

I hope you'll enjoy reading THE SILKEN WEB. . . .

Sandra Brown
February 1992

Chapter One

꧁ ꧂

The children began shouting and shrieking as one discordant voice when the kite dipped and spun crazily before it started to nose dive.

"Look out!"

"Kathy, don't!"

"Pull up!"

"No, Kathy, no!"

Kathleen, her eyes never leaving the erratic kite, clamped her teeth over her bottom lip and pulled the string taut. She took several running steps backward, raising the kite string high over her head and dodging the sneakered feet of a dozen excited children.

"Let out on it a little, sweetheart."

The voice was deep, masculine and totally unexpected. Kathleen didn't have time to fully register it before she barreled into the man who'd materialized behind her.

Startled, she dropped her arm, and the kite went into a steep nose dive.

It smashed into an oak tree and was hopelessly impaled on a limb, its tail enmeshed in the leafy branches. The children scrambled through the branches of the tree, issuing orders to each other and suggesting possible solutions that were met with guffaws and aspersions.

The man directed his gaze to the scene, then turned his head and fixed his blue eyes upon Kathleen. "I apologize," he said humbly, placing his hand over his heart. The gleam in his eyes made Kathleen doubt his sincerity. "I thought I was helping."

"I could have handled it."

"I'm sure you could have, but I mistook you for one of the kids and it looked to me as though you needed some help."

"You thought I was one of the children!" With her hair tied back into pigtails, her heart-shaped face bereft of makeup and her navy shorts and white T-shirt with the summer camp's logo on the front, she could see where he *might* make that mistake.

"I'm Kathleen Haley, one of the camp directors." He gave her a once-over that said she wasn't dressed for the part. "I double as a counselor," she added, extending her right hand.

The blond giant with the thick mustache shook hands with her.

"My name is Erik Gudjonsen, spelled G-u-d-j-o-n-s-e-n, but pronounced Good-johnson."

"Am I supposed to recognize your name, Mr. Gudjonsen?"

"I'm the videographer who'll be shooting the documentary for UBC. Didn't the Harrisons tell you that I'd be coming?"

If they had it had slipped her mind. "They didn't say it would be today."

The Mountain View Summer Encampment for Orphans was to be featured on the nationally televised magazine show *People*. In an attempt to generate public awareness of the camp, and thereby contributions, Kathleen had approached a network producer with her story idea. After several letters and lengthy telephone calls to New York, she had sold the producer on it. She'd been told that a photographer would be assigned to videotape the activities of the children sometime during one of the summer sessions.

She hadn't given any thought to the videographer, nor what he would be like. Weren't all photographers a bit myopic? Didn't most wear baggy trousers and have light meters like identification badges dangling from cords around their necks? Her ideas on the profession in general had certainly never conjured up a picture that in any way resembled Erik Gudjonsen.

His appearance was as Nordic as his name. He had inherited a body from his fiercest ancestors. Viking blood must surely course through that tall, muscular body that radiated strength and vitality. Even standing still in a deceptively casual pose, he seemed capable of great power.

Erik Gudjonsen's hair shone like a golden helmet in the sun. It was thick, luxurious, falling around his aristocratic head in casual disarray. His darker mustache added to the sensuality of his wide mouth. Strong white teeth glistened from beneath the brush of the thick mustache and contrasted handsomely with the tan, weather-roughened face.

His jeans were well worn and tight. They rode low on his slender hips and hugged the muscles of his thighs like a glove. The chambray shirt fit almost as snugly. The sleeves had been rolled back to reveal sinewy arms. The blue fabric was stretched tightly over a broad chest that was matted with tawny hair. It was difficult not to stare at the deep V that his unbuttoned shirt revealed. His hands were long, with tapering fingers that denoted strength and yet the sensitivity required to operate a complex videotape camera.

For some inexplicable reason, Kathleen felt a strange constriction in her chest when her eyes traced the corded column of his neck, the proud, somewhat stubborn chin, sensual mouth and slender nose, up to the blue eyes.

And when her green eyes clashed with the full impact of his, she had a sinking feeling in the lower part of her body that was both delightful and disturbing.

"You look better suited to hard news stories."

He shrugged noncommittally. "I go where I'm assigned."

"Well, I hope you're not looking for an angle on us because you'll be disappointed. We're strictly on the up and up."

"I never said otherwise. Why the third degree? Do you mistrust newsmen?" Leaning down, his mustache only partially concealing a smile, he whispered, "Or is it men in general?"

In a voice as cool as her expression, she said, "Go up the hill and take the left fork. Follow it until you drive through the main gate. The building immediately inside and to your right is the office. You'll find either Edna or B. J. there."

"Thank you." Still smirking, he sauntered in the direction of his parked Blazer.

Kathleen couldn't determine a logical reason for her irritability the rest of the afternoon, though she handled the energetic children with her usual aplomb. Of all the counselors, they adored Kathy, as they called her, the most. It was a reciprocal affection.

Today, for some reason, ever since meeting Erik Gudjonsen, she was irascible and anxious for the sun to move closer to the horizon. Then, at five o'clock, everyone would migrate toward cabins for a rest hour before dinner in the large, noisy dining hall.

Now, as the children cavorted in the roped-off section of the Kings River that threaded its way through the Ozark Mountains of northwestern Arkansas, Kathleen basked in the sunshine as she sat on the shore. She was ever watchful of the campers, but for a few moments she could revel in relative peace while they were occupied with their own antics in the clear water.

She sighed deeply and closed her eyes for a moment against the glare of the sunlight on the water. She loved this place. Each summer, it was as much a sabbatical for her as it was helpful to her friends, the Harrisons, for her to serve as a counselor at the camp.

For sixty days, Kathleen Haley, fashion buyer for Mason's Department Store in Atlanta, ceased to exist. She retreated from the frantic pace she lived the other ten months of the year and renewed herself with the mountain air, regular meals, early hours and exhausting exercise. Yet despite the rigorous schedule, the camp work was restful, for her mind as much as her body.

Few career girls would give up their valuable time to serve as a camp counselor, but to Kathleen it was a labor of love. She knew firsthand the desperation of these children as they sought love and attention. If she could give back only a particle of the affection she had found here years ago, her time and efforts were more than worth it.

"Hey, Kathy, Robby is going past the rope."

She opened her eyes to see a self-righteous tattler pointing an accusing finger at the boy breaking the stringent rule.

"Robby!" Kathleen called. When the offender's head broke the surface, she gave him a threatening stare. It was enough to make him dive back under the boundary and poke up to a standing position in the shoulder-high water. To show him she meant business, she warned, "Once more outside the rope and your swimming days are over. Do you understand?"

"Yes, Kathy," he mumbled, and hung his head.

She smiled secretly, knowing that her disapproval was usually enough punishment to keep even the most contrary of the children in line. "Why don't you practice that handstand you were trying to do the other day? See how long you can stay under."

His eyes brightened immediately, knowing he was back in favor. "Okay! Watch me!"

"I will." She waved at him from the bank and he set about to show her his trick.

"Jaimie, thank you for calling my attention to Robby, but it's really not polite to tattle. Okay?"

The thin boy with dark hair and eyes looked slightly crestfallen, but he smiled timidly and said, "Yes, ma'am."

Each summer, there was one child who touched her deeper than any other. This summer, it was Jaimie. He was smaller than the others, awkward, introverted. Sports didn't come easily to him and he was usually the last one chosen when they divided into teams. He was quiet, serious and shy. But he was the most avid reader and the most talented artist of the group. His dark liquid eyes had melted Kathleen's heart the first day of camp, and though she tried not to show partiality, she had an undeniable soft spot for Jaimie.

She stood up and walked to the water line. Sitting down on the damp sand, she pulled off her tennis shoes and socks and put her feet in the cool stream. Cupping a handful of water, she trickled it over her tired leg muscles. An unwelcoming image of Erik Gudjonsen came to mind.

At twenty-five years old, Kathleen had dated many men, had fancied herself in love with a few of them, but the last thing she wanted was close contact with a man. Wasn't that what she was running away from?

A shrieking laugh brought her back to the present and she hastily checked her wristwatch. Ten till five!

She blew the silver whistle that was suspended around her neck on a blue ribbon. With whining protests, the children trooped up the pebbly shoal and slipped on their tennis shoes. They'd wear their swimsuits back to the cabins, letting the sun dry them during the walk. After each picked up his or her own belongings, they were ready to leave. While they grumblingly obeyed her dictates, Kathleen put her own shoes back on and then formed the group into a reasonably straight line for the hike up the hill.

She started a song with an infinite number of verses as they tramped up the steep incline. Kathleen marveled again at how much she loved this countryside. The red gravel road that led up to Mountain View Encampment was hot and dusty, but no pavement would ever spoil its natural state. The camp administrators had wisely left the environs as wild as practicality would allow. For children who lived in orphanages in large cities, this was their only exposure to any landscape that wasn't crowded with buildings and spanned with concrete.

All seasons were spectacular in the Ozarks, but since the spring had been an unusually rainy one, this summer the mountains were green with oak, sycamore, elm and pine. Grapevines draped the trees, and the ground was carpeted with lush undergrowth.

The Kings River was running swift and full. In the shallows, the water was so clear and pure that one could count the rocks that lined the riverbed.

Kathleen loved it all. She loved the mountains, the trees and the people who lived in this rural setting, farming or ranching in pastoral simplicity.

How vastly different were their lives compared to hers in Atlanta, where she knew constant stress and unrelenting pressure. As fashion buyer for a major department store, she must continually be making decisions. She bought merchandise for several departments, including young adults, women's sportswear, better dresses, coats, and "after-fives" and formals.

But even with all the headaches that came with it, she loved her job. That was why her friends and associates were astounded when she had resigned her position at the beginning of the summer.

"Kathy, make Allison stop tripping me. She's doing it on purpose," said the bespeckled Gracie with a pout.

Kathleen came back to the present with a jolt and automatically said, "Allison, how would you like for me to trip you? Cut it out."

"She did it to me first," argued Allison.

"Then why don't you be my example-setter and show the others how to turn the other cheek?"

"Okay."

The sun beat down on Kathleen's back, and as the rough cedar gate of Mountain View came into sight, she used her T-shirt to blot a bead of sweat that rolled down between her breasts.

The campers were fractious and in need of the allotted rest time. They divided by sexes and trudged listlessly toward their dormitories.

"Everyone get showered before the supper bell. I'll see

you then. Les, keep your hands to yourself and leave Todd alone.'' Kathleen saw them safely into the cabins and then turned toward the group of buildings assigned to counselors. Her position on the board earned her a private cabin. As she went through the screen door, she flipped on the switch of the overhead fan.

Drained of energy, she fell onto her back across the bunk and sprawled like a rag doll. Forcing herself to breathe slowly, she soon felt the heat and tension ebbing out of her body. Her eyes closed, and involuntarily, her thoughts returned to her hasty departure from Atlanta.

Mr. Mason, disconcerted and anxious over her sudden resignation, had asked for a reason. Her answer to his inquiry wasn't truthful. She didn't tell him that she could no longer work with David Ross

David was the accountant for Mason's, and handled all the department store's bookkeeping, from the purchase of light bulbs to the enormous payroll. He was demanding of his subordinates, but affable and likeable when outside the office. Kathleen had enjoyed their shared coffee breaks and the few occasions when they had gone to lunch together, as often as not in a group of department executives.

Soon the lunches had become more private, the "chance meetings" more frequent and the casual touches more lingering. At first Kathleen thought his increasing interest was her imagination, but it became apparent that he was serious, and she couldn't mistake the hungry look in his eyes each time they fell on her.

Overnight, she cooled her attitude toward him and began to rebuff his covert passes. David Ross was very intelligent, very good looking and very married. He had three children and an English sheepdog who lived with him and his attractive wife in the suburbs of Atlanta.

Kathleen rolled over onto her stomach on the narrow bed and buried her face in the pillows as she recalled her last encounter with David.

It had been the end of a long, tiring day, and Kathleen was

already exhausted. She had been opening boxes of merchandise that had just arrived, unloading it and checking it against her order form. The store had been closed for an hour and nearly all the employees had gone home.

David came into her office and shut the door behind him. He smiled engagingly and crossed to the desk, leaning on his widespread hands and lowering his head close to hers.

"How about dinner?" His voice was as efficient and precise as his account books.

She smiled. "Not tonight. It's been one of *those* days, and I'm tired. I'm going to go home, take a bath and go directly to bed."

"You have to eat sometime, somewhere," he reasoned.

"I think I have one slice of bologna in the fridge."

"That doesn't sound too appetizing." He grimaced comically.

She laughed brightly, almost too spontaneously. "Well, that's what I'm having for dinner tonight."

She took her purse out of her desk drawer, stood up and reached for her blazer hanging on a halltree near the door. Before she could pull it down, David stilled her hand. He turned her around to face him, eased her purse out of her hand, placed it on the desk and put his hands on her shoulders.

"The fact that you're tired isn't the real reason you won't go out with me, is it?"

She met his eyes levelly. "No."

He drew a heavy sigh. "I thought as much." His fingers brushed her cheek caressingly, but she stood unaffected and stoic. "Kathleen, it's no secret that I'm attracted to you. More than attracted. Why won't you at least go to dinner with me?"

"You know why, David. That's no secret either. You're married."

"Not happily."

"I'm sorry, but that's none of my concern."

"Kathleen," he groaned, and pulled her closer. She shrugged away from him, but couldn't escape his firm hands.

Deciding to try another tack, he asked, "If I weren't married, would you be interested in seeing me?"

"The point is moot. You—"

"I know, I know. But if I *weren't* married, would you be interested?"

His eyes compelled her to answer, and as always, Kathleen was harmfully honest. "You're an attractive man, David. If, *if* you weren't married, yes, I would want to see you—"

Before she could finish, she was crushed to him in a desperate embrace. His arms wrapped around her like closing pincers and his head lowered to capture her mouth under the bruising pressure of his.

He knew how to kiss. For one brief moment, Kathleen thrilled to the sheer masculinity of him, to the fervent lips moving over hers, persuading them to open. She didn't consciously surrender, but suddenly his tongue was inside her mouth, greedy and intrusive. His hand slid down her spine onto her hips and he drew her tighter.

Frantically, she began pushing him away. Her fists made several futile attempts at pounding on his back. Then she flattened her palms against his shoulders and pushed with all her strength, kicking at his shins at the same time until he released her.

His eyes were wild with lust and his chest heaved with exertion. He took one step toward her, but the rigid lines on her resolute face and the green ice of her brilliant eyes halted him. He knew he had gone too far.

"Stay away from me," she gasped in a strangled voice. "If you ever touch me again, I'll file a formal complaint of sexual harassment."

"Crap. Even if you had the guts to carry it that far, who'd believe you? Dozens of people have seen us together. You've put out signals. I've acted on them. It's as simple as that."

"You're what's simple if you can't distinguish between friendship and a come-on!" she said angrily. "We're coworkers. That's all."

"For the time being."

"Forever, Mr. Ross."

He made a scoffing sound as he straightened his clothing. "We'll see."

He left, but Kathleen knew that she had merely stalled him. He was probably planning his next course of attack. She sat down at her desk and covered her face with her hands. Now what?

Damn him, he was right—she wouldn't file charges of sexual harassment. She could probably make them stick, but she didn't want to invest the time and energy it would require to see it through. Even if she won, she would still be working at Mason's, and recently she had come to feel that the formal department store wasn't providing her with enough challenge. It was staid. She wanted to work in an environment where the attitude toward fashion was progressive and innovative.

David Ross was the catalyst she had needed to make the difficult decision of leaving the safe and familiar for the unknown.

At least that's what she had told herself. What she refused to acknowledge was that rather than confronting a problem, she had run away from it. Retreat had been her strategy since the loss of her parents. Some things were so bad that one's only choice for coping was to flee.

Inexplicably, Erik Gudjonsen's face was suddenly emblazoned on the backs of her eyelids. His self-assured expression was all too reminiscent of David Ross's. What was it with men even remotely good looking? Was a handsome face supposed to allow them special privileges? Did they think all women were ready to fall into bed with them? To surrender to practiced hands and lips? To . . .

She ignored the sudden acceleration of her pulse and the tingling feeling that prickled the erogenous parts of her body. For a fleeting instant, she wondered what it felt like to be kissed by a man with a mustache.

To hell with that! Kathleen told herself emphatically, and swung her legs over the side of the bunk and stamped into the bathroom.

She showered in tepid water with her special moisturizing soap and, after toweling off, laved herself with an after-bath splash. Her heavy hair was released from the restrictive rubber bands and brushed vigorously. She thought of leaving it to hang free, but decided against it. Even after the sun dipped behind the mountains, the evenings could still be warm. She gathered her hair into a ponytail at the nape of her neck and tied a navy-blue ribbon around it. The wisps that framed her face were damp from her shower and curled beguilingly against her dewy skin.

She didn't wear much makeup while at the camp. A light sprinkling of freckles across her nose and high cheekbones only accented her apricot-tanned skin and called attention to the red highlights in her auburn hair. She smoothed a blushing gel onto the hollows under her cheekbones, gouged out a scoop of peach-flavored lip gloss with the tip of her little finger and applied it to her lips. After whisking her mascara wand along the tips of long black lashes, she was finished.

Kathleen slipped into lacy bikini panties, which was the one feminine luxury she allowed herself during the summer, and the uniform pair of navy shorts. However, for dinner she usually replaced the camp T-shirt with a blouse. What I'd give for an evening to really dress up, Kathleen thought wistfully as she slipped on clean white tennis socks and sneakers.

She crossed the compound in the direction of the mess hall just as the dinner bell sounded. Meals were the one thing the children were eager to line up for, and she joined them at the door.

"Hey, Kathy," called one of the other counselors. Mike Simpson was a brawny college boy majoring in physical education at the University of Arkansas. His size belied his easygoing manner and gentle patience with the kids. He coached them in the more vigorous sports, like soccer, softball and volleyball.

"Hi, Mike," Kathleen shouted over the loud racket the children made while they stood in squirming lines waiting to invade the cafeteria.

"The Harrisons asked that you join them in their office before dinner. They're waiting for you."

"Okay, thanks," Kathleen flung over her shoulder as she descended the steps.

Behind her, she heard Mike say, "Very funny. Which one of you wise guys pinched me? Huh?" His question was met with shrill laughter.

She was still smiling as she pushed open the door to the air-conditioned building that housed the administrative offices of Mountain View.

"Kathleen, is that you?" Edna Harrison called out to her as she shut the door behind her.

"Yes," Kathleen answered. She crossed the outer office toward the Harrisons' private living quarters.

"Come in, dear. We've been waiting for you."

By now, Kathleen was standing framed in the doorway and she came face-to-face with Erik Gudjonsen. He stood up from his seat on the early-American sofa. His back was to the Harrisons.

"Kathleen Haley, meet Erik Gudjonsen," Edna said. "He's the photographer from UBC. Erik, Kathleen is one of our board members. We simply couldn't run the camp without her."

"Oh, I've met Ms. Haley. We bumped into each other this afternoon."

Chapter Two

꙰꙰

Kathleen wished she didn't lack the nerve to slap his smug face. For the benefit of her friends, she said politely, "Hello again, Mr. Gudjonsen."

"Come in and sit down, Kathleen," B. J. said. "Mr. Gudjonsen was asking some questions about Mountain View, and I told him you were the one who could best explain the concept of the camp, since you had lived it. We'll go to dinner shortly."

Because Edna and B. J. Harrison were seated in the only two easy chairs in the room, Kathleen had no choice but to sit beside Erik on the sofa. Self-consciously, she tugged on the legs of her shorts as she sat down.

"How was your day, Edna, B. J.?" she asked.

The couple was as dear to her as parents. In their early sixties, they were still robust and healthy. The love and concern they showed the orphans who came to their camp each summer was inspiring.

Kathleen always thought of the Harrisons as a unit, and oddly enough, they resembled each other. Both were short and plump. While Edna's eyes were warm brown and her husband's gray, they both reflected open friendliness. They

14

walked with the same purposeful stride. Their gestures when they talked were almost identical.

Kathleen doubted that either of them had ever had an uncharitable thought about even the most unscrupulous character. They found goodness in everyone and everything. As she thought on it now, Kathleen realized that the similarities that had developed between them weren't so surprising since they had been married for more than forty years.

"We had a leaky pipe in one of the cabins and I tinkered with that today," B. J. was saying. "I think I saved a plumber's fee. We'll know in a day or so." He chuckled.

"Thank you, dear." Edna patted his knee. "Tomorrow you can work on that ornery air conditioner."

"You see, Erik?" B. J. opened his hands in a gesture of helplessness. "They're never satisfied."

"Oh, you!" Edna exclaimed softly, shoving her husband's shoulder lovingly. She turned her attention back to the photographer, who was enjoying the older couple's display of affection. "Erik, Kathleen first came to our camp when she was fourteen. I don't want to embarrass you, Kathleen, but I'm sure Erik would like to hear your story." Her kind eyes were anxious, but the smile on the young woman's face reassured her.

"No. I'm never reluctant to talk about Mountain View." Kathleen forced herself to face Erik. Sitting so close beside him on the small sofa made her uncomfortably aware of him. His raw masculinity was a tangible quality that touched her and left behind prickly sensations.

"My parents were killed in a boating accident when I was thirteen. They had no living relatives, and I had no brothers or sisters. Friends in our church placed me in an orphanage in Atlanta. It was well run and reputed as one of the best in the country. But having lived in a family environment as an only child, I found it difficult to adjust. My grade average dropped significantly. I became belligerent. In short, I was a brat."

B. J. laughed, but Edna shot him a reproving look and it subsided.

"The next summer, the orphanage sent me here. I had a terrible attitude toward the idea, as I had about anything at that time. I thought I had been dealt with unjustly by everyone, by God. But that summer, the whole course of my life changed."

Her voice became charged with emotion and she smiled tremulously at the Harrisons. "B. J. and Edna refused to let me destroy my life with bitterness and hatred. They taught me how to love again by loving me when I was most unlovable. I started acting like a human being again and not a wounded animal. I owe them a debt of gratitude that I can never repay."

"You've repaid us a thousand times over, Kathleen." Edna turned her tear-laden eyes to Erik. "You see, Mr. Gudjonsen, Kathleen came back to our camp each summer until she grew too old. Then, during her college years, we asked her to serve as a counselor. Since she knows the pain and disillusionment most of our campers harbor, she is better able to relate to them than anyone. We've seen her work miracles with even the most maladjusted children. When a position on the Board of Directors came open, we offered it to Kathleen. She was reluctant to accept it, but we insisted. No one has been disappointed. Last year she singlehandedly raised enough money to air condition the mess hall and install two basketball goals."

Kathleen blushed under what she considered unearned praise. Her discomfort was heightened when she lifted her eyes and saw that Erik was staring at her.

Aware of her embarrassment, he turned his attention to his hosts. "I want to hear more about your success here, but right now I'm starving. May we continue our conversation in the dining room?"

"A boy after my own heart!" B. J. exclaimed jovially as he stood up, slapping his palms against his thighs.

"Don't count on being able to conduct a conversation over dinner, Erik," Edna cautioned. Using his first name came quite easily. "Our dining room isn't exactly conducive to serious debate."

He laughed as he casually took Kathleen's arm and steered her through the outer office to the front door. "It doesn't matter. I want to capture the spirit of the camp, anyway."

"Oh, well, if it's spirit you're after, you're at the right place." B. J. laughed.

"Would it be against the rules to take my camera in there?" Erik asked.

"It wouldn't matter to us," Edna said. "You're making the rules for as long as you're here."

"Thank you, Mrs. Harrison."

"Edna," she corrected.

The smile he gave her could have graced the cover of *GQ*. "Edna. I'll just run to my car and join you in a minute. Save me a place in line, B. J."

"Sure thing. Kathleen, why don't you go along with Erik and make sure he doesn't get lost."

She started to object, but what could she say that wouldn't sound ungracious? For some reason, she was hesitant to be alone with him. Perhaps his easy charm was disturbingly reminiscent of David Ross's. Or maybe, as Erik himself had suggested, she was suspicious of journalists. Mountain View's program had no hidden agendas, and, because the camp was so dear to her, she would naturally resent anyone poking around looking for scandal where none existed.

"You two hurry up now, or all the food will be gone. We won't let anyone go back for seconds until you have gone through the line," Edna said.

The older couple strolled off arm in arm in the direction of the dining hall. "Where is your car?" Kathleen asked.

"Parked by my cabin."

She turned around and struck off on the path through the trees that led to the cabins reserved for visitors.

It wasn't far, but by the time they reached his parked Blazer, she was winded. Probably because she had covered the distance in record time. He seemed to know that she was uncomfortable with him. As he lowered the tailgate, she thought she detected a dimple partially hidden by his mustache.

He opened a black plastic box and removed a videotape cartridge. He then loaded it into the video camera. Kathleen had never seen one of the complicated cameras up close, and in spite of herself, she was intrigued.

"Can you carry that?" Nodding his head, he indicated a long tubular carrying case.

"Sure," she said, reaching in. Her arm was nearly wrenched from its socket when she tried to lift it. She hadn't expected it to be so heavy.

"What's in here?"

"A tripod."

"It weighs a ton," she complained.

"Yeah, I know. That's why I asked you to carry it." He winked. "Besides, no one but me touches my camera."

Deftly, he raised the tailgate with one hand and they started back toward the compound. They didn't speak. Kathleen doubted she could. The weight of the tripod case had her puffing by the time they reached the dining hall.

Gallantly, Erik held the door for her and she gave him a withering glare as she stumbled past him and went inside. The dull roar of two hundred children's voices greeted them.

"Where can I stick this?" he asked as he surveyed the room.

"That's a loaded question, Mr. Gudjonsen," she muttered under her breath.

"Tsk-tsk, Ms. Haley."

"There you are." Edna interrupted Kathleen's well-chosen comeback by bustling up to them. "Erik, why don't you put your equipment on the dais. No one will bother it there. Hurry up and get your food and join us at the far table. It's marginally quieter over there."

Erik retrieved the case from Kathleen and placed it and his camera where Edna had indicated.

"Shall we?" Erik enthused, rubbing his hands together and nodding toward the cafeteria line.

"By all means," Kathleen said coolly. "I think you'll be surprised by the food. It's better than most home cooking."

"Right now, anything sounds good. I haven't eaten today."

"Watching your figure?" she asked snidely, for if anyone didn't need to worry about his shape, it was Erik Gudjonsen.

His eyes twinkled as he looked down at her. "No. It's a helluva lot more fun to watch yours."

She bit her lip to keep from saying what she thought of his sexist comment. She was obliged to introduce him to the ladies who ran the kitchen for Mountain View and managed to provide the campers and staff with three delicious meals a day. Most of them were old enough to be Erik's mother, but they simpered and basked under his inordinate commendation of the meal.

Their plates were heaped with pot roast and vegetables as they passed down the line. Kathleen was reaching for a glass of mint-sprigged iced tea when Erik caught her hand and sniffed the air.

"Do you smell peaches?"

Peaches? Her lip gloss? She fought her impulse to lick her lips nervously. His eyes raked her face, as if trying to detect something elusive.

"Peaches?" she asked innocently. "Oh, there are your peaches. Peach cobbler for dessert," she said, relieved.

Turning back to him triumphantly, she was startled to find that he wasn't so ready to accept her explanation. His warm stare on her face was alarming, and she tugged on her hand several times before he released it.

"Good. I love peaches," he said. Kathleen was uneasy at the tone of his voice, for in some way it held a threat to her.

They joined the other counselors and the Harrisons at a separate table off-limits to the children. Introductions were made all around, and Erik apologized in advance if he couldn't remember everyone's name for the first few days.

He ate heartily, but courteously answered any questions directed to him. Kathleen thought the other female counselors sickeningly attentive, but Erik treated them all, no matter how homely or pretty, in a friendly manner.

A real ladies' man, she thought snidely.

"Tell us about yourself, Erik," B. J. said around a mouthful of potatoes.

Erik shrugged modestly. "There's really not much to tell."

"Now, Erik, we all know that you're well known in your field. Weren't you in Asia?" Edna asked.

"Yes," he answered. "I've had some good assignments. I was in Saudi Arabia during Desert Storm."

"Have you ever been in danger?" asked one of the younger girl counselors breathlessly.

He smiled. "A few times. Usually, I shoot just run-of-the-mill stuff."

Try as they did, no one could get him to recount any tale of valiant struggle, though they were sure there had been some. Before he was sent to the camp, Edna had been told by the network officials that Erik Gudjonsen was one of their most accomplished photographers, as well as one who could add a human-interest touch to any story, no matter how mundane or extraordinary.

When he had finished eating, Erik stood up and excused himself. "I'd better do some shooting before the natives get too restless," he said, indicating the children.

"Good idea," B. J. agreed. "Anything we can do to help?"

"No, just act normally. I really hope I don't attract the kids' attention. I want them to behave just as they are now. I could use the able assistance of my key grip here, though."

Kathleen didn't realize he was referring to her until a silence fell on the group. She looked up at him. *"Me?"* she asked in astonishment.

"If you don't mind. Now that you're familiar with the equipment."

"But I only—"

"Please, Kathleen, time is of the essence," he cut in.

She glanced around at the expectant faces and realized she had no choice but to get up and follow him.

"What are you trying to pull?" she asked out of the corner of her mouth as they crossed the large room. "I'm not at all familiar with the equipment."

"No, but I need you anyway."

"Why?"

They had reached the small dais that B. J. used whenever

he had to make important announcements to the whole group. Erik turned on the camera, slung it upon his right shoulder and placed his eye to the viewfinder. Kathleen noticed that he didn't shut his left eye. That must be hard to do, she thought objectively. How could he focus his vision?

"Just stand still a minute," he said as he turned toward her.

She was appalled when he placed the lens of the camera to within inches of her breasts and began turning the awesome dials that ringed the lens.

"What—" She jumped back in shock.

"Just stand still, I said." He reached out with his spare hand and drew her close again.

"Would you get that thing away from me? I know you think you're very funny, but I don't."

He took his eye away from the viewfinder and fixed her with an exasperated expression. "I'm only using your white blouse for my color balance."

"Exactly what does that mean?" She was partially pacified, but still suspicious.

"It means," he said with the slow, measured tone one would use on a simpleton, "that I have a meter built into the camera. Each time I shoot a scene, I have to check my lighting and balance the color level against something solid white. I promise you my motives for using your blouse are honorable."

"Why didn't you use a tablecloth?"

One corner of his mouth tilted into a sardonic grin. "I only promised that I was honorable. I'm not stupid."

Kathleen shoved past him and strode back to the table. When she had flopped into her chair, B. J. turned to her and asked, "Everything all right? Is Erik set to shoot?"

"I think so," she mumbled, and didn't add that Mr. Gudjonsen's actions were no bloody concern of hers!

For the next half-hour, she chatted with the other members of the staff and studiously kept her eyes off Erik, who managed, despite his size, to remain almost invisible as he moved among the tables recording the antics of the children as they launched into a series of organized games. When he finished, he whistled loudly to get everyone's attention. His voice boomed out across the room. "My name is Erik. Would any of you like to be on television?"

The response was deafening. Kathleen knew a smug satis- faction when he was stampeded by clamoring children all demanding equal time to cavort idiotically before the camera. As he did everything, he handled the mob with aplomb.

For another half-hour, he let the children ham in front of him. When he called it quits, he safely returned his camera to the dais and strolled to the staff table, wiping a perspiring forehead with his sleeve.

"You are either a saint or a glutton for punishment." Edna laughed. "Why would you put yourself through such torture?"

"I've learned that there is nothing more intimidating than the lens of a camera. Even the most gregarious become tongue-tied and inhibited in front of it. So, I thought I'd let them act as foolish as they wanted to, let some of the mystique wear off. Tomorrow night, I'll show them the tape on the monitor. Hopefully, the magic will have worn off and they'll start ignoring me. That's the only way I'll get candid reac- tions."

"You missed your calling, my boy," B. J. said. "You should have been a child psychologist."

The night bell sounded and the children began to grumble objections and pleas for a fifteen-minute extension. As they knew it would be, it was denied, and they didn't need much persuasion to troop off to their cabins.

Each counselor, except Kathleen, who again was saved by her seniority, was responsible for checking to see that every- one was properly tucked in. Goodnights were called across the compound, and gradually the crowd dwindled down to the Harrisons, Kathleen and Erik.

"Erik, we start early," Edna warned. "Breakfast is at seven-thirty."

"I'll be here. Do you think one of the ladies in the kitchen would brew me a thermos of coffee to take along tomorrow?"

"Sure," B. J. said. "How do you like it?"

His white teeth flashed in the darkness. "Black as pitch and hotter than hell."

B. J. slapped him on the shoulders and laughed. "I'm beginning to like you better and better, my boy. Come on, honey, I'm tired."

Edna rose. "Kathleen, I'm assigning you to Erik, since you know more about the camp than anyone. He'll stay with your group for the next few days and observe. Any problems with that?"

An awkward silence ensued, with only the cicadas in the trees brave enough to break it. Kathleen wasn't thrilled with the idea of being observed by either the camera or the photographer.

"Kathleen?" Edna's worried voice penetrated the darkness.

"No, there are no problems. I was only trying to think of . . . uh . . . of interesting things we could do."

"I've given that some thought," Erik said. "I've typed up a very loose script. It's in the car. Walk back with me and I'll give it to you tonight. We can talk about the feasibility of my ideas in the morning."

"That's a good idea," B. J. said. "Now, let us old folks go to bed. Edna?"

"Okay. Goodnight."

"Goodnight," Kathleen and Erik said in unison.

The couple was swallowed up by the blackness that was almost absolute. Here, on the mountaintop, there was nothing to interfere with the night. No city lights robbed the darkness of its glory or the sky of its truly infinite scope. It was blanketed with stars that one forgot were there when they were obscured by man-made light.

Kathleen was seething inside, but she refused to let her anger show and give Erik Gudjonsen the pleasure of knowing he had upset her. She walked by his side, surefooted in the darkness, and stifled a gratified giggle when she heard his muffled curse as he bumped his head on a low limb.

He was carrying both the camera and the tripod case, but

she noticed that his breathing remained normal. Apparently, he was accustomed to that particular exertion. Just wait until she put some of her plans into action! That would show quick enough who was hale and hearty.

"Let me open the car door so we'll have some light," he said as he opened the passenger side of the Blazer. "I think that script is back here," he said, going to the rear of the truck and lowering the tailgate. He replaced his camera in its padded case with the care of a mother toward her infant.

He straightened up and faced Kathleen. Before she realized his intention, he splayed his hands on her back and pulled her close. Ducking his head, he let his tongue lightly trace her lower lip. Then he kissed her hard and quick.

She was aghast. "Just what the hell do you think you're doing?"

"That much should be obvious."

"I'm not amused or interested, Mr. Gudjonsen. And if this video didn't mean so much to the camp, I'd send you packing. As it is, I'm forced to cooperate."

"Just what I thought. Peaches!"

"Where is that damned script?"

"There isn't one. I lied about that just to get you alone in the dark woods."

Kathleen turned her back on him and stalked away.

Like a taunting challenge—or a sweet promise—he called to her, "I'll see you first thing in the morning, Kathleen."

Chapter Three

✻ ✻

The beginning of the next day was inauspicious. Kathleen hadn't slept well, and her cranky disposition didn't improve when she arrived at breakfast to find Erik already there. He was smiling, teasing the children, flirting with the counselors and looking rested and exuberant.

Normally, she indulged in the homemade biscuits that were lighter than air and melted in the mouth, though she wasn't a regular breakfast eater. This morning, the biscuits could have been chalk, which she chewed mechanically and washed down with lightly creamed coffee. The aroma of freshly grilled bacon and scrambled eggs wasn't at all appetizing. It was as if overnight her whole world had gone sour. It was Erik Gudjonsen's fault, and she resented him for it. She had resigned from her job to escape the unsolicited attention of a man with an inflated ego. She now thought David Ross an amateur compared with the videographer.

Only in the secret parts of her mind would she admit how his kiss had affected her. It had been quick, almost playful, but effective. When she felt the tip of his tongue against her lips, a spear of pleasure had penetrated her breasts and pierced downward to her very center, leaving a wound like a hollow emptiness.

Kathleen admitted now, as she covertly watched him from beneath the screen of her black lashes, that she had played right into his hands. Everything she had done since meeting him had been a defensive reaction to his masculine forcefulness. Obviously it amused him to goad her.

Resolving not to let him provoke her, Kathleen made plans for the coming day. She was a capable, independent woman, and by the end of this day, he'd know it. As for her attitude toward him, she would treat him with cool politeness, professionalism, and meet his insinuating bantering with condescending tolerance.

Determinedly, she stood up, checked her wristwatch and then imperiously blew the whistle around her neck. "All of you in Group Four, meet outside on the steps. Pronto." She was proud of the strong confidence in her voice, and carried her head high when she returned her tray to the large service window leading into the kitchen.

As she sailed out the door and strode toward her group, Erik turned to face her. He stood ramrod-straight and saluted briskly, making all the children laugh.

"Reporting for duty, Sergeant."

Swallowing her vituperative comeback, she said graciously, "Have you got everything you need?"

"Yes, I'm ready," he said solemnly.

That's what you think, Kathleen thought to herself. "All right," she said aloud. "Let's go."

She had a full schedule of exhausting activities. Hoping to put Mr. Gudjonsen in his place, she was disgruntled to find that he did everything well, indeed excelled in everything. He took to the steep, rocky trail up the mountain like a goat, and all the while carrying his camera on his shoulder, ready to use it at an instant's notice. How could he do that? she asked herself in exasperation when they had reached the turnaround point of their nature hike. She collapsed on a grassy area to rest.

Meanwhile, Erik was taping the children as they uncapped their canteens and took great gulps of water, emptied gravel out of their sneakers or ventured off into the woods seeking new discoveries.

Kathleen's eyes were closed as she leaned against a tree trunk. They flew open when she felt Erik's large body plop down beside her.

"Whew!" He expelled his breath in a long sigh as he blotted his forehead with a handkerchief. "How do you do this every day?"

"You're tired?" she asked with a trace of incredulity.

"Sure. Aren't you? If I did this kind of thing all the time, I'd be dead within a week."

He smiled and she answered with a soft laugh. Was that one small point on her side of the scoreboard?

After they had returned to the compound and eaten a hasty lunch, they traipsed to the archery grounds for target practice. The children pressed Erik to try his hand with the bow. His aim was far better than Kathleen's, and the children clustered around him in awe as he repeatedly zinged the arrows into the heart of the targets. Then his ever-present camera was slung back onto his shoulder and he taped the children's efforts as Kathleen coached them.

By the middle of the afternoon, she had put down some of her bitterness and afforded Erik a grudging respect. He never forgot his job. The camera was like an extension of his arm and he guarded it constantly. But his rapport with the children surprised her. He was patient, answered their multitudinous questions, joked, teased, admonished and placated with equal aptitude.

When she blew the whistle for swimming, they shouted excitedly and dashed for the river. As she ran to keep up with them, Kathleen glanced over her shoulder to see Erik walking back toward the compound. She shrugged off her faint disappointment and followed the campers to the river.

She had worn a bikini, though a conservative one, under her shorts and T-shirt. She stripped these off unselfconsciously and ventured out into the swift current. It didn't take

long for the children to include her in their horseplay, and
soon she was struggling to keep her head above the water as
they tried to dunk her.

Finally, laughing and shrieking, they heeded her pleas for
mercy and released her. She came up out of the water, pushing
the clinging hair off her face.

That was when she saw Erik standing on the shore, stripped
down to swimming trunks but with his camera up to his
eye and aimed directly at her. She hesitated, then smiled
tentatively before turning away to commission the kids not to
get too rambunctious.

She walked up the shoal and wrung the water out of her
hair. "I thought you had called it quits for today," she said
unevenly, wishing he would look somewhere else besides at
her body in the cinnamon-colored bikini.

He had secured his recorder and camera up on a high, dry,
flat rock under a shade tree. The breath caught in her throat
at the sight of his physique without the camouflage of clothing. The crinkly carpet of blond hair that matted his chest
tapered to a silky line that disappeared into the low waistband
of his blue trunks. His legs were muscular and tanned that
same dark color as the rest of him and sprinkled with blond
hair that showed up in sharp contrast.

"I had to get another tape and put on a swimsuit."

"Are you going in?" she asked.

"Yes. I can't resist. I nearly melted up there." He indicated
the steep hill that they had taken on their nature hike.

She sat on the bank while he went in the water. He played
rough with the boys, more gently with the girls, but none were
deprived of his attention. Even Jaimie, who had followed Erik
around all day like a worshipful puppy, was included.

Kathleen had been combing through her hair with her fingers, and it was almost dry by the time Erik called "uncle"
and came out of the water.

"If I stay here too long, I'm going to need more vitamins,"
he said as he fell onto his back. The skin on his stomach
stretched taut and formed a deep cavern beneath his ribs. His
chest rose and fell with heavy breathing.

She laughed. "You don't have any trouble keeping up."
Before she could rationalize her motivation, she confessed,
"I was trying to trip you up today."

He rolled over onto his side and looked up at her with his
piercing blue eyes. She refused to meet them and stared at
the splashing children.

"Why?" he asked softly. He wasn't smiling.

Shaking her damp hair, she said, "I don't know. Maybe I
have an instinctive aversion to someone who follows people
around with a camera as though trying to catch them in some
compromising situation. I think I had you pegged as a cynic,
looking for ulterior motives behind our program here. Mountain View is ecumenical and supported strictly by private
donations. Edna and B. J. take very little out for their own
salaries and work hard each fall and spring to book groups
for sales meetings and such. The money they make off of that
goes right back into the camp. They've assumed this summer
camp for orphans as their personal mission, but they also
leave themselves open for criticism. I guess I saw you as a
modern-day witch-hunter."

To her surprise, he laughed. "A few years ago, you would
have been right."

"Oh?"

"Yes. I *was* a cynic. I thought the world and everything
in it stank. I knew all the answers to make it right, of course,
but I wouldn't share them with anyone. That would put me
on the same low plane with all the other idiots who tried to
rectify universal injustices." He laughed bitterly at himself
and sifted several small pebbles from one hand to the other.

"What made you so bitter toward the world?" Kathleen
asked. "You see, I excused myself for feeling that way. My
parents had been taken from me."

"That's the hell of it. I had no excuse. I think I acted that
way out of immaturity and boredom more than anything else.
I was a perfect example of the 'me' generation. If the whole
world was bent on destruction, then I was determined to show
it that I didn't give a damn if it went to hell in a bucket. I
would look out for Number One. Me."

"What changed you? Not that I don't think you're still a smart-ass," she qualified.

He laughed at her admission, but then grew serious. "I was sent to Ethiopia on assignment. I spent six months there. I went convinced that the whole world was ugly."

"And you found even more ugliness?"

"No," he said gently. "I found beauty."

She shook her head in bafflement. "I don't—"

"Let me explain. If I can. One day I was in a refugee camp. God, Kathleen, you can't even imagine the deprivation, the misery. We have no concept of . . ." He made a helpless gesture with his hands. "There's just no way to describe the devastation, the . . . the putrification." He rubbed a hand over his eyes as if to wipe away the image.

"Anyway, I was shooting tape, and in my eyepiece, I saw a young mother with her baby. Both of them were well past critical as far as starvation levels go, emaciated, really. But unaware of my seeing her, the woman squeezed the last drop of milk out of her breast and put her nipple in the baby's mouth. She wept. The infant reached up and touched her cheek. It was as though he knew that was all she had to give and was grateful for it."

He became quiet, staring off into space. Even the sounds the campers were making seemed to be absorbed by his intensity.

"Amid all that ugliness, I saw something beautiful. I don't mean to get too preachy, but I think I realized that there could be something good found in everything if you look hard enough. The world just might be worth saving after all, if only for the sake of one child."

Kathleen was strangely moved by the story. "Your camera must find all sorts of nuances that the naked eye would miss. It doesn't discriminate, does it? It isn't closed by prejudgment."

"Come here," he said suddenly, grabbing her hand and hauling her to her feet.

"Where?" she asked. "The children—"

"No, no. We're just going over here. Very few people are allowed this privilege. I hope you appreciate it."

He steered her toward the boulder where his camera was. Hands on hips, he squinted his eyes at her appraisingly and then looked at the heavy camera. "Let's see. How are you going to do this?" he muttered. "If I put that on your shoulder, you'll sink into the ground."

"What—"

"Here! I know." He flipped several switches as she had seen him do last night, turning on the machine. "Okay, you move over here." Placing a hand at her waist, he pulled her nearer until she was facing the rock and almost eye level with the camera.

"Now, stand up on tiptoe until you can fit your right eye against the eyepiece. Can you see the monitor in there?"

She did as she was told. It was hard to concentrate on anything after the contact his hand had made with her bare midriff. But her eyes found the tiny television monitor that was about an inch square.

"Is that what it looks like? It looks just like a black and white television. I thought it would be like looking into the lens of an ordinary camera," she exclaimed.

"If you're shooting film it is, but with videotape, you can see exactly how it's going to look on a television screen, except for the color. That's why you need a white balance." He cleared his throat loudly and got an elbow in his ribs. "What do you see? Tell me which way to move it."

"Well," she hesitated. All she could see was a blurry image of the tree a few feet in front of them. "It's out of focus," she admitted.

"Say when," he said close to her ear. "I'll try to focus for you."

She watched as the trunk of the tree gradually became clearer, until she could see the patterned detail of the bark. "When!" she cried excitedly.

"Now which way do you want to go? Left? Right? Up or down?"

"Up a little, more into the branches." He took a half-step closer to adjust the camera and she felt his warm, hard chest against her back. His arm rested on her shoulder as he reached in front of her to maneuver the dials around the lens. Her heartbeat quickened.

"Now to the left," she said breathlessly. "Keep going. Wait! Right there. There's something . . . it's a spider and . . . oh, the web is huge. It spreads from limb to limb. He's so busy at work. Oh, Erik, can you move closer, I mean, make him bigger?"

He chuckled and she felt his breath stirring the hair at the back of her neck. "Sure. But I'll have to roll focus again. Can you see him better now?"

"Yeees! There! Now focus again. Perfect. He's perfect."

"Would you like to record an afternoon in the life of a spider?"

"Aren't we?"

"No, I have to press the record button."

"Would you mind?"

"Of course not."

Once they began recording, she expected him to return his left hand, but he didn't. Instead, he laid it on the rock so that she was pressed between the hard, cool surface of the boulder and the warm vibrance of his body. It would be hard to discern which was the stronger and more impregnable.

"How's he doing?" he whispered in her ear. For a moment, she thought she felt the brush of his mustache against her lobe.

"Fine. He's beautiful." She could feel his knees against the backs of her thighs and unconsciously adjusted her legs to those muscular columns.

"Your hair smells like honeysuckle," Erik murmured. This time, there was no mistaking that his lips were moving against her ear. His hips shifted and Kathleen realized that it was only the tight spandex of her bikini bottom and his cotton swim trunks that separated his virility from the soft curve of her buttocks.

"Erik," she said hoarsely.

"Hm?" His nose was investigating the area behind her ear.

"I think . . . I've . . . the spider . . . We'd better stop now." She didn't know for sure if she was talking about stopping the videotaping or the forced proximity of their bodies that was quickly becoming an embrace.

He sighed. "Okay." He clicked off the camera and the tiny monitor in the eyepiece turned gray again. He stepped away from her, and when she felt it was safe, she composed her features and faced him. Unable as yet to meet his eyes, she spoke to the ground. "Thank you. It was wonderful."

"Was it?" His voice was ragged but intuitive, demanding of her an honest answer. She lifted her eyes quickly, and was instantly impaled by the sharpness of his. Her green eyes were held mesmerized until his slid down her face and rested on her trembling lips. Then they moved up again to search the inner turbulence that shone from her eyes.

"Kathy. Kathy."

The small, quiet voice finally penetrated the desire-clouded perimeter of her brain. She backed away from Erik and looked down distractedly at Jaimie.

"Kathy?" he asked uncertainly. "My feet are getting pruney."

Kathleen clasped her hands to flaming cheeks and glanced hurriedly at her watch. "Oh, my God! It's five-fifteen."

Erik started laughing at her, but she ignored him and ran to the riverbank, reached for her whistle, which had been shed along with her clothes, and blew it loudly.

"Hurry, hurry, kids. We're late. Get into your shoes and line up quickly."

She finally gave attention to the small hand tapping on her arm and looked down to see Jaimie again. His dark eyes were shining and bright. "It was neat having Erik here today, wasn't it, Kathy?"

Kathleen looked back toward the rock where Erik was

hauling his camera onto his bare shoulder. "Yes," she said
shakily. "It was neat."

🦋 🦋

Erik hurriedly ate his dinner and then began setting up
the television monitor on which he could play back his
videotapes. He had promised the campers they could see
themselves on television and he was keeping the promise.
Many of them skipped the meat and vegetables and went
straight to the chocolate pudding, hoping to speed the meal
along.

When Erik saw what was happening, he announced loudly,
"Nobody gets to watch until everyone's plate is clean."

There was a congregational groan, but the food on each
plate was then attacked with voracity. Within a half-hour, all
two hundred children were fanned out in a semicircle before
the dais.

"Okay. Here are the ground rules. The first boy who stands
up and blocks someone's view has to wrestle me. The first
girl who does it has to kiss me." The children shrieked with
laughter as Erik scowled darkly. "I mean it. If all of you
cooperate, everyone will get to see. Okay?"

"Okay!" they chorused.

He started the playback, and soon they were convulsed
with laughter at their images on the screen.

"Isn't he marvelous with the children?" Edna said glow-
ingly. She, Kathleen and the other counselors were still seated
at their dinner table, relaxing over cups of coffee or glasses
of iced tea.

"He's very competent," Kathleen said.

"Oh, I know he is. He wouldn't work for the network and
have been assigned so many impressive jobs if he weren't.
But he could have had an artistic temperament and been
cranky with everyone. He manages the children beautifully."

Kathleen crossed her arms in a defensive gesture. She
didn't want Erik to be marvelous. She examined him for

flaws. She wanted to see him make a mistake, commit a small transgression. His perfection disturbed her. His presence disturbed her. *He* disturbed her.

Ever since they had returned the children to the compound and gone to their separate cabins, her mind had been in a whirlwind. Much to her chagrin, she caught herself remembering how it felt to be close to him, something he had said into her ear, his warm, fragrant breath and how it caressed her cheek and the back of her neck.

Then, impatiently, she berated herself for acting like a fool. She was a mature woman, too old to be behaving this way. Too old to have that shortness of breath and fluttery heartbeat each time she reflected on the image of him as he had walked toward the river, his body naked except for the swath of cloth around his loins that enhanced rather than hindered his sexuality. Never had she given so much thought to the male anatomy.

She had resisted the temptation to wear something to dinner besides her navy shorts and white knit T-shirt. But she did succumb to the urge to dab Mitsouko onto the pulse points of her body. Not because of him, she had averred even as she leaned down to stroke some on the backsides of her knees.

Now, Edna's enthusiasm for Erik only made her more determined not to become too attracted to him. He was a world-traveler. He was several years older than she. How old? Thirty? Thirty-five? Chronological age didn't matter. Even if he were younger than she, he would still be years older in experience.

Surely he had known women in every part of the world. A man who looked like Erik would not stay celibate for long. His virility radiated from him like an aura of light that touched everyone, especially women. The only persuasion he would ever have to use would be to get women *out* of his bed once he was finished with them. To get them into it would be no problem.

Disobediently, her mind conjured up a picture of Erik lying on a wide bed. Someone was with him. It was she. She was

helpless beneath him. He was nuzzling her neck with his
mouth. His mustache—

What was she doing? Kathleen shook her head. Glancing
around furtively, she noted that neither the Harrisons nor
anyone else had been watching her strange behavior. They
were all engrossed in the unedited tape that was being played
through the monitor a second time at the request of the
viewers.

No one noticed when Kathleen stood up and left the mess
hall, shutting the screen door quietly behind her.

No one but Erik.

He watched Kathleen as she strolled to the edge of the deep
porch and sat down on the top step, tilting her head back to
gaze at the sky. He saw how the tendrils that had escaped the
knot of hair secured to the top of her head lay like strands of
silk against the stark whiteness of her shirt.

Closing his eyes briefly, he could almost smell the honeysuckle essence of her hair that had filled his head and made
him drunk this afternoon.

It was hard to tear his eyes away from the poignant picture
she made sitting out there in the shadows. For the sake of his
captive audience, he returned his gaze to the tape. But not
his mind. It was still on the girl on the porch.

Girl? Woman? That was the hell of it. For some reason,
none of the labels he usually attached to women fit Kathleen
Haley. She had elements of every other woman, yet she was
none of them. She had a classiness, an indefinable distinction,
that made her different and impossible to categorize.

But she was woman. God! She was woman. Every time he
saw her, his body threatened to make it embarrassingly evident how much of a woman he thought her to be.

That was another thing that didn't fit into the scheme of
things. She wasn't his type. The Harrisons had told him she
worked in the fashion industry. He should have guessed that
right away. Who else could make a simple pair of shorts and
a T-shirt look haute couture? It had never mattered a tinker's
dam to him what a woman wore. He preferred them without

anything on. And then, he liked lush bodies, round hips, big breasts.

She was almost boyishly slender, but that tight little fanny nearly drove him crazy. He wanted to cup his hands over it, just to see if it was as firm and taut as it looked. Those long, slender legs didn't try to be provocative, but he had caught himself watching the play of muscles as she walked ahead of him on the mountain trail earlier in the day. Her breasts were small, but full and beautifully shaped. When she had come out of the cold, rushing river, her nipples had stood out invitingly, eager and pert.

Dammit! He was fantasizing about a woman barely mature enough to be deemed such. He liked women, but he liked them naked, silent and in bed. He never thought of them as people with careers. Never did he seek one out for the sake of an enlightening conversation. Yet today he had shared with Kathleen thoughts that he hadn't even catalogued in his own mind. It was her rapt, intense listening that had opened up his own brain, making him see things clearly that had been nebulous before.

The kiss last night hadn't been spontaneous. He had planned it right down to the last detail. He had wanted to match his mouth to hers. But rather than satisfying him, he now craved more than one kiss. He had to see if she tasted as good as that one brief appetizer had indicated she did.

The tape running through the machine clicked off, and Erik was thrust out of his pleasant surmises by the enthusiastic applause of the children.

"Again, again," they chanted.

Erik laughed. "I don't think so."

"Children," B. J. called over the roar, and clapped his hands. "Children, the night bell is about to ring, so let's all start toward our cabins, please. Counselors, round up your groups. We've had a real treat tonight. Let's all give Mr. Gudjonsen a big thank you."

The words were screamed at him, the campers taking full advantage of being as loud as they wanted to be.

Kathleen had reentered the room when all the commotion started. Erik managed to wade through the throng toward her. "I'd like to show you the tapes I shot today. They're not edited, but I thought you might like to see what I've got so far."

"Well, I . . ." She hesitated. She didn't know whether she wanted to be alone with him or not.

"Come on," he urged. "Look at it as a free movie." He cuffed her on the shoulder with a gentle fist.

She laughed. "All right."

They said their goodnights to the other counselors and to the Harrisons, who hurried out of the building, declining Erik's offer for them to stay, so B. J. could get back to their cabin before the ten o'clock news came on. The ladies who managed the kitchen had been cleaning up the dinner dishes while the tape was playing, so the building was now deserted.

"Let me load this first tape," Erik said. "Why don't you catch the lights? We can see it better."

Kathleen moved to the large panel and flipped off the switches. Only the diffuse light from one small bulb in the kitchen illumined the room as she made her way back to the benches.

"Ready?" Erik asked over his shoulder, and smiled.

"Ready."

He started the tape and Kathleen took a seat at one of the long dining tables. Erik sat down beside her, propping his elbows on the table behind him and stretching his long legs out in front of him. Kathleen looked down at her own bare leg, a scarce few inches from his thigh. She didn't move farther away.

They watched the raw footage that he had shot and were soon chatting amiably about the moods he had captured. Kathleen couldn't help but laugh when the camera rolled in on Gracie's splotched, tear-streaked face. She had fallen down and scraped her knee on the morning hike, and had wailed disproportionately to the injury.

"Oh, Erik, how cruel," Kathleen admonished, even though she was laughing.

He chuckled. "Maybe so. But I couldn't resist. You know, one day, when she's older, the braces come off and she can wear contact lenses, I'll bet Gracie will put the rest of them in the shade." His hand found its way to Kathleen's shoulder.

"I hope so. She deserves some happiness. Her parents and little brother died in a car crash. She was hospitalized for months with injuries. She was eight at the time, and as sad as it is, that's often considered too old for adoption. She'll probably live at an orphanage until she's eighteen when, hopefully, she can go to college."

"God, what a bummer."

Kathleen sighed. "Yes. Most of the children here were orphaned under similar circumstances. Some of them have one parent, usually a father who isn't able to keep them with him. Very few were born in a home for unwed mothers or lost their parents in infancy. Most infants are easily adopted." Just then, a close-up of Jaimie filled the small screen.

"Jaimie is the exception to that rule. His father never married his mother. She gave him up for adoption at birth. He was never placed because he's biracial."

Erik's hand moved from her shoulder to her neck in a comforting gesture that changed into a caress. "He's rather special to you, isn't he?"

"Yes. I try not to let it show, but he is." She was glad Erik had to take his hand away when he got up to change tapes. She was finding it hard not to lean against him.

He had shot four twenty-minute tapes, and each time he got up to rewind the one just played and exchange it with another, he returned to his seat and replaced his hand on her neck or back or shoulder. In some way, at all times, he was touching her.

Kathleen buried her face in her hands when her videotape of the spider came up. They laughed over the erratic movements of the camera, which made the spider look as if he were dancing on his web.

"I'm glad I didn't aspire to be a videographer!" she exclaimed.

"You were h ndicapped. You couldn't hold the camera

yourself. My excuse is that I couldn't see what I was taping.''
He moved closer to her and settled his lips against her ear.
''And I was distracted.'' His mouth made a feather-light
pass across her cheek. Then the video machine clicked off.
''Damn,'' he cursed softly under his breath as he got up to
put in another tape.

Kathleen stood up. Her knees were trembling. ''I'd better
be going . . .'' she said nervously.

''No. There's one more. Sit,'' he ordered.

Kathleen lacked the will to resist, and honestly wasn't sure
she wanted to. She dropped onto the bench again. Boldly,
Erik placed an arm around her shoulders when he resumed
his seat.

For several minutes, they were silent as they watched the
children cavorting in the river. The screen went gray for a
few seconds, then Kathleen gasped as she saw herself coming
slowly out of the water.

She was the exclusive focus of the moving picture. The
background of trees that lined the opposite side of the river
was like a green curtain behind her body, outlining it in detail.
She came out of the water with unintentional provocative
grace. Her cinnamon-colored bikini almost made her appear
naked. Wet hair clung to her neck and shoulders seductively,
like the fingers of a lover. The water, sparkling in the sunlight,
rolled down her limbs, her chest, her stomach, her abdomen,
in glistening drops that looked like diamonds against her skin.
On the tape, the tentative smile she had given him seemed
alluring—shy, yet inviting.

The screen went blank again and a heavy silence pervaded
the room. Kathleen, unable to move, continued to stare directly in front of her. The tape finally ran out and the machine
clicked off. It sounded like a cannon's boom. Still she sat
motionless with her heart pounding, employing all the energy
left in her body.

Erik touched her face with the back of his hand and, with
sure fingers, turned her chin around to face him in the darkness.

"For my private tape library," he whispered, and lowered his head to brush his lips across hers.

She pushed away from him in breathless caution. Standing up hastily, she took two steps toward the dais. "Your recorder . . ."

He came off the bench like a spring. His hand reached out with uncanny speed and clasped her around the waist. "Forget it," he said gruffly. He swept her into his arms and against that hard, masculine body. Deftly, he released her hair from the barrette which held it atop her head and raked his fingers through the heavy skein. Entwining his fingers in it, he pulled her head back, forcing her to look at him. "Forget everything. Think only of this."

His mouth closed over hers, assuming total possession and brooking no arguments to the contrary. But it was a gentle assault. His lips sipped at hers while his mustache tickled and teased until her lips opened in welcome. Then each secret of her mouth was discovered by the hungry exploration of his tongue.

Without her having been conscious of it, her hands had come up to caress the sides of his face. Now her fingers were weaving through that glorious blond hair and touching the strands that lay against his collar.

His hips moved against hers, and quite naturally she answered the movement and settled against his manhood. She felt, rather than heard, the breath catch in his throat, and then he moaned her name. His hand smoothed down her back, stopped long enough to appreciate her tiny waist, then moved to the soft swelling of her hips. The hand became bolder as he cupped her tenderly and pressed her tighter to him.

His mouth nibbled her earlobe and worked its way on a sensuous trail down to her neck. "What is that fragrance?" he breathed, and Kathleen groaned when she felt the tip of his tongue in the sensitive triangle at the base of her throat.

"Mitsouko," she whimpered.

"Never heard of it."

"No?"

"No. But I'll never forget it now."

His hand was on her rib cage and moving up. *Oh, God, yes! Yes!* His hand covered her breast. His palm fit over her as if it were made for that complementing purpose.

It began a slow, learning, rotating circle that suspended her in some euphoric atmosphere. Lowering his head to replace his hand, he nuzzled her with his nose and mouth. His breath was moist and hot through the cotton of her shirt. His lips formed her name around her nipple. She heard a sharp little cry, not realizing she had made it.

Once again, his hand was on her breast, and his thumb had taken over where his lips left off, gently raking her ever-tightening nipple. His mouth was at her ear, doing something delicious as he asked huskily, "Where do you want to go?"

"What?" she asked weakly, absently.

"Your cabin or mine?"

The words finally made it past that fog of sexual oblivion and doused her arousal like an icy shower. The flames of passion that were licking her body and igniting her spirit were extinguished with that one simple question.

She shoved herself away from him and fought to fill her constricted lungs with oxygen, taking several deep, uneven breaths.

"Kathleen, what—"

"I can't . . . can't be . . . be with you," she said quickly, before she changed her mind.

"Why the hell not?" He broke off and looked at her for a moment before saying softly, "I'm sorry. That was an ungentlemanly thing to ask." He shook his head ruefully and plowed frustrated fingers through the hair that was still mussed from her caresses. He chuckled without mirth. "I just wish you had told me this was 'that time of the month' fifteen minutes ago."

It took her a moment before she realized what conclusion he had jumped to. Had it not been so dark, he would have seen how embarrassed she was by his supposition, but it was better to have him think she was having a period than for him to know the real reason she wouldn't go with him.

He closed the gap between them and took her face in his hands. "Goodnight," he said softly, and kissed her lightly on the lips, then once on her forehead.

"Goodnight," she murmured. She had to keep herself from dashing out of the dining hall while he stood there and watched her.

Chapter Four

🌿⁂ 🌿⁂

I just had the most wonderful idea!'' Edna exclaimed the next morning as they sat at breakfast.

"What's that, honey?" B. J. asked, biting into a biscuit.

"Kathleen should take Erik to the Crescent Hotel for dinner.''

Kathleen's fork clattered to her plate and she jerked her head up to see the amusement glimmering in Erik's blue eyes.

"What's the Crescent?" he asked the Harrisons without relieving Kathleen of his stare.

"Erik, you'd love it. It's a hotel in Eureka Springs that was built in the 1880s and has been restored to its original Victorian elegance. Their dining room is sumptuous!''

"I don't—'' Kathleen started.

"How far is Eureka Springs?" Erik interrupted.

"About thirty miles, though it takes about an hour to get there. We don't have super interstate highways up here.'' B. J. laughed. "You really ought to go see the town. We call it the Switzerland of America. Eureka Springs is built right on top of the mountains. The houses and buildings are quaint, usually several stories. One floor might be level with the street, while the back of the house is supported by stilts thirty feet tall.''

"You talked me into it," Erik said enthusiastically. "I've heard of Eureka Springs, but I've never been there.''

"Good. Then it's all settled," Edna said.

"Wait!" Kathleen fairly shouted, then flushed hotly when three pairs of eyes turned toward her. "I can't just go off like that. I mean . . . the children . . . tonight . . . it's against the rules.''

"You're a board member. You can't break the rules." Edna smiled. "We need to give Erik a break. He's not accustomed to being isolated from civilization the way we are.''

Kathleen looked at Edna suspiciously. What the older woman said had merit, and it was possible that Edna truly did want to relieve Erik of one night in the noisy dining hall, but Kathleen also thought that Edna was dabbling in some good old-fashioned matchmaking. There was no gracious way to decline the offer of a free night, so Kathleen swallowed the nervous lump in her throat and said softly, "I suppose it would be nice to get away for a while.''

"You can leave as soon as you bring the kids back this afternoon," Edna said with the briskness of one who had accomplished a mission. "Erik, the Crescent also has a lovely, secluded club with a dance floor in the basement.''

"It's sounding better all the time," he said to the Harrisons, then turned his back on them and winked at Kathleen.

Oh, God, she groaned to herself. It had taken all the courage she could muster to enter the mess hall for breakfast this morning after her behavior the evening before. What had come over her? She must have taken leave of her senses. She had stopped him just in time, but still he had gone further with her than any man had ever been allowed to go. And she had known him only two days! Her ready reactions to him were frightening.

But, self-righteously, she absolved herself of guilt. The way his hands had roamed her body with easy familiarity was an accomplished technique. His mouth, the heat of his embrace, were all too practiced. He'd detected in her a susceptibility and had capitalized on it. He had told her a poignant story about his assignment in Ethiopia, and she had fallen for the emotional blackmail like a pioneer housewife at a medicine man's show. How many times had he used that same story to break down barriers with a woman? The tale might not even be true!

Kathleen held herself in too high a regard to dally with casual affairs that led nowhere, relationships that did nothing to enrich one's life but fed on self-deception, disillusionment and pain until one was left with only a feeling of emptiness. Hadn't she fought David Ross like a tiger?

Before she had finally fallen into a restless sleep, Kathleen had resolved that the next time Erik made any sexual overtures, she would inform him in terms that left no room for doubt that she wasn't interested in a romantic entanglement.

Now, Edna had arranged a date for them! A date that would take hours if they drove all the way to Eureka Springs on the two-lane state highway that ribboned its way through the mountains.

It was with mingled relief and regret that she learned Erik had chosen to accompany Mike Simpson's group today as they went on a horseback trip to the other side of the mountain. It would be an all-day event. How Erik was going to carry his camera, Kathleen didn't know, but she was sure he would manage. He is a man of rare talent, she thought sarcastically as she watched him striding across the compound with his equipment and several of the inquisitive children in tow.

The hours of the day were easily filled, and Kathleen's group was trudging up the hill to the compound just as Mike's group was returning. Secretly, she hoped that Erik would be tired and saddlesore, anything to prevent him from wanting to keep their date. But he was smiling and exuberant when he hailed her from across the wide yard.

"Hey, Kathleen, wait up." He said a few words to Mike, ruffled the hair of one adoring little boy and cuffed a little girl under her chin before he jogged up to Kathleen.

His white knit shirt was soaked with perspiration, and his hair clung damply to his forehead, but he had never looked more appealing as his eyes squinted into a smile.

"How was your day?" he asked.

"Fine. The children missed you." And so did I, dammit, she added to herself. "How was the riding?"

"I was rusty for a while, but I finally worked the kinks out." He seemed admirably humble.

Knowing she looked about twelve years old with her pigtails and shorts and tennis shoes, she shifted uncomfortably under his perusal. Did he remember last night? No sooner had the question entered her mind than his eyes lit on her lips and lingered there. Yes, he remembered, and she felt herself blushing under her deep tan.

"How did you haul your camera?" she asked, with a curiosity she couldn't restrain.

He smiled, his teeth creating a white slash in his dark face. "It rode in front of me on the saddle."

"Very ingenious," she said dryly.

"I've learned to improvise." He smiled deeply again. *Was* that a dimple under his mustache? "When can you be ready?" he asked suddenly.

"Do you still want to go?" she demurred. "We don't have to, you know."

"I know. But I want to," he leaned down and whispered conspiratorily. "Why do you think I volunteered for that damn packing trip? I didn't think I could be with you all day, anticipating tonight, and keep my hands off you. I don't think sex education is included in the curriculum, is it?"

What had happened to all those carefully chosen words she had rehearsed all day? Where, in her befuddled brain, were all those epithets hiding? The sound logic she had pieced together had fled, being replaced by titillating possibilities. Her tongue couldn't function at all, much less deliver the blistering refusals she had memorized.

She couldn't meet his gaze. It was too unsettling, too disturbing, too hypnotic. She darted her green eyes at the trees, the flagpole where the flag hung limply in the still afternoon, and toward the straggling campers and counselors who were wending their way tiredly to their cabins. "About an hour?"

He took a tendril of hair between two of his long, slender fingers. He tugged on it gently before tucking it behind her ear. "Fifty-five minutes," he said huskily, before he turned on his heel and strode off in the direction of his cabin.

Her thoughts were running rampant as she hastened to her own cabin. What could she wear? She didn't have anything appropriate! With longing, she thought of her closet at home in Atlanta, where she had designer dresses, gorgeous shoes and racks of accessories, all of which she could buy at wholesale prices because of her job.

Now, she stared bleakly at the one metal rod in the narrow closet and bemoaned the meagerness of her wardrobe at hand. The cotton print shirtwaist or the voile sundress? She gnawed the inside of her cheek. The print was soft, simple and sweet. And safe. The sundress was soft, simple and sexy. Not so safe. After her shower, she was still debating with herself.

With an impatient shrug at her own silliness, she took her sundress off the hanger. The voile felt like a cloud settling over her flesh. The bodice was cut like a camisole. Lace-trimmed straps about an inch wide spanned her bare shoulders. She was saved from total immodesty because the front was tucked and pleated on either side of a row of pearl buttons that stopped at her waist. That provided two layers of the sheer fabric over her breasts. The skirt was full, but she wore flesh-toned panties and a half-slip as meager protection from its sheerness. The sea-green color accentuated her own vivid eyes and highlighted the honey-apricot tone of her skin.

She slid her bare feet into the only pair of high-heeled sandals she had brought with her. She disdained panty hose in the sweltering heat, but had shaved her legs to glossy smoothness and applied a rich lotion that made them silky to the touch.

She twisted her hair up into a knot on the top of her head and secured it with a long gold clip decorated with a nautilus shell. Small gold loops were inserted into her pierced ears.

She dabbed herself liberally with Mitsouko just as Erik knocked on her door.

Instinctively, her fluttering hand flew to the base of her throat where she could feel the pounding of her pulse. *Stop this!* Kathleen ordered herself to no avail. She was far more nervous now than she had been on her first date when the young man had picked her up at the orphanage.

Somehow she forced her reluctant legs across the room toward the screened door. Erik's silhouette filled the twilight-tinted opening.

"Hi," she said with affected casualness.

He made no pretense of his feelings. His mouth hung open at a ridiculous angle as he toured her body with his wide, stupefied eyes. "Are you the same girl who was in pigtails a mere hour ago?"

"Fifty-five minutes," she corrected teasingly. His face then returned to normal and he smiled that dazzling smile that always left her feeling dizzy. She had never seen him dressed in anything but jeans. The swimsuit hardly counted as clothing. His appearance left her breathless and lightheaded. His blue shirt fitted his torso to perfection. The camel-colored slacks hugged his hips and thighs like a second skin, the straight legs broke with tailored preciseness on the vamp of polished loafers. The navy blazer was stretched over bunched shoulder muscles as he placed his hands on his hips and eyed her appraisingly.

"You, Ms. Haley, are amazing. Out there," Erik indicated the camp with a backward jerk of his head, "you look like someone's beautiful kid sister. Now you look like someone's beautiful . . . uh . . ."

"What?"

"Never mind," he growled. "What I had in mind to say could get me in trouble. Let's go."

He ushered her out the door and toward the Blazer, parked a few yards from her cabin. "I hope you know the way, because I drove here with one eye on the road and one on an obsolete map."

Kathleen laughed as she slid into the passenger side of the

truck. "I do, but only after coming here for years. Only the natives truly know their way around up here."

"I believe it," he said. "Which way?"

She gave him directions to get them underway and then settled against the back of the seat, which was still warm from the truck having been closed up all day. A soft flow of air from the air-conditioning vents soon remedied that. "You don't seem like the Blazer type to me," she said musingly.

Erik laughed easily and reached for the dial of the radio. "What type am I?" he asked, amused. He found a congenial radio station, and his arm extended across the backs of the seats until his fingers brushed her bare shoulder, making her tremble on the inside.

"Oh, you know," she said smoothly. "The Miata type. Or maybe a Corvette."

He laughed again, deeper this time. His laugh was so natural, so easy, so masculine. It literally rumbled from his chest. "How about a Dodge van?"

"You're kidding!"

"No. This car belongs to the television station. Actually, when I'm at home, I drive a Dodge van. Nothing fancy. No fur-covered mattresses, no quadraphonic CD systems, no murals on the outside. But very functional for hauling all my equipment."

"I can't believe it," Kathleen said honestly. Then, raising her knee to the seat and turning toward him slightly, she asked, "You live in St. Louis, don't you?" The Harrisons had told her that much about him.

"Yes. Have you ever heard the term 'O and O'?"

"No," she said, shaking her head.

"Well, actually you wouldn't unless you worked in the television industry. 'O and O' stands for owned and operated. And that applies to television stations that are actually owned by the networks. According to FCC regulations, each network can own five VHF television stations. UBC has one in St. Louis. Really it's only an address for me. They send me anywhere they need me."

"That's intriguing. I'm afraid I don't know very much about the television industry."

"I'm afraid I don't either," he said, smiling. "All I know about is my camera and how to use it. I aspire to doing much more creative things than network news stories. I really consider my affiliation with them as an apprenticeship. One day, I'd like to have my own production company and produce commercials, industrial films, things like that. Unfortunately, a setup like that costs a lot of money."

"Surely the network pays a valuable employee like you well."

"Well, but not extravagantly. The glory guys are the ones in front of the cameras, not the ones behind them." His index finger tapped the end of her nose. "Now it's your turn. I know nothing about the 'rag trade.' "

Kathleen laughed and launched into a brief outline of her work, but to her surprise, he was genuinely interested and asked intelligent questions until she found herself talking animatedly. "I attend several fashion markets a year, not only in Atlanta, but in Chicago and Dallas as well. I go to New York every few months."

"That sounds glamorous," he said, obviously impressed.

"Not so much so." She laughed. "I must often placate the alterations seamstress when a garment proves unalterable. And there's always a wealthy customer who *must* have a dress by the night of the country club dance. She places me at the mercy of a shipping clerk in a warehouse who has a heart of stone. Salesladies are constantly running out of goods that manufacturers swear are no longer available." She paused and drew a deep breath. "Had enough?"

He laughed. "But you'll be eager to return in the fall."

Suddenly reminded that she had nothing to return to, she looked away quickly. "Yes," she answered vaguely. She didn't want to discuss her resignation from Mason's or the reason for it.

Sensing her withdrawal, Erik shifted his attention away from the road and peered closely at her through slitted eyes.

Kathleen adroitly avoided pursuing this line of conversation by saying, "Slow down a little. You need to make a left-hand turn up here at the crossroads."

※ ※

The Crescent Hotel stood sentinel over the township of Eureka Springs. Looking very European with its gray brick walls, blue roof and red chimneys, it depicted the period in which it was built. Broad verandas on each floor ran the length of the building where guests could sit in rocking chairs and enjoy the mountainous panorama. The corners of the building were square and topped with pyramid-shaped roofs.

Erik parked the car and helped Kathleen out with a hand under her elbow. He was impressed with the old hotel, but Kathleen was slightly embarrassed that Edna had made so much of it to a man who had been all over the world. Nevertheless, his comments were appreciative.

The lobby had white Grecian columns connecting the Persian rug-scattered hardwood floor to the high molded ceiling above. An open white marble fireplace was free-standing in the room, and one could enjoy the fire from four sides. Of course, on this hot summer night, the logs were stacked, but no fire was burning. Instead, patrons sat on the Victorian furniture in air-conditioned comfort.

The dining room looked like a room out of *The Unsinkable Molly Brown*. The walls were covered with red and gold flocked paper. The oaken floors gleamed with the patina that only age and careful maintenance can produce. The table-cloths were also red, showing off the china, crystal and silver. One corner of the room was dominated by a grand piano, where a man in a black tuxedo was playing softly.

On their behalf, Edna had made the reservation. They were shown to their table by the maître d', who held Kathleen's chair for her with an old-world flourish. He took their drink orders and then discreetly withdrew.

"What in the hell is a spritzer?" Erik asked.

"It's white wine and club soda on the rocks with a twist of lemon."

"Whatever happened to healthy, substantial drinks like scotch and water?" He leaned his elbows on the table and propped his chin on his fists as he teased her.

"I don't like anything that tastes alcoholic. I like things that taste like punch or are very tart or made with ice cream."

He grimaced. "What do you do when you need a good swift kick in the butt?"

"I take a vitamin pill."

He laughed and saluted her with his highball glass, which had just arrived. After they had sipped their drinks, he said, "I've got to taste a spritzer. No one should go through life without having done that."

He took the frosted wineglass out of her hand and deliberately turned it around to place his lips on the lipstick-smudged place hers had been. He watched her over the glass as he took a small drink. When he handed it back to her, he said softly, "Delicious."

Kathleen's stomach did a somersault, but she was unable to tear her eyes away from the power of his. He hadn't been referring to the drink when he had made that one succinct description. He was reminding her that he had tasted her mouth thoroughly, knew it, recognized it and liked it.

She could have hugged the waiter when he returned to the table with the menus. "What will I have tonight?" She feigned interest in the bill of fare. Actually, she didn't think she'd be able to eat a thing. Her heart seemed to have swollen in her chest and compressed her lungs until her breathing was little more than light panting.

"I already know," Erik said, closing the menu decisively.

"What?" She laughed.

"Fried chicken. Only in the South can you get real fried chicken."

"You should come to Atlanta sometime. I think it must be the fried chicken capital of the world."

He watched her mouth as she spoke, and then raised his

eyes to meet hers. "I will." It was a promise, and again her heart did that erratic dance that she now knew from memory.

"What are you having?" he asked when the waiter came back with a pen poised over his tablet.

"The trout. Broiled, please. And I'd like some extra lemon wedges," she said to the waiter.

After he left, Erik leaned across the table toward her once again. "Would you like another spritzer?"

"No, thank you. But order yourself another drink if you like."

"No. I'm drunk enough as it is." He reached for her hand, encircled her wrist with his strong fingers and brought it to his lips to press a fervent kiss against her pulse. "Mitsouko. Do you always smell so good?" His mouth mumbled the words against the back of her hand as his thumb stroked the sensitive palm in heart-melting rhythm. The question was rhetorical and needed no answer, so none was offered. "Tell me about you, Kathleen."

"What do you want to know?" she asked breathlessly.

"Everything. Was it tough on you when you lost your parents?"

She hadn't intended to, hadn't even thought of it, but she reached out with her other hand and covered the masculine one that was holding hers. She stared at the clasped hands for a long while before she spoke.

"I wanted to die, too. I was angry. How could God do this to me? I had always been obedient, a good student, eaten all my vegetables, you know, the kind of things a kid thinks are exemplary." She sighed. "I was spending the night with a friend because I had had a cold and Mother didn't want me out in the boat. I didn't even find out about the accident until the next morning, when my friend's mother heard about it on the radio."

Closing her eyes, she relived all the pain she had felt on that day. "I am almost twenty-six years old. I only lived with Mamma and Daddy half of my life, yet they are still so much a part of me," she said softly. "Memories of them are more vivid than things that happened subsequent to their deaths."

"You were put in an orphanage."

"Yes." She smiled gently. "I remember being angry at my parents' friends, who said they were worried about me but wouldn't ask me to live with them. They were all very kind. I realize that now. But then, I was bitter about the rotten deal I was getting out of life. I wasn't too charitable toward anyone."

"You were entitled to a little bitterness, I think." He raised her hand and kissed it quickly, then asked, "Where did you go to school?"

"At the orphanage. It was a church-supported institution—how I hate that word! They had classes through the ninth grade. Then I went to public high school. That helped prepare me for living 'on the outside.' "

"And college?"

"I had good enough grades to be offered a scholarship by benefactors of the orphanage, but I also worked in a dress shop near the campus to subsidize the scholarship."

He smiled knowingly. "You don't fool me, Ms. Haley. You worked so it wouldn't look like you were taking charity."

"Perhaps that was part of it," she conceded shyly.

"Go on."

"You know the rest. Or virtually all of it. After I graduated, I worked as a salesgirl in retail stores, gradually being promoted until I applied for the position at Mason's two years ago." Hurriedly, Kathleen switched the subject away from the job she had so recently given up. "What about your family? By your name, I take it you are of Scandinavian descent."

"Yes, my father was Danish. He was first-generation American. His parents came over from Denmark when he was an infant. My grandfather was a watchsmith. My grandmother never even learned English. All I remember about her is her white hair pulled back into a tight bun and her home-baked cookies, which were the best I've yet to taste."

"Maybe that's because you were young," Kathleen suggested with a smile.

"Maybe."

"Your parents? What did your father do?"

"He was a hard man, determined. He worked his way through college, served in the war, and then came home and married my mother. He worked for Boeing in Seattle, where I grew up. He was a big, brawny guy, with a fierce temper. But I've seen him weep over a sentimental movie."

"You speak of him in the past tense," she commented gently.

"Yes. He died ten years ago. Mother, who is as petite and soft and timid as Dad was boisterous, still lives in the Northwest."

Their conversation was interrupted by the arrival of their food. Kathleen was surprised that she was able to eat, after all, and did unladylike justice to her plate. The dining room at the Crescent was reputed to combine good country cooking with elegant service. Erik complimented them on achieving that as he dunked yeast rolls into the rich natural gravy of his fried chicken, which he declared surpassed any other.

Kathleen declined his offer of dessert, but was persuaded to eat one of the remaining rolls dripping with rich, thick honey as they sipped their after-dinner coffee.

When Erik was presented with the bill, her suggestion that she pay for her half was met with a glowering look.

"But it was Edna's idea that we come."

"Ms. Haley, I'm all for equality between the sexes—to a point. Buying a lady her dinner is one of those points. I'll pay the bill."

She could tell by the strong set of his jaw and his firm tone of voice that the issue was closed.

"Where is the lounge with the dance floor?" Erik asked as they left the dining room and traversed the lobby.

"We don't have to go there," Kathleen protested quickly.

"Oh, yes, we do. Edna will want a full report, and I'm afraid I'd lose favor if I didn't dance with you at least once."

By the determined look on his face, Kathleen knew it was pointless to argue, so she said, "It's downstairs."

He ushered her down the broad staircase with the carved banister to the basement, where a quiet cocktail lounge had been hollowed out. It was an unsophisticated room, barely more than a tavern. Behind the bar, animated neon signs flashed the names of various beers. Few people were in the lounge on this weeknight, but there was a three-piece ensemble playing music in front of a tiny dance floor shrouded in darkness.

Unaffected by the small crowd and the fact that no one else was dancing, Erik took Kathleen's hand and led her onto the floor, drawing her into the circle of his arms.

The group played slow ballads. They danced twice in the traditional way, though Erik's arm around her back held her to him possessively.

On the third song, he raised her hands and placed them around his neck, putting both his arms around her waist. He dipped his head close to hers and whispered into her ear, "I like it better this way. It's like making love to music."

Kathleen's breath was suspended for a moment when he drew her closer. His readiness to make love was apparent as he pressed against her. He nuzzled her hair with his nose, treating it to the sweet scent. His mouth brushed across her ear as he whispered her name. Then it came to rest on her lips, parted them and kissed her tenderly. "You feel so good against me. I love the way your body moves with mine. I love the way you look, and smell and taste." His tongue made quick, darting forays into her mouth that made her cling to him in desperation, wanting more.

It was several long seconds before she realized the music had stopped and the trio was putting down its instruments to take a break. Kathleen pushed away from Erik shyly.

"You'd better get that hot little number home quick, buddy. Looks to me like she's primed and ready."

The stranger's intrusive words abruptly brought them back to earth.

Chapter Five

🌿 🌿

Kathleen swiveled around toward the obnoxious, nasal voice and saw two young men sitting at one of the small tables. They were propped back in their chairs, their expressions stupidly insolent. Cowboy hats with feather hatbands were tilted back on their heads.

Her face flooded with hot color. Turning away quickly and not waiting for Erik, she raced for the door. The crash of furniture against the hardwood floor brought her to a jolting halt.

Acting with the instinct of a jungle cat, Erik pounced on the two young men who had spoken unwisely. One he caught under the chin with a right fist. The cowboy flew out of his chair under an impact like Thor's hammer and landed unceremoniously on the floor in an undignified heap. The other young man had stood up in hopes of making a show of self-defense, but his belly was plowed into with an iron fist, and then, as he leaned over in agony, he, too, knew the rocketing pain of Erik's punch to his jaw.

Bleary-eyed, they stared in fear up at Erik from their humiliating positions. "Have one on me to cool off a little, boys," Erik said cheerfully. He flung a five-dollar bill onto the table.

58

Then, with the dignity of a monarch, he met Kathleen at the door and escorted her out of the silent room.

When they had mounted the staircase and were crossing the lobby toward the front door, she asked shakily, "Erik, are you all right?"

"Sure. Why shouldn't I be? They deserved to be knocked on their cans for what they said about you." He smiled down at her and squeezed her arm reassuringly. "They'll live. I promise. I didn't hurt them near as much as I could have."

That was what worried her. For an instant, when he had turned on the two young men, she had seen an expression on Erik's face that caused a prickle of fear to chill her spine. His teeth were bared in a feral grimace and his hands were clenched into fists that hung loosely at his sides as he crouched in the menacing position.

He had spoken of his father's fierce temper. Apparently, his Viking blood, which felt each emotion strongly, wasn't immune to anger.

🐾 🐾

"Can you please point me in the right direction? The streets in this town are like a maze," Erik said once they were in the truck and he was backing it out of the parking lot.

Was this affable man the same one who had attacked the two cowboys in the lounge only a few moments ago? Kathleen laughed nervously as she said, "Straight ahead for the next few blocks."

"*Straight?* You've gotta be kidding!" Erik said as he took the first sharp curve.

Indeed, most of the streets in Eureka Springs were unique. Each wound around the hills, seemingly without destination but somehow managing eventually to converge on the wider and more uniform thoroughfares.

The narrow, twisting streets were lined with historic houses decorated with "gingerbread" trim, jeweled with dormer windows and flanked by beds of geraniums, petunias, periwinkles and marigolds. Most of the century-old houses had been fully restored and painted in gaily contrasting colors that made the neighborhoods look more like Disneyland than a small community in the Ozarks of Arkansas.

"Would you like to stop someplace else?" Erik asked when they reached the highway that led back to Mountain View.

"No. It's been lovely to get away for a few hours, but the grind starts again tomorrow, and then, the day after, we're taking a busload of the older kids to the Buffalo River for a day of tubing on the rapids."

"Hey, now, that sounds great. Can I come along?"

"Of course." She smiled across the dark interior of the truck.

Erik must have read the invitation in her eyes, and there was no masking the desire in his voice when he commanded her huskily, "Get over here."

She moved as close to him as possible considering the console between them. Their thighs touched. "That's better," he said, smiling down at her and risking kissing her fleetingly on the mouth.

When his eyes returned to the road, he lifted her hand to his mouth and planted a hot, moist kiss in the palm. Not releasing her hand, he placed it high on his thigh. Her fingers trembled, but his own imprisoned hers where they were.

Having reached the main highway, Erik knew his way back to the encampment. Kathleen was lulled by the humming of the car's motor, her full stomach and the soft music emanating from the dimly lighted dashboard. Her head fell back against the seat. Her eyelids gave up the struggle to remain open.

Slipping under her skirt, his hand stroked her thigh, caressing the smooth skin. When he found the softest spot, his hand stilled and rested. Only occasionally did she feel his fingertips brushing her.

Drowsily, she could smell the intoxicating fragrance of his cologne—potent, but not overwhelming or cloyingly sweet. It was brisk and clean and sharp, conjuring up thoughts of sea air or autumn breezes. The image of a Viking sailing his warship into a fjord was projected onto her mind. The Viking had Erik's face, and the girl wildly waving at him from shore looked like her.

The dream grew even more pleasant as the returning warrior bounded off the ship onto shore and gathered the girl into his brawny arms, raiding her mouth, tickling her ear with his mustache. She, giggling, clutched at his back and drew him to her.

Kathleen was still smiling at her fantasy when the truck pulled to a stop outside her cabin. She lacked the energy to move. "Are you awake?" Erik's breath ghosted over her neck as he whispered to her.

"No," she answered sleepily.

He chuckled. "That's what I thought. We're home. Come on."

Before she realized what was happening, he had opened the passenger door and was reaching inside, catching her under the knees and around the shoulders, lifting her out of the front seat and carrying her to her cabin.

He opened the squeaky screen door and caught it with his back as it closed, not wanting it to slam shut. Then he moved through the moonlit room toward the bed.

He laid her gently on the pillows and kissed her forehead. Leaving her for a moment, he went back to the electric panel next to the door and switched on the overhead fan, but left off the lights. He shrugged out of his coat and tossed it onto a chair.

Kathleen was strangely languorous. She couldn't remember ever feeling quite this helpless. All her muscles seemed to have dissolved, yet they all strained toward Erik as he lay down beside her on the narrow bed and gathered her to him.

His lips claimed hers hungrily. There was no persuasion in his kiss this time, no subtlety. His lips and tongue were greedy for her, but they were robbed of a conquest as she met their eagerness with a reciprocal response that surprised even her, opening her mouth, welcoming the pillage, contributing to the seduction.

Gradually, the initial hunger abated, though it was by no

means appeased. Pausing only to draw a breath, Erik's lips were still resting lightly on hers as he murmured, "I've waited all day for that. Every second of last night, I spent tasting you, trying to get the way you smell and look and feel out of my mind so I wouldn't go completely insane. And now, I can't get enough . . . I can't . . . I can't . . ." Once again, his lips descended on hers.

Kathleen received them confidently. He moaned deep in his throat as she ran her tongue along his bottom lip and then under the brush of his silky mustache. "God, Kathleen, I want you." That was all he could manage to say before he hooked his thumbs under the straps of her bodice and lowered them.

He nibbled her lightly, sampling each morsel of her throat and chest as if he were a gourmand at a feast. Kathleen's hands cradled his head, luxuriating in the feel of his hair between her fingers. When his mouth reached the top curves of her breasts, it lingered, hovering over her, waiting.

He raised his head and looked into her eyes, searching them for signs of objection. His fingers manipulated the top button on the camisole until it came open. When she didn't protest, only stared up at him with wide, trusting eyes, he released the second. The third. The fourth. All lay undone under his fingers, and still he continued to pierce her with the laser-light quality of his blue gaze.

Then, slowly, prolonging the anticipation, he lowered his eyes and parted the front of her bodice until he was looking at her breasts. "I wish I dared a light," he said hoarsely. "I want to see you. Your color. I want to see what you look like when I do this." As he spoke, he touched one bewitching crest with the tip of his finger and felt it pucker under the merest suggestion of stimulation. Then he rolled it gently between his fingers.

I should stop this. I should stop this. The words were repeated in her head like a catechism, but she was powerless to carry out the intention. Erik's fingers were gentle and yet demanding as he explored her, learned her, stroked her, brought her to a pitch of arousal she had never known before.

And she was to find that it had only begun. He lowered his head and covered her with his mouth. She was enveloped in a sweet, hot, wet trap from which she didn't want to escape. His tongue curled around her nipple even as his cheeks flexed to draw her deeper into the enchanting cavern of his mouth.

She felt his hand moving up her thigh in a sensual caress. When had she raised her knees? Why were her hips rotating in an erotic rhythm out of some pagan ballet? It didn't matter. Nothing did as he continued to pleasure her with his mouth on her breasts.

His hand was alarmingly close to the center of her body where the heat was becoming unbearable. Every nerve ending in her being was pulsing toward that one point that ached to be relieved.

Did she murmur his name? Did she beg him to touch her with a healing hand? Did he sense a silent plea? She never knew, but was helpless to resist when his hand settled over her with an accuracy that startled and thrilled her. She gasped in mingled shock and delight when his fingers insinuated their way under the lacy, elastic leg of her panties. With infinite tenderness, he touched her, finding her bathed with the sweet moistness her body had provided at the coaxing of his fingers.

She was catapulted out of her lethargy when he left the bed and started unfastening his shirt, virtually ripping the buttons from the fabric.

For the first time since they had entered the cabin, Kathleen realized the dangerous game she was playing. *My God! What am I doing?*

Erik had his shirt off and was furiously working at his belt buckle, muttering impatient deprecations to the suddenly stubborn metal.

"Wh— What are you doing?" Kathleen asked shakily.

"Well, you may like it wearing clothes, and I'll admit that it can be fun, but it's too hot tonight. Besides, I prefer nakedness."

"No!" she cried in a stage whisper, and bolted from the bed, clutching her bodice over her heaving, bared breasts. "No!" she repeated, shaking her head.

He stopped his frantic efforts and jerked his head up to stare at her in bafflement.

"What do you mean by 'no'? Do you mean 'No, we leave our clothes on,' or 'No, period'?"

She averted her head to keep from looking at him. "No, period," she mumbled to the wall.

"*Why?* Damn you, why?"

Why? She was ashamed of the real reason, and even if she told him, he wouldn't believe her. Who, in this day and age, remained a virgin to the ripe old age of twenty and five? No one. No one except Kathleen Pamela Haley.

"I . . . I don't . . ." She had started the sentence timidly. But then she gained conviction and raised her head stubbornly, meeting his eyes defiantly. "I don't want to."

"Like hell you don't," he said savagely.

For a moment, she was too startled by his ferocity to speak. His arrogance was unequaled. Who did he think he was? She was? Had he never been turned down before? Well, she was no one to trifle with, and he might just as well learn that now. "I said I don't want to, and I meant it," she hissed loudly.

The chiseled lines on either side of his mouth hardened, and his eyes went cold. "Well," he drawled in a voice that was deceptively calm, "I hate for you to have gone to all this trouble without knowing the fruit of your labor."

His arm went around her waist with the speed of a striking snake, and his other hand clenched her wrist. He dragged her hand downward until she gleaned his intention and gurgled, "Nooo!"

"Oh, yes. I don't know what *your* game is, but we're playing by *my* rules now." He flattened her hand against his manhood, which stretched the front of his trousers.

"Stop this, Erik. I'll never forgive you if you don't," she warned in a hard voice.

He laughed scoffingly. "Do you think I care? Go ahead, Kathleen. Touch me. Feel me. I want you to know how all your careful teasing paid off." He rubbed her hand up and down the hard shaft while his breathing became more labored.

Then, abruptly, he flung her away from him in a gesture of utter disgust.

She covered her face with her hands to halt the angry, debasing tears that were coursing down her cheeks.

"Goddammit!" he cursed. "I don't know why I'm bothering myself with you." The quiet room was filled with his harsh breathing. He turned on his heels, grabbed his shirt and coat and stalked to the screen door. Kathleen heard it squeak as he opened it. He paused before he went out.

"You know, the boys in that nightclub weren't wrong. You are a hot little number. And you *were* primed and ready."

The next morning, Kathleen walked on leaden legs toward the dining hall. She dreaded meeting Erik face-to-face because she wasn't sure what she would do when she saw him. Would she feel compelled by rage to slap his face for the insulting words he had flung at her? Or would she want to weep because he thought her capable of intentionally leading him on? Every time she recalled the revulsion in his voice, she shuddered. Yet by what right did he expect her to sleep with him? Wasn't the choice hers? After a sleepless night of debate, she still had no answers.

He wasn't in the dining room when she went in. She behaved normally, responding to the hellos the children called to her. When she joined the other counselors at their table, she offered the obligatory pleasantries, though it was impossible to hide the red puffiness of her gritty eyes.

Her heart leapt to her throat when Erik stalked in, but he stayed only long enough to retrieve a thermos of coffee from the kitchen, then slammed out, having looked neither right nor left. His back was ramrod stiff.

The other counselors curiously shifted their eyes toward Kathleen, and there was a noticeable cessation of conversation. She sipped her coffee nonchalantly, trying to act as though she hadn't even seen him.

Edna was standing on the porch when Kathleen left the dining room after pretending to eat a hearty breakfast. The older woman went straight to the point. "Things didn't go too well last night, did they?" she asked with uncanny intuition.

Kathleen was tempted to brazen it out, to respond happily, but she knew it would be useless. She had known Edna too many years, had grown up under her watchful care. This woman knew Kathleen's heart and mind probably better than most mothers knew their own daughters.

Kathleen sighed heavily. It was with relief that she let her shoulders, which she had been holding so proudly for the benefit of the staff, slump in dejection. "No."

"I'm sorry. I was foolishly trying to play matchmaker. B. J. warned me to leave well enough alone, but you two seemed to be attracted to each other. I think you look beautiful together. He's so masculine and you're so——" Edna was startled into silence by Kathleen's uncharacteristically bitter laugh.

"Not being attracted to each other isn't our problem," she admitted.

A light dawned on Edna's kind face. "Ahhh. Then may I presume that quite the opposite is true?"

Kathleen looked away guiltily. "Yes," she mumbled. "He's much more . . . He's sophisticated and I'm . . ."

"I think I get the picture," Edna said sadly. "Come on. Let's walk. I've asked Mike to take your group to the soccer field with him."

How had Edna known that she didn't feel quite up to coping this morning? Affectionately, Kathleen placed her arm around the older woman's waist. They strolled toward a tributary of the river, little more than a stream, which flowed at the back of the Harrisons' cabin. By mutual consent, they sat on the clover-carpeted ground. It was shady and peaceful. The campers had filed off to their first morning activity. From somewhere, the purr of B. J.'s lawn mower could be heard. The birds chirped as they flitted through the sun-dappled branches of the trees. Noisily, a squirrel and bluejay argued over territorial boundaries. The brook bubbled over its rock-strewn bed, unaffected by grief, indecision or hurt.

"Are you in love with him, Kathleen?" Edna asked gently.

Kathleen shook her head, the ponytail whipping her neck like a brush. "I don't know. Honestly, I don't. I've only known him a few days."

Edna laughed with genuine humor. "My dear, time has very little to do with love. Some people know each other all their lives and love each other for that long. Others meet and fall in love in the space of hours. Love doesn't have a timetable. Nor does it discriminate. It happens to the best of us, you know. Are you afraid of loving, Kathleen? I don't mean physically," she stressed. "I mean are you afraid of losing Erik as you did your parents?"

Love? Only in the last few hours had Kathleen realized that Erik was a man she could care a great deal for. She wasn't quite ready to attach the label of "love" to the emotions he brought to the surface. But those emotions were too strong to be taken lightly or to dismiss completely.

That was another problem. Erik was interested in her. She knew that. The chemistry between them couldn't be denied. But if she slept with him, what then? He would go on his way, to another assignment anywhere in the world, to another woman, with a new scalp dangling from his belt. What of her? She would be left with nothing except a sense of loss— of the man and of her self-respect.

Most contemporary women would hoot over her old-fashioned code of morality. That didn't bother her. It was important to her. But was that the only reason she had resisted him?

Perhaps Edna was right. She was afraid. Pure and simple. What to her would be a commitment, to Erik would be an episode. Yes, she feared that. But she wasn't ready to confess it. "He's arrogant and extremely selfish and spoiled," Kathleen said crossly.

"Yes, he is," Edna agreed. "And B. J. is a procrastinator, downright lazy sometimes, and snores. But I'd be a basket case without him, even though at times I feel like killing him." She grew serious again and took Kathleen's hand in hers. "You loved your parents, and in your young eyes, they deserted you at a vulnerable time in your life. You've overcome all the obstacles of that trauma and grown into a beautiful woman. But you'll decay and dry up from the inside out if you don't share all that beauty with someone, Kathleen. Don't be afraid of loving."

Tears gathered in the corners of Kathleen's eyes. She placed her hand on Edna's shoulder and said softly, "I love *you*."

Edna reached up and patted Kathleen's hand briskly. "I know you do. But that's hardly the problem right now." She got to her feet with an economy of movement unusual for a woman her age. "It may make you feel better to know that your misery's got company. If Erik's mood this morning is any indication, I'd say he's got it bad, too. He was as cranky as a bear with a bee sting in the butt."

"Where is he?" Kathleen asked quietly.

"He's in the office. He asked permission to look through the case-history files for background information."

"Oh," Kathleen said indifferently as she stood up and dusted off the seat of her shorts.

She and Edna returned to the compound, and for the rest of the day Kathleen exhausted herself with activity. If thoughts of Erik interfered, she put them down, refusing to think of him for more than moments at a time. Thus, he was constantly on her mind.

He didn't make an appearance at lunch. She was disappointed that he didn't see how unaffected she was by the night before, how calm she was, how indifferent to him.

He was at dinner.

He came through the screen door of the dining hall with the bearing of his most regal ancestors, charming whomever came under the light in his eyes, smiling from beneath his mustache with the ease of a worshiped movie idol.

Kathleen chatted with Mike Simpson, who was surprised and delighted with her attention. She sat beside him at the table and engaged the others around them in a steady stream of lively conversation.

After getting his tray, Erik swung his long leg over the bench across the table and down from Kathleen. He sat next to a female counselor who flirted unabashedly. Kathleen gnashed her teeth whenever the girl's high, shrill giggle reached her over the noise in the dining room. She refused to look in their direction.

When the Harrisons joined the table, Edna assessed the situation at a glance, and when her eyes met Kathleen's, the girl noticed that Edna's were highly amused.

What's so funny? she wanted to demand.

After she finished eating, she picked up her tray to return it to the kitchen. Without going out of her way, it was necessary for her to walk past Erik and his adoring companion. She resolved to ignore them.

She stood up and tugged on the bottom of her T-shirt, straightening it, not knowing how the automatic gesture outlined and defined her figure. Casually, she stepped over the bench and took two purposeful steps toward the kitchen.

"Hello, Kathleen."

She practically tripped as her tennis shoes screeched to a halt, almost as if her feet had usurped her brain's authority and given an independent command.

She arranged her face into a bright, cheerful smile, then turned her head to look at him.

The girl was draped over his arm, and Kathleen had the wild impulse to set her tray down and yank the girl's long hair from her head. Instead, she said sweetly, "Hello, Erik, Carol." Her voice dripped with saccharin and her smile was brilliant. She was the only one who couldn't see the green fire smoldering in her eyes. "How was your day?"

"Erik stayed cooped up all day in the office, but then he joined my group at the river for their swimming time." Carol rolled her eyes toward him as if they shared a great secret. Then she met Kathleen's eyes again. "He didn't even bring his camera. He said he was there strictly for pleasure."

Kathleen loathed the smug expression on the other girl's

face, but she was made more furious by the mirthful twitching of Erik's mustache. "How nice!" she said with false enthusiasm. "He's been known to need cooling off."

"Is the tubing trip still scheduled for tomorrow?" Erik asked, all but laughing out loud at Kathleen's clever slur, which the other girl was too dim to catch.

"*I'm* still going," Kathleen said, with emphasis.

"Then so am I," he said.

"Suit yourself." She turned her back on them all and, after returning her tray to the window, left the hall.

He was impossible! How dare he be civil! All but laughing at her! She had wanted to shun him, to put him in his place, and he hadn't even had the gallantry to give her that trite satisfaction. He had forced her to be polite.

How could she have ever entertained the idea that she was falling in love with him? She didn't love him. She didn't even like him. She would put him out of her mind and think about something else.

Why, then, when she returned to her cabin, did she forget things? Why, when she started searching for something, did she forget what she was looking for? Why, when she stretched out on her bed, did she recall vividly how his gentle hands and burning mouth had delighted and tormented her body?

His mustache wasn't prickly at all. It was soft. When he closed his mouth over her nipple, his mustache nudged the plump mound of her breast in a caress all its own.

She rolled over onto her back with a feeble groan, willing her body not to throb with remembrance. Unable to stop herself, her hands sought out the places that had known his touch and tried in vain to rub out the recollections. But the nerves were too alive, too raw, and rather than help, her hands made her even more agitated.

She flopped over onto her stomach and pressed her face into the pillow, unable to rid herself of his image. It was hours later that her mind finally slipped out of the real world into the one dominated by dreams.

And, still, Erik was there.

Chapter Six

The morning dawned bright and clear. Kathleen had wished that some whim of nature might prevent today's trip to the Buffalo River. Apparently, that wasn't to be, so she dressed and packed a small duffel bag to take with her.

Preparing for any emergency, she crammed Band-Aids, antiseptic lotion, insect repellant, suntanning cream, zinc oxide, for those who asked for the suntanning cream too late, tissues, Chapstick, antacid tablets, aspirin, extra towels, extra socks and a change of clothes for herself into the canvas bag. Certain that she was forgetting something she would critically need, she zipped the bag, slung it over her shoulder and left her cabin for the center of the compound.

Breakfast was routine, and she ate resolutely, striving not to notice Erik as he came in and became a part of the noisy, active beehive. The children who were scheduled for the trip were almost too excited to eat, and when the bell rang, they raced for the bus parked outside, competing for the choice seats next to the windows.

"Have a good time, but be careful." Edna waved to the children hanging out the windows.

"We'll get back in time for dinner, which I'm sure they'll be ready for," Kathleen said, laughing.

"I'll look for you then." Out of the corner of her eyes, Edna noticed Erik climbing aboard the bus. She looked at Kathleen as though she wanted to say something, but only patted her on the hand and said, "Have fun today."

Kathleen spoke pleasantly to the driver, who had driven the ancient school bus for her in years past. Erik's extra equipment had been secured on one of the vacant seats near the back of the bus, but he had insisted on keeping his camera with him. He took the seat across the narrow aisle from Kathleen.

At last, everyone was settled, the driver engaged the reluctant gears and they pulled out of Mountain View's gates. Conversation was impossible while the children loudly sang, argued, challenged and scoffed, accompanied by the unique clamor of the bus.

In her seat directly behind the driver, Kathleen became more relaxed with each passing mile. When she finally deigned to look at Erik, she saw that he was watching her unabashedly. He smiled at her tentatively at first, and then, when she didn't turn away or stare back at him stonily, his grin widened and she couldn't resist answering it.

Every few miles, they drove through one of the many sleepy mountain towns that lined the two-lane highway. The names of the towns were unimportant. They all looked the same. Each had a gasoline station combined with a grocery store. Some had a post office. Often it was nothing more than a mobile home converted for that purpose, yet the American flag flew proudly from makeshift flagpoles.

The houses, which were usually situated directly on the highway, all looked the same, too. Washing hung on outdoor lines to dry. The front porches—and each house had one— were equipped with chairs suitable for rocking away the evening hours. Each home, almost without exception no matter how humble, was blessed with a panorama of the mountains. Gardens, heavy with summer produce, nearly all sported scarecrows. The crops in those small plots weren't for sport. They often provided a family with food for many months.

It was in one such town that Kathleen took time to let the children use the restrooms in the gas station and pick a cold drink out of an antiquated electric cooler chest with "Grapette" emblazoned on its side.

Ever sensitive to his presence, Kathleen suddenly missed Erik amid all the confusion, and looked around to see him crossing a dusty lane toward a lone house perched on a tree-shaded hill.

Instinctively following him across the road, she saw what had attracted his attention. On the rickety front porch of the house sat an old man playing a fiddle. His seat was a metal bus-stop bench with a faded Rainbo Bread sign barely distinguishable in its rusty, peeling paint.

His skin was brown, dry and rivered with deep wrinkles. Sparse white hair stuck out from his head at comical angles. He wore denim overalls, with only one shoulder strap clasped. Without a shirt to hide it, his flabby chest jiggled as he played the fiddle.

Possibly in a more refined setting, the instrument tucked under his double chin would have been classified as a violin, but Kathleen was sure that no instrument, even a Stradivarius, had ever been more cherished. With callused fingers that were dirt- and nicotine-stained, he coaxed a lilting melody from the fiddle, though none but he knew the tune.

When he saw Erik approach, he smiled a toothless welcome and patted his horny, bare foot on the unpainted slats of the porch.

Kathleen stood in awe as Erik's camera began to hum. He moved toward the old man, who wasn't in the least affected by this contraption that seemed not of the same century as he. Erik moved closer until he was crouched on the porch near the old man's feet, pointing the camera directly into the intriguing face.

The screen door opened and an equally old woman came out, drying her hands on a dingy towel. She smiled and, when she saw Erik's camera, self-consciously brushed back wisps of white hair that had escaped the tight bun on the back of her head. Her faded calico dress hung loosely on her spare frame; her feet were as bare as her husband's and almost as callused. She flipped the towel onto her shoulder and began clapping in rhythm to the music.

When the man finished the tune, she leaned over him and kissed him smackingly on the cheek. "That's my favrit," she cackled.

Erik stood up to his full height and took the woman's hand, brought it to his lips and kissed it softly. She laughed and fluttered her scanty, colorless eyelashes at him like a coquette at a ball.

"Thank you both," was all Erik said before he turned around and hopped off the porch. Three lazy hounds lying in the shade under the porch did no more than raise sleepy eyes at the intruders.

Erik spotted Kathleen standing between him and the rutted road. When he was even with her, he smiled and touched her face with his free hand before silently indicating with his head that they should return to the bus, the horn of which was honking imperiously.

"Why did you do it?" she asked when they were once again underway. "Why did you want to put them on tape?" The children had lapsed into a less rigorous camp song, and conversation was easier.

"Because they were beautiful," he answered simply. "Didn't you think so?"

She did now. But she wouldn't have thought so before. She wouldn't have even seen them, noticed them, unless Erik had guided her to them.

"Yes," she said gruffly. "They were beautiful."

His steady gaze shifted down to her mouth, and a fleeting expression of despair and longing filled the cerulean eyes. "And so are you," he said, for her ears alone. When his eyes met hers again, she melted under the impact. "I'm sorry about the other night," he said in a low voice. "It was your prerogative to say no." He and B. J. had shared a can of beer and a lengthy conversation before dinner the previous night. It had been an enlightening discussion for Erik. He understood her refusal now, and that understanding had doused his anger.

More than anything, Kathleen had wanted to hear him apologize, to see him groveling at her feet, begging for forgiveness. Now that she heard the remorse in his voice, she admitted her own blame. "I wasn't playing fair."

"I threw the rule book away when I met you, Kathleen Haley. From now on, we make up our own rules as we go along. Is that fair enough?"

The gentleness of his smile and the earnestness in his eyes were too hard to resist, and Kathleen agreed eagerly, "Yes, Erik. Yes."

Surreptitiously, he mimed a kiss, and she blushed, lowering her eyes briefly before raising them once again to the warm directness of his.

A few miles beyond the town of Jasper, the driver turned right and wound the recalcitrant bus down a dirt road that eventually led to the banks of the Buffalo River.

Eons ago, the river had gouged a deep canyon out of the Ozarks. At many places along the Buffalo, cliffs rose out of its banks and towered over the swift-running water. Gray stone walls, clothed with vines, hung over the river and were reminiscent of the Hanging Gardens of ancient Babylon. The Buffalo was popular throughout that part of the country for canoeing, fishing and other water sports.

Kathleen had been coming to this particular spot for years, and had seen it grow from a playground known only to locals to a thriving tourist attraction. During each of the two-week sessions of the camp, she brought the children for one day's fun on the white water rapids. Inner tubes were rented from a nearby store. The sporting tuber climbed up the rocky hill along the bank until he had gained the area above the smooth rocks over which the water boiled. Then, sitting in his inner tube, he rode it over the rocks and let the swift current carry him about a half-mile down the river where the rushing water finally calmed enough for one to stand up.

It was quite an adventure, but since the water was never more than three or four feet deep, it was safe. Nevertheless, Kathleen was ever watchful. Today Mike Simpson's group and another one, under the supervision of a female counselor named Patsy, came along, making the number of children close to forty.

Erik spent the first hour after their arrival with his camera, climbing the rocky ledges with the children, recording the anticipation in their faces and voices, then catching their elated expressions as they rode down the white, roiling water. When he had all he needed, he returned his equipment to the bus for safety and then stripped down to bathing trunks.

His physique was perfect, his skin without blemish. He splashed, played, hollered and thoroughly enjoyed himself with the children, who vied jealously for his attention.

After a picnic lunch, the counselors and Erik insisted that the children rest a half-hour before going back into the water.

It was about two o'clock when Mike Simpson pulled himself out of the river and plopped his inner tube on the rocky shoal. "Hey, Kathleen, we haven't had a head count since lunch. Think we should?"

"Yes," she agreed. Everyone had been having so much fun that she hadn't thought about it. At Erik's insistence, and much to the campers' delight, she had ridden the rapids a few times herself. Now she, Erik, Mike and Patsy began ticking off names and heads bobbing in the water.

"Someone's missing," she mused aloud, not quite ready to panic.

"Some of them are still up there above the rapids," Erik said reassuringly.

But the minutes went by, and though they counted again and again, they always came up one short.

"Jaimie!" exclaimed Kathleen. "Where's Jaimie?" She looked about her frantically, as though willing him to appear. "Has anyone seen him?"

"Let's not jump to conclusions," Mike said. "I'll ask around and see if anyone has seen him."

"I'll do the same," Patsy offered.

"Don't alarm the other kids," Kathleen cautioned. "Keep it low-keyed."

"Yeah, sure." Mike jogged away.

Erik said, "I'll go up into the woods on the opposite bank. You look around here."

"Thank you. Erik . . ." She placed her hand on his arm.

"I know," he said with uncanny understanding. "We'll find him."

She walked to the concession stand and asked about for Jaimie. Nobody had seen him. She went into the store where the inner tubes were rented. The owner hadn't seen Jaimie, but someone had brought in a tube they had found in the river tangled up in some low-hanging branches. Fear gripped Kathleen's heart. Had Jaimie been sucked into the swift river and washed downstream before he could regain his footing? He was so small. Not athletic. He could swim, but not very well.

The thoughts that raced through her mind were out of her worst nightmares. *Jaimie!* her mind screamed. *No!* She ran back to the river, hoping against hope that Mike's search had produced the lost child. But his face was as grim as Patsy's when she rejoined them at the riverbank.

"Kathleen, what should we do?" Mike asked. For the first time since she'd met him, his open, optimistic face was showing signs of stress.

"We should call the police. The forest rangers." She spoke with more calmness than she felt.

Just then, Patsy said excitedly, "There they are!"

Kathleen followed the direction of her pointing finger and whirled around to see Erik and Jaimie climbing down one of the steep cliffs on the opposite side of the river. "Thank you, God," she prayed as they waded into the river and made their way across.

When they reached her, she didn't know whether to clasp the boy to her or scold him. She did neither. Erik seized control again.

"Hey, Kathleen, look what our little scout found!" Erik said to her cheerfully but with a warning in his eyes.

"Yeah, look, Kathy," Jaimie chimed. He held out a piece of stone, roughly resembling an Indian arrowhead. "Erik says it could have been from the Creeks or the Cherokees or the Chickasaws. Do you think it's real? Erik says he's sure it is. What do you think, Kathy?"

The eager brown eyes looked up at her guilelessly, and she longed to reach for the thin, little body and hug it to her.

She spared Jaimie the embarrassment by answering in as calm a voice as she could muster, "I'm sure it's real, though I don't know which tribe it could have come from. Maybe you could look it up in one of B. J.'s books when we get back."

"Okay," he said, scampering away.

"Jaimie," she called after him. "We'll be leaving before long, so don't wander off again, please."

"Okay," he called back, and ran toward the river to show off his prize to his comrades.

Now that the ordeal was over, she felt the weakness in her knees and would have collapsed onto the hot rocks of the shore had Erik not put out supportive arms to draw her against his hard body.

Mike and Patsy, looking somewhat embarrassed, hurried off to watch the children. Everyone had been sobered by the last hour's worry.

Kathleen turned around to face Erik. "Where did you find him?" she asked tremulously.

"Come here," he said and, taking her hand, pulled her behind the parked bus to afford them some privacy. When they were out of sight of the others, he cradled her against him as though she were the one who had been lost and was now home.

The hair on his chest tickled her nose as he pressed her head into it, and he stroked her back with a comforting hand. "Jaimie didn't know he was missing. That's why I signaled you not to chastise him. He told me he had to go to the bathroom." A rumbling chuckle formed deep in his chest. "Number two, he said. Wanting absolute privacy, he decided to go into the woods. After he had done the deed, he got a little carried away with his exploring, and I found him investigating that piece of rock, which I assured him must be an arrowhead. He was in a world all his own and didn't realize how long he'd been gone or how worried we'd been."

"Erik, if anything had happened to him . . . to any of the children, I . . ." She shuddered, not able to complete the thought.

"I know, I know, but it's all over now and no harm's been done. Later today, I'll tell Jaimie that he shouldn't ever go wandering off by himself like that."

"Thank you," she whispered into the hair-roughened skin beneath her lips.

"Don't I get a reward of some kind?" he asked tenderly, and placed a finger under her chin to lift her face up to his.

He was close. He was strong. She needed him, his strength. And she only nodded numbly in answer to his question before his head descended toward hers and she felt his warm lips move over hers. It was a kiss rife with caring. When he withdrew his mouth, Kathleen continued to cling to him for a few moments.

They walked back to the riverbank with his arm secure around her shoulders. Kathleen tried to behave normally, but for the remaining time they were at the tubing site, she was jumpy, nervous and overcautious with the children. The hands on her wristwatch moved with infinite slowness, but at last it was time to blow the whistle and call everyone for the trip home.

She sat beside Erik on the way back and made no pretense of not wanting to. As soon as everyone was aboard the bus and she had made the final head count, she plunked down on the uncomfortable seat beside him and didn't refuse when he offered her his hand to clasp tightly.

When they arrived at Mountain View, everyone was already in the dining hall. For this day, the rules were suspended, and the children were allowed to have their dinner without having first showered and rested. They clambered off the bus, eager to share their day with the other campers. The weary adults were less exultant, and they made a bedraggled picture as they entered the hall.

Briefly, Kathleen recounted Jaimie's disappearance to B. J. and Edna when they asked about her bleak expression and pale face. They agreed that she had handled it correctly in not scolding him, but they also thought that B. J. should talk to him and caution him again about the dangers of separating himself from the others.

Under Erik's stern and watchful eye, Kathleen managed to choke down some of her dinner, but she was still too upset by the day's frightful incident to enjoy it. Never was she so glad to hear the evening bell as she was that night.

As she trudged down the steps of the dining hall, planning to go directly to her cabin, her upper arm was gripped firmly. "Come on, you're going with me," Erik said decisively.

"What?" She tried to release her arm, but it was a futile effort. "I'm going to bed."

"Yes, you should. But first you're going to unwind a little bit. If you try to sleep now, you'll only have nightmares about what could have happened today."

No doubt he was right about that, but she still didn't give in too easily, especially since they were trekking in the direction of his cabin. "Where are you taking me?" Kathleen asked.

"For a drive."

That wasn't the answer she had expected to hear, but when had Erik Gudjonsen done anything she had expected him to? "A drive?" she asked weakly. "Where?"

He smiled down at her, and his teeth gleamed in the tanned face. "Wait and see," he taunted, and slung his arm across her shoulder, pulling her closer.

Obediently, she went with him, lacking the will and the strength to argue, and at the same time, glad to relinquish decision-making control to him. She had been solely responsible for her life for so many years, forced by necessity to make each decision. It was a relief to submit to someone else for a while.

He helped her into the Blazer before climbing in himself. He drove toward the compound and then out the main gate.

"This is the way to the swimming area," she remarked when he took the turn.

"Yeah, but we'll have to walk a little way to get where we're going. I want to show you something."

Again she didn't argue. The night was cool and there was the merest hint of rain in the air. Erik had left the windows down, and Kathleen leaned her head against the seat and closed her eyes, letting the cool breeze blow across her face.

When the Blazer stopped, she opened her eyes and saw that they were indeed parked at the swimming area. "It's lovely, but I've seen it," she said dryly.

Erik laughed. "You're feeling better. Your glib tongue has been restored to full power." He opened the passenger door and hauled her out. "Come on, smart aleck. You have to walk from here."

Instead of going toward the river as she had expected him to, he traipsed off into the woods, dragging her behind him.

"Erik," she said worriedly. "Are you sure—"

"I know where I'm going?" he finished for her. Even the faint moonlight couldn't penetrate the thick branches of the trees that umbrellaed them. "Yes, I know where I am. I found this place the other night when I was rather . . . agitated . . . and needed a place to cool off." He squeezed her hand tightly and she blushed.

They walked for a few more minutes in silence. He did seem acquainted with the surroundings, for he helped her avoid vines and boulders. "Where are—"

"Listen," he interrupted her. "Can't you hear the river?" They stopped and she listened. She could hear the sound of rushing water.

They walked through the last barrier of trees, and the moonlight revealed Erik's destination. There, beside the river, was an expanse of white sand finer than sugar. It led directly into the pebble-lined riverbed. There were some large rocks about a hundred feet upstream that caused the gentle rapids. At the sandy beach, the water was quite swift. Huge oak and elm trees spread their limbs like natural canopies over the river, which was narrow at this point, creating a feeling of intimacy and privacy. It was beautiful.

"How did you find it?" Kathleen asked in awe. She was amazed that in all her years of coming to the camp she had failed to find this spot herself. But then, it was off the beaten path and in an area too dangerous for nature hikes with curious children.

"I told you I was walking out my frustration." He smiled. "Come on."

They ran toward the water's edge. Erik had brought a blanket from the Blazer and he spread it on the sand. Kathleen paused long enough to whip off the clothes she had worn home from the tubing trip. Earlier in the day, she had untied the neck strap of her bikini in order to get full benefit of the sun and tied it in a bow between her breasts. It was designed to be worn either with the strap or without, so she went into the water unselfconsciously.

"Oh! It's cold!" she cried as the water gurgled over her ankles.

"Not when you get used to it," Erik assured her.

He waded out a little farther, but the water never got any deeper than his knees. He squatted down on his haunches, fighting the current, and then sat down on the pebbly bottom, putting his back to the rapids. "It's like a whirlpool," he said.

The swift water threatened to unbalance her at any moment as she timorously made her way out into midstream to join Erik. She put her hand on his solid shoulder when she reached him and eased down into the water. Its numbing frigidity almost took her breath away.

"How can you stand this?" she asked as her bottom finally touched the riverbed and she stretched her feet out in front of her.

"You'll get used to it," he said. "It's great, isn't it?"

After a moment, she was willing to concede that it was. The swirling water, with its bubbling lullaby, was soothing, whisking away her tension as it rushed past her. She supported her torso on her hands and leaned back, lifting her hips and allowing her legs to float in the current. As delicious as it was, her position caused a problem. The water was so swift that it gushed under the cups of her bikini bra.

"I think I might be in danger of losing my bikini." She laughed nervously.

"Well, I can fix that," Erik said.

Chapter Seven

❧❧ ❧❧

Before she knew what had happened, her bra had been whipped from her body and was bobbing away in the swirling water.

"Erik!" she shrieked, and covered herself with crossed arms. "What did you do?"

"I saved you from worrying about losing your top. Now that it's lost, you've nothing to worry about." He shrugged happily. His smile was dazzling . . . and dangerous.

"You unhooked it on purpose!"

"Guilty," he said easily. "Now relax and enjoy the water." He tilted his head back and raised his face to the sky like some of his pagan ancestors who worshiped the heavens. His eyes were closed.

Kathleen's main concern wasn't the swift water, but the rapid beating of her heart. She was here in the wilderness, in the middle of the night, with this virile and arrogant man, sitting virtually naked within inches of him.

In spite of the growing uneasiness, she felt a twinge of pique and annoyance when he didn't even look at her. He seemed totally detached, disinterested. Gradually, she began to relax and resumed her previous position by leaning back on her hands, making sure that the crests of her breasts, which were contracted to hardness by the cold water, were under the surface. For long moments, Kathleèn and Erik were quiet, with only the sound of water around them. When his voice caressed her ear, she jumped in alarm.

"Did you hear that?"

She could hear nothing over the thudding of her pulse in her ears. "What?"

"See that owl on the outer branch of that tree?" He pointed toward one of the oaks, but she couldn't see anything. "No. Where?"

"There. See that branch . . . Wait a minute. This is no good." He moved behind her and placed his muscled thighs on either side of her hips. Her back knew the sturdy support of his chest. One of his arms extended past her head as he pointed to the designated tree. "See him? On that lowest branch over the water."

She strained her eyes in the darkness, but she could see no sign of an owl or anything else. "I can't see him," she sighed.

"I'm not surprised. There's nothing there." His lips settled against her ear as his arm came firmly around her waist, imprisoning her against him. "I lied. I had to get you close to me."

Halfheartedly, she squirmed away from him, but he was sensitive enough to know that she really didn't want to be released. "You're going to get in trouble doing that some-day," she warned him in a soft, ragged voice. "That's the second time you've tricked me."

"Mm-hm. And it's worked both times." His breath was warm as he made the admission against the back of her neck. He held up her hair in a gentle fist while he kissed the scented skin beneath it. But the hand didn't remain idle when he dropped her hair back to her shoulders.

He massaged her neck with magic fingers, then moved his hand down her spine slowly, as if counting each vertebra. Tantalizingly, he slid his hand, palm opened and fingers wide, around her rib cage until he flattened it against the smoothness of her abdomen. His fingers brushed her lightly, though his palm remained stationary. Kathleen wanted that hand to move. His fingers teased her, slipping periodically under the elastic band of her bikini but refraining from touching her.

"Your skin is like wet silk," he murmured into her ear. His tongue became involved with the velvet texture of her skin directly behind her lobe. Imperceptibly, his hand moved upward.

He cupped the underside of her left breast gently. "Your heart is pounding, Kathleen. Is that for me?"

She purred as his fingers lightly stroked the undercurve. "Yes."

"Kathleen."

Then both his hands covered her, alternately flattening her, pressing his palms against her, then kneading her carefully, lifting her, teasing the aching tips of her swollen breasts with his fingertips. Reluctantly, he sacrificed the pleasure of one breast to cradle her jaw and turn her head toward him. He pulled her back, leaning her across his thigh to meet the fervent kiss he offered her.

Their mouths melded together. They tasted, savored while they sipped each other, then delighted again in a deep kiss. Never had she kissed with such abandon and such promise. Her hands went unrestrained as she tangled her fingers in his hair.

His hands moved over her with exquisite precision, examining each hollow, each curve, each plane. They moved down her sides, over the firm belly to glory again in her breasts. Those inquisitive hands and his masterful mouth brought her a pleasure she had never known before. And a seed of desire was planted deep inside her and began to grow until it flowered into full bloom.

Lost in their kiss, she moved against him. It was his tortured gasp against her cheek that brought her out of that euphoric silken web he had spun around her. She realized that her hip was rubbing against his erection.

"I'm sorry," she whispered as she leaned her head against the wall of his chest.

"No apology is necessary." His voice wasn't quite normal. "You're going to be frozen solid if we don't get you out of here." Disengaging their limbs, he rose to his feet and extended his hand for her. Modestly, she came up out of the water, and as hurriedly as the current would allow, she waded past him toward the shore.

Scrambling onto the sand that was still warm from having absorbed the sun's rays all day, she moved away from him, keeping her back to him and primly crossing arms over her chest. Somehow, as tenuous a protection as the water was, without it, she felt totally exposed.

She heard the wet rustling of cloth and knew that he had peeled off his swimming trunks. Quiet footpads brought him to stand close behind her. "Kathleen." He placed his hands on her shoulders and turned her around to face him. Her chin was buried in her chest and her eyes were squeezed tightly shut.

"You've never been with a man, have you?" When she didn't answer, he placed his index finger under her chin and lifted it, forcing her to look at him. "Have you?" he repeated as she opened her eyes to his penetrating gaze.

She could only shake her head "no."

He gathered her to him tenderly, wrapping his arms around her but allowing her own shielding arms to remain between them. He rested his forehead against hers and his breath fanned her face as he whispered, "B. J. intimated as much. My poor, dear girl. I'm sorry. How could I have known that you were a virgin? Though I should have realized it from the first." He chuckled softly, and the vibrations that emanated from his body were transmitted to hers.

Her hands, which she had clasped protectively to her own shoulders, began to relax and finally settled on his chest. "A virgin is such a rare thing, I didn't even recognize one when I met her." His comment was self-deprecating. He sighed deeply, in regret, and said, "No wonder you were afraid of me."

Her head came up quickly. "No, Erik. I was afraid of what was happening, but I was never afraid of you," she said earnestly.

"And now?"

Now? she asked herself. *Now?* Now she knew that she loved him. This morning when he had taken the old couple's picture, she had known it. When he had kissed the lady's hand as if she were a countess, Kathleen had felt an unfamiliar tug at her heart. His concern for Jaimie and the calm, steady way he had handled the crisis only emphasized how vital he had become to her life.

Yes, she loved him. She wanted him to know the full extent of her love. She wanted to express it. Shyly, she placed her hands on his shoulders and looked up into the fathomless eyes. "I'm not afraid now, either."

His breath was strained through clamped teeth as she moved half a step closer and her breasts were molded against his bare chest. Carefully, treating her as if she were a precious piece of porcelain that might shatter at any moment, he put his arms around her waist and drew her closer. The contact was electric and jolted them both.

"Kathleen," he rasped into her hair. "Come lie down with me." Compelling. Urgent. Soft.

As one unit, they moved toward the blanket he had spread out on the sand. He sat down and looked up at her, again offering her his hand. She hooked her thumbs under the sides of her bikini and eased it down her thighs, past her knees, and then daintily stepped out of it.

He reached for her as she sat beside him. Then, slowly, he lay down, bringing her with him. He rolled onto his side and pulled her against him until they lay face to face.

"If I hurt you in any way, I want you to stop me."

"You won't," she said, brushing back a lock of silver-gilded hair from his creased forehead.

"Yes, I will. I wish I didn't have to."

"Then I want you to hurt me. I want this."

He spoke her name softly before it was trapped by his lips

as they captured hers. His tongue outlined her mouth, taking in each nuance, memorizing her unique taste, painting her lips with the nectar of his own mouth. Reaching for her hand, he planted an ardent kiss into its palm and then settled it on his chest.

"I want you to know me, Kathleen. Touch me. I won't do anything until I know you want me as much as I want you."

She watched his eyes as her hand began to explore the wonders of his chest. Her fingers waved over the crinkly hair and massaged the hard muscles under the surface. She grew shy when she accidentally touched one of the hard brown nipples nestled in the mat of tawny hair. Erik drew in a sharp gasp, then ceased to breathe altogether, as if in anticipation of her touching him again. Putting down maidenly shyness, her fingers returned to that turgid bud of flesh and examined it with curious fingers.

His swallow was audible. "Am I allowed the same privileges?"

She laughed softly. "By all means."

She adjusted her position to make her breasts more accessible to him. His hands cupped her, lifted her. The crests knew the sweet aggravation of his thumbs before he lowered his head. She was amazed how hot his mouth felt against her cool skin. What he did with her was so subtle that Kathleen couldn't describe it. All she knew was that she felt that finessing at her breast deep within her womb, and cried out for him never to stop.

Arching against him, she felt his male heat against her belly. Why had she been frightened of him before? His manhood wasn't a thing separate and of itself. It was Erik. His essence.

Her hand worked its way down the taut, flat stomach, followed the trail of silken hair on his abdomen until it blended into a thicker, rougher thatch. Then her fingers closed around him.

"Oh, my God, Kathleen. Sweet . . . yes, yes." The words were unimportant. The tone of his voice, the urgency underlying the words, said more, told her in a language more forceful than the spoken word that she was pleasing him. His reaction gave her confidence and she grew bolder.

His palm settled on the delta at the top of her thighs and massaged circles over her. Slowly, his fingers traced down that feminine curve until he found her soft and pliant and moist. He moved carefully, slowly, until he lay between her thighs.

Then she felt him gently enter the threshold of that secret place. "I'll make it as easy as I can. I swear it," he vowed in a whisper, then gave her all of himself.

Despite her determination not to, she cried out. Her heels dug little cups in the sand underneath the blanket, and her nails made crescent-shaped impressions on the skin of Erik's back.

"My love," he whispered. "I'm sorry. Relax, relax."

For long moments, they lay locked in that most intimate of embraces. Timeless. Eternal. He kissed her, lifted the unwanted tears from her cheeks with solicitous lips. His hands smoothed her hair from her face and then threaded the heavy strands through his fingers before burying his face in its radiance and breathing deeply of its scent.

Unknowingly, Kathleen moved, tightening her muscles around him. His quick, shuddering intake of breath sounded like a miniature hurricane in her ear. Realizing she had stirred him, she tried the internal movement deliberately, and this time his response was less subtle.

At first, his thrusts were tentative, but then nature took over and there was no stopping him from reaching that ultimate goal. It was as natural for Erik, at that moment of fulfillment, to cry her name, as it was for the whippoorwill to call plaintively to his mate.

There was something primeval and innocent about their nakedness. The rushing river, the whisper of the wind, the black, starry sky, were all testimonies to the forces of life. No less were Kathleen and Erik.

They became one with the night.

⁂ ⁂

" Kathleen?"

"Hm?"

"Are you sure you're all right?"

She snuggled closer against him and laughed softly. "What must I do to convince you? That's the fourth time you've asked me that since we came in."

He placed a hand on her shoulder and stroked the smooth skin, reveling in the feel of her. Ever wandering, his hand slipped under her arm and found the fullness of her breast. "I know. I just want to make sure you're not uncomfortable."

She laughed again. "Believe me, I'm comfortable." Moving closer, she fit her hips against his abdomen as they lay on the narrow bunk in the guest cabin.

She had never imagined that love could be this consuming, this absolute. Even though an hour had passed since they lay together beside the river, the magnitude of the experience hadn't diminished. She relived each second of it.

Erik had put his trunks back on, and Kathleen had pulled the T-shirt over her bikini bottom. They had laughed over the destination of her top and wondered who would eventually find it. After they had folded the blanket and began walking back to the Blazer, their arms entwined around each other, she had said, "Erik, it was wonderful."

"For me it was." He kissed her fleetingly on the forehead. "It will get better for you. I promise."

How could it get any better? She thought it had been beautiful, though she didn't feel that satisfied weightlessness she had read about. Her body still ached with some indefinable longing.

"Do you think we'd be expelled from camp if you spent the night in my cabin?" he had asked her as they drove through the main gate. He had extinguished the headlights of the car and was creeping across the compound at a snail's pace.

"Not if no one catches us," she said in a singsong voice.

"I knew I liked something about you, Kathleen Haley. You're a lady of adventure." He caressed her knee.

"Wait!" she said suddenly. "Pull around to the back of the kitchen."

His grin was devilish. "Did you work up an appetite?"

As punishment for his question, she kissed him soundly on the ear. "No, but I want to get something."

"Well, hurry up, or we'll get caught."

"I'll be right back," she whispered as she opened the car door.

In less than a full minute, she was back, carrying a brown paper sack. "What's in the bag?" he asked as he quietly engaged the gears of the truck again and tried to find his way down the darkened drive toward his cabin.

"Wait and see," she teased as he maneuvered past the last tree.

When they got inside and accustomed their eyes to the darkness—they didn't want the disruption of bright lights—Erik declared that a shower was in order.

"I wish we had a deep bathtub, but we'll make do with what we have," he said in a voice feigning martyrdom.

The shower had been an orgy of warm water, soap, naked skin, curious hands and insatiable mouths. "Wash my hair, woman," he commanded playfully as he dropped to his knees and tossed her the slippery plastic bottle of shampoo.

She laughed but fell to the task enthusiastically, working the soap into a rich lather and squeezing it through the strands of his hair. She was only distracted from the labor of love when his mouth relentlessly navigated her stomach. His hands caressed the backs of her thighs and hips as his mustache played havoc with her navel. When he stood up again, Kathleen was trembling.

The small reserve of hot water for the cabin began to run out and the water cooled. "Are you clean?" Erik asked her as he continued to massage her soapy breasts.

She leaned against the tiles of the shower stall, oblivious

to anything but the gifted hands that touched her so expertly. "Squeaky clean," she murmured.

"Are you sure?" Something in his tone caused Kathleen to open her eyes, which had fallen shut in sleepy contentment. That hungry desire she had come to know quickened in her again as his hand moved down her body to the tight auburn nest between her thighs. His eyes grew smoky with passion as his sudsy fingers stroked her.

"Erik," she pleaded, lifting her arms around his neck and rotating her hips against the erection that had replaced his hands. She was pressed to the tile wall as he kissed her long and deep until the water became quite cold.

They dried off, but remained unclothed. Kathleen presented him with the paper sack she had picked up in the kitchen. "For you," she said. The sack was full of ripe, luscious Arkansas peaches.

"Thank you!"

They sat on a rug on the floor, and with a small paring knife she had remembered to bring along, Kathleen peeled a peach for him slowly with a tempting Eve-in-the-Garden look in her eyes. They ate lustily, sharing two of the peaches, letting the juice run down their bodies in appealing rivulets.

"Your face is sticky," she observed.

"It sure is. Do you mind?"

She shook her head and with a naughty glint in her eyes said, "Uh-huh." Leaning toward him, she placed her lips against his and licked them lightly. Erik had long since ceased to breathe even before her mouth left his lips for his chin and beyond to his neck. When her lips moved over the skin of his chest and her small pink tongue found his nipples, he groaned and wound his fingers through her hair.

Now, after another, briefer shower, they lay on his narrow bed, their limbs entwined. He murmured love words into her hair and continued to examine the mysteries of her breasts and take pleasure in the changes in them that he could bring about with his caressing fingers.

Tiny tremors began to dance in Kathleen's veins. She loved

the feel of his hair-matted chest against her skin, the long legs rubbing hers. The scent of his masculine soap, combined with his unique muskiness, made her eager to know him once again.

"Erik?"

"Shhh. You're supposed to be asleep."

"Erik, please—" She couldn't speak as her distended nipple was gently pressed between his fingers. His mouth was at her ear, provoking it with a persuasive tongue. "Erik, love me again."

"Kathleen, you'll be sore, darling, and—"

"Please."

"Kathleen . . ."

She heard the indecision, the hesitation in his voice. Purposefully, she rubbed her hips against him. His heartbeat became irregular and accelerated. Slowly, his hand slipped to the back of her thigh and gently pushed it upward until her knee was close to her chest.

He probed her slightly, easing himself into her and then withdrawing gradually. The hand on her breast smoothed down to her abdomen and flattened there, bringing her closer. Then his fingers brushed downward through the auburn curls.

Kathleen sighed and murmured something incoherent, but Erik seemed to understand. Even as he sank more surely into her, his searching fingers found that sensitive bud that silently cried out for his touch. Her whole body quivered. He touched her again ever so lightly, but with infinite caring and a need to give.

Kathleen felt her soul swelling, expanding, and she soared with it. In rapid succession, tiny explosions erupted within her, rippling outward from that flowering of pleasure, igniting each nerve, firing her spirit. She pushed her hips against him, forcing him deeper, crying his name in wonder and love.

He let her come back from that seductive oblivion slowly, welcoming her return with words she expected never to hear from a man's mouth in reference to her. Was she that beautiful? Was she that woman he praised so highly for her femininity? She hoped so. She wanted to be that for him.

But when he left her, she stared at him in surprise. "Erik, you're still—"

He smiled down at her tenderly. "Yes. That time was for you," he said before settling his mouth against hers and kissing her deeply. "I want to watch your face."

She was an eager pupil but afraid of disappointing him. "I don't think . . . I mean, just now . . . so soon . . ."

He laughed as he stretched over her. "You have a lot to learn, Ms. Haley, and I'm going to love teaching you." He dipped his head and flicked his tongue across the straining pink crests of her breasts in turn.

Raising his head, he studied her face as he slipped his hand between her thighs and trailed his fingers along the dewy skin. "You feel so good."

"So do you."

"You're so soft here." His fingers went beyond the protective folds.

Her neck arched. "Oh, Erik. I can't believe that you're touching me this way."

"Believe it." He leaned down and kissed her on each breast, then on her parted lips. "You are incredibly sweet," he grated as he continued to stroke her from the inside out.

She knew then that he had been right about his ability to arouse her again. She was more than ready when he poised above her and then filled her. Sighing, she surrendered to every sensation that inundated her. Her body rushed toward that now-familiar crescendo. She opened her eyes and saw that he was staring into her face. He clasped her to him and plunged deeper than he had before, giving her all he had to give. And when the wave crashed over them both, his lips formed her name, but his eyes spoke of love.

※ ※

They met at breakfast. Whenever their eyes locked, they laughed at each other like guilty children who shared the delicious secret of having committed some mischievous transgression and gotten away with it. Indeed, they had. Unseen, he had walked her back to her cabin just before dawn.

Edna eyed them suspiciously, but they were unaware of it. The other adults were too despondent to notice anything except the rain outside. Rain spelled disaster to a camp counselor who would be forced to spend the day indoors with two hundred cantankerous children.

Thank heaven for Walt Disney, for he was on the agenda for today. They would show one movie in the morning, have lunch and then show another movie after crafts session in the afternoon.

Erik took the change in itinerary with the gladheartedness with which he was accepting everything this morning. "I can show how you handle a rainy day. And I'm not quite finished looking over those files," he explained to Edna.

An hour later, the children were seated around a large-screen TV. The film was started over much hand clapping and foot stamping. Erik set his camera on the tripod, but the moment he turned it on, he knew that it was malfunctioning. He cursed softly under his breath, but the soundtrack of *Lady and the Tramp* made it inaudible to anyone except Kathleen, who was standing with him.

"It's too difficult to explain," he told her when she questioned him about it. "But these cameras are so specialized that when the least little thing goes wrong, they're out of commission. I know what's wrong, but I don't have the part that needs to be replaced." Agitated, he raked his hair as he said another low "damn."

"What can you do?" Unseen in the darkened room, she slid her hand under his sleeve and up the inside of his upper arm.

"Stay in bed with you all day," he suggested with a comical leer as he leaned toward her.

"I'm serious."

"So am I."

She cleared her throat authoritatively. "I mean about the camera."

"Oh, about the camera." He pretended sudden enlightenment. "Well, I'll have to go to St. Louis and have it fixed."

"Erik," she whispered despairingly.

He cuffed her under the chin and said, "Wait here. I'll be right back." He left her and slipped out the door.

Forlornly, she watched the cavorting, singing characters that flickered on the moving screen, but couldn't even appreciate the ingenious animation when she thought of spending the day without Erik.

When he came back, his walk was jaunty despite the fact that his shoulders and hair were rain-dampened. "I called the airport in Fort Smith. They have flights to and from St. Louis today. If we leave right now, I can catch a two-thirty flight, get my business done and return tonight. I've called the engineers at the television station. They're tracking down the part I need and will have it by the time I get there."

"You'll be gone all day," she moaned.

"And you'll be with me. At least, part of it." He pressed a finger against her lips when he saw the rapid questions forming there. "I asked Edna if you could drive me to Fort Smith. She said because of the rain, you could be spared. That is, if you don't mind fooling around in Fort Smith until I come back tonight."

"Oh, no, Erik. I'll go to a movie or do some shopping. And we'll have all that time in the car together." Impulsively, she wrapped her arms around his waist and buried her face in his damp shirtfront.

"Careful," he whispered as he disengaged himself. "The movie won't be all that engrossing if we're providing a better show, and besides, we have to hurry. I'll pick you up outside your cabin in fifteen minutes. Okay?"

"Yes," she answered eagerly.

When he honked the horn for her in the specified amount of time, she dashed to the Blazer wearing a tight pair of jeans, a green silk blouse and a clear plastic windbreaker as protection against the rain.

"Do you always look sensational?" he asked as he leaned

over to caress her firmly on the mouth. What had been intended as a brief, perfunctory kiss became as passion-filled as all the others. With the merest contact, their mouths became hungry for each other and wouldn't be denied. When at last they breathlessly pulled away, Erik grumbled, "This is going to be the longest day I've ever spent in my life."

She gave directions to the highway that would take them to Fort Smith and he drove as fast as the rain-slickened road would allow. It took them the better part of three hours to reach Fort Smith, and that barely allowed Erik time to catch the 2:43 flight to St. Louis. He picked up his reserved ticket at the counter and turned toward Kathleen. "I'll be on the flight arriving at eleven-ten tonight. That's almost nine hours Can you entertain yourself for that long?"

"I'll think about last night."

"That ought to keep you busy." He grinned. Then his face sobered. "Keep an eye on the Blazer. I'll have the camera with me, but all my other stuff is in there, so lock it up if you leave it."

"I'll guard it with my life."

"Don't ever say that." He placed his camera on one of the turquoise vinyl and chrome sofas that were scattered through the small air terminal and gripped her shoulders. "Our lives are too precious now to be gambling away."

"Oh, Erik," she pleaded, "kiss me."

Impatiently, he looked around the waiting room. Outside the large plate-glass windows, he saw the arrival of the turbo prop airplane that would be his flight. "Come here," he said as he grasped her hand and dragged her toward a telephone booth.

He squeezed them inside it and tried to close the door. "Damn this door," he muttered as he tried unsuccessfully to unjam it. "What the hell. Let them look." His arms went around her in a possessive clench. His mouth opened hers, his tongue dipping into that sweet recess between her soft lips and promising greater fulfillment when time and circumstance allowed.

Shakily, he pushed her away from him. "We'd better get out of here before we're arrested." He tried to laugh, but the imminent departure was too close, and neither wanted to be separated from the other.

His flight had been announced over the public-address system, but they were granted a few more precious minutes to cling to each other while the aircraft was refueled.

"We're being silly," he whispered into her hair as he embraced her one last time. "I'll see you in just a few hours." He kissed her hard on the mouth. "I'll see you tonight."

"I'll be here," she said, smiling.

He went through the security check, nervously watchful of the attendants who examined his camera. He blew Kathleen a kiss before he ran through the door toward the portable steps that led up to the fuselage of the waiting airplane. Just before he climbed aboard, he took the camera off his shoulder and cradled it in one arm. With the other, he waved to Kathleen, who stood behind the glass where nonpassengers were consigned, and then he disappeared from her sight.

A lump swelled in her throat and she swallowed it impatiently. What was wrong with her? She would see him tonight. *Silly!* she admonished herself.

The airplane door was closed. The portable steps were wheeled away. Slowly, the airplane taxied to the end of the field and turned to its takeoff position. It waited for a private plane, which had just landed, to cross the runway on its way to the terminal.

Kathleen, from her position behind the glass, heard the roar of the engines as the pilot revved them, preparing for takeoff. The pilot accelerated and the aircraft barreled down the runway. Kathleen was just about to walk away when her eyes were drawn to the single-engine plane that had entered the intersecting lane off the runway. It began to spin crazily on the wet pavement, and with horror she saw it swerve back onto the runway and in the direct path of the oncoming larger airplane.

She didn't know then that the dampness she felt in her

palms was blood from the deathgrip with which she clenched her fists, driving her nails into the soft flesh. All she was aware of was the inevitable crash of the two airplanes in front of her.

"No!" she screamed at the moment of impact. The smaller plane careened into the nose of the larger one and immediately burst into flames, disintegrating before her eyes.

"No!" she screamed again, held in suspension for an expectant eternity. Then there was a rumble that shook the earth and shattered her world as the full fuel tanks on Erik's jet exploded in a blinding light.

Chapter Eight

❧ ❧

Kathleen hurled herself toward the glass door, and when it wouldn't open, she frantically pounded the glass with her fists, unconscious of the bruising she was giving them. She screamed without ceasing, frantic, her fingernails torn away in futile efforts to open the mechanized door.

Pandemonium had broken out in the terminal. Sirens sounded, people were rushing toward the doors and windows to witness the carnage spread out before them. Ticket counters were deserted. Kathleen fought her way through the onlookers, unaware of the wild, desperate gleam in her eyes. She raced out the front door and around the west side of the building, sliding on the muddy ground. The periphery of the airfield was surrounded by a high cyclone fence that seemingly offered no gates for entrance.

Without any thought to safety, Kathleen began to climb the fence. Her hands were ripped by jagged metal, and her clothes torn by pricking barbs, but still she continued to climb until she gained the top and was able to drop to the ground on the other side. Her palms and knees were scraped by the rough concrete as she landed.

She ran toward the blazing wreckage and its suffocating black column of smoke. It looked like a funeral pyre.

"No. He must be alive," she insisted, even as she ran.

By now, emergency vehicles were surrounding the aircrafts. The smaller plane was barely recognizable as such. There was no doubt as to the fate of its pilot and passengers. Only the front section of the larger aircraft was burning, and firefighters were valiantly trying to put out the life-taking flames.

"Hey, lady, are you crazy?" Kathleen was tackled from behind and flung to the ground. "How'd you get out here, anyway? Stay the hell out of our way."

The fireman's face was smoke-smudged and haggard. He was wearing the yellow slicker and hat associated with his job. What he said was true. She shouldn't be hindering them if they were trying to save Erik's life. She refused to believe that he had no life left to save.

Kathleen pushed herself to her feet and moved away, watching while firemen worked to put out the blaze as other survival teams were unloading passengers from the rear emergency exit of the craft.

She watched with growing panic as passengers were gingerly lifted out. Some were able to crawl out under their own strength, others needed support. Most were bleeding, some were unconscious, some were dead. It was from these that Kathleen averted her eyes. Erik wasn't dead. She knew he wasn't dead.

Her attention riveted on a passenger being unloaded now. Apparently, he was heavy, for two brawny men were having a hard time hauling him down out of the jet. Kathleen's heartbeat escalated, though she hadn't thought that was possible. Then she saw the shining blond hair, blood-streaked but no less brilliant in the gray light.

"Erik!" The name was pushed out of her lungs and she ran toward the men who had strapped him on a stretcher and were whisking him toward a waiting ambulance.

"Wait!" she shouted as they were collapsing the legs of the stretcher to shove it into the vehicle.

She ran up to them, gasping for breath. "He's . . . Is he . . . ? I'm . . ."

"He's not dead," the paramedic said gently. "As a matter of fact, all I could see was a bad bump on the head. Now, please, let us get him to the hospital."

"But the . . . the . . ." She pointed toward the portable oxygen mask covering Erik's nose.

"He's on oxygen. He's got a lung full of smoke. Now, please—"

"I'm going with you," Kathleen said determinedly, even as she gazed down into Erik's waxen, still—too still—face.

"No way." The other paramedic spoke for the first time. "We've got injured people who need medical attention. Get out of the way."

Obediently, she stepped back and allowed them to place Erik in the back of the ambulance. One of the men climbed in behind the stretcher and slammed the door, obliterating her view.

What if Erik had internal injuries that weren't visible? Internal bleeding? Hemorrhages!

The ambulance's motor started and she ran around to the driver's side. Beating on the window, she shouted, "Where are you taking him?"

"St. Edward's," the paramedic shouted as he drove away. "Just follow the sirens."

❧ ❧

St. Edward's Mercy Medical Center was only about a five-minute drive from the airport. Kathleen followed the wailing ambulances with their grim cargoes into the emergency entrance of the modern medical complex.

She watched the ambulance Erik was in as it pulled up to the covered porte cochere and unloaded the stretchers it was carrying. She parked his Blazer, automatically locking it securely as he had directed her to, and scrambled up the incline to the automatic doors. Kathleen had just run through them when she saw Erik being wheeled into one of the treatment rooms with a crew of medical personnel following. She was glad to see that the hospital was manned with a disaster team adequate to handle an emergency like this.

Kathleen knew it was useless to attempt to follow Erik, so she nervously sat down on one of the uncomfortable chairs in the colorless, cold waiting room.

And she prayed.

She was certain that St. Edward's would have a chapel, but for some reason, she didn't feel the need to seek its solace. She wanted to remain as close to Erik as she could. Her faith had always been deep and abiding and she had called on it frequently in her life. Now was one of those times, and she bargained with God for Erik's life, promising circumspection, anything, in the way people are wont to pray in times of crisis.

The next few hours passed in a blur of confusion, heartache and fear. Each time someone would come out of or go into the room where Erik was, Kathleen would hasten to them, her eyes pleading for information, but she was either brusquely pushed aside or given a compassionate look which told her nothing. Relatives of the most unfortunate crash victims were summoned into rooms where crying and anguish could be heard in bone-chilling volume.

Telephones rang, patients with minor injuries came and went in an endless parade, elevator doors whished open and whirred closed, doctors and nurses rushed about and Kathleen was oblivious to it all. Her eyes remained glued to the door behind which Erik might be fighting for his life. If only she could see him, maybe her presence would make a difference in his condition. Could she imbue him with enough strength to pull him out of danger?

When she didn't think she could stand it any longer, she crossed to the crescent-shaped reception desk and cleared her throat loudly to attract the attention of the nurse who was poring over a chart.

"Yes?" The nurse looked up at Kathleen.

"Miss—" Kathleen glanced down at the name tag pinned

to the white polyester uniform. She corrected herself. "Mrs. Prather? Could you . . . would . . . Mr. Gudjonsen . . . He was brought in from the airport. Could you tell me something, anything, of his condition? Please."

"Are you a relative?" Mrs. Prather asked peremptorily.

Kathleen was tempted to lie, but she couldn't and she didn't think the worldly-wise Mrs. Prather would believe her anyway. She looked down at the gray tile floor and said quietly, "No. We're . . . uh—"

"I think I understand," Mrs. Prather said. Kathleen jerked her head upward and looked into the gray-blue eyes that had softened slightly. For some reason, this young woman with the emerald eyes, auburn hair and torn clothes had touched a soft spot in Mrs. Prather's heart. "I'll see what I can do." She turned on silent, rubber-soled feet, and then said over her shoulder, "I'll bring you back some antiseptic for your hands, too."

Kathleen glanced down at her hands and for the first time saw that they were purple with bruises and bleeding from numerous abrasions. She had no fingernails, only bloody stubs. When had that happened? When she looked up again, Mrs. Prather was gone.

Anxiously, she waited at the desk, counting the number of times the elevator door opened and closed.

"Thank you, I'm fine," she answered in monosyllabic words when another nurse inquired if she could be of assistance.

Finally, Mrs. Prather bustled through a swinging door and came to the front of the desk, handing Kathleen a square of gauze with some smelly, yellow lotion in its center.

"Wipe your hands with this. It'll burn like hell, but you need to clean those cuts out."

"Erik?" Kathleen asked in desperation.

"He's been X-rayed and examined carefully. They see no signs of internal injuries or broken bones."

"Thank God," Kathleen whispered, and shut her eyes against the wave of dizziness that swept over her.

"However," Mrs. Prather qualified, "he hasn't regained consciousness. He's still comatose and has a nasty gash on his head. Several stitches were taken on his scalp. The sooner he wakes up, the better."

Kathleen stifled the cry that almost found its way out of her throat. "Maybe if I could see him, talk to him . . ."

Mrs. Prather was already shaking her head. "Not now. I'm sorry, but it's really better for him if you don't. I'm sure that when he wakes up and his condition stabilizes, the doctor will let you see him for a very few minutes. Until then, I'm afraid you'll have to wait."

Kathleen reached out and touched Mrs. Prather's sleeve. "Thank you," she said quietly as she turned away to resume her vigil.

Dusk became darkness, unnoticed by Kathleen. The lights came on automatically in the parking lot outside the emergency room. Traffic on the busy thoroughfare now bore the glare of headlights and winking red taillights, and still she didn't leave her post.

Mrs. Prather went through the swinging doors frequently, but each time she returned to the desk, she looked toward Kathleen and shook her head sadly. There was no reason for words. She already knew Kathleen's question.

Mrs. Prather had been gone for some time now, Kathleen mused hopefully as she glanced down at her watch. Maybe she'd be back soon with some news. Just then, the automatic door from the outside swung open and a woman rushed through it.

Kathleen's eyes were inexplicably drawn toward her. She was small, blonde and extremely attractive. Her perfect features were marred with anxiety as she swept toward the desk. She was wearing a straight cotton skirt that fit her tiny figure to perfection. A soft cotton blouse molded over small, round breasts.

She rested her palms on the high desk and strained toward the nurse who was briefly relieving Mrs. Prather.

Her voice was husky and the words tumbled over each other

in their rush to get out as she said, "I'm Mrs. Gudjonsen. I was called by a Dr. Hamilton about Erik Gudjonsen. The doctor knows I'm coming."

"Yes, certainly, Mrs. Gudjonsen. Go in there." The efficient nurse pointed the beautiful young woman toward the swinging doors that had held Kathleen's unwavering attention for the past hours.

Mrs. Gudjonsen whirled away from the desk, and her dainty, swift feet took her inside the treatment room, the door closing behind her.

And just as soundly, just as impregnably, a door closed around Kathleen's heart.

She sat perfectly still, afraid that if she made the slightest movement, she would shatter into a million brittle shards. Heat washed over her head and throbbed in her earlobes until they felt as if they were on fire. Her lungs constricted, squeezing out her life's supply of oxygen, and she couldn't swallow the bile that rose to the back of her throat.

She was lightheaded and feared that she was about to faint. The roaring in her head must surely be heard by everyone around her, though they all seemed to go about their business unperturbed. Didn't they realize that she, Kathleen Haley, was dying? Now. They could be witnessing the slow, agonizing, torturous death of someone's soul. And they didn't see. They didn't care.

She had to get out, away.

Knowing better than to listen to Edna's gentle advice, she had followed it nonetheless because it had been what she wanted to do. But again she had loved and lost. She had found the courage to love again, but just as her parents had deserted her, Erik would, too. Only she wouldn't be around to let him. She'd be gone before that happened.

Carefully, hoping she wouldn't fly apart and vanish into thin air, Kathleen stood up and crossed to the desk. Taking up a blank prescription form lying on the desk, she wrote Erik's name on it and, with shaking fingers, pushed the paper through the gold ring that held his car keys. She placed the keys with the identifying paper where she knew Mrs. Prather would be sure to see them.

As Kathleen turned away, she bumped into a tall, husky, blond man who was hurrying up to the desk. She ducked her head, not wanting anyone to see the tears that flooded her eyes and coursed uncharted down her face.

Minutes later, Mrs. Prather's quick, light footsteps reflected her lifted spirits. That good-looking Mr. Gudjonsen had awakened, recognized his brother and sister-in-law, and spoke to them. Then he had asked for someone named Kathleen.

There was no doubt in her mind who Kathleen was. With the doctor's approval, Mrs. Prather spun on her heels and struck off down the hall and through the swinging doors.

But when she pushed them open and scanned the waiting room, the lovely woman with the brimming emerald eyes and the auburn hair, the scratched hands and the anxious, love-filled face, had disappeared.

"Would you tell me where she was if you knew?" Erik demanded. His eyes pierced the deep hollows into which they had sunk. Fine lines of fatigue, worry and recent illness were etched around his hard mouth and the weary, red-rimmed eyes. "Would you, dammit?" He pounded his fist on the pine table.

"Erik, calm down and quit shouting at us," B. J. said reasonably. "We've told you we don't know where Kathleen disappeared to, and we don't. We are as worried about her as you."

"Oh . . ." Erik breathed an expletive with all the despair and hopelessness in the world in his voice. He slumped into the easy chair and covered his face with his hands.

This was the second time in the last month he had come to Mountain View and begged the Harrisons for information of Kathleen. And both times they had sworn to him that they didn't know her whereabouts.

For two weeks, he had lain in that goddam hospital, unable to find out what had happened to her. When he had regained consciousness and started asking for her, a nurse said that a woman matching his description of Kathleen had been there, but had left. He had become frantic with worry. The doctor had ordered a hypodermic to sedate him, lest he worsen his condition.

But when he awakened again, anger at his own uselessness and frustration over the patronizing platitudes of Bob and Sally had made him even more desperate.

"I'm telling you that this was no fly-by-night roll in the hay, Bob!" he had shouted at his brother. "Dammit, she wouldn't have left like that without a word. Maybe she was mugged or murdered or raped or something. Have you thought of that? *Huh?*" The veins had stood out from his bandaged temple in a frightening way, and the nurses had been called to forcibly give him another sedative despite his Herculean struggles and vituperative curses to prevent them from doing so.

When he reawakened, Bob and Sally were with him, their nerves frayed, their expressions stricken. "Erik, she left your keys at the desk with a note attached. She couldn't have been abducted. She left purposefully and calmly." Bob looked to his wife for support, but Sally's concern was directed toward her brother-in-law, for whom she felt a good deal of affection.

"Maybe . . . uh . . ." Bob stuttered, "maybe you misinterpreted her . . . uh . . . feelings."

"Get out of here. Go home—anywhere. I don't care," Erik mumbled. "Just leave me alone." Then he had turned away from them to stare bleakly out the window with that hard, bitter look on his face that was to characterize his expression for the following weeks.

Despite his indifference toward regaining his health, he

recovered. He terrorized the nurses and cursed the doctors, but he recovered. The headache lessened a little each day, and the wound on his scalp hurt, then itched, then became unnoticeable as it healed.

Bob and Sally left after the initial danger was over, but returned to accompany him home to St. Louis. They took turns driving the Blazer while he sat in the backseat, brooding.

He had telephoned the desperately worried Harrisons each day while he was in the hospital, asking about Kathleen. They had told him nothing, swearing that they didn't know anything. They hadn't seen Kathleen since she had left with him that rainy morning. He told them that as soon as he could, he would return to Mountain View.

He had read the newspaper accounts of the airplane wreck and knew that he was lucky to be alive. Eleven passengers and the pilots weren't so lucky. Still, sometimes he wondered why he considered himself fortunate. Without Kathleen . . .

Why had she disappeared without a trace? When she left, she hadn't even known the extent of his injuries or if he would recover with all his faculties. Something had driven her away, but what?

He began his search for her at Mountain View after spending several frustrating weeks in St. Louis recuperating. The Harrisons swore that they had received no word from Kathleen except one handwritten note that had been mailed from her address in Atlanta.

Erik read it. It told nothing other than that she was well and would contact the couple later. She implored them not to worry about her, apologizing profusely for deserting them in the middle of the summer. That was all.

Now, on his second fruitless trip to Mountain View, where the leaves were beginning to display the paintbrush of autumn, Edna brought him back to the dismal present with a gentle urging.

"Tell us again what you found in Atlanta."

He sighed and straightened himself slightly in the chair. "She had been there right after the accident. She bought off the lease to her apartment, paid up all her utilities, packed everything and left. With no forwarding address. I went to Mason's Department Store. Did you know she wasn't working there any longer?"

"No," the couple said in shocked unison.

"She quit at the beginning of the summer. Yet every time we talked about her work, she made it sound as if she were going back this fall."

"She loved her job, Erik. Why would she quit like that?"

"I had to bribe one of the salesgirls with lunch to find that out. It seems that one of the male employees had the hots for Kathleen. He was married."

"Well, that explains that. Kathleen would never become involved with a married man," Edna declared firmly.

Erik snorted rudely as he stood up and went to the window. When he faced them again, anger oozed from every pore in his body. "How do you know? Maybe she's a scheming, lying little slut that deceived us all."

"Now just a minute, young man." Edna flew off the couch and rounded on Erik, shaking her finger in his face. "Don't talk that way about Kathleen. You know it's not true just as I do. I'll not have you stand here in my house and bad-mouth her."

"Then why did she run away like some guilty or frightened child?" he demanded.

Edna's anger evaporated and her body sagged with dejection. She rubbed her temples as if they pained her. "I don't know," she said slowly.

"Maybe she *is* a frightened child," B. J. spoke quietly from the couch. "Maybe with you lying injured, possibly dying, she couldn't face it, she couldn't risk it, couldn't stand the thought that she might lose you. I think I'm safe in assuming that she had formed quite an attachment to you." B. J. narrowed his eyes on Erik, waiting for a confession, but when none was forthcoming, he went on. "I grant you this. She's setting a dangerous precedent in her life, always running from adversity. One day, she'll have to meet a prob-

lem head-on. And it won't be easy for her. She hasn't prepared herself for it.''

Erik seemed to reflect on that for a moment, but then his
features dropped back into an impenetrable mask. ''Well, for
whatever reason, she ran away from you and me and made it
quite clear that she doesn't want to be found.'' He picked up
his discarded denim jacket from the back of the chair and
walked to the door. ''I've wasted two months of my life
looking for her, and I don't intend to invest any more. I'll let
you know when the piece about the camp is going to air.
Thank you for all your help.'' The words were clipped, curt
and, Edna thought, forced. Underneath that stern resolve, she
thought she detected an unspeakably painful disillusionment.

She was sure of it when she watched Erik walk to his
Dodge van, get in and slam the door. He rested his bowed
head against the steering wheel in utter desolation before he
seemed to gain enough initiative to turn the key and start the
motor.

Chapter Nine

❧ ❧

Kathleen tugged on the skirt that rode slightly above her crossed knees in a ladylike gesture that caused the middle-aged secretary to smile. Such an attractive girl, she thought.

Kathleen returned the smile. She was the paragon of professionalism as she sat in the beautifully decorated outer office awaiting her interview with Mr. Seth Kirchoff, owner of the exclusive department store Kirchoff's in San Francisco.

Her calm facade belied the tumult within. Could anyone guess that inside Kathleen was shivering with anxiety? She needed this job so badly. It went beyond economic necessity. She needed it to restore her sanity, her equilibrium, both of which had been unbalanced since she had sat in that hospital waiting room in Arkansas and watched Erik's wife rush to his side.

Unconsciously, Kathleen squeezed her eyes shut in a vain attempt to blot out the pain the vision still caused. Immediately, she opened them and darted a glance at the secretary, hoping that the woman hadn't seen that moment of weakness. She hadn't. She was leaning over a file cabinet behind her desk.

After two months, one would think the agony would have subsided, the ache would have become only a dull reminder; but the memory was there constantly, an open, gaping wound, still raw and bleeding.

Kathleen turned her face toward the wide picture window and gazed out at the San Francisco skyline. She noted the Transamerica Building and, far in the distance, the Bay, sparkling like a great sapphire in the brilliant sunlight.

How could she have been so naive? Why hadn't she even considered the possibility that he was married? It had not once occurred to her. She had been so dazzled by the man, held by his magnetism, that she hadn't looked beyond the obvious.

His seeming to care for her was all a sham. Tears of shame and humiliation clouded Kathleen's eyes when she remembered how she had responded to him both physically and emotionally. His tutelage had been expert and she had been all too willing. The intimacies that had seemed so sacred when they had shared them now offended her.

At the hospital, when she had heard the pretty woman identifying herself as Mrs. Gudjonsen, by virtue of her name having the right to stand by Erik's bedside, be privy to the information that had been withheld from Kathleen, she had wanted to flee, to run until she was exhausted and then slip off the edge of the earth to be swallowed up by oblivion.

She *had* fled. She had returned to the airport and waited there through the night while cleanup crews hauled away the wreckage of the crash and restored the field to operational capacity. Boarding the first plane going east, she had returned to Atlanta.

In the space of a few minutes, Kathleen Haley had grown up. Before, she had considered herself to be a mature woman, wise to the ways of the world, well acquainted with heartache and suffering.

What a fool she had been. Erik had robbed her of her innocence in more ways than taking her virginity. He had shown her just how self-serving a man could be. David Ross was an amateur compared to Erik Gudjonsen. Kathleen hadn't known such intentional deceit could exist. Now she did. Never would she walk so blindly into any kind of relationship. The young woman she'd formerly been was gone. In her place was a woman with bruised hands and a bruised heart. Both would be a long time in healing.

She bought a Little Rock newspaper for several consecutive days, avidly poring over the accounts of the accident. Erik's name never appeared on the list of casualties. To relieve her own mind, she called the hospital and was told he was mending well and would soon be released. When asked if she wished to be connected to his room or to leave a message, she declined.

Uppermost on her list of priorities was to close this chapter of her life. If she could have rubbed it out of her history, she would have done so, but that wasn't possible. Her only hope was to put it behind her, chalk it up as a learning experience and go on from there. She wanted to start over, in another place, as another person, so she emptied her apartment and moved into a modest hotel until she could decide what to do.

For weeks, nothing happened. She read the classified ads in all the out-of-town newspapers she could buy on the Atlanta newsstands. She mailed letters of inquiry to major department stores all over the country, but if she received any reply at all, it was usually a polite but impersonal rejection. All the while, her bank account dwindled as surely as her spirits, which hadn't recovered from the death-blow they had been dealt.

Then she saw a classified ad in a trade journal. There was no name, no telephone number, only a post office box to which to send a résumé. According to the ad, several jobs were open, but they weren't listed specifically. Mechanically and without hope, she mailed the requested information, knowing that it was a shot in the dark.

To her surprise, she received an answer within a few days. If she was still interested in a job as fashion buyer, she was to call the enclosed telephone number and make an appointment.

If she was still interested! Quickly, Kathleen checked her bank balance and decided that if she lived frugally, it would be worth it to gamble on a trip to California.

"Ms. Haley?"

She jumped out of her reverie when the composed, assured secretary called her name. Another woman, chic, slim and fashionable, was coming out of the inner office. She eyed Kathleen with a calculating, shrewd look as she passed her on her way out the door. This applicant wanted the job, too.

"Mr. Kirchoff will see you now," the secretary said graciously. "I'm sorry you had to wait."

"Thank you," Kathleen answered in kind. "I didn't mind."

She walked on trembling legs toward the austere door and went in. Why was she nervous? This wasn't like her. She was usually so sure of herself. Was this to be another legacy of Erik Gudjonsen's? This uncharacteristic self-consciousness and insecurity?

With determination to put down her feelings of inferiority, she tilted her chin back and crossed the luxuriantly deep blue carpet toward the intimidatingly large desk.

The man behind it glanced up at her with a detached expression, then almost did a double take as he lifted his dark eyes in a full, long appraisal. "Ms. Kathleen Haley?" he asked in a well-modulated voice.

"Yes," she said, smiling.

"Sit down please. I'm Seth Kirchoff." Though he didn't stand, she accepted the well-manicured hand proffered across the desk and shook it.

"Thank you, Mr. Kirchoff," she said as she sat down. "I'm pleased to meet you." She was gaining her momentarily lost confidence now. She knew that she looked the part of the stylish, competent fashion buyer. Her linen suit was lightweight, as was dictated by the season, but the antique gold color bespoke the end of that season. The slim skirt fit her size six body to perfection. The short jacket was crisp but softened to femininity by the cream crepe blouse underneath it. Her brown pumps and matching clutch bag were a treat to herself from Gucci she had splurged on during a trip to New York the year before. The gold spheres in her ears were the correct amount of jewelry. Her dark auburn hair, enriched by the color of the suit, had been pulled back into a loose bun at the nape of her neck, but again was spared from severity by the natural wisps that lay on her cheek. She had artfully applied her makeup, the carefully chosen colors coordinating with her ensemble and her own coloring.

She looked at the man across the desk and took in his own handsome features. His hair was dark and wavy, hugging close to his well-shaped head. He was very good looking in a sensitive sort of way. He was not ruggedly virile like—

Stop that! Kathleen commanded herself as she continued to assess Mr. Kirchoff. His mouth was sensual, soft. His nose was long, narrow and sculpted to harmonize with the rest of his face.

Handsome as he was, it was his eyes that arrested Kathleen's attention. They were a rich chocolate-brown, deep, dark, but not mysterious, as such eyes were usually characterized. They were open, warm, and bespoke sincerity and . . . what? . . . Compassion?

Kathleen's green eyes slid down over the molded chin to the well-defined shoulders. There her gaze froze. Where she had expected to see an oversized leather chair, befitting a man of Mr. Kirchoff's position, she saw the incongruous shine of chrome. Seth Kirchoff was sitting in a wheelchair.

Her fondest wish at that moment was that he hadn't detected her shock, but he had. "It is rather gruesome when you first see it, isn't it?" he asked, looking down at the arms of the chair. "But once you get used to it, it isn't so bad." He raised those compelling eyes to hers and smiled.

"I don't find it gruesome," she replied honestly. "It's just that it was unexpected."

He grinned winningly. "I've often considered putting a sign outside that read 'Beware: Man in Wheelchair Inside.' "

Kathleen laughed spontaneously. "You might weed out a lot of tedious interviews that way."

"I might at that. Maybe I should do it." They smiled at

each other, each frankly approving of the other. "At the risk of sounding piteous, I'll tell you straightaway that I was in an automobile accident the night of my college graduation. Three of my fraternity brothers were killed. I was spared, but a broken back left me paralyzed from the waist down."

"You were very lucky."

He propped his chin on his fists, supporting them with his elbows on the arms of his chair. "That's a very unusual response, Ms. Haley. Most people would say, 'I'm sorry,' or something to that effect. Over the years, I've catalogued people's reactions to my disability. They either express pity or embarrassment, and won't look me in the eye, or else they ignore it totally, as though if they don't see it, it will go away. You have done none of those. I think I like you, Ms. Haley."

She grinned. "I think I like you, too."

He laughed good-naturedly. "Would you like some coffee?" Without waiting for her answer, he pressed a button on his desk component, and within seconds the secretary was in the office.

"Ms. Haley, this is Mrs. Larchmont. She insists that I call her that in spite of our friendship."

"I wouldn't want anyone to suspect that we're carrying on a hot and heavy love affair," retorted Mrs. Larchmont. Claire Larchmont was a woman in her early fifties, Kathleen guessed accurately. Kathleen thought she was an executive's dream for an attractive, competent assistant.

It was apparent that these two shared a mutual affection and were secure enough in that relationship to tease each other. She turned to Kathleen. "You may call me Claire."

"Ms. Haley, would you like some coffee?" Seth asked her again.

"Yes, with cream please," she addressed Claire.

"And I—" Seth started.

"I know what you want, Mr. Kirchoff," she said as she left the office.

"She's priceless, isn't she?" Seth asked Kathleen.

"The two of you seem to work very well together," she said.

"Yes, we do." He clasped his hands together on the desk and said, "Now, I want to tell you what I'm looking for."

He launched into a brief history of the department store, which had been established by his grandfather in the 1920s. Over the years, through the Depression and World War II, Kirchoff's had managed to survive. Seth's father had taken control of the business after the war and had increased its volume of business and profits. He had died three years ago.

"One might think that the business would have naturally fallen to me, but it was specified in my father's will that the reins of power go to my uncle. You see, Father thought that when the rest of me had been paralyzed, so had my brain. He never quite forgave me for becoming a cripple."

There was no bitterness in Seth's voice, only a deep-lying sadness. "Anyway, my uncle died last year quite suddenly, and virtually by force, I moved into this office."

He paused in his story long enough to accept a silver tray from Claire. On it were china cups and a carafe of coffee. When the coffee had been poured and served, Claire withdrew, leaving them alone again.

"Ms. Haley, Kirchoff's has the potential of being an important name in the fashion industry of San Francisco, but it has been in the hands of old men with no vision, my father included."

He sipped his coffee, then continued, "When I seized control, I began to lop off heads—figuratively, of course." He smiled and Kathleen was blessed with the full impact of his charm. "It wasn't an easy thing to do, since some of the people I fired had been here for twenty years or more, but nonetheless it was necessary. I gave the supervisor of each department ample time to restructure his or her section. When he or she didn't, he was excised. Forgive me." He paused. "Would you care for more coffee?"

"No, thank you," she said, replacing her cup on the tray.

"I'll get to the point of this interview, Ms. Haley. I know you must wonder where all this is leading."

"I haven't been bored, Mr. Kirchoff."

He returned her smile and then pressed a lever that engaged

the gears of his motorized chair. He steered it around the desk until he was beside her chair. Judging from the length of his body and legs, he must have stood tall before his accident.

"I'm looking for someone to coordinate all the fashion buying for my store. And I'll share a secret with you. There will be two more stores under construction by the end of the year. By next Christmas, there will be three Kirchoff's in the Bay Area."

"How wonderful!" she exclaimed sincerely.

"I hope so. But I want our image to grow with the expansion. For years, we have catered to a particular customer. She buys four to six dresses a year. She is very conservative and budget-minded. Her taste is reserved. Her imagination, nil."

"I know the customer well. The scourge of every fashion merchant," Kathleen said dryly.

He laughed. "That's why we need to update our image. I want the clientele of Kirchoff's to change. I want the customer who buys four to six ensembles a *season*. She is stylish, fashion-minded, courageous, a trendsetter. She's a mover and shaker. Active in civic affairs. Professional. Possibly both. In either case, she dresses the part. She also outfits her children as stunningly as herself."

"Wow," Kathleen said, impressed. "You have done your market research."

"Indeed I have. I want an updated misses' department that handles everything from sexy lingerie to debutante gowns. I want an extensive junior department that will carry mother's little darling from her first training bra to her bridesmaids' dresses."

Kathleen's mind was ticking. "Price range?" she asked.

"Expensive to very expensive."

"Accessories?"

"Only the best. If a customer needs a three-hundred-fifty-dollar belt to set off her silk evening skirt, I want her to know she can come to Kirchoff's and find a large selection of them."

"Men's and children's?"

"I've hired other buyers for those departments, but you'd have the authority to check their orders and make certain they're keeping pace with your departments."

"Do you want to stay with domestic designers?"

His brow creased in concentration. "Not exclusively, but I prefer to buy out of New York rather than Europe. Yankee pride, I guess."

"Your buying budget?"

"At this point, it's unlimited. We'll be jumping in all the way."

It was a dream come true! Unconsciously, Kathleen gnawed her bottom lip as she envisioned all she could do with such unrestricted license.

"When can you start?"

The question was so abrupt that Kathleen jumped in surprise and riveted her wide, glowing eyes on Seth. "Wh— What? You mean . . . I . . . ?"

"Yes, you have the job. If you want it. The salary is forty thousand dollars a year, excluding sales bonuses and employee discounts. Is that satisfactory?"

Satisfactory? She didn't know what to say. "Mr. Kirchoff. are you sure? I mean, yes, I want the job, but aren't you interviewing others? Maybe you should wait—"

"No, Ms. Haley. I knew you were what I wanted the moment you walked through the door. I despise women who barnstorm their way in here, spouting all their grandiose ideas and not listening to what I'm saying. You're a good listener. You have style and experience. I can tell that by the way you dress and by your résumé. Your taste is impeccable. Yet, and this is very important to me, you're extremely feminine. I want my customers to want to look like you—assured but soft, independent but entirely female."

She blushed under his close scrutiny.

"I gladly accept your offer, Mr. Kirchoff. And in answer to your question, I'm available immediately. Or as soon as I can find a place to live and move my things from Atlanta."

"Very good. Shall we say," he consulted a calendar on

his desk. "Monday the sixteenth? That will give you ten days. If you need more time, let me know."

"Thank you. That should be more than sufficient. I'm anxious to begin."

His smile was warm. "Good."

She extended her hand, which he shook heartily. His grip was strong and comfortable. "Thank you, Mr. Kirchoff. I won't let you down."

"I'm not afraid of that. I only ask that you drop the Mr. Kirchoff stuff and call me Seth."

"Then I'm Kathleen."

"Kathleen," he said softly, as if savoring the sound of her name on his lips.

She stood up self-consciously, aware of the fact that he must remain seated. But as she walked toward the door, she heard the soft whirring sound of the wheelchair's motor as he followed her.

"I'd break my back again if I could have the privilege of opening the door for you, Kathleen, but would you mind too much doing the honors?"

She laughed with him. "Not at all." She held the door while he wheeled through it and then followed him. A man in a dark gray suit was standing beside the secretary's desk.

"Ah, George," Seth said. "Is it time to go already?"

"Yes, Seth. You have a lunch appointment with your sister."

"George, I want you to meet Kirchoff's newest employee, Ms. Kathleen Haley."

"So you hired her!" exclaimed Claire Larchmont from behind her desk. "Oh, I'm so glad."

"Why?" Seth teased. "I may have hired her to replace you."

"Never," she said, unperturbed. Then she smiled graciously at Kathleen. "Welcome aboard, Ms. Haley."

"Kathleen," Kathleen said. Claire smiled at her and nodded, then turned back to her computer terminal.

"Kathleen, George goes with the territory. He's my valet,

chauffeur, therapist, drinking buddy and best friend. George Martin.''

"Mr. Martin," Kathleen said, smiling.

"Please call me George, or I might not hear you," he said. He was a tall, thin, middle-aged man who radiated a strong moral character and dependability. His smile was welcoming.

"Now everyone is on a first-name basis except you, Mrs. Larchmont," Seth said. Claire turned around to face him, as usual, unscathed by his taunt. "Please see to all the bureaucratic red tape of putting another employee on the payroll—insurance, things like that. Also, issue Kathleen a check for five thousand dollars to cover her moving expenses."

Kathleen started to object, but Seth stopped her. "I won't have it any other way. If we were a large corporation transferring an executive, you would receive that kind of consideration. And I look upon you as an executive."

"Thank you," she said, flabbergasted at all that was happening. After she put the check in her purse, she shook hands again with Seth. "I'll see you on the sixteenth," she said.

"We all look forward to it." He smiled that sincere-sad smile as he clasped her hand tightly.

She nodded her goodbyes to Claire and George. While waiting for an elevator, she looked at her wristwatch. She congratulated herself. A full half-hour had transpired since she had thought of Erik.

❧ ❧

Her move to San Francisco was accomplished with relative ease, considering that she moved from one side of the country to the other.

After her interview with Seth, Kathleen went directly to a downtown lunchroom and purchased a newspaper. Over a tuna-salad sandwich, she began perusing the classified ads for a suitable apartment.

Some listings she was able to eliminate after a telephone conversation. Others required expensive cab rides, only to prove that they weren't what she was looking for. Finally, at sunset, she checked into a hotel and spent a dreamless night, exhausted and exhilarated after the day's events.

The next morning, she found a place that was more what she had in mind. It was one of four apartments carved out of an old house. The furnishings were outmoded, but clean and quaint, as was the exterior of the house. Only the occupants had keys to the main door, and Kathleen's apartment was on the ground floor. It was small, having only a combination bedroom-living room, a tiny kitchen alcove and a small bathroom, but that was all she would require for a while. She put down the requested deposit and first month's rent with the landlord and then made flight arrangements back to Atlanta.

In the southern city, she sold her car to a used-car dealer, sacrificing it, she knew, but saving the time and trouble of selling it herself. She didn't want to drive it to San Francisco. Since her former apartment had been furnished, she had little in the way of household items to discard. Most of these she donated to charitable organizations. What few personal items she had she packed in boxes to be shipped by air on her return flight. Within a matter of days, she was ensconced in her new apartment in the Bay City.

She reveled in this jewel of a city, gloried in the climate that, with the fall season, was brisk and invigorating. She jogged in Golden Gate Park, went sight-seeing on Fisherman's Wharf.

She bought a used compact car, making a small down payment with some of the money Seth had given her for "moving expenses," and signing a note of credit for the balance. With a map in one hand, she set out, by trial and error, to learn her way around the hilly streets of her new home. She enjoyed the time off, the freedom to be lazy, but by the Sunday evening before she would start her new job, she was ready to get down to work.

"Tomorrow I start over," Kathleen averred to the darkness as she lay on the convertible sofa bed that came with the apartment. "In a few months, I won't even remember him."

She pulled the pillow from under her head and hugged it

to her. "I won't remember. I *won't*." She pressed her face into the softness, and even as she vowed she would forget, she saw his face vividly. Tears managed to eke out of the squeezed lids as she saw him wave to her as he disappeared into the fuselage of the airplane.

"Erik, Erik," she sobbed. "Why did you do that to me? Why?"

Did he ever think of her? What was he doing this very moment? Was he sleeping? Making love to his pretty wife? Was he stroking her with those treacherous hands and lying to her with his persuasive lips?

Did he make love to his wife as ardently as he had to Kathleen? Was she perhaps cool to his fervor? Was that why he sought lovers? Obliging ones. Like herself. Kathleen buried her shame-scalded face in the pillow.

As jealous as Kathleen was of that blonde woman who rightfully claimed Erik's love and name, she felt a great wave of pity for her. Did she know of his unfaithfulness? Was Kathleen his first extramarital dalliance? No, of course not. He couldn't have seduced her so smoothly, without the least shred of guilt, had he not been adept at it.

She wanted to hate him. She did hate him! But as she turned to her side and raised her knees to her chest in a position of self-protection, she ached to feel his hard, lean body next to her. She was chilled without the warmth of his embrace. One night in his bed had spoiled her to needing his strength during the night, to awakening periodically in the security of his arms, to hearing the rich, steady cadence of his breathing.

And this night, like all the others, she felt a pain, more cruel than death, eating at her, squeezing her heart, destroying her spirit.

❧ ❧

The next morning, she got up early, ate a piece of dry toast and drank two cups of coffee as she put on her makeup. Determinedly, she shed the shroud of despair that blanketed her each night, and looked forward to her new job with renewed enthusiasm. This would save her. It must.

She chose her dress carefully. It was essential to create a good first impression with both her new employers and her subordinates. The tailored navy dress had a designer label, but she had bought it as a sample on a buying trip to New York and had paid barely a fourth of the retail cost.

It had a round, collarless neck and buttoned down the left side, over her bosom to her knee. The long sleeves were slim. It hung as a chemise, but she belted it with a copper leather belt that matched her shoes and bag. It wasn't a coincidence that the leather was almost the exact color of her hair. A gold pin held a paisley scarf around her neck. It was a rainbow of navy, copper and green. Small gold loops were in her ears, and her hair was pulled back into a functional, professional-looking bun.

In the full-length mirror on the back of the door, she critically surveyed the results of her half-hour in the bathroom and decided that she was the best that she could be.

Having familiarized herself with the streets of San Francisco, she negotiated rush-hour traffic with only a modicum of trepidation. If she could survive Atlanta's famous traffic jams, she could survive anything.

Arriving at the skyscraper building where the corporate headquarters was located, she identified herself to the garage attendant. He smiled at her and said, "Yes, ma'am. Mr. Kirchoff said to give you this. Stick it on the fender of your car and you can park here anytime."

"Thank you," she said as she drove into the dim cave of the garage.

She arrived at the twentieth floor and went into Seth's office. As she expected, Claire Larchmont was already busy at her desk. She waved merrily, though she was speaking into the telephone cradled between her shoulder and chin.

"Right. Mr. Kirchoff said those proposals must be ready by the end of the day and subject to his approval." She hung up. "Kathleen! This is your big day. Are you excited? Did you get moved in all right? Is there anything you need?"

Kathleen grinned. " 'Yes' to the first question. 'Yes' to the second. And 'I'll let you know' to the last."

"I'm sorry." Claire laughed good-naturedly. "Seth tells me all the time that I'm a motor mouth."

"Seth? I thought it was strictly Mr. Kirchoff."

Claire winked. "I only do that to irritate him."

Kathleen laughed. "Is he in?"

"Not yet. This is his morning for physical therapy. He and George exercise in his pool on Mondays and Thursdays, so they're always an hour later. Ms. Kirchoff is in there. His sister. You might as well meet her now, I suppose."

Kathleen looked closely at Claire's face, which had lost some of its animation.

"Oh?" Kathleen asked leadingly.

"Find out for yourself," Claire said guardedly, and Kathleen had to respect the secretary's reticence in talking about her employers.

"I'll bring in some coffee," Claire said as Kathleen's hand closed around the doorknob.

She pushed the door open and went into the room, seeing immediately the straight back of the woman standing at the window. Kathleen closed the door behind her so that the latch clicked audibly to alert Ms. Kirchoff that she wasn't alone.

"Claire?" she asked, and turned around on the heels of her pumps. "Oh," was her only comment when she saw that she had made a mistake.

"Hello, Ms. Kirchoff, I'm Kathleen Haley." Kathleen closed the distance between them, but for some reason unknown to her, didn't extend her hand to be shaken. The other woman's rigid posture and arms folded defensively across her chest spoke a very eloquent body language.

"Ms. Haley, I'm Hazel Kirchoff," she said, nodding her head like a feudal lord greeting a serf. "My brother told me that he had hired you."

How did one respond to a comment like that? There was nothing to say, so Kathleen merely inclined her head, much in the same way Hazel Kirchoff had only moments before.

There was an uncomfortable silence while the two women squared off and assessed each other.

Hazel Kirchoff was a short woman with a matronly, though well-proportioned, figure. Her tussah silk suit was impeccable in cut as well as fit, and her blonde hair was worn in a short, soft style. If anything was a trifle overdone, it was her jewelry. She wore two diamond-encrusted rings on each of her third fingers, a diamond watch and three bangle bracelets. At her ears were small diamond studs. Her makeup was attractively applied but couldn't completely camouflage faint, weblike lines around her eyes and mouth. She was considerably older than Seth, Kathleen thought, and well established in middle age.

Her eyes, like her brother's, held one's attention. Though unlike his, which shone with compassion and tolerance, hers were cold and haughty. They weren't the same rich chocolate-brown of Seth's but a colorless gray that reflected no life, no spontaneity, and were chilling in their blank, piercing stare that revealed nothing, yet saw everything.

"I trust you have found our city to your liking," she commented at last.

"Yes," Kathleen said. Then she smiled and laughed under her breath. "It's certainly different."

"Indeed."

There was another one—a sentence for which there was no easy response. Undaunted, Kathleen tried again. "I'm looking forward to working at Kirchoff's. Seth has outlined some very attractive prospects."

"My brother often does and says things impulsively."

Had Hazel Kirchoff been better acquainted with Kathleen, she would have realized that the glimmer of green fire that suddenly flashed in her eyes was a warning of the temper now lying close to the surface.

Kathleen pushed her caution aside even if she was facing a new employer. "And you think hiring me was one of these impulsive gestures?"

Hazel smiled, though there was no humor in the expression.

"Many young women would love to work for Kirchoff's, but Seth was quite taken with you. He came home with a glowing report of your physical attributes. He described you perfectly." The gray eyes raked down Kathleen's body as if they were looking at something distasteful. "You are not the first opportunist to take advantage of my brother."

Kathleen was aghast at the blatant insult. "I did no such thing! I am qualified for this job and I'll work hard for Kirchoff's. Seth is a very intelligent, visionary man—"

"He is a cripple," the woman snapped. "I must constantly protect him from women preying on that fact. He depends on me for everything." She had almost impassioned herself to anger, and just in time saved herself that indignity. She pulled herself up to her full height and turned away from Kathleen in a gesture of dismissal. "However, nothing we say matters. I'll see to it that you're not with us for long. Your type never is."

Before Kathleen could issue the furious retort on the tip of her tongue, George swung the door open and Seth wheeled into the office. "So! My two favorite ladies! I see that you've met."

Chapter Ten

❧ ❧

Yes, they had met, but to Kathleen it seemed more of a confrontation. That first morning set the tone of each subsequent encounter she had with Hazel Kirchoff. Since Hazel was general manager of the store, her path crossed Kathleen's often. Whenever they were alone together, she was aloof and snide, but within Seth's hearing, she was charming and gracious.

Kathleen had never seen a temperament more deadly than Hazel's and kept her dealings with the woman at a minimum. It didn't take long to observe that Hazel was disliked by most of the employees at Kirchoff's. She was critical, capable of reducing even the staunchest personality to tears with her vicious tongue. But that same tongue dripped honey when Seth was around. For her brother, she smiled and praised his ideas, which she scorned outside his hearing.

She was fiercely possessive of him. Even George took a backseat when Hazel was around to see to Seth's needs. Often, the handicapped man seemed embarrassed by her constant coddling, but he never berated her for it. He accepted her unwanted help with the kindness that characterized all his dealings with other people.

As his sister was disliked, Seth was adored by his employees. It was difficult to pity a man who didn't pity himself. He joked constantly about his wheelchair, referring to it as his chariot. He flirted with the women employees, shared a camaraderie with the men, and made even the newest clerk feel important to the company. He paid his people well, and they knew it. In return, he expected diligence from them, and they gave it. For this reason, patrons of Kirchoff's were faithful and were treated with a deference that other department stores could learn from.

Those first hectic days, Kathleen and Seth spent mostly in his office going over the books, checking orders that the former buyer had placed, seeing what goods had been received and which were still forthcoming for the holiday season. Some were not too bad, others were atrocious, and Kathleen and Seth groaned in despair.

"We'll make do the best we can. In October, I want you to make a trip to New York and buy to your heart's content for spring. That's when we'll make our first big breakthrough."

"In the meantime," Kathleen said, "I'll call some of the houses I've bought from and ask if they can send me a few of their better pieces. I hope it's not too late."

He agreed and Kathleen set about to learn the "personality" of the store. She and Seth visited it together, riding there in his specialized van. George escorted them out the front of the office building to the van, parked in a reserved space only a few feet from the doors. The converted van was painted silver and had a black interior. A hydraulic lift raised Seth's wheelchair into it. The van was luxurious, and Kathleen commented on it as she sank into the rich leather upholstery while George locked down Seth's chair.

"Yeah, it's okay," Seth conceded dryly. "I wanted a Ferrari, but the damn chair wouldn't fit in one."

Kathleen laughed easily.

Much to Seth's surprise, Kathleen asked that a small storage room on the ground floor of the seven-story building be given over as her office rather than the one he had designated as hers on one of the upper floors.

"It's much more convenient. Really," she argued convincingly. "I can catalogue goods as they come in, check them against the manufacturers' invoices and inspect them before they're ever sent to their departments."

"But, Kathleen," he protested, "we have subordinate employees who do all that."

"I know. They can help. But I like to do most of it myself, or at least supervise." In the end, she got her way.

The first week of October was upon them and she was anticipating the trip to New York scheduled for the end of the month. She was unloading a box of evening gowns, hanging them on hangers to be steamed before consignment to the after-five department, when a wave of dizziness assailed her.

For a moment, she gripped the edge of a nearby table and shut her eyes, hanging her head in an effort to supply it with the needed blood. Finally, she straightened up slowly and took a deep breath.

The girl operating the hissing steam machine had noticed. "Kathleen? Are you okay? You look like you're about to faint."

"N— No. I'm fine. Just a little dizzy. I think I may need to start eating a bigger breakfast." Sometimes she became so involved with her work that she delayed lunch or forgot it altogether, so that toward the end of the day she was shaky with weakness. The problem was that she had never been a big breakfast eater, and lately, the last thing she wanted in the morning was food.

Only this morning when she was brushing her teeth, the flavor of the toothpaste nauseated her to the point of gagging. Besides the morning queasiness, an annoying indigestion had plagued her evenings. Each afternoon, it seemed that her stomach enlarged, crowding her lungs and making her feel stuffed when she was really hungry.

Kathleen hadn't put all these symptoms together until they persisted and had now developed a pattern that couldn't be ignored. Almost blacking out at work for the third time in one week brought them to the forefront. For the rest of the day, she took things easy and went to bed as soon as she got home, determined to feel better by the time she woke up the next morning. But the moment she opened her eyes, she knew she wasn't well.

"I don't know what's wrong with me," she had murmured to herself as she stared down perplexedly at the meter on her scale, which indicated she had lost another two pounds. Then her eyes glazed as she looked at her ten polished toenails and they multiplied to twenty before her blurred eyes. Slowly, her eyes traveled over the bathroom fixtures until she was looking at her own pale face in the mirror over the small sink. "No," she mouthed. "No, it can't be."

Instinctively, she placed her hands on her abdomen and felt only the flat, taut muscles that were usually there. But she knew that something was vastly different. It was no longer supple, but turgid. She had thought her swollen, tender breasts were harbingers of her long-overdue period.

Her period! When had she last had one? June? July? Yes, the first of July. She remembered that she was having one during the Fourth of July celebration at Mountain View.

And Erik had arrived a week later. The middle of July. And she hadn't had a period since then. She had attributed its absence to the emotional turmoil she'd been through.

She looked at herself in the mirror and raised a frantic hand to smother the small scream she felt on her lips. Then she forced out a laugh that sounded hollow even to her own ears. "You're being silly, Kathleen Haley. Hysterically jumping to the wrong conclusion. Things like this don't happen to grown-up women like you. They just don't. It's something else. Besides, everyone knows that you gain weight when you're— It's something else."

But it wasn't.

She telephoned a gynecologist she found in the Yellow

Pages, not wanting to ask for a recommendation from one of the ladies she worked with for fear of stirring up curiosity. Luckily, the doctor had an appointment open the next day at noon. She took it, glad that she could go on her lunch hour and be back in the office for the rest of the day.

The next thirty hours were the longest Kathleen had ever spent, with the possible exception of the long hours she had sat waiting in the hospital emergency room in Arkansas.

Almost in defiance of her upset stomach, she ate a huge dinner that night at a Chinese restaurant that had been praised as one of the best on Grant Avenue. It was a stupid thing to do. Because of the volume of food, one should never go to a Chinese restaurant alone. But she cleaned the silver serving dishes they brought her after eating all of the wonton soup and two egg rolls as an appetizer.

Feeling that she had proven her worst suspicion was just that, she drove home. But her confidence was short-lived when she raced to the bathroom the moment she opened the front door and emptied her full stomach with violent spasms. Depleted and sick with worry, she went straight to bed, already dreading to hear the doctor's verdict.

Lunch hour finally came, and she took her car out of the garage and drove straight to the doctor's office only a few blocks away. She hadn't eaten since her bout with nausea, and her hands were trembling as she gripped the wheel.

She walked into the comfortable office in the high-rise medical building, introduced herself to the nurse behind the glass window and then sat down to fill out the forms required of all new patients. When that was done, she returned them to the nurse, who said, "Thank you, Ms. Haley. We'll send for your records in Atlanta soon. Now, if you'll have a seat, the doctor will be with you shortly."

It was another nurse who opened the door and called her name. Kathleen jumped in startled reaction. She had been watching a young woman with a very active toddler sitting in her lap. The mother was trying to read a Raggedy Andy book to the restless little boy, but he was more interested in terrorizing the gold fish in the aquarium.

Kathleen followed the nurse down the hallway and went into the room with a large red "2" stenciled on the door. "Are you having any problems, Ms. Haley? Or is this a routine checkup?"

"I think . . ." She bit her lip. "No, a routine checkup." As ludicrous as it was, she thought it better not to bring up the subject of pregnancy. It was a childish game—to deny what one didn't want to believe.

The nurse made a notation on the chart in the folder. "Why don't you undress, and then we'll do all the preliminaries before the doctor comes in. There is a drape in the cubicle."

Kathleen went into the small enclosure, undressed and pulled the square of printed cotton over her head. It barely covered her hips. "Charming," she muttered as she stepped from behind the curtain.

"Let's weigh you first," the nurse instructed her. When that was done and her weight duly noted on the chart, the nurse took Kathleen's blood pressure and a sample of blood out of her pricked middle finger. Her hands were so slippery with perspiration that the nurse teased her about being nervous and commissioned her to relax. Kathleen smiled weakly.

"Are your periods regular?" the nurse asked as she leaned over the chart.

"Yes."

"Your last menses?"

Kathleen blanched. "Uh . . . let's see . . . I can't remember exactly. Maybe two weeks ago."

She was then directed to collect a urine specimen in the tiny adjoining bathroom. She handed the nurse the plastic cup, hoping that the contents wouldn't be incriminating.

Left alone for several minutes, Kathleen tried to calm her rapid breathing and slow her heartbeat, but to no avail. By the time the doctor bustled in, she was quaking with nerves.

"Ms. Haley, I'm Dr. Peters. No wisecracks about my name, please. Most of my associates often suggest that I should have been a urologist." He laughed at his own ribald joke, and Kathleen smiled. Who could be afraid of a kindly, middle-aged man with white hair, half-glasses that continually slipped down his nose and the countenance of Santa Claus? She was grateful for his blustery attempt to put her at ease.

The examination was routine. He listened to her chest, felt the glands in her neck, looked into her ears and throat, then had her lie back on the table while he did a rudimentary examination of her breasts.

"Are they sore?" he asked her.

Her throat closed around the lump that had suddenly formed there. Erik had asked her that. The following morning. She could still hear the gravelly inflection of his voice, the concern as he touched her . . .

"A little," she replied.

The doctor stuck his head out the door and called to the nurse, who came in to assist Kathleen place her legs in the stainless-steel stirrups. They were cold against the soles of her feet.

"I'm sorry about that," the doctor said as he heard her slight gasp. "I've asked my wife to knit some booties or something for those, but she's too busy playing tennis. Now just relax while I open your legs a little more. Scoot down just a tad. There, that's fine. Now relax."

Again. Erik. He had whispered that in her ear, even as he took her virginity. Relax. Relax. While I'm being unfaithful to my wife and deceiving you, relax.

The speculum was cold, too, and when it opened inside her, Kathleen cringed and gripped the loose cloth over her breasts, clenching her jaw. She didn't release her fists until the doctor's gloved fingers were withdrawn.

Finally, he was done. He didn't say anything except, "When you're dressed, I'll see you in my office," before he went out, his coattails sailing after him.

She dressed while the nurse chatted as she cleaned up the examination table and prepared it for the next patient. When Kathleen told her where she worked and what she did, the nurse was impressed. "What a wonderful, exciting job!"

Yes, Kathleen thought. And not exactly made to order for

a pregnant lady. But then, she wasn't pregnant or the doctor would have said so. She took a tissue and dabbed at the perspiration on the palms of her hands.

"Come in," the doctor called as she timidly knocked on his office door. In a courtly gesture, he stood up as she entered and indicated the chair opposite his desk. When he was sure that she was comfortable, he folded his hands on his desk and looked at her disarmingly over the tops of his lenses.

"Ms. Haley, forgive me for being so blunt, but did you suspect that you were pregnant?"

The words hit her like a shot from a cannon. The energy seemed to seep out of her body slowly, like air leaking out of a balloon with an insufficient knot at its end. She was deflated by slow degrees until she felt that there was nothing left inside her. But there was. Erik's baby was inside her.

She bowed her head as tears spilled over her lower lids. "Yes," she admitted in a low voice.

"When was your last period?" he questioned gently, knowing that she had lied to the nurse.

Putting pretense aside, Kathleen said, "The first week of July."

He did some silent mental figuring, then said, "That adds up. I estimated by the size of your uterus that you are about ten weeks pregnant." He cleared his throat delicately, giving her time to assimilate what he had said. "Everything seems perfectly normal. Your blood sugar is right, although I think you'd better start eating and gain some weight. You should deliver—"

"I can't have the baby," she blurted out before she lost her nerve. She swallowed hard and dashed the tears off her cheeks with balled, impatient fists. "I want an abortion."

Dr. Peters was somewhat taken aback by the resolution in her voice and the stubborn set of her chin. She didn't look the type to make a hasty decision, especially about something as important as this. "Is this your first pregnancy Ms. Haley?"

She laughed bitterly. Little did he know that it had been

her first time with a man. It had never occurred to her that she should be protecting herself against disease and pregnancy. Good Lord, most teens were more sexually responsible! What had she been thinking? Kathleen laughed again, and the brittle sound caused the doctor's brow to crease. She certainly hadn't been thinking about getting pregnant. "Yes, this is my first pregnancy."

"Then are you sure of your decision?"

She looked down at the soggy tissue in her hand. "As sure as one can be about killing something."

"Ms. Haley, you have a couple of weeks, no more than that, to reconsider before you make up your mind to terminate the pregnancy. Perhaps you should consult with the father—"

Her head came up instantly. "That's impossible. Besides, there's nothing to reconsider. I must have the abortion. Will you do it? Or must I go somewhere else?"

He stared at her for a long moment, thinking that much of her determination was contrived. She seemed so helpless, so vulnerable, so innocent in spite of her age. He sighed heavily. "Very well."

He picked up the telephone on his desk and asked his receptionist to make an appointment for Ms. Haley. "D and C. Termination of pregnancy." When he replaced the receiver in its cradle, he said to her, "Check with Maxine on your way out. Until I see you, you can always change your mind, you know."

She walked to the door, but didn't leave immediately. Instead, she turned around and faced the doctor again. This time, the tears ran unchecked down her face. "Please don't think I take what I must do lightly, Dr. Peters. I have no choice. You see," she sniffed back her tears bravely, "the child's father is married to someone else."

※ ※

Saturday morning. Two days. Could she wait that long? The nurse named Maxine had informed her that she wasn't to eat anything Friday evening past midnight and that she was to go to the hospital that night and have all the lab work done. Dr. Peters, it was explained to her, always had his patients put to sleep to spare them even the most minor discomfort. So she was to have a chest X ray at the hospital at the same time they did the blood test.

Seth called her on Friday afternoon and asked her if she would go to dinner with him. Her nerves were jangling. Hazel had come to the store that day and had countermanded an order that Kathleen had issued. The poor clerk who was carrying out Kathleen's innovative method of checking inventory came under Hazel's waspish tongue and was reduced to tears.

"Does Seth know what you're doing down here?" Hazel had demanded when Kathleen interrupted the scene. "We've always handled the inventory my way."

Kathleen resisted giving her opinion of Hazel's archaic system and answered levelly, "Yes, and he approves."

Hazel sized her up with those deadly eyes before she turned away. Her straight back and imperious footsteps were grim indications of her hatred for Kathleen.

Now, Seth's kind voice was coming to her over the telephone, and his tone was so friendly and confidence-inspiring that she was momentarily tempted to pour out her whole sordid story.

But though they had become close during the past several weeks, Kathleen knew that she couldn't burden him with her problems. If she couldn't call Edna and B. J., she couldn't tell a virtual stranger. Guilt at the way she had deserted the Harrisons gnawed at her. Not only had she forsaken their friendship and support, she had abandoned them in the middle of the summer when they still had two sessions of the camp to contend with. And she wasn't being falsely modest when she realized that finding someone with her experience to fill her shoes wouldn't have been easy for them. Additionally, her fund-raising attempts had been temporarily suspended. She would resume them, of course, but later. When she had healed emotionally. Now she had quite enough to deal with.

She ached with the longing to talk to the Harrisons, but was afraid some mention of Erik might be made. At this point in time, she wasn't ready to handle what they might have to tell her. It was better to wonder if he had sought her out after his recuperation than it was to know for certain that he had never come looking for her at all.

"After dinner, we can go dancing." Seth's pleasant voice brought her back to the present. "Of course, it's hard for me to dip."

Kathleen smiled into the telephone. How could she feel sorry for herself and wallow in this miasma of self-pity when someone in Seth's condition could joke about his plight? "That's okay," she said as cheerfully as she could. "I can't dip either."

"But I'm a devil at cha-cha. Push forward twice. Brake. Back one-half spin. Brake."

Now he had her laughing. "You're crazy, Seth Kirchoff."

"Yes, I am. About you." His voice became quieter now, more serious. "Fortune smiled on this old crippled boy the day you walked into my office, Kathleen. You're perfect for the job. You're smart as a whip. You're beautiful and wonderful to have around just to delight the eye. And on top of everything, I like you. Now why won't you have dinner with me?"

"Seth—"

"My conduct will be above approach, I promise. If I get too far out of line with a lady, George won't empty my tee-tee bag."

"Oh, Seth, how awful!" she cried, but she was laughing. "Please, Kathleen."

"No, I really can't tonight, Seth. I have other plans."

"A date?"

"No, no, nothing like that," she rushed to assure him. "I . . . It's some personal business." She'd better cover her bases now. "As a matter of fact, I'll be tied up all weekend."

There was a long pause before Seth asked, "Is everything all right? Work? Money? Everything?" The concern in his voice touched her heart. Being as he was, he would naturally be atuned to someone else's pain.

"Yes, Seth. I'll see you on Monday."

"Okay."

"Goodbye."

"Goodbye." She was just about to hang up when she heard his voice again. "Kathleen?"

"Yes?"

"You know that if you ever want anything, all you need do is ask. I'm your friend."

So simple. No questions. No strings attached. No qualifications. Unconditional friendship. Love. Her throat tightened painfully. "Thank you for that, Seth. Goodbye." She replaced the telephone before the tears that had gathered in her eyes could burst free.

After the blood was drawn and the X ray taken and she had filled out the necessary forms, Kathleen was told to go home to bed and to report to the reception desk at six-thirty the next morning.

She followed the instructions but was unable to fall asleep, no matter how exhausted she was. In her mind's eye, she could see the instruments that Dr. Peters would use on her to rid her of the "products of conception." Not "the baby." Not even "the fetus." The products of conception.

Her limbs felt like lead but her head seemed too light to hold onto her pillow as she tossed and turned through the night. Her brain refused to release her from consciousness. It forced her to remember, to speculate, to fear.

Long ago, she had vowed that before having children, she would be sure beyond a shadow of a doubt that her mate was her mate for life. She knew the pain of growing up without parents and had promised her as-yet-unconceived children that they would never have less than two parents, a real home, a complete family unit. If she were to call off the abortion and decide to have the baby alone, she would be breaking her promise, robbing her child of a parent. No. Never.

What would Erik think if he knew that she was carrying his baby? Would he even want to know? Would his reaction be one of anger at her for not being mature or responsible enough to take birth-control precautions? Would he feel pity and offer to help her by absorbing half of the financial burden? God! She couldn't have stood that.

Or would his reaction be quite different? Would his blue eyes fill with that warmth that she had read in them as he looked at her body and caressed it lazily, exploring it with inquisitive hands while his eyes worshiped it with appreciation?

Would he kneel before her, cupping her hips with his strong hands, drawing her to him and pressing his face against her abdomen in silent communication with his baby? Would his lips plant thankful kisses into her skin while he nuzzled her? Would he glory in the maternal fullness of her breasts?

No! No! Why was she torturing herself this way? A baby might mean nothing special to him. He might already have one. For all she knew, he and his wife might have an entire family of little Gudjonsens that meant no more to Erik than fidelity did.

Kathleen tried to blot out the euphoric fantasy, but it wouldn't go away. Rather, it expanded. She saw herself being wheeled down a hospital corridor toward the delivery room with an anxious Erik striding beside the gurney, clasping her hand and declaring his love.

Then they were standing at the nursery window, looking down in adoration at their son. Son? Yes. Erik would have to have a son.

Then they were walking down a tree-shaded lane, each holding the hand of their sturdy toddler. He had blond hair, slightly waved and defying control. His eyes were a piercing blue. Just like his father's . . .

Kathleen was still awake when the alarm went off beside her convertible sofa. She pulled herself up with tremendous effort. The only good thing about this morning was that it spelled the end of the hellish night she had spent, and at the end of this day, her ordeal would be over. She would be rid of the last remnant of Erik and could begin to live her life again.

At least that's what Kathleen told herself as she went through the routine steps of dressing. Without conscious thought, she drove herself to the hospital, parked the car and checked in at the reception desk. She was directed to the third floor, where she checked in at another desk.

"I'm Kathleen Haley," said the automatic voice that Kathleen didn't recognize as her own.

"Good morning, Ms. Haley. Come right this way."

She followed the nurse, sickeningly fresh and pert for this hour of the morning, down the hallway to a room with six beds in it. Only two other patients were already there.

The nurse slipped a clear plastic identification bracelet on Kathleen's arm. "Undress in there and put your personal belongings in the locker. There is a hospital gown in there for you. Be sure to take off your jewelry. And use the commode if you have to. I'll be back to start your IV."

She was gone and Kathleen was left alone with the other women in the cold room. One was younger, seventeen at the most. Was she in here for the same reason Kathleen was? Her heart went out to the girl, but the worldly-wise, insolent eyes that met hers didn't seem too upset. The other woman was older and weeping softly into a handkerchief. No doubt her D and C was therapeutic. Her abortion had been forced by nature. How awful.

Kathleen went into the bathroom and did as the nurse had told her to. I won't think, she told herself. *Don't think about what you're doing. Just do it and get it over with.*

She climbed into the high hospital bed and lay back on the rock-hard pillow. In a few minutes, the nurse came in carrying a bottle and a tray.

Without speaking, she bathed the crook of Kathleen's elbow with alcohol. Thankfully, it was the opposite arm from where they had drawn blood the night before.

She had always had an aversion to needles. As a child, she had been terrified of getting shots. As an adult, her fear wasn't much different. She turned her head away and winced as the nurse sought a vein, and then, after finding it, jammed the needle in and taped it to her arm.

"What is this?" Kathleen asked timidly.

"A pre op," the nurse said succinctly. "You're scheduled for seven forty-five so just take it easy for a while." Then she raised Kathleen's hand before dropping it back to the bed impatiently. "You've got on nail polish. We can't put you to sleep if you've got polish on your nails."

"I'm sorry," Kathleen apologized meekly. "No one told . . ."

Her voice trailed off. The nurse had already gone out the door.

❧ ❧

One patient, the woman who had been crying, had been wheeled out. The other girl was chewing gum and flipping through a *Rolling Stone* magazine. Just when Kathleen was about to break the silence and ask the girl if she knew the time, the door opened and Dr. Peters came in.

He had on a green surgical suit. The mask had been untied from around his nose and hung on his chest. His hair was comically mussed, but his eyes were kind and bright.

"Ms. Haley," he said softly as he took her hand. At least he hadn't said "good morning." He wasn't that hypocritical.

"Hello, Dr. Peters."

"Are you feeling well under the circumstances?"

"Yes. Hungry."

He chuckled. "You can eat all you want tonight."

"She took off my nail polish." Kathleen was dismayed that her bottom lip was quivering. She thought she had suppressed all those emotions.

"That nurse who brought you in here?" Dr. Peters asked. When Kathleen nodded, he leaned over and whispered, "She's a real bitch." He coaxed a smile from the tremulous lips. "But it is required that you take off nail polish before surgery. Otherwise, if you shouldn't be getting enough oxygen and your nails were to turn blue, we couldn't see it." Unnecessarily, he checked the IV. "Are you feeling drowsy?"

She wanted to answer "yes." She begged her mind for oblivion, but she was wide awake and told him so.

"Well, we'll get you under so you won't feel any discomfort. I promise. Briefly, I want to go over the procedure with you, so you'll know what's happening."

He hitched a hip to the side of her bed and partially leaned, partially sat on it. "First, we dilate the cervix. That's the opening to your uterus." She nodded. "Then, when you are dilated, I'll insert a hollow tube into the cervix. It's attached to a vacuum—"

"No," she gasped, and reflexively gripped his hand. "No, please, don't tell me." Her breathing had accelerated to an alarming pace and she felt a blackness closing over her as though she might faint at any moment.

"Ms. Haley—"

"I don't want to know. Just do it. When will it be finished?"

He covered her hand with his and patted it gently. "Not very long. You'll probably wake up in a couple of hours, and then, when you feel it's safe enough to drive, you can go home. I'll try to get as much of the lining of your uterus as is safe, so you won't have too much residual bleeding. But use napkins. No tampons until your next period." He hesitated over the next question. "Would you like to discuss birth-control methods?"

Birth control? For what reason? A hysterical laugh almost escaped her lips. Maybe the IV was working after all. She suddenly felt giddy. "No. That won't be necessary."

"I suggest using condoms. And not only for birth control."

"Of course." She couldn't understand herself why she hadn't taken commonsense precautions before, so she didn't try to explain her carelessness to Dr. Peters.

"I'll see you in the OR in, let's see," he checked his Japanese, stainless-steel wristwatch, "in about twenty minutes."

Thirty-five minutes went by before the orderlies came in with the gurney and needlessly moved Kathleen onto it. She felt capable of getting up and walking around but knew that that was out of the question. Self-consciously, she glanced at the girl in the other bed.

She surprised Kathleen by speaking for the first time. "It's no sweat. Really."

Had she been through this before? Stunned, Kathleen could only murmur, "Thank you." They pushed the gurney through the door.

The lights on the corridor ceiling rolled past her. They turned the corner and Kathleen gripped the edges of the gurney, dizzy, afraid that she was going to fall onto the floor. She was wheeled through two sets of double swinging doors, then left to rest in the pre op room.

A nurse checked the bracelet on her wrist. "Ms. Haley?"

"Yes."

The nurse smiled. This one wasn't so bitchy. Maybe she understood. "I'm going to give you a little more juice," she said as she adjusted a clamp on the IV tube. The bottle had been moved with her. "You'll be getting very sleepy soon."

Indeed she did. Seemingly within a matter of seconds, the room began to tilt and images loomed largely close and then receded to the size they are when one looks into the wrong end of binoculars.

No discomfort. Dilate. The products of conception. Vacuum. Vacuum. Kathleen tried to move her hand protectively over her abdomen, but wasn't sure she made it.

Not the products of conception. A person. A baby. Hers. Erik's.

Erik. Erik. Erik, where are you? I loved you! I still love you. And they're going to kill our baby. Why aren't you here to protect me?

Why aren't you here to see your son born? Your baby. But there will be no baby. A vacuum.

The nurse leaned over and said something to Kathleen, but she couldn't hear her. She saw the ceiling moving again, and then she was in another room and the lights were extremely bright. Someone was draping her knees over the high stirrups at the end of the table. Her legs were so heavy. She flinched against the cold bath someone was giving her genitalia.

Dilate. No baby. Erik's baby. She loved him. Would it be so wrong to want the results of that love? She could live with his deceit if only she could have something of value from their time together, something that would make the pain of loss more bearable. What could be a better testimony to the love she had borne the man than to have his baby? A baby would love her back.

A blond baby. A boy. She knew it was a boy. Blue eyes. Erik's eyes. Erik's baby.

Some disembodied voice was crooning to her and covering her nose and mouth with a mask. She couldn't breathe. She refused to. She heard someone screaming over and over and realized it was she. "No!" She fought the restraining hands. "No, don't touch me."

"Dr. Peters," an alarmed female voice said from beside Kathleen.

"Leave me alone. I love him. I want the baby. I'm not asleep. I'm not delirious. I'm awake and I want my baby." Her panicked voice sounded maniacal to her own ears, but she had to convince them. In desperation, she repeated the words with all the force and conviction she could muster.

"Ms. Haley."

She knew that voice and turned her thrashing head toward it. "Dr. Peters," she gasped. How could she make them understand? They mustn't take the baby. She tried to pull her knees together, but something kept them wide apart. "The baby, don't hurt it. My baby. Erik's. I love him. It's a boy. I know it is. I want my baby. Erik . . . Erik . . ."

The dark oblivion that Kathleen had craved she now anathematized. Nonetheless, it blanketed her, black and absolute.

Chapter Eleven

Kathleen studied Seth as he tried to assimilate what she had just said to him. His features were devoid of expression, as though he were stunned.

"I can't believe that I heard you correctly," he said at last.

Kathleen wore a forced mask of poise. Little did she know how huge her green eyes looked. Nor did she realize that the severity of her hairdo, peeled away from her pale face, emphasized the sharpness of her cheekbones. It was obvious to everyone but herself how rigidly she held her body, how tense she was.

"Yes. You heard me correctly. I have to resign. I will, of course, stay for two weeks while you look for a replacement."

"Damn the replacement!" Seth slapped his palms on the polished surface of his desk. It was the closest he had ever come to showing a temper. Never had she heard him raise his voice to that level. She squirmed under the prodding of his deep eyes. "Why, Kathleen? For godsake, *why?* I thought you liked us, liked your job here."

Unable to look at him any longer, she turned her head toward the large picture windows that framed the skyline of the city. "I do. But as I understand my job description, I'm to be the buyer and fashion coordinator for your store, soon to be *stores*. As such, I should look the part of a high-fashion-minded individual, keep pace with trends."

His dark brows arched over his eyes in puzzlement. "So?"

She turned her gaze from the foggy scenery and looked at him directly. "That's not so easy if you're pregnant."

Again that blank, unwavering stare, as if what she had said was so incomprehensible that he couldn't grasp it. His eyes fluttered down to her flat midsection. Then back to her face. "You're telling me that you're pregnant?"

She squared her shoulders. "Yes."

It was mid-October. Two weeks had gone by since Kathleen had awakened in the hospital's recovery room, frantically demanding to know if she still carried Erik's baby. Dr. Peters had been there to reassure her.

"I want to have this baby."

"Am I to understand that you're a single parent?"

She nodded.

"You'll do fine." He patted her hand and Kathleen was grateful for his encouragement.

The last two weeks hadn't been easy. She was still nauseated in the mornings and indigestive in the afternoons, but Dr. Peters had prescribed some tablets for her to take when she became too uncomfortable.

What pained her most was the mental anguish she was going through. She was again tempted to telephone Edna and tell her everything, but Kathleen refrained from doing that. The Harrisons would only worry about her more than they no doubt already were doing. So she would have to work out this untenable situation for herself. She would survive. Women, even single women, had babies all the time.

Seth would have to know immediately. His plans for expansion were in full force, and he was on the telephone every day to manufacturers in New York, lining up appointments for Kathleen when she went on the buying trip scheduled for the end of the month. He had to be told, and yet, Kathleen dreaded that more than anything. She hated to let him down professionally, for she was aware of the faith he had placed in her abilities. Even more, she didn't want to disappoint him as an individual whom he respected. The greatest hurt would be seeing the disillusionment in his eyes.

Now she had told him, but she didn't read in his face any of the disgust that she had expected. Instead, his eyes seemed to shine with wonder and happiness. He wheeled around the corner of the desk, drew up beside her chair and took her hand in the security of his.

"I suppose congratulations are not in order." It wasn't a question and not intended to be flippant, but Kathleen laughed mirthlessly.

"Not exactly." She gazed into the fathomless depths of his dark eyes and saw no censure there. She could be totally honest with this man and never fear ridicule. "I didn't know when I took this job. I swear it. I almost had an abortion, but . . . but . . . ." To her chagrin, tears began blurring her eyes. How much could one human being weep before running completely dry? She must be close, for it seemed she had cried endlessly during the last month.

"I'm certain that, for you, having the child is the right decision. Why didn't you confide in me before now?"

"I was confused, uncertain what to do."

"And now you know?"

She shook her head dismally. "No. I'm just trying to live one day at a time and keep my head above water."

He placed his hands on her shoulders and pulled her toward him until her head rested against his chest. She cried quietly, the sobs shaking her body as he stroked her back with a conciliatory hand and murmured solicitous phrases in her ear. Finally, the flow of tears was stemmed and she sat up, accepting the handkerchief that he took from his breast pocket.

"The father?" he questioned her softly.

She considered lying and telling Seth that the father was dead, but she couldn't. "It was a one-night stand. He was gone the next day." His finger slipped under her chin and raised her face until she was forced to look at him.

"You loved him, didn't you?"

She looked away from him, her eyes darting around the room, resting first on one object and then another, anything to keep them busy and away from Seth's discerning gaze.

"Kathleen?"

Then she did look at him, and his face was full of such tenderness that she collapsed under its compassion. "Yes," she sobbed, and buried her face once again in the handkerchief. "And I still do. God forgive me, but I do."

"Does he know about—"

"No!" she cried. "He never will. I'll never see him again. He has another life, a . . ." She couldn't tell Seth that Erik had a wife. She'd retain that much honor in his eyes. "To me, it's as though he's dead."

She got up and walked to the window. Her arms were wrapped defensively around her waist. She hadn't heard the motor of his wheelchair approaching her, and jumped when he spoke directly behind her.

"Why are you leaving Kirchoff's?"

Kathleen whirled around in disbelief that he needed to ask. "Why?" she said incredulously. Hadn't he heard a thing she had said? "Why? I think the reason is obvious. I'm pregnant, Seth. In a few months, I'll be as big as a blimp. And a few months after that, I'll have a newborn baby to take care of."

"I know the facts of life, Kathleen," he said without emotion, but he was smiling. "There's no clause in your contract that says pregnancy would prohibit you from doing your job. That's illegal, and besides, we're not as stuffy and unenlightened as that! Professional women are no longer restricted from having children. Are you afraid it would be too much for you?"

She answered slowly, a glimmer of hope beginning to shine on an otherwise bleak horizon. "No, but—"

"What did you intend to do?"

"Well," she said evasively, "I thought I'd get a lower-profile job. And then, after the baby came, when I was able to go back to work, I'd put the baby in a day—"

"In a day-care center, where he'll grow up without you, without the proper attention an infant needs?"

"No," Kathleen said angrily. "I'd make sure that it was a good one."

"That's still unacceptable, Kathleen. Come here." He took her hand and pulled her down toward his lap.

"Seth," she gasped. "What are you . . . I'll hurt you," she said as she landed with a plop on his thighs.

He laughed. "How I wish you could!" Then he sobered and drew her closer, placing one arm around her back and the other around her waist. "Kathleen, I wish I could feel something in my legs. Even pain. I can't feel anything from the waist down. It's dead." His eyes pierced into hers. "Do you understand what I'm trying to say?"

She looked away, momentarily embarrassed, then back at him. It was hard to remain embarrassed with someone as unpretentious and open as Seth. "Yes, I think so," she murmured.

"Then you know that I'll never be able to have a baby, a family, though that was one of my fondest desires. And as much as I'd like to in my mind," he stroked her cheek with fleeting fingers, "I couldn't impose any physical demands on a woman." He raised her hand to his lips and kissed the tips of her fingers. "Will you marry me, Kathleen?"

It was her turn to stare now. The unexpected proposal had import enough, but what was even more astonishing was that it had come when she had just divulged that she was carrying another man's child and that she loved that man. Had Seth gone mad?

"Seth, you—"

"I want you for my wife," he finished simply. "I love you, Kathleen. I have from the moment you walked into my office that first day. I know you don't love me. You love the father of your baby, and I truly would think less of you if you didn't. But he isn't here. I am. I want you. I want your child.

Please, Kathleen, come into my life. Such as it is." He smiled sadly, and only one side of his sculpted mouth lifted at the corner.

"I'm asking a lot, I realize," he continued after a moment. "I know that a healthy woman like you needs more of a man than I can be." His voice took on a touching desperation. "But I can give you security, a name for your child, an opulent lifestyle—"

"Seth, please." She pressed her fingers against his lips to still them. "Your wealth doesn't matter to me. What you're offering is too generous even to consider. Your side of the giving far outweighs mine."

"Let me worry about that," he said, drawing her against his chest and placing her head on his shoulder. "Live in my house, let me see you every day, work with me, help me realize my vision, imbue me with your lively spirit."

"Seth," she whispered against the warm, fragrant skin of his throat. Could she do it? Was this the answer to her dilemma? She had the highest regard for him. Maybe it bordered on love. He was honest, idealistic, trusting and tolerant. What more could one ask of a man?

His physical limitations didn't even figure into her decision. She had loved once. To Erik, she had given her body, all she had to give, and she was certain that she could never love any man with that single-minded passion again. She would never see Erik again. Even if she did, he belonged to someone else. They could never have a life together.

She still loved him. No longer did she try to deny that indelible fact. She loved him. A life with Seth wouldn't be as blissful, as electric. She wouldn't get breathless each time she anticipated seeing him and, upon sight, have even the highest anticipation dimmed by the reality. She would never know again that transcendence of body, soul and mind, that oneness with another being that could only happen through loving.

But her life with Seth would be a good one. He would cherish her and her child. It would be quiet and peaceful.

They would work side by side, each doing something they loved. She would know kindness and . . . honesty.

"You don't have to give me an answer today, but I'd be elated if you'd say yes right now," Seth said.

She sat up and placed her hands on the lapels of his coat. "Do you know what you're bargaining for?"

"Yes."

"Then I'll marry you, Seth. Happily and without hesitation."

He kissed her softly on the lips. It was a kiss empty of passion, but tender. It sealed the covenant. When he pulled away, he said, "We're of different . . . tribes, so to speak. Does it bother you that I'm Jewish?"

"Not if it doesn't bother you that I'm Christian."

He laughed. "All I ask is that if the baby's a boy, we have him circumcised on the eighth day of his life according to our tradition."

"Of course. And may he celebrate Christmas and Easter until he's old enough to decide religions for himself?"

"Certainly." His eyes wandered leisurely over her face, adoring each feature. Finally, he said gruffly, "I love you, Kathleen."

She banished the picture in her mind of azure eyes that sparkled like water, hair that shone golden in the sunlight, a mustache that framed flashing white teeth, and tried to focus her attention on the dark, loving face close to hers. "I know you do, Seth, I know."

❧ ❧

"Surely you're joking." Hazel Kirchoff was seated in her beautifully, tastefully, expensively decorated living room on the peach silk cushions of her half-circle couch. Her hands were folded gracefully in her lap, her ankles crossed with exemplary deportment, her posture straight, as had been taught her in the private school she had attended as a young girl.

"No, I'm not. Kathleen and I are getting married this Sunday afternoon in Judge Walters's chambers. He owes us a favor. Remember? We ordered that mink stole for Mrs.—"

"Seth, I'm well aware of the favor we did for the judge," she snapped. "Would you kindly tell me what you can possibly be thinking when you say that you're marrying that little . . . Ms. Haley."

Seth grinned as he wheeled over to the antique rosewood sideboard and poured himself another scotch. "Surprised? I am, too."

"The only thing that surprises me is that my rational, intelligent brother is babbling like an idiot. You can't really mean that you and Ms. Haley are getting married. It's preposterous!"

"I agree!" he said cheerfully. "But strange as it may seem, it's true."

The agitation on Hazel's face didn't reveal a fraction of the fury raging within her. She had known that girl meant trouble. Beauty and brains were incompatible attributes. What her brother considered intelligence, Hazel recognized as cunning. Kathleen had schemed her way into the corporation, the thing that Hazel held most dear. Now she was invading her family and home, too. She had craftily besotted Seth, who, God knew, would welcome the attention of any woman.

Their mother had died when Hazel was twenty-four. Seth, a late-in-life baby, had been only eleven. Hazel had taken care of and protected him ever since. It wasn't an obligation she had asked for or particularly enjoyed, but damned if she would be usurped.

Belying the tumult inside her, she smiled and said, "Why don't you tell me about it, Seth, dear."

Eagerly, Seth launched into an account of Kathleen's merits. The more Hazel listened, the more she cursed her brother for the fool she had always thought him to be. His acts of generosity irritated her. His patience, his acceptance of his disability, all grated on her. Why didn't he feel anger, bitterness? He was weak. Just like their father, for whom she had always harbored the deepest disdain.

When Seth finally paused long enough to take a sip of scotch, she put her lips to her sherry glass, though she really didn't drink any. She despised the stuff. Her solace came from the secret bottle of vodka stashed in a drawer in her bedroom.

She smiled sweetly, the expression on her face barely more than a grimace. "I know how talented and beautiful Ms. Haley is, Seth." The words stuck to her throat like bad-tasting medicine. "But what do we know about her?"

"She was raised in an orphanage after the death of her parents." He went on to capsulize Kathleen's life for his sister, much as Kathleen had done for him the afternoon he had proposed.

The more he talked about Kathleen, the brighter his eyes shone and the more the burning, sinking feeling in her stomach pained Hazel. "Seth, darling," she said gently, "forgive my indelicacy, but you can't . . . I mean . . . it won't be a traditional marriage." She managed to force a blush and look awkwardly down at her hands, all the time thinking that her brother couldn't satisfy that slut in a million years. She had seen the way Kathleen used those beguiling eyes and that small, lithe body to full advantage, torturing her stupid brother into thinking that he was a man again.

"I know, Hazel," Seth said sadly. "However, providence has compensated for that. You see, even now, Kathleen is carrying the Kirchoff heir. She's expecting a baby in the spring."

The words had a devastating effect on Hazel's false composure. "What!" she gasped. Her face grew hideous, all the ugliness in her soul suddenly becoming evident in that moment when the facade was down. The whore was pregnant! That didn't surprise Hazel. What did surprise her was the bitch's audacity to try to dump her bastard on the Kirchoffs. "You're going to marry a whore pregnant with someone else's bastard? You intend to name that scum as your heir?"

Seth was momentarily shocked by Hazel's coarse tirade. Since her one love affair had gone awry many years ago, Seth knew his sister avoided men except on a professional basis.

He placed his highball glass on the parqueted top of the coffee table and wheeled his chair closer to her. He knew she must be extremely upset to react so violently. Perhaps he should have broached the subject more gently, instead of letting his happiness run rampant and without discretion.

"Hazel," he said kindly, "I know that this comes as a surprise to you, and you're naturally suspicious of Kathleen's motives, but I must ask you not to speak about her in those terms. I love her very much."

Hazel stared at him in disbelief, wondering if he had any inkling as to how imbecilic he sounded.

"The man . . . the father of her child hurt her deeply. She loved him. Kathleen couldn't have given herself to him had she not."

That's what you think, Hazel sneered silently. *That whore would open up her long, slender legs for any man. And you, my stupid brother, are sadly lacking in that department.*

"Please give her a chance, Hazel. I know you'll come to love her as I do. And the child. It will be your niece or nephew, after all." He smiled.

Hazel forced her face to remain inscrutable. What choice did she have? If she spit out the harsh words that were churning inside her, clamoring for release, Seth might possibly turn on her. He was obviously besotted with the woman.

As it was, she still held the reins of control over him. The best guarantee she had of keeping them was to accept this tramp into her house and, in Seth's view, play the simpering spinster sister-in-law. It wouldn't be difficult. It wasn't far from the role she had been playing for years—the doting sister—when all the while, the very sight of Seth repulsed her. She must protect her first love, the store. Hazel forced herself to ask calmly, "What about her job at the store?"

"She'll retain it. I've insisted. But I want her to hire an assistant to be in training to take over when the baby arrives."

That wasn't the best option to Hazel's mind, but she could work around it. Even to herself, her smile felt false as she said, "Forgive me, Seth, for what I said. I was too stunned to think rationally." She raised her hand to his dark hair and brushed back a few vagrant strands. "I guess I'm having a typical jealous reaction. You've been more like a son than a brother. Now I'm losing you to another woman."

He caught her hand and pressed it to his cheek. "You're not losing me. We're going to be a family. All of us together."

"Yes," she murmured as he wheeled away to ask George to bring a magnum of champagne. Of one thing Hazel was certain, if she had to murder the woman, her bastard and Seth himself, that slut wouldn't inherit one red cent of the money that rightfully belonged to Hazel Kirchoff.

❦ ❦

"I just can't believe it, B. J." Edna said. "She's married?"

"That's what the letter says, but I'm damned if I can believe it either." He raked his hand through his grizzled gray hair. "Who is the guy again?"

"She says his name is Seth Kirchoff and that he owns the department store she's working for. In San Francisco, of all places. They were married last Sunday. She says she's moving into his house this weekend."

"You figure he's rich?"

Edna scanned the paper she was holding in her hand. "Well, if this stationery with her new initials embossed on it is any indication, I'd say yes," Edna commented caustically. As she read the letter again, she asked, "B. J., aren't you surprised?"

"Nothing surprises me anymore," he grumbled.

Edna spun around and glared at him. "Will you put down that damn newspaper and talk to me about this! You aren't going to hide behind that screen. I know that you're hurt by her behavior, too. Now let's talk about it."

"There's nothing to talk about. Kathleen's got a new husband and a new life. That's all there is to it," he said firmly.

"No, that's not all there is to it. Don't you think we should tell him—"

"No!" B. J. said adamantly. There was no doubt in his mind to whom Edna was referring.

"But we promised to let him know if we heard from her."

"We did no such thing, Edna, and don't try to trick me into thinking we did."

She gnawed her lip as she thought of a new tack. "Maybe we should just let him know that she is alive and well—"

"And living in San Francisco with a new rich husband. Do you think that would be kind?" he demanded.

"No," she sighed, and slumped down in a chair at the kitchen table where they had been enjoying a leisurely breakfast until the mail had been delivered.

"All right then," B. J. said, grateful that the unpleasant issue had been settled. "Pour me some more coffee."

Erik stared down into the amber liquid in his glass as if it held the answers to all the mysteries of the universe. Maybe if he looked at it hard enough, deep enough, he would find the solution to his own misery.

The sound of laughter came from the other side of the bar, from a booth where three couples were sharing a pitcher of beer and congenial conversation. He turned his back on them as a wave of loneliness struck him. Had he ever been part of a group, fit in anywhere? At one time, his peers at work had included him when they went out after hours for a drink. But his drinking had become too serious, his mood too morose, his temper too volatile to be attractive to other people.

When he had finally been able to go back to work after the airplane accident, he was angry to the point of madness. He had finally produced the piece on the innovative orphanages he had been assigned to do, but each day he worked on it was torture. Each time he played the videotapes of Mountain View, his gut would be wrenched anew. If he saw Kathleen's image on the monitor, he would smash his fist into his palm as though wishing it were she he was crushing.

"You took your sweet time, ol' buddy," his producer said when he finally submitted the piece for air play.

"Go to hell," Erik grumbled as he headed for the door.

"Wait a minute, Gudjonsen," the man called him back, but quelled under the forbidding look Erik leveled at him. "Listen, I know it's none of my business," he said bravely, "but ever since you came back after that airplane accident, you've had a burr up your ass. There are some people around here who are getting pretty fed up with this attitude of yours. I like you, Erik. You're a terrific talent and I hate to see a career wasted and shot to hell because of a chip on someone's shoulder. If there's anything I can do—"

"As you said, it's none of your business," Erik snarled, and slammed out the door.

That had been late last fall, and now it was spring. Each day, unlike the emergence of life around him, spelled further deterioration for Erik.

The standards of perfection he had always demanded from his work were less stringent. He was sloppy in the things he produced. He drank too much, usually until he was in a somnolent stupor. No surcease from his depression was found with women. None appealed to him. Plenty were available, just as they had always been, but he spurned them. Try as they might, none could arouse him to that pitch of passion that Kathleen—

"Another one, please," Erik said abruptly to the bartender, and watched as the scotch was splashed into the glass. Months ago, he had given up water or ice or soda, anything that diluted the drugging quality of the liquor that made the pain bearable.

However, he welcomed the pain now. That slow, smoldering heartache was almost a comfortable companion, and virtually the only friend he had left. They knew each other well. For a while, he had wiped the image of her face from his mind each time he had unwillingly conjured it up. Now, he let it alone. He savored the sight of her even if it was a figment.

Last summer. Had it been that long ago? Those days, so few when compared to his lifetime, had brought him immeasurable pleasure and unspeakable sorrow. One thing good had come out of them. Bob and Sally had adopted little Jaimie.

Erik smiled in spite of his dejection. For years, his brother and Sally had tried to conceive, almost desperately, using clinical techniques he couldn't even fathom. Once he was able to talk about Mountain View, he told them about Jaimie. They became interested in the child and asked Erik to show them tapes of Jaimie. Excited, but trying not to build their hopes too high, they contacted the orphanage in Joplin, Missouri, where Jaimie lived. Before two months had gone by, he was theirs. Then, at Christmas, Sally had proudly announced that she was pregnant. Jaimie was as thrilled by the news as the rest of the family.

One good thing had come out of last summer.

How long was he going to go on like this? He wasn't the first guy to be thrown over. This was just the first and only time it had ever happened to him. Dying a slow, useless death wasn't exactly his idea of valor. He had alienated his friends and driven his brother to distraction with worry over him. His associates despised him, but no more than Erik despised himself. He didn't want to regress to the cynic he had been before Ethiopia and other such experiences had opened his eyes to the pain others in the world suffered.

This was April. April in Paris would be nice. Slowly, almost regretfully, Erik pushed away the full glass of whiskey and stood up. He looked at the sallow, unkempt, disreputable-looking man that stared back at him from the mirror over the bar.

Walking toward the door, he knew what he had to do.

❧ ❧

"A baby! A boy!" Edna exclaimed as she held the announcement in her hand. "She didn't even mention that she was pregnant when she sent us that long letter at Christmas."

"Read it to me again," B. J. said.

"Theron Dean Kirchoff, eight pounds five ounces, twenty-one inches long, born April twelfth."

"April twelfth," B. J. mused aloud.

The birth announcement was slowly lowered as Edna's eyes lift to confront those of her husband.

"It couldn't be," she whispered hoarsely.

"Have you ever heard of an eight-pound-plus premature baby? She didn't marry that guy until October. She hadn't even met him until the end of August, first of September."

"What are you doing?" Edna asked as she followed close behind B. J. into the living room to the telephone.

"I'm calling Erik Gudjonsen. Not telling him about Kathleen's whereabouts for his own good was one thing. Having a son is another."

B. J. was on the telephone for fifteen minutes, but the results of the long-distance call were less than satisfactory. Yes, this is the television station where Mr. Gudjonsen was employed, the girl at the switchboard told B. J., but he no longer worked there. He had quit without notice just a few days ago. No, no one knew where he was working now, but it was thought that he had gone abroad.

Chapter Twelve

❧ ❧

Theron, please!'' Kathleen shouted, and dodged the thrashing legs that threatened to shower her again with the clear water of the swimming pool. Theron shrieked with delight and renewed his efforts to drench his mother.

"You're a pest. Do you know that?" she teased, and grabbed his chubby body around the waist, lowering her head and nuzzling his neck while he strove to escape this show of affection. At seventeen months old, he was already developing an aversion to maternal protection and asserting his newfound independence. Only when he ran into trouble of some sort did he come to Kathleen seeking solace.

He was active, curious and headstrong, determined to have his way against all odds. On the days Kathleen was home, she spent nearly every minute in his company, basking in a glow of pride and love.

When Theron was born, Seth wanted her to quit working. He saw how time- and energy-consuming being a mother was. But Kathleen had been adamant.

"Before I was your wife, I was your employee. You hired me to do a very difficult job. Until I feel like I've accomplished what you outlined for me to do, I'll continue working at least three days a week. With the new store in Stonetown and the boutique in Ghirardelli's now open, you need me more than ever.''

He acquiesced, but only if she would accept her current salary. Each week, she endorsed a paycheck and deposited it into a savings account. Seth wouldn't let her spend any of that money, but gave her a sizable ''household account.''

She had hired an assistant to help her, but was never far from the telephone when not actually in the stores or at her office.

Her assistant was a young man named Eliot Pate. He knew the retail clothing business inside out, had a flair for style and an uncanny instinct about what merchandise would sell quickly. They had recognized each other's talent, and an immediate friendship had sprung up between them.

She accepted his alternate lifestyle. He overlooked her flagrant femininity, and she overlooked his occasional bitchiness. When she was off, spending her days with Theron, she knew that Eliot had things well under control.

Today was one such day. She and Theron were languishing away the late afternoon hours in the Kirchoffs' pool. Kathleen never thought of this estate in Woodlawn as her house. It was too large, too ostentatious, and Hazel never passed up an opportunity to let Kathleen know who was mistress of it.

When Seth had first brought her here as his bride, Kathleen was intimidated by the apparent show of wealth, but gradually she had become accustomed to it, which was strange considering where and how she had grown up.

The traditional house was fashioned after those found in the English countryside. The lawn surrounded it in a broad expanse of green, perfectly clipped and trimmed. The interior was decorated with the most meticulous attention to detail. But to Kathleen, the rooms looked like settings in a magazine instead of where people actually lived. Hazel's personality was reflected in everything, and for that reason alone, Kathleen had never felt that she belonged here.

Her favorite rooms were those occupied by herself and Theron. Seth had generously offered to let her redecorate them to her own taste. She rid the rooms of the somber, cold, formal decor that Hazel had installed, and put in its place her choice of furnishings, which were lighter, brighter and much more conducive to everyday living.

Downstairs, what had once been a library had been converted into a den for Seth, which connected to a solarium that had become his specialized bedroom. Seth's den was cheerful and pleasant, and they often sat in it in the evenings, talking over the stores' progress and Theron's precociousness.

Now, as she bounced her child in the water, she marveled again at how well things had turned out. When she had married Seth almost two years ago, she'd had no reason to expect that she could be this . . . content. The word *happy* had almost formed in her mind, but that really couldn't describe her. Yet she felt a deep sense of satisfaction with what she had made of her life, when at one point it had seemed so hopeless.

Her relationship with the Harrisons had been restored. She had heard from them soon after letting them know of her marriage. Their congratulations were reserved.

But when she notified them of Theron's birth, she was deluged with presents and advice on parenting. Since then, they corresponded often and telephoned periodically, on birthdays and such. If that closeness they had once shared had cooled since that pivotal summer, Kathleen was at least glad that the lines of communication remained open.

She shared their happiness over Jaimie's adoption. When they told her about it, she felt only a momentary pang of jealousy for the family who had taken the boy into their lives. She often thought about the child who had touched her heart that summer.

With Seth's full endorsement, she continued as an absentee board member for Mountain View, making anonymous and sizable contributions to it. The checks were always drawn on an account Seth had in a New York bank and signed by his attorney. One, Kathleen specified, was to be used to build some tennis courts. For years, the Harrisons had wanted to add that sport to the summer curriculum. Kathleen tried to convince herself that her donations weren't made as recompense for the dreadful way she had treated the couple who had loved her so much.

Seth knew of the Harrisons, but not the extent of Kathleen's former relationship with them. She had never told him that she had been at Mountain View only weeks before coming to San Francisco. That subject was better avoided.

The stability and peace of mind she was feeling this afternoon had been hard to come by.

"Do you want to go under?" she asked Theron. "Huh? Hold your breath." She sucked in her breath with an exaggerated motion, and then quickly pulled the small, sturdy body under the surface, only to bring it up again. Theron blinked his blue eyes and gasped for air, then crowed with laughter. He began bucking, indicating that he wanted to do it again.

Laughing, Kathleen said, "Hold your breath. Ready? Here we go." She dunked him again, and this time there was no delayed reaction. When he came up, he was already slapping his hands on the surface of the water.

His laughter and her own hoots of praise for his brave accomplishment prevented her from hearing Seth's van as it pulled into the driveway. Nor did she hear the sound of the hydraulic system lowering his chair to the ground, or the muffled voices as they came around the flagstone path toward the swimming pool.

"Kathleen! What's going on? We could hear you all the way on the front drive." Seth's voice, as usual, was warm with happiness. Keeping her full attention on her wet, wiggling son, she called over her shoulder, "Come see what Theron can do. He's very proud of himself."

"You be careful with that boy, Kathleen," George said from behind her. "He's getting almost too big for you to handle."

"He is at that," she agreed. Theron was now even more

excited with his ardent audience, and waved his chubby arms at them before Kathleen told him again to hold his breath and dunked him under.

Everyone applauded when he broke the surface and smiled, revealing almost a full set of shiny white baby teeth. "That's enough for now," Kathleen said, laughing. "I'm pooped!" She lifted Theron out of the pool onto the redwood deck and he toddled toward Seth. George leaned down and picked up the little boy, swatted him affectionately on the rump and sat him in Seth's lap, disregarding the fact that his diaper was dripping wet.

Only when Kathleen turned around and walked up the mosaic tile steps out of the pool did she notice the other man standing quietly behind Seth's chair. There was something vaguely—

My God!

"Kathleen, I've committed the cardinal sin usually attributed to inconsiderate husbands and brought someone home for dinner without giving you notice."

Kathleen's heart was pounding so loudly that she could barely hear Seth's words as Erik stepped from behind the wheelchair. "This is Erik Gudjonsen. Erik, my wife, Kathleen."

Her heart seemed to swell and then burst, showering the universe with infinitesimal fragments of herself. And as it did, her world disappeared and was replaced by a smaller one comprised only of her and the man in front of her. Standing so close. Close enough to see, to hear, to smell, to . . . touch.

No, she mustn't touch him. If she did, she would die of the pleasure and the pain. But the decision was taken from her as Erik extended his hand. She watched that hand as it closed the distance between them. And then, almost in wonder at this miracle, she reached out and grasped it with her own, closing her fingers around it as though to verify that this was no dream, but actuality.

The gentle squeeze she received in return made it abundantly clear that he was real. Her eyes lifted from the studied attention she gave their clasping hands to his chest, over the firm, strong chin, past the sensuous mouth under that mustache which, even now, she fantasized about, along the slender, aristocratic nose, to his eyes, which bored into her.

There the exultant celebration in her breast was squelched. His eyes resembled pieces of blue ice, hard and unyielding beneath the shaggy, sun-bleached brows. Lying deep in their depths was a terrifying hostility.

"Mrs. Kirchoff," he finally said in acknowledgment of Seth's introduction. The world came back, righted itself and demanded that she behave according to custom.

"Mr. Gudjonsen." Her voice sounded foreign to her ears, and she only hoped that no one else noticed. His voice was poignantly familiar—deep, husky, befitting his size.

Then Seth was speaking excitedly. "Kathleen, Erik and I have been corresponding for the last several months. We're working on a project for the stores. I've wanted to keep it as a surprise for you. Now that Erik's here, we'll go over all the details after dinner."

Her smile was stiff, contrived, and she felt dizzy and nauseated, fearful that she might disgrace herself by throwing up at any moment. After the initial astonishment of seeing Erik here in her own backyard, feminine vanity had set in. She was all too aware of the wet hair that clung to her shoulders. She hadn't put on any makeup all day and was dripping wet, her apple-green maillot suit clinging to her shivering body.

"I can't wait to hear what you've been planning, Seth. If you'll excuse me now, I'm going to take Theron inside and clean him up before Alice gives him his dinner. I'll meet you on the patio in an hour for cocktails."

"Okay, but bring Theron back. I want Erik to see him when he's more presentable."

"He seems like quite a live wire," Erik commented as he looked down at Theron for the first time.

"Yes, he is," Seth said proudly. "You ought to see him try to negotiate the stairs. He's fearless."

With growing horror, Kathleen saw Erik peer down into

Theron's face. The boy looked up at him with reciprocal interest.

"I have to get him inside," Kathleen said, and barged between Erik and Seth to pick up Theron. "Excuse me," she said as she held the child and hurried toward the house.

She practically ran through the kitchen door and, when she was safe inside, leaned against the wall weakly.

"Goodness, Kathleen, you look like you've seen a ghost. What in the world is the matter with you, girl?" Alice asked with concern.

Alice, George's wife, acted as housekeeper/cook and ran the house with the competence of a ship's captain. She was as soft and plump as George was hard and lean, but they complemented each other perfectly. Kathleen knew that the couple had lost a teenage son to muscular dystrophy. While Seth was still in the hospital after his debilitating accident, George had come to see him on behalf of a paraplegic association. He had offered his full-time services to Seth. The couple had been with him ever since.

Now, Alice crossed the tiled kitchen floor, wiping her hands on a towel.

"Oh." Kathleen laughed nervously. "I think I got too much sun. When I left the pool, I felt a little dizzy." She took a deep breath. "What's on the menu tonight? Seth brought Er— a guest home for dinner. I hope that won't inconvenience you," Kathleen said, despising her breathlessness.

"No. I'd planned on roast beef, so it's already in the oven," Alice replied absently. She was more worried about Kathleen's pale color than how many people there would be for dinner. "I'll fix a fresh fruit compote for an appetizer, then serve salad and vegetables with the main course. Instead of a heavy dessert, what do you think of a crème de menthe parfait?"

"Sounds wonderful," Kathleen lied. The thought of eating was repugnant. "Well, Theron needs a bath."

"I'm sure he could use one," Alice said, laughing at the

toddler, who was emptying a drawer of plastic measuring cups.

"Come on, Theron," Kathleen said, taking his hand and leading him out of the room. "If you need any help, Alice, call me." She always offered, but Alice never took her up on it.

"Don't worry about dinner. You just dress up pretty for the company."

Kathleen was glad that Alice didn't see her footsteps falter as she walked across the wide entrance hall from which the broad staircase rose majestically.

As she bathed Theron, her mind was spinning with a million questions she hadn't allowed to surface before. They did now. What was Erik doing here? What kind of business venture could he possibly have with Seth? Where had he been these past two years? What had he been doing? Was his wife with him?

He looked the same. No, he looked different. What was it? He was older. Time had etched tiny lines at the corners of his eyes. The creases on either side of his mouth were harder, less inclined to tilt mirthfully. His eyes—she shivered—his eyes didn't dance any more with devilish humor. They were cold, cynical, callous.

She placed Theron in his playpen and indulged herself with a bubble bath. *What was he doing here?* Why had he come back into her life when things were going so well? Why hadn't he come sooner?

She avoided the most important question, the one that plagued her more strongly than the others. Would he recognize Theron as his son? If he did, what would he do about it?

She toweled dry and padded into her bedroom with a bath sheet wrapped around her. Standing at her closet, she selected an ensemble, discarded it, then moved to another until she finally settled on a pair of white silk evening trousers. The accompanying strapless blouse was multicolored stripes in metallic colors. Her waist was swathed by a shocking-pink cummerbund. She slipped into white high-heeled sandals and put gold disks into her pierced ears. Two dainty gold chains encircled her suntanned neck.

Putting on makeup had never been so difficult. Her hand shook with the effort, and she smeared mascara that had to be wiped away before she could apply more. Since her butterfingers couldn't quite cope with intricate clips and combs, she decided to let her hair hang free and loose on her shoulders.

She had learned that in the Kirchoff household it was customary to dress for dinner. In the almost two years she had been here, she had rather come to enjoy that tradition. Besides, Seth liked to see her wear fine clothes.

When she was ready, she dressed Theron in a navy-blue playsuit with "Ahoy, there!" appliquéd in white letters on the front. As she brushed his thick cap of blond curls, she marveled again at the miracle of his birth. She had known before Dr. Peters had made the proud announcement in the delivery room that the child was a boy. Her early visions of him had been mystically accurate. She shuddered whenever she thought back to the time when she had contemplated abortion. What a tremendous sacrifice it would have been never to have known the joy of loving Theron.

Would Erik feel that affinity that she did each time she looked at Theron? Did fathers have that same oneness with their children that mothers did?

She swung Theron down from his padded changing table and took his hand. "Are you ready?" she asked, the question really directed to herself. The unqualified answer was "no." She was torn between her burning desire to feast her eyes on Erik once again and the anguish of seeing him dangerously near his son. But if she didn't hurry, Seth would wonder what was keeping her. She couldn't arouse his suspicions in any way. At all costs, she must remain cool and collected around Erik, for Seth must never know their former relationship. He must never be hurt. She prayed he wouldn't see the resemblance between Theron and their dinner guest.

They descended the stairs hand in hand. Kathleen slid open the glass door that led out to the patio, and, released from her restraining hand, Theron barreled past her toward the man sitting at the round, umbrella-shaded table sipping a drink.

Erik, taken by surprise, laughed and reached down to ruffle the curls on the head pressed against his knee. "Ahoy there, Captain. Where's your—"

At that moment, he glanced up and saw Kathleen standing in the doorway. *God, she's beautiful*, Erik thought, and impatiently swallowed the lump in his throat. He had considered himself cured, able to take anything fate threw in his path, but when he had seen her coming up out of that pool this afternoon, his heart sang with joy while his mind cursed the gods who had played this despicable trick on him.

From the back, he had thought the young Mrs. Kirchoff looked familiar. Her hair had a radiance that he had seen only once before. When she had turned around and he saw the face that had haunted him for years, he had ridiculed the desire that coursed through his veins like a raging fever, threatening to ignite him from the inside out until he disintegrated to ashes. Standing as she was, wet and glistening, time rolled back to another time he had seen her coming out of the water. He still had that tape of her. Only on the most depressive days did he indulge—and torture—himself by watching it. Today she had been no image captured on electronic machinery.

Somehow he prevented himself from vaulting past Kirchoff and taking her in his arms and devouring her with a mouth that was still hungry for the taste of her lips. But the other man was in the way. The man in the wheelchair. The man whom, over the past few weeks, Erik had come to admire and respect for his courage, integrity and shrewd business acumen.

Seth Kirchoff had talked about his wife endlessly, praising her talents and beauty to the hilt, but had he ever called her by name? No, surely not, or Erik would have reacted to that name. But who would have thought that Kathleen, *his* Kathleen, would end up as the wife of this San Francisco entrepreneur?

That was when his previous flare of joy at seeing her turned to bitter bile in his soul. Of course. She had run away from the struggling videographer when she had been given a golden opportunity. She had probably been disgusted with herself for allowing his hands to taint her. She obviously aimed for higher things. How had she felt about giving away her most valuable bargaining asset? It hadn't mattered to Kirchoff, Erik supposed, because she had gotten him to marry her. *Congratulations, Mrs. Kirchoff. You're a very wealthy woman.*

Seth had every reason to be proud of his wife, Erik thought as she crossed the patio toward him. She was lovely, graceful, motherhood having smoothed away some of her coltish angles and replacing them with feminine curves.

She was still slender, almost too much so. No one looking at her would believe that she had carried a child. Her stomach was flat, the results of fifty faithful and vigorous situps a day. If it weren't for the generous fullness of her breasts, no one would ever know that she was a mother.

Her heels tapped on the patio. He heard the rustle of her clothes as she knelt down to pick up the child at his knees. The silk covering her breasts gapped slightly and blessed him with a glimpse of the smooth, bare flesh beneath. Her fragrance wafted up to him as she stood. Passionate longing raced through his body and centered in his loins, making him throb with desire.

"Mitsouko," he spoke aloud, though he hadn't intended to.

Kathleen stood stock-still and stared at him. "Yes," she answered. Moving away from him, she took a chair across the table, keeping the boy on her lap. "I see you have a drink," she said breathlessly. She didn't look at him.

"Yes."

"Where is Seth?" she asked, almost in desperation.

"He went inside with George to change clothes. He said he'd be out shortly."

"Hazel?"

"Hasn't made an appearance." He took another sip of his drink and said, "So we're all alone, Kathleen."

Her head snapped up. He looked rakish in his crisp white shirt and navy blazer. The shirt was unbuttoned halfway down his chest and provided a view of the tanned column of throat and hard, hair-matted chest. Her fingers tingled in remembrance of how that hair felt over the contour of muscle. His beige slacks hugged the hard thighs and molded over taut hips and . . .

She raised her eyes quickly, hoping he hadn't noticed the direction of her gaze, but he had. He insulted her by tipping his glass in a mocking salute.

"I must congratulate you, Kathleen. You've come a long way from the camp counselor in the Ozarks. How long has it been now? Let's see." He squinted his eyes, feigning concentration. "Two years? Yes, two years. There was an accident at the airport in Fort Smith. It was costly in lives and equipment, but I managed to survive. It happened on July sixteenth at two forty-three in the afternoon." His tone was hard, intentionally hurtful, and Kathleen felt the tears swimming in her eyes.

"I'm glad . . . you . . . you survived."

"Yeah. Your concern at the time overwhelmed me," he said sarcastically.

What gave him the right to be angry with her? "I couldn't very well join the crowd around your bed, could I?" she asked tersely.

Crowd at his bed? What in the hell was that supposed to mean? There had been no one there except Bob and Sally, and she had never even met them. He had quizzed them enough to know that.

Before he could pursue her enigmatic question, George helped Seth onto the patio. Erik had noted that everywhere there were steps, ramps had also been built to accommodate Seth's wheelchair. Light switches and thermostats on the walls were also placed low so Seth could easily reach them.

"Well, I'm glad to see that you two are getting better acquainted. You look ravishing, darling." He wheeled over to Kathleen and she got up, setting Theron on the patio. Placing both hands on Seth's shoulders, she leaned over to meet his chaste kiss. He held her hands as she straightened. "Isn't she gorgeous, Erik? I'll bet you thought I was exaggerating about her, didn't you? Have you ever seen coloring like this, or skin so soft?"

Kathleen paled by several shades. Erik had seen much more of her skin than Seth ever had. Since he had brought her to this house, they had gone to separate bedrooms each night. He had only been in her room once, and that was when George had carried him up the stairs to see her completed redecoration. They kissed a warm goodnight each evening. But she went up to her room, while Seth went to his with George, who would get him into bed for the night.

"Your wife is indeed beautiful, Seth," Erik said, but Kathleen could hear the underlying mockery in his voice.

"George, would you please tend bar? I'll have a scotch on the rocks and Kathleen her usual spritzer."

Involuntarily, Kathleen's eyes went to Erik, who, unnoticed by Seth, again saluted her with his glass. They both remembered another time. Kathleen's recollections were warm. Erik's were obviously those of the triumphant seducer.

❧ ❧

The scene on the patio set the mood for the remainder of the evening. If anything, Kathleen felt more strain when Hazel joined them for predinner drinks. As usual, she was polite and played the sweet sister-in-law and aunt like a grand dame of the theater, but Kathleen knew it to be an act. When they were alone, Hazel vented her hatred and resentment on Kathleen. Sometimes Kathleen would catch Hazel with a malevolent look directed toward Theron. She refused to leave Theron alone with the woman, whom Kathleen considered to be pathological in her possessiveness toward Seth.

By the time Alice announced dinner and relieved Kathleen of the squirming Theron, she was a tangle of nerves. Often, she had noticed Erik staring at the child. For once, she was thankful Theron always ate dinner in the kitchen in a high chair under Alice's supervision. Kathleen had disapproved of this banishment, thinking that he should be included with the rest of the family. But early after his birth, Hazel had made clear her wish that he not be at the table with them. Seth had agreed by saying, "I think you need that time to relax and enjoy your own dinner, Kathleen. Hazel's only thinking of you."

They went into the dining room, and Kathleen was disconcerted to find that Erik sat directly opposite her, since Seth sat at one end of the table and Hazel at the other. The delicious food that Alice served so aptly stuck in her throat, and she was barely capable of eating a third of her portion.

She hated this room. It always seemed to stifle her. The walls were covered with dark blue moire, a fabric she had always disliked. The furniture was dark and heavy, the china overpatterned, and the chandelier too ornate.

"Exactly what is this project that you and Seth are working on, Mr. Gudjonsen?" Hazel asked in her unctuous tone.

Erik laughed easily, in the manner Kathleen remembered so well, lifting the corners of his mustache and teasing at the possibility of a dimple hiding beneath it. His eyes shone a brilliant blue in the softly lit room. In spite of her earlier anger, her heart turned over at his masculine beauty.

"I'm sure that you, Ms. Kirchoff, and you . . ." he hesitated before he said, "Kathleen, are wondering why I suddenly burst upon the scene."

"This is your show, Erik. You tell them what we want to do," Seth said.

"Well," Erik said slowly. "I'm a photographer, working mainly with videotape instead of film. I worked at a network affiliate television station for a while." He darted a quick glance at Kathleen. "Last year, I went to Europe and knocked around for a while. Missing the States, I came back with hopes of establishing my own production company and thought that the Bay Area was a good place to settle. Some financial backers, whom I was lucky enough to find, referred me to Seth. Not only has he agreed to invest in my new company, but he has also dubbed Kirchoff's as my first major account. We plan to produce commercials for the stores that will be innovative and unique. Hopefully, when they begin to air, they'll generate more clients for my company. Kirchoff's is, after all, a very prestigious name to have in one's portfolio. Eventually, I'd also like to do industrial films, documentaries, things like that.''

"That's wonderful, Erik!" Kathleen cried, her enthusiasm for his new venture bubbling forth before she could stifle it. The other three at the table turned to her in surprise. Flushing, she looked toward Seth and said, "This is what we've needed to do, Seth. I couldn't be more pleased with your decision."

He grinned and reached for her hand. "I knew you'd feel that way. I'm counting on you to help Erik."

Her eyes flew to Erik, then back to her husband. "In . . . in what way?" she stammered.

"I want you to act as a consultant for him. He knows a lot about production, but he claims not to know a lot about fashion. He wants your expert opinion on all that before each commercial is made." His dark eyes shone with excitement and, despite her own misgivings about Erik's sudden resurgence in her life and the prospect of their working together, she couldn't help but be glad to see Seth's exuberance.

"Hazel, what do you think?" Seth asked. She had remained ominously silent.

The older woman smiled sweetly at Erik and said, "I'm afraid I am ignorant about television commercials. I'll reserve judgment on Mr. Gudjonsen's craft until we've had time to see the results of his labors." On that dim note, she suggested that they go into the living room for coffee.

Erik ushered in Hazel, while Kathleen walked beside Seth's chair, holding onto his free hand. No sooner were they settled than George carried in a large silver tray with a coffee service and china cups and saucers on it. He set the laden tray on the coffee table. Alice came in with Theron straddling her broad hip. "The little prince is ready for bed, but he wants to kiss everyone goodnight."

Kathleen noticed Hazel's expression of stern disapproval, but Alice set the toddler on the floor and he immediately ran to Erik after his mother had given him the first goodnight kiss. With a naturalness that surprised Kathleen, Erik picked up the pajama-clad boy and hauled him onto his lap. With the indiscrimination of a child, Theron wrapped his chubby arms around Erik's neck and gave him a smacking kiss on the mouth.

Theron pulled away and rubbed his face comically. The mustache had tickled and he was instantly intrigued by this new, fun toy. His fingers reached up and plucked at it.

"Ouch! That's attached, Captain," Erik said, but he didn't deter Theron's curiosity. He laughed and stroked Theron's back, staring down into eyes that Kathleen knew were mirror images of his own.

She watched Erik's face in suspense. At first she read incredulity, then bewilderment, then enlightenment. Her heart stopped. Erik raised his eyes over the top of Theron's head and she shook under their piercing accusation.

Theron clambered down and toddled on his sturdy little legs to Hazel. She accepted his kiss with a gushing falsity that sickened Kathleen. Then he was beside Seth, climbing unassisted onto his lap.

"Isn't he wonderful, Erik? Was ever a man so lucky to have a son like this?" Theron got down from Seth's lap and went once more to Kathleen, who knelt and hugged him to her fiercely. He indulged her by allowing her to cover his face with soft, quick kisses before he was again handed over to Alice.

"Thank you, George. I'll serve the coffee," Kathleen said quietly as the couple left the room to carry Theron to bed before eating their own dinner in the kitchen, another custom that irked her. Why couldn't they all eat together like the big family they were?

Seth extolled Theron's virtues and recounted escapades for Erik while Kathleen poured the coffee, first serving Hazel, who drank hers black. Both Erik and Seth had ordered theirs with a splash of brandy. When she handed Erik his cup, her fingers had momentarily made contact with his, and it was like an electric bolt that ran up her arm and aimed directly for her heart.

Shakily, she poured Seth's coffee and was carrying it to him when Erik said, "He's quite a boy. How old is he? When did you say his birthday is?"

That was when Kathleen's trembling hand lost control of the cup. It slipped off the saucer and into Seth's lap, splattering it with scalding coffee.

Chapter Thirteen

Kathleen stared stupidly at the hot liquid being absorbed by the fabric of Seth's trousers. Finally, conditioned reflexes took over and she cried, "Oh, Seth, darling, I'm sorry." She lunged for the tray and picked up a linen napkin, then came back to him quickly, blotting up the hot coffee in his lap before he could protest.

"Kathleen," he said, laughing. "Dear, don't bother yourself." Anguished moans were coming from between her tense, colorless lips. "The one good thing about my paralysis is that it takes something pretty painful to even bother me. Remember?" he asked gently, taking the stained napkin out of her hand. "Go drink your coffee. You look like you could stand some."

She walked like an automaton to the couch and sat down, but she didn't pour any coffee. She didn't think her shaking hands could handle it, so she clasped them tightly in her lap while Seth wheeled over and served himself another cup.

He was chuckling under his breath. "I think the dry cleaners can get this stain out, but if they can't, I'll buy a new suit at Kirchoff's. I hear their fall lines are terrific."

He looked toward his guest with a broad grin, but Erik

didn't share the humor. He was staring at the spot on Seth's lap that had just been doused with scalding liquid and yet displayed no feeling. *No feeling*.

A half-hour later, Erik stood up and said his goodnights. "I've enjoyed the evening. I was getting tired of eating out. Thank you, Hazel. Kathleen." He crossed the room with his long-legged stride and stopped in front of Seth's wheelchair. Shaking hands with the man, he said earnestly, "I'm looking forward to doing business with you."

"Same here," Seth said firmly, and smiled his heart-melting smile. "If you'll excuse me, I'm going to let Kathleen show you to the door. I think I'd better let George get me out of these clothes as soon as possible."

"I'll take you as far as your door," Hazel said solicitously to her brother, assuming a proprietary position behind his chair.

Kathleen's knees would barely support her as she rose and walked with Erik to the wide arch leading into the hall. "Oh, Kathleen," Seth delayed their departure, "I promised to show Erik how we've lighted the pool. Would you be so kind as to take him around back and show it to him before he leaves?"

The blood pounded in her ears. She would have to be alone with him! "O— Of course."

"I'll say goodnight then." Seth blew her a kiss and then he wheeled away, Hazel following him.

As soon as the double front door with the etched glass windows shut behind them, Kathleen faced Erik belligerently. "Must you see the pool?"

"Absolutely." The well-mannered mask had been dropped. His features were set and hard. He gripped her arm and virtually dragged her along after him. She tripped and stumbled in her high-heeled sandals and finally gasped his name. "Let go of me," she said. It did no good. He neither slowed down nor relieved the pressure on her arm.

When they were past the cabana beside the pool, he flung her against the dark side of the building and pinned her there with his body.

His hands came up to each side of her face, not in a gentle gesture but in an imprisoning one, crushing. His face was fearsome. She had seen it that way once before, just as he was about to slug the two cowboys in the lounge at the Crescent Hotel.

"I want to know. And I want to know now. Is he my son?" The voice wasn't Erik's. It wasn't the same voice that had lulled her to sleep while whispering love words in her ear. This voice vibrated with fury and hatred.

She struggled against him but his body only thrust against her harder, and he flattened her arms on either side of her head with iron fists that threatened to crack her fragile wrist bones. "Answer me, damn you! When is his birthday? Your little *accident* in there isn't going to prevent me from finding out."

He thought she had spilled the coffee on purpose! "Let me go." The words were literally pushed past her lips, which were rigid with anger.

"Not a chance," he growled. "Not until you tell me the truth. *Is he my son?*"

He pressed against her, and despite her anger, that tight coil of desire that had lain dormant inside her for two years slowly began to uncurl and wind through her body with an awareness of the hard muscles, the masculine scent, the virility that speared into her belly.

She fought it. She closed her eyes briefly, partly to block out his furious face so close to hers. "Would it make a difference?" she asked at last in what she hoped was a disparaging tone.

"To a lying slut like you, probably not. But it does to me."

She choked on a sob. How cruel and unfair he was. She had loved him! He was the one who had been unfaithful, cheating on his wife. Yet he insulted her like this.

Kathleen wanted to hurt him the way she had been hurt. "Yes!" she hissed. "He's your son. And a fat lot of good it'll do you to know it." Her head went back against the hard surface of the wall and she defied him with every fiber of her being.

First his face revealed suspicion as he searched her own features for signs of deception. Then a look of wonder and awe broke across the face that she loved. An infinite sadness replaced that. Finally, the anger returned as he snarled down at her, "I wonder if Seth knows what a hot little number his wife is?"

Again Kathleen struggled, and again it was futile to expect escape. "You called me that once before. It wasn't true then and it isn't true now. You know nothing about me, Erik."

His head lowered a fraction and he brushed across her forehead with his mustache. "Don't I?" he breathed. "I can prove how well I know you."

"No," Kathleen begged softly as she felt his thigh insinuating itself between hers. "No," she said again, wanting to convince herself. His hard thigh was pressing her to the wall, rubbing against her femininity through the thin silk pants.

His thumbs made mesmerizing circles on the pulse points of her wrists until her balled fists relaxed. He covered her palms with his, making even that simple touch erotic. His breath was hot and agitated against her face as he promised, "I'll exorcise you from my mind yet, you hot little . . . hot . . . hot . . ." His mouth took hers hungrily, working her lips apart with his tongue.

Kathleen made outraged sounds deep in her throat that soon changed and became little more than murmurs of ecstasy. His hands traveled from her palms, down her arms to her shoulders, then around her back to lower the short zipper of her top. Weakened by the power of his kiss, she didn't— couldn't—resist. Nor did she want to.

He pulled down the strapless blouse. Her breasts spilled into his waiting hands. He buried his face in the deep cleavage, drinking up the intoxicating fragrance and reveling in the texture of her skin as he massaged her gently. His mouth closed around her, eager and wet, and she arched against the long, strong leg between her own.

He found the dusky center of her breast, which was swollen and tingling with passion, and worried it further with his tongue. Then he suckled her gently, drawing on her sweetly, begging for sustenance. Unconsciously, her arms went around his neck, pulling his head nearer and holding it there. At the small of her back, she felt his hands lifting her onto his thigh.

He strained against her and urged her with beseeching hands under her hips. Upward. Closer. Wider. The hard bulge in his trousers fit snugly into her welcoming vulnerability. Only clothing prevented the sexual union from being complete. He moved. She responded with an answering pressure. Most intimately, his body stroked hers.

Kathleen felt herself being drawn into that frenzied height she had not forgotten. She flew toward it before she was aware of her flight and in control enough to call herself back.

Her fingers dug into the muscles of his back, and she rotated her hips against that beloved invader between her thighs. His mouth withdrew from her breasts a fraction and only his tongue remained to lash gently at her nipples. The tumult rolled over her, bathing her with liquid fire. "Erik, Erik," she cried as each spasm seized her.

When it was over, she clung to him limply while she gasped for breath. His own breathing was ragged against her neck. Her fingers wound through the golden strands of his hair, which she had memorized by touch long ago. "Erik," she sighed in exhaustion, replete with love.

Suddenly, he slung her away from him against the wall. The lips that had brought her so much pleasure moments before were now curled in cynical derision. "You see, Kathleen," he mocked. "You've just proven my point. You are no fit mother for my son."

🌿 🌿

Days later Kathleen was still distraught over what had happened. She didn't even want to listen to Eliot as he persistently shook the invoices under her nose.

"Kathleen, pay attention. I asked you if you had canceled this order. Seth is on the telephone. Hazel," he grimaced eloquently, ''is with him, complaining that our customers are looking for the new Polo shirts in the fall colors and none are to be had.''

She dredged herself up to a level of consciousness where his words finally registered. ''Aren't they in yet? I ordered a dozen shirts in every color in varied sizes for each of the three stores. How can there not be any in stock?''

''Damned if I know,'' Eliot said, raking his slender fingers through his artificially but beautifully streaked hair. ''But will you talk to Seth? I've never heard him so upset.''

She picked up the telephone and spoke calmly into the receiver. ''Hello, Seth. I don't understand the problem, but I'm sure I'll get it straightened out.''

''Kathleen, the problem is that we don't have any of our most staple item, and you created that problem. What I want to know is why.''

Kathleen had never heard such exasperation in Seth's voice. And it was directed toward her. ''*I* created the problem?''

''Yes. I called the shipping department directly. The goods were received by us—by you—on July thirteenth. You refused them, initialed the return slip and sent them back. How could you do such a thing?'' he demanded.

''I didn't!'' she shouted, causing Eliot to raise an expressive brow. He had never heard one cross word between Kathleen and her husband. She rubbed her forehead with frustrated fingers. Why, when she was already upset, did something like this have to happen? She tried to be reasonable. ''Seth, there is some mistake. I never even saw the goods. I never initialed anything.''

''Then how is it that I'm looking at a very good carbon copy of the order and staring at your initials? I ought to know my own wife's signature when I see it, for godsake!'' She bit her lips in an effort not to scream back at him. She was well aware of Eliot observing her shrewdly and knew Hazel was gloating on the other end.

Hazel.

A light began to dawn. Could the woman do such a thing?

Would she sacrifice the welfare of the stores in order to cause friction between Kathleen and Seth? Kathleen had given Hazel more credit than that, but maybe she had been too generous.

"I never sent back that order, Seth," she said matter-of-factly.

Seth sighed heavily. "I'll call Ralph Lauren again and try pleading with them to send us the shipment. In the meantime, we'll have to hope that our customers don't go somewhere else."

"I'm coming over to the offices in a while. I'll see you then," Kathleen said before she heard the click on his receiver that ended the conversation.

She replaced the instrument slowly and stared at it for a moment. She saw Eliot out the corner of her eye as he moved toward her and placed his hands on her shoulders, turning her around to face him.

"Sit down. We're going to have a talk."

She obliged him, in too much inner turmoil to object. "What's been happening to you, Kathleen? For the past three days, you've acted like a zombie. You look like hell."

"Thanks."

"You know what I mean, sweetheart. Where's that bouncy vibrance we're so used to seeing? Where's our Little Mary Sunshine? Hm?"

She could never get too perturbed with Eliot. He was too nice to look at. His tall, lank frame was created to hang clothes on and he wore them with élan. The well-maintained bleached hair was boyishly casual. His tan was perfectly tawny, and Kathleen suspected it covered his body. Straight white teeth and a delicate mouth made his smile engaging. His heavily lashed gray eyes were direct and, at times, insolent. It was that perpetually contemptuous attitude in which he held the world that prevented him from being completely beautiful. But he was her friend.

She avoided his eyes as she said grumpily, "I haven't slept well lately. That's all."

"Un-uh. It's more than that, but if you don't feel inclined to tell me, don't. What do you think happened to that order?''

"I don't know."

"And I'm the King of Siam." He sat down on the corner of her desk and swung his expensively shod foot.

Baby blue linen shoes indeed! she thought with a smile.

"Do you remember when Mrs. Vanderslice ordered that ball gown for her daughter? You ordered a size ten, but a size twelve was shipped. The old bitch threw a bloody fit, accusing you of thinking her daughter was fat? Do you remember all of that?''

"All too well, but   ''

"Hear me out," he went on. "Do you remember when you sold the identical dress to two old broads attending the Opera gala? Do you remember the ruckus they raised?''

"Yes." How could she forget? Her brow wrinkled in perplexity. "Eliot, what are you trying to say with this long, convoluted story?''

"That someone is sabotaging your work, dear girl.''

"But who?''

"You know as well as I do." He leaned down and whispered in a stage whisper, "Hazel Baby.''

Kathleen stood up and walked to the only window in her tiny office. "I didn't order that Vanderslice girl a size twelve and I wouldn't sell the same dress to two society women.''

"Precisely.''

"But why would Hazel do those things?" Kathleen asked, admitting unwittingly that his surmise might be correct.

"Because she's so jealous of you that the poison darts literally fly through the air every time she looks at you." He made a gesture with his hands that was so descriptive and so comical that Kathleen laughed in spite of the seriousness of the subject. *"And,"* Eliot continued, "if you ask me, as far as Seth goes, she doesn't give a shit.''

"Eliot, please," Kathleen said. His blunt language had been one thing she could never tolerate.

"All right, Chastity Ears," he said with exaggerated politeness. "Hazel doesn't give a *damn* about him, except to control him and keep him eating out of her hand. The way she manipulates him is sickening. As if that weren't enough, he can't see through her. He doesn't know he's being had."

Kathleen didn't want to admit it, but Eliot was right. Where his sister was concerned, Seth's handicap wasn't his paralysis. It was blindness.

"Watch that bitch, Kathleen," Eliot warned. "She's out to hurt you. I know."

Kathleen tried to laugh at Eliot's dire prediction, but the sound she uttered was little more than a strangled breath. Eliot came up behind her and kissed her lightly on the neck. She was accustomed to his displays of affection and didn't mind them, knowing that they meant nothing more than friendship. Today she shrugged away from him and folded her arms across her chest protectively. She shivered with cold, though the temperature was only seasonably cool for mid-September.

"What is it, Kathleen? It's more than Hazel Kirchoff, isn't it?"

"I don't know what you mean," she said evasively.

"Yes, you do. You're jumpy and distracted. Neither your mind nor your heart is in your work. What is it?"

My former lover and the father of my child has come back to torment me. There. Was that what she was supposed to say? Should she tell Eliot, everyone, what was the matter with her? Would they believe her? She grinned wryly. Eliot would. Some of the stories he had told her of his escapades had made her hair stand on end. This would neither surprise nor shock him.

But she had been shocked to the very core of her being by Erik's reappearance in her life. What had happened behind the cabana was disgraceful. She wasn't surprised that he had tried to make love to her. No, not love. Sex. And it had been doled out like punishment. If he was enough of a cad as a married man to seduce the innocent she had been two years ago, he was perfectly capable of wanting to pick up the shabby affair where it left off, even though she was married now, too.

What surprised Kathleen was how she had reacted. Why hadn't she fought harder? Instead, she had welcomed the feel of his body against hers. She had reveled in the taste of his mouth and the heady scent of his cologne mingled with his own unique essence. The expert touch of his hands had brought her to—

God! She covered her face now with shame at the remembrance.

"Kathleen? Are you all right?" Eliot asked, his voice laced with anxiety.

"Yes, yes, I'm fine. I'm just tired. If you can take over here, I'm going over to the main office and then home. I want to spend the rest of the day with Theron."

She gathered up her things and left, but as she drove the few blocks to Kirchoff's executive offices, she felt again that stabbing fear that had pierced through her when Erik had spoken his parting words.

He wouldn't do anything to separate her from her child, would he? He wasn't that cruel. Besides, even if he wanted to, he'd never get away with it. Theron was hers. Erik had had another wife when the baby was conceived. She could always cry desertion if it came to that. But he hadn't really deserted her. She had deserted him.

The fear of a custody trial was secondary to the initial havoc Erik would wreak on her life if he told Seth about them. It would devastate her husband. He considered Theron to be his. Since the day he had proposed marriage to her, he had never referred to Theron's father. It was never "your child" but always "our child" when he talked about the baby during her pregnancy. He never failed to call Theron "my son." If people speculated on Theron's parentage, they were polite enough not to mention it. For all practical purposes, Theron belonged to Seth.

Kathleen had been scrupulously faithful, never giving anyone room to question her devotion to her husband. Seth often told her to go out more, to make friends, develop outside interests, but she had refused, pleased to be home with him. He was truly remarkable. He went more places than anyone had a right to expect of him. They took Theron on outings to Golden Gate Park. They went to Ghirardelli's for ice-cream sodas. They went to movies and to dinner. Of course, George always went with them and handled the complicated transportation problems, but Seth had tried his utmost not to let her give up anything she liked to do for his sake.

Lately, though, he had shown a fatigue that she hadn't noticed before. He seemed less inclined to want to go out, and seemed much more at ease sitting beside the pool while she swam or they sipped drinks and talked. His color hadn't looked good either. She had questioned George, but his answers had been vague and patronizing. She took it upon herself to phone Seth's doctor, but his lengthy answers to her inquiries into her husband's health, though sounding professional, told her nothing.

These thoughts had been revolving in her head like a macabre carousel for the last few days, ever since Erik's untimely visit to their home. They were still circulating in her brain when she arrived at Seth's offices and found them deserted. However, there was a note on his door telling her that he and Hazel had gone to lunch and would be back shortly. She was to make herself at home. Claire's computer was covered. She was out to lunch as well.

Kathleen swung open the wide door and closed it behind her, poignantly reminded of the first day she had walked through it. She still liked this room. Going over to the stereo components on the bookshelf, she turned the radio to an FM station. She went to the windows and drew the blinds, plunging the room into semidarkness. As long as she had to wait, maybe she would get in a nap. She hadn't slept at all for the last few nights.

Taking off her shoes, she lay down on the comfortable leather sofa and closed her eyes. It was dim and quiet. In no more than a few minutes, she was asleep.

The dream was particularly pleasant. Erik was there. But he wasn't the angry, bitter man who had pinned her against the wall of the cabana. He was the old Erik, the one with laughter in his eyes, and lips prone to smiling.

In the dream, he leaned over her and, with his little finger, lifted a curl away from her cheek. She could feel the warmth of his breath on her face. Then his lips were on hers, moving over them with precision, urging them to open, encouraging her tongue to join his in an erotic adventure.

His hand was firm on her waist, but it began to move. Slowly, it crept over her ribs, so painstakingly he may have been counting them. She felt him cup the underside of her breast, cradling her in his palm.

The dream changed, the tempo increased as his mouth became more imperative. She could feel the pressure of his body as it covered hers. Through the thin knit of her Diane von Furstenburg dress, she could feel his exploratory fingers finding the budding center of her breast, caressing it with increased desire.

It was so real. His kisses were so warm. His hand was so accurate as he coaxed her into deeper passion. Round and round, his thumb circled her. His body was so heavy. So heavy . . .

Her eyes flew open and her subconscious fear was confirmed. It was no dream. Erik was lying beside her on the narrow sofa! She thrashed her arms and legs against him. "Let me up, Erik," she commanded with venom. "Get away from me."

Unexpectedly, he did as she asked. Rising from the sofa, he laughed with satanic glee. "I wondered when you were going to wake up. Or was that little pornographic dream you were having all an act?" His eyes slid to her breasts, which still evidenced his touch. "No, it was no act," he sneered.

"Shut up. I don't even want to be in the same room with you." Kathleen shoved her feet into her shoes and made ineffectual attempts to straighten her hair.

"Why?" he asked casually as he sprawled into one of the

deep easy chairs. "Are you afraid of losing control? Having a replay of the other night? I must say, you had a good time, though I was left high and dry. No pun intended."

"You're disgusting," she said, jumping to her feet.

He laughed again. "I don't think you were disgusted the other night. As I recall—"

"Will you stop talking about it!" she screamed, and covered her face with her hands. She drew several restorative breaths while she tried vainly to compose herself. "The repulsion I feel for you can in no way measure the disgust that I feel for myself for letting you touch me in the first place. Now, are you leaving or am I?"

The muscles in his jaw were working and she knew that she had struck a nerve, but she couldn't afford to be merciful.

"I have an appointment with your husband," he said tightly.

"Fine. I'll see him at home."

She managed to get to the door. She was even allowed to open it. That was as far as she got. Erik's large, tanned hand came from around her, slapped against the door and slammed it with emphasis. At the same time, his body trapped her between him and the oak door, both equally impregnable.

"Not so fast, Mrs. Kirchoff. You have something of mine that I want."

The blood in her veins froze and she closed her eyes against the vertigo that shook her. Wedged as she was between him and the door, she barely managed to turn and look up at him with imploring eyes. "Wh— What?" she asked tremulously.

"My son."

She shook her head and mouthed words soundlessly. Finally, she croaked, "No. He's *my* son."

"I ought to wring your neck for having my child without notifying me. I would gladly kill you for that."

Kathleen didn't doubt what he said for one moment. "How would you have explained Theron to your *wife*?"

Erik stared down into her face. There was no guilt, no remorse that she had discovered his deception, only a stunned blankness. Slowly, he stepped away from her, still with that stupefied expression on his face. His arms dangled loosely at his sides.

She pushed past him, moved to the window, and opened the blinds, flooding the room with harsh, revealing light. The stereo components were switched off peremptorily. She immediately regretted having done that. The cessation of the music only made the silence more palpable.

She returned to the window and stared out, looking down at the traffic far below. His words, when they came at last, were hoarse and full of incredulity, dispelling any doubt of their veracity.

"Kathleen, I don't have a wife. I've never been married."

She spun around and looked at him with naked bewilderment. Between them stretched a gulf of misunderstanding. Her eyes scanned his face for signs of deceit, but there were none. His own shattered features reflected the hopelessness she felt.

Before either could move or speak, George opened the door and Seth wheeled through it. His good mood had been restored. His voice was cheerful when he saw them both, and he said, "What a nice reception. Had I known you were waiting for me, I would have cut lunch short. How are you, Erik?"

Still stunned, responding reflexively, Erik turned and shook Seth's outstretched hand. "Fine." He cleared his throat and said again, "Fine."

"Good. Are you ready to start on our project? Have you found a place to live?" As usual, Seth's face was open and guileless, ready to help, understand and . . . forgive.

"Yes," Erik answered. "I bought a condo. Right now, it's four empty walls. I've got to furnish it."

Seth laughed. "Then you're in luck. Kathleen is great at that. I'm sure she'll be glad to help. Won't you, Kathleen?"

Chapter Fourteen

Kathleen darted a quick glance at Erik and then looked back at her husband. "I . . . I'm sure that if Erik wanted a decorator, he would engage one," she said safely. What had Erik just told her? What had he said? He had no wife? *He had no wife!* And never had!

"Oh, but decorators are so . . . professional. If he hires a decorator, his place will look like our living room—too perfect for people to live in."

That was the first time Kathleen had heard Seth make even a veiled criticism of his sister. Right now, that wasn't important. Indeed, it barely registered. Her mind was still circulating around what Erik had said. He had no wife. *I've never been married.* The words were repeated in her ears like a chant. The statement meant everything in the world to her.

"Kathleen is too busy to get involved with decorating a bachelor's apartment," Erik said.

Had he stressed the word bachelor?

Seth wheeled behind his desk and yawned politely behind his hand. "Excuse me," he said. "I ate too much lunch."

Seth seemed oblivious to the tension in the room, an aftershock that vibrated off the walls, a lingering remnant

195

of the revelation that had been spoken moments before. "Tomorrow is Thursday, isn't it? That's one of your days off. Did you have anything special planned?"

"No, but I—"

"Erik, you?"

"No."

"Great. Tomorrow you two can shop all day. When you're finished, come back to the house and I'll grill steaks out on the patio."

Since neither of them said anything to the contrary, Seth considered the matter closed and went on to other things. Kathleen excused herself, leaning down to kiss Seth goodbye and nodding to Erik as she left.

That evening at dinner, the matter of the canceled order came up again. This time, it was Hazel who broached it. "I think," she said, wiping her mouth daintily on the linen napkin, "that Kathleen has far too many responsibilities. How else could she have made such a costly error?" Seth missed the stinging implication and heard only his sister's concern.

"I didn't make the error," Kathleen replied calmly.

"Darling, it doesn't matter," Seth said soothingly. "Everything has been taken care of now. We should have the goods within the week."

"It *does* matter if someone is accusing me of being incompetent when I am no such thing," she protested vehemently.

"Hazel didn't mean that—"

"I'll decide if and when I have too many responsibilities and deal with it myself. I won't need anyone else advising me." She stood up abruptly. "If you'll excuse me, I'm going upstairs to play with Theron."

Kathleen left the two of them in the dining room and didn't go down again until she knew Hazel had come upstairs to her suite of rooms.

As she descended the last steps, Seth was being wheeled into his room by George. She was struck by the fatigue she saw around his eyes and mouth. His complexion, which was usually healthfully tanned by the hours of therapy he spent in the heated pool, was gray. Violet shadows under his eyes, which had appeared faint in the daytime, now looked drastically darker in the evening.

"Seth," she said, squatting down so she could rest her head against his knee. She noticed that George had tactfully withdrawn. "I'm sorry if I sounded out of sorts at dinner. I can't explain what happened, but you must know that I didn't cancel that Polo order, no matter what other crises I may have had on my mind at the time."

She felt the steady pressure of his hand as he stroked her hair. "My sweet Kathleen. I don't know what happened either, but I'd forgive you no matter what you did. I love you." His voice was soothing, and his words, which she knew he meant deep in his soul, pierced her heart. She burrowed her head closer against the legs that couldn't feel the tenderness she felt for him.

"I've been worried about you, Seth," she said quietly. "Are you feeling well these days?" She raised her head and looked closely into his eyes, which were clouded with something she couldn't define. All she knew was that they didn't shine with the exhilaration she usually saw there.

"I'm fine. What could be wrong?"

"I don't know," she said slowly. "You'd tell me if you didn't feel well, wouldn't you?"

"If it would guarantee your love, I'd tell you my deepest, darkest secrets." He smiled, but his jest fell flat.

"I *do* love you, Seth." She meant it. Who couldn't love this man? He represented everything that was good and kind in the world.

His face turned serious but was warm with love. "I know you do," he whispered. "You and Theron mean so much to me, Kathleen, that sometimes my love is painful. It's as if my body can't contain it, as if I'll burst for loving you so hard. Do you understand?"

Yes, she did. She knew the emotion he was trying to convey. She had felt it for the past two years, and with as much anguish over its unrequited state as Seth's.

"You are beautiful, Kathleen. Truly beautiful. I want to

memorize your face for the time I'll spend in eternity." His fingers followed the path charted by his eyes as they traveled over her features.

His intensity and choice of words frightened her, and she cried softly, "Seth," as she gripped his hand.

"Come now," he said briskly, pulling her up to receive his kiss on the cheek. "Let a hard-working man go to bed. Besides, you've got a busy day ahead of you tomorrow. You *do* like Erik, don't you, Kathleen?"

She could see how important her opinion was to him. "Of course. And I think what he's going to do for Kirchoff's is fantastic. You made a wise decision."

The relief on Seth's face was worth any turmoil she would suffer from being and working closely with Erik. "I'm glad you approve. I want the two of you to get along. You don't mind that I offered your services as a decorator, do you? I know you enjoy that kind of thing, and you spend far too much time here with only me, George and Alice, and Hazel for company. Not to mention the demands Theron makes on you."

"Don't worry about that. You're my family. But I don't mind helping Erik if you want me to."

"Good." He seemed satisfied. "Goodnight, sweetheart." He pulled her down and, this time, kissed her sweetly on the lips.

Sensing that their private time was over, George came out of the shadows. He said goodnight and opened the door to Seth's bedroom, closing it quietly after Seth had steered his chair through.

Kathleen had never been invited into that room. She never questioned Seth about its absolute privacy. Perhaps the trappings of his disability were too visible in his bedroom. She accepted his decision and respected it. If she could help it, she would never do anything to embarrass or injure the man who had given her a future when she had had none.

What could she wear? Kathleen pondered the contents of her three closets. With a typically feminine anxiety, she decided that nothing she had was appropriate.

She scolded herself for acting like a silly teenager. She wasn't going on a date with a special beau. She was only going shopping with Erik, and he had seen her both dressed to the nines and wearing the navy shorts and white T-shirt that were the Mountain View uniform. He had also seen her in nothing at all.

Kathleen blushed at that thought. Gloriously naked, she had lain in his bed, and he had seen her in his shower with soap and water combining into foaming rivers all over her body that he navigated with his hands and mouth. Did he ever remember? The stain in her cheeks became deeper. The familiarity with which he had touched her in the past few days proved that he remembered her body well.

Finally, she selected a pair of brown leather jeans that Seth had insisted she buy. He was proud of her figure and often coerced her into modeling in the lavish fashion shows she had instigated at Kirchoff's. He was too generous with his gifts, urging her to buy at least one garment for herself from each house she visited when she went to New York.

When they went on their frequent tours of the stores, if Seth saw something in Kathleen's size that he liked, he stripped it off the hanger and handed it to her with a beguiling smile. "You'd look swell in this, kid," he'd say with a Humphrey Bogart slur. She never argued with him. If she could please him by wearing pretty clothes, she was all too glad to do it. There was so little she could do for him.

Kathleen felt a pang of guilt at her jittery nerves as she finished dressing. Was she being unfaithful to Seth by anticipating the outing with Erik? No, she argued with herself. Seth was the one who had planned it. She was really doing this for him. But as she looked at herself critically in the mirror, she knew that she was doing this for herself, too.

She had put on a silk shirt with the pants. The electric-blue color deepened the emerald-green of her eyes. The toes of her imported Italian boots shone with the same saddle-brown of the jeans. She let her hair hang loose so it waved around her face and shoulders like a copper scarf.

She ran lightly down the stairs just as the doorbell was ringing. It was only natural that she call out, "I'll get it, Alice," but her footsteps faltered noticeably on the stairs.

Gripping the doorknob as though it were a lifeline, she swung open the door before she could chicken out.

Erik stared at her over the threshold. He didn't say anything as he raked her with greedy eyes. The muscles in his throat worked convulsively. When at last his gaze rose to meet hers, he said, "Good morning."

"Good morning." It took all the breath she could muster to speak, for he looked gorgeous. He was as slim-hipped as ever, as the tight jeans emphasized. A dark plaid cotton shirt was stretched over the muscles of his broad chest and shoulders. A camel-colored cardigan was knotted casually around his neck. "Come in," she murmured, stepping aside to let him enter. She could smell his cologne as he walked past her. "Seth wanted to say goodbye. He's having breakfast with Theron." Erik stopped, turned around and looked at her, and then nodded. "I'd like to see him, too."

She didn't know if he was referring to Seth or Theron and felt it was safer not to ask. She walked a few steps ahead of Erik, leading him through the labyrinth of the first floor until they reached the bright, sunny breakfast room off the kitchen.

They were greeted with peals of laughter as Kathleen pushed open the swinging door. "What's going on in here?" she asked brightly. Too brightly?

The center of attention was Theron, who was still pajama-clad and sitting in his high chair. In his hand, he held a long banana and was trying his best to peel it.

"Hi," Seth said. "Alice, get Erik some coffee, please. Sit down. We're having a time here. He's been trying for five minutes to figure out how to get to the inside of that banana, but he won't let any of us do it for him. Watch."

Seth leaned over closer to the high chair and said, "Theron, let me peel the banana for you." He reached for the fruit, but the little boy hugged it tight to him until Seth's hand was withdrawn, and then he renewed his struggle to peel it himself.

"Isn't he something?" Seth asked rhetorically with pride.

"Yes, he is," Erik answered gruffly, and Kathleen whirled her head around to look at him. By the unnatural sound of his voice, she almost expected to see tears in his eyes, but to her relief there were none. He only stared at his son as possessively as he had looked at her minutes before. She knew a quickening of pity for him. How torturous it must be to see his son and not be able to claim him.

A triumphant gurgle drew her attention back to the boy as he finally conquered the banana. Within seconds, the skinned banana was being shoved into his mouth until it disappeared altogether.

"He's the stubbornest baby I've ever seen," Alice said, shaking her head, predicting dire outcomes for such hardheadedness.

"Are you going to work out in the pool this morning?" Kathleen asked Seth, whom she was glad to see looked rested and more himself than he had last night.

"Yes. Then I'm going to let Theron play in there for a while."

"You don't think it's too cold?" she mused with a wrinkled brow.

"I'll keep him in the water once he gets wet, and then rush him inside when we're finished."

She acquiesced, knowing that the water's temperature was carefully maintained so that Seth and George could go through their exercises in comfort year-round. "Just be careful with him. He's slippery as an eel and has no fear of the water yet."

Seth's eyes softened and he said, "You know I will. George will be right there with us all the time. I wouldn't risk my son's life for anything in the world." He reached across the table and clasped her hand.

She dared not look at Erik, but somehow she knew that his

body had tensed perceptibly with Seth's words. She could feel her own tension.

"Let Alice cook you some breakfast, Erik."

He declined Seth's offer. "No thanks. I'm already bumming one meal off you today. I picked up a doughnut on the way over." His smile was as genuine and dashing as ever. It gave away none of the turmoil he felt inside. "If Kathleen's ready, I am."

"She's ready," Seth said with a faint scowl. "I never have been able to get her to eat a sensible breakfast. She's too figure-conscious."

"I can see that," Erik said as he looked at her appreciatively.

"You should have seen her when she was pregnant," Seth said. Erik's attention didn't waver. His eyes stayed glued on her as Seth continued, "I've never seen a woman carry a child more gracefully. From the back, you couldn't even tell that she was pregnant. She looked ravishing right up to the day of delivery."

"She would have," Erik said.

The warmth of his gaze affected her too much, and the topic of conversation was too uncomfortable. She stood up quickly and upset Theron's cup of orange juice. Thankfully, it had a sealed cup with a perforated spout to prevent such accidents. She nervously righted it and said, "We'll be back well before dinner. Alice, do you need anything?"

"No. Seth's going to do most of the cooking tonight." She laughed.

"Well, then," Kathleen said absently. She had suddenly run out of excuses not to leave with Erik. "Goodbye, Theron," she said, leaning down to receive his banana-flavored kiss. "Mommy will see you tonight. Maybe I'll bring you a surprise."

"Bye-bye," he said happily, waving a chubby fist.

Everyone laughed. To Kathleen's dismay, Erik walked around the table and ruffled Theron's hair. "Goodbye, Captain."

Kathleen stammered the rest of her goodbyes, kissed Seth quickly, and then she and Erik were walking out the front door and down the flagstone walk to a waiting sports car.

She turned around in surprise. "A Corvette," he said dryly. "A woman I once knew told me I was this type." His eyes were dancing with only a ghost of their old humor.

As she slid into the sleek silver car with the rich maroon interior, she asked, "What happened to your Dodge van?"

"I still have it. But this car is good for the professional image. Who trusts a videographer who shows up at business meetings in a van with a wheezing carburetor?"

He steered the car down the tree-lined driveway and then turned onto the major thoroughfare. "I thought I'd take you to the condo first and let you see what we've got to work with."

"Okay."

That was the extent of their conversation until they reached the site of his condominium. It was in an impressive complex of garden homes. Each unit was built in a different style of architecture, but they blended well together. The grounds were well maintained and there was a pool in the center of the complex for the exclusive use of the home owners.

"This is very nice," she commented.

"It ought to be," Erik said. "I'm paying through the nose for it."

He unlocked his door and stood aside. She entered the foyer of the contemporary structure. Their footsteps made hollow echoes as they went through the empty rooms while Erik pointed out features. He whispered, as one is wont to do in an empty house.

The condo was a study in glass and wood. One wall of the living room was redwood, while a stone fireplace was set between two floor-to-ceiling windows on another. The kitchen had every conceivable built-in appliance, but still retained an inviting coziness.

"Upstairs are two bedrooms and a bath for each. I'm not going to do anything to them just now. And I can't spend a

lot of money, Kathleen. I'm not as rich as your husband."
His tone was snide and she walked away in anger, instantly
wishing that she had paid more attention to where she was
going.

She found herself in a large master bedroom, dominated
by a king-sized bed, by the look of the mussed covers, recently slept in. That was all that was in the room.

"It's rather austere at this point," Erik said from close
behind her. She moved away, ostensibly to look out the
wide, drapeless window, but actually to put distance between
herself and his overwhelming male magnetism.

Kathleen gave careful attention to the skylighted high ceiling, the louvered doors that opened into a huge walk-in closet
with a built-in chest of drawers. He was close behind her
again, and she retreated through another set of louvered doors.

The master bathroom was sumptuous. There was a shower
with a clear glass door, two basins, a private commode and
a bathtub. Kathleen was intrigued by the bottles of shaving
lotion, a bar of woodsy-smelling soap, an old-fashioned shaving mug and brush, and a mustache comb. A blue toothbrush
hung on a brass rack. His hairbrush was tortoise shell. The
grooming items were intensely personal. She quickly averted
her eyes from them, though she would have loved to handle
each article.

A redwood hot tub situated beside a picture window afforded an unrestricted view of a private patio, landscaped
with evergreen plants and seasonal flowers, now blooming in
fall colors.

"Wow."

He chuckled. "This room was almost worth the price of
the house."

The sensuality and intimacy of the room, added to the
predatory gait with which he stalked her, set her nerves on
edge, and she went back into the bedroom, where she automatically looked at the bed. Had Erik slept there alone? Yes.
There was only one pillow. Still, hadn't they shared the same
pillow?

"Kathleen." She felt his hands on her arms, turning her around. He lifted her chin with his finger and looked deeply into her eyes. "How is it that you thought I was married?" His voice was gentle. He could have been speaking to a bewildered and confused child for all the tenderness in his tone.

Tears flooded her eyes. She gulped her words. "I . . . I saw her. I had waited all day, knowing you were hu— hurt . . in pain. They wouldn't let . . . tell me . . . I was so scared. Then she came in and said she was Mrs. . . . Mrs. Gudjonsen. They took her right in to you . . . and I . . . I . . . She was tiny, and blonde, and pretty, and she . . ."

"Sally."

Kathleen blinked back tears as she looked up at him. 'Sally?"

"My sister-in-law. My brother Bob's wife."

Kathleen's knees finally succumbed to the weakness that invaded her body with a debilitating effect and she slumped against him. He gathered her to him tightly, almost blocking off her breath with the ferocity of his possessive embrace.

"God, Kathleen, what did we do to deserve this?"

Their bodies swayed together, each giving comfort to the other. They stayed locked in that wordless, communicating embrace for long minutes while Erik whispered incoherent messages to her hair.

He kissed her. His mouth encompassed hers. His hands rubbed her back as though she were a healing lotion that he wanted to be absorbed into his skin.

Then, with a supreme act of will, he pushed her away from him. He sat down on the corner of the bed, spreading his knees wide, clasping his hands between them and staring down at his rigid white knuckles.

"How could you possibly have construed that I was married after . . ." She heard a touch of irritation in his voice. "Did you think no more of me than *that*? Dammit, Kathleen, how could you?"

"I don't know," she wailed. "I was overwrought, sick

with worry for you and afraid, so afraid that you'd . . . afraid of everything.'' There was no explanation. There was no remedy.

Erik knew it, too. When he spoke again, the anger was gone. ''I was a raving maniac when no one could find you. I thought something terrible had happened to you, that you'd been kidnapped or something. Then, when it was finally evident that you'd left on purpose and with the deliberate intention of covering your tracks, I went through a period of rage that is probably unequaled in human history. I couldn't figure out why . . .''

His voice trailed off as he stared forlornly at the tight fists his hands had formed. Kathleen was leaning against the windowsill, staring bleakly into space, seeing nothing, hearing only the desolation in Erik's voice, which matched that in her heart.

''When I saw you the other night, I wanted to kill you.'' He laughed mirthlessly. ''No. I wanted to make love to you first and then I wanted to kill you.''

They were silent for a while, lost in their own thoughts. Erik was the one to break the stillness. ''Why did you marry him, Kathleen?''

She took a deep breath. She could feel his eyes stabbing into her back, but she refused to look at him. If she did . . .

''I discovered I was pregnant with Theron.'' She swallowed the lump in her throat that grew there each time she remembered her first visit to Dr. Peters's office and the decision she had made. ''At first I thought the answer was an abortion. I went to the hospital and even to the operating room. I stopped them just before they put me to sleep.''

''My God,'' he breathed.

''Exactly. God was with me that day. I might never have had Theron—'' She broke off when a shudder shook her entire body. When she recovered, Kathleen went on and told him about Seth's proposal and their marriage. ''He's been so good to me, Erik. He never once drilled me about you—the father. He accepted me and Theron without censure. He treats Theron as his own.''

"But Theron's not his. He's *mine*. Mine, Kathleen."

She spun around and faced him, the color slowly draining from her face. "You wouldn't—*couldn't*—hurt him, Erik. Please. I beg you."

"Sonofabitch!" he cursed savagely as he stood up and crossed the room to stand beside her at the window. He didn't look at her, but shoved his hands into the pockets of his jeans. He stared out the window with as much disinterest as she had done.

Suddenly, he turned and shouted, "How do you compete with a man like that? A paraplegic. Do I become the world's worst villain and claim Theron my own? Should I grab up the child he loves as his son when fate has already kicked the man in the teeth? What am I supposed to do, Kathleen? Theron's my son, goddammit!" He slammed his fist into the wall of his new house, seeming impervious to the pain it must have caused him.

"It would be easier if Seth were a real sonofabitch. Just my luck. The man's a saint." The bitterness in his voice stung Kathleen's ears. It was heartwrenching to witness the torturous struggle of a man's conscience.

"He's been generous beyond my wildest hopes in loaning me money to start my business. It wouldn't have been possible to buy the equipment and rent the building I needed without his backing. Not only that, he's put me in touch with all the businessmen in San Francisco who are potential clients." Erik leaned back against the wall and closed his eyes. Frustration was evident in every line of his body. "Now, how should I repay him for all that? Walk out with the child he considers to be his and tell him I have a terrible lech for his wife?" He dug into his closed eye sockets with the heels of his hands as if he wanted to block out every thought pattern, wipe the slate of moral score-keeping clean, erase all the scruples he was battling. He released his breath slowly, lowered his hands and looked at her. "You can't imagine what a sacrifice you're asking of me, Kathleen."

She looked deeply into his eyes. Her voice was ragged with emotion as she said, "Yes, Erik. Yes, I can."

He heard the words and in her swimming eyes he read the ones left unspoken. Erik cupped her face between his palms and his soothing thumbs stroked and stilled her trembling lips. Resting his forehead against hers, his eyes closed against the torment of holding her and not being able to have her.

This is hell, he thought. For over two years she had ruled his thoughts, both conscious and subliminal. He knew her body better than he knew his own, for he had studied it more and it had been indelibly recorded on the pages of his mind. Time hadn't dimmed the sensation of being held within her. No woman had ever held him so tightly, surrounded him so sweetly, entrapped him so completely.

He had loved her for that. And he had loved her spirit and the bravery with which she had overcome the adversities of her childhood. Ironically, he loved her now for the commitment she gave her husband. He couldn't speak to her of love now. He couldn't have her. He wasn't a thief and he wouldn't take what didn't belong to him. But, God! How was he to survive giving her up?

"We'd better go," he said at last, and released her, opening a chasm of regret between them.

※※

In the most poetic recesses of Kathleen's mind, she deemed the day "star-kissed." By tacit agreement, they pushed all their heartaches aside and reveled in the day they had been granted alone together.

Kathleen made the first attempt to talk about something other than the painful past and the hopeless future. She chose a subject she knew would interest Erik greatly.

"Guess what? Jaimie has been adopted," she said, thinking she would surprise him. He was helping her into his car.

"I know," he replied lightly, shutting the door.

"You know!"

As Erik got behind the wheel, he laughed at her shocked expression. "Yeah. And before you did, I'd bet. Who told you?"

"B. J. and Edna, of course," she answered, still dismayed by the twist in the conversation.

"But they didn't tell you *who* adopted him."

"No."

"Bob and Sally." He enjoyed the thrilled smile that lit up her whole face. "He's a Gudjonsen and is wild about his uncle Erik. He has a baby sister named Jennifer."

"Oh, Erik, how wonderful. Sally and Bob have truly been blessed."

"Yes. They have." Only a touch of bitterness tinged his words.

As they drove through the city, Kathleen launched into a variety of ideas for Erik's condo, until he laughed and said, "I don't care what you do, short of decorating it in pink and purple satin. I'm sure your taste is as good as mine." He dug an elbow playfully into her ribs as he pulled the sports car to a stop at a traffic light.

"But what do you like?" she asked in exasperation.

He slid a glance in her direction that more than suggested what he liked, but he refrained from making the sensual comment that came to mind. "I like browns, you know, different shades. I like that rust color like maple leaves in fall."

She smiled. "Earth tones?"

"Yeah. That oughta do it." She shot him an impatient, disparaging look, then they both laughed.

By the time they reached the shopping area, her head was whirling with ideas. She gave him a crash course in decorating. Erik stood back and let her take charge. She selected linens for his bed and bathroom, picked out twin love seats for his living room. A coordinating chair, a large coffee table and two end tables were also selected. She asked his opinion on lamps. He picked up one with a china base of a seventeenth-century shepherd and shepherdess in a tight clench. Kathleen stared at it in horror, but one look at his twinkling eyes over the frilly shade, and she knew that he was teasing her. They settled on two with clay urns and linen, pleated shades.

At lunch they ate in a restaurant on Fisherman's Wharf that provided a panorama of the Bay and, in the distance, the Golden Gate Bridge. As they ate, Kathleen's heart was overflowing with happiness. Mere days ago, she had thought she would never see him again. Now he was here, across the small table from her, his knees touching hers under the curtain of the tablecloth. They were breathing the same air. She could look at him all she wanted to and didn't have to worry about curious eyes that might intercept those looks so unguarded and filled with love.

She called home from the restaurant and talked to Alice. Seth had gone to the office. Theron had been fed and was down for his nap. "He's fine and not missing you a bit," Alice assured her.

"I know," Kathleen said with a pout. "That's what bothers me."

On their way again, Erik took her hand companionably as they strolled through the shops of Ghirardelli Square, avoiding Kirchoff's Boutique. Erik looked longingly at all the amenities that he couldn't yet afford to add to the meager furnishings he had already picked out.

In an art gallery, he expressed a liking for a wall hanging done in woven yarns of brown, beige and sienna. Kathleen sent him on an unnecessary errand and tried to purchase it for him as a housewarming gift from her and Seth. She was disappointed to learn that it was only a sample, but another one could be ordered from the artist. She placed the order and left her telephone number where she could be contacted when it was finished. It would look perfect on the redwood wall of his living room and give some warmth to the room.

Selecting window treatments was tedious, and Erik was happy to leave it to Kathleen and a decorator who agreed on a time to meet him later in the week at the condo to take exact measurements.

"You may want a headboard later on, but for now you might consider painting the wall behind your bed a vibrant color and then tossing hundreds of bright pillows against it."

"Hundreds?" he teased as he slurped his chocolate soda. They were taking a break in Ghirardelli's Chocolate Manufactory.

"Well, maybe only dozens," she conceded with a smile as she licked the last foamy sweet drop off the end of her spoon. When she looked up, she was alarmed to see that Erik was watching her mouth, as though envying the right of her tongue to disappear inside it. The blue eyes raised slightly, seeking hers, and there was a moment of sexual awareness that rocketed through them.

"What's next?" he asked hoarsely, trying to reestablish the ease with which the rest of the day had passed. His eyes, however, were mutinous, and lowered to take in the agitated rise and fall of her breasts. Sensing his eyes on them, her nipples communicated an enticing message all their own.

"Well, as I was saying about the bedroom," Kathleen said breathlessly, all too aware that his interest was wandering in a dangerous direction and that she was following his lead right to the edge of the enchanted abyss. Safety lay in meaningless, idle chatter. "Let's pick out the color you want on the wall, buy the paint, and then we'll search for pillows. We may get lucky and find an inexpensive chair to go in there, too. What would you think about a wicker trunk at the foot of the bed? That's a functional piece, and decorative as well."

He leaned over closer to her and placed his lips directly on her ear as he whispered, "I can think of only one decorative and functional item I want near my bed. She's got auburn hair that shines in the sunlight like fire. Her eyes are green and radiant and bewitchingly outlined with dark lashes. And if she didn't want me to talk like this, why did she wear a silk blouse and tight leather pants that fit her sexy little fanny like a glove?"

He pulled away from her, and Kathleen caught herself before she swayed against him. She was held hypnotized by his words and the tone of his voice. His eyes were glowing with desire and his mustache twitched around an insolent curl on his lips. He knew he had disoriented her. She wanted to pay him back.

"There's something I always wanted to ask you. Do you have a dimple under the right side of your mustache?"

"Maybe, maybe not. Why don't you find out," he challenged.

Suddenly, the tables had turned again. She wasn't taunting him as was her intention. He was still one point ahead. But who cared? The game had its own reward. "I might sometime," she promised softly as they stared at each other.

"I'll look forward to that."

They completed their shopping within the next two hours and headed for his car, Erik grumbling that he hoped he could remember when he was supposed to meet which delivery man.

When they drove up the lane at the Kirchoff estate, they were still basking in the warmth of each other's presence. He came around to the passenger side of the car and opened the door for her. She was looking up into his face as they walked toward the front door, but intuition caused her to glance toward the side yard. Her heart lurched to her throat, and she shoved away from Erik as she broke into a dead run.

"Theron!" she screamed.

Chapter Fifteen

❧❦ ❧❦

The toddler heedlessly ran the length of the diving board of the pool. At the end of it, he stopped, looked down at the inviting water that he loved, laughed happily and then jumped.

"Theron!" Kathleen screamed again, but this time her cry was soundless. Panicked fear had sealed her throat, prohibiting her from making a sound. She raced forward as she saw his tiny blond head swallowed up by the deep water.

She had almost reached the redwood decking when footsteps thundered past her and Erik all but knocked her to the ground as he sped past. Without a moment's hesitation, he vaulted off the deck and dived head-first into the pool. What seemed like an eternity to Kathleen, as she stood at the pool's edge, was actually only a few seconds before Erik broke the surface, his arm around Theron's chest.

Theron gasped for breath and choked up water as Erik kicked them to the side of the pool. He lifted the boy up into the anxious arms of his mother.

Kathleen heard her own whimpers, though she didn't realize it was she making that piteous sound. "Theron, Theron," she cried feebly as she held his sturdy little body to hers.

Theron had survived the near-fatal incident, but now that he was safe and aware of his mother's anxiety, he too began to wail in a delayed reaction.

"My baby, my precious," Kathleen crooned as she pushed back the sodden curls and felt each feature of his face to assure herself that he was alive.

Erik dragged himself out of the pool. Water gushed from his clothes as he knelt beside mother and child and added his own conciliatory words to them.

"Erik," Kathleen looked at him and gasped, "I saw him go under. I thought . . . I—" She broke off, unable to go on, and leaned weakly against his wet shoulder as she grasped a wiggling Theron to her.

"I know, Kathleen, I know. I died a thousand deaths myself," he said emotionally.

When they had all quieted down somewhat, and Theron was slapping Erik's knees to see the water squirt out of the cloth, Kathleen looked up and saw Hazel on the patio. Where was everyone else? Now that the initial panic was over, the enormity of the accident hit Kathleen full force.

"What was Theron doing out here all alone?" she asked.

"I'd like to know that myself." Erik had picked up Theron and was holding him protectively, possessively.

Hazel came rushing across the lawn toward the pool just as George and Alice were helping wheel Seth out the patio door.

"What's happened?" he called in an alarmed voice.

They descended on the trio, bombarding them with questions.

Erik held up his hands, taking charge. Kathleen was reminded of the day Jaimie had wandered away from the river. He had calmed everyone that day, too. "All we know is that when we drove up, Theron was on the diving board. He jumped in, but thankfully, I was able to go after him within seconds."

"I . . . I couldn't help it," Hazel began to blubber. Everyone turned as a group to stare at her. Kathleen had never thought to see tears in the woman's eyes, but they were evident now. "We were playing on the patio with his little trucks. He . . . I . . . I was going through a magazine. When I heard Kathleen's scream I looked up. I didn't even know he was near the pool. He got there so fast. I . . . I . . . Oh, Seth." Her face crumpled and she covered it with her hands, shaking her head in disbelief of her carelessness.

"Hey, hey, everything is all right now," Seth said soothingly. "Theron's safe. But you're going to have to watch him more closely, Hazel. You know how curious he is."

Hazel continued to moan into her hands while everyone turned their attention to Theron, who seemed to have recovered and was as good as new.

Kathleen watched Hazel. For comic relief after the calamitous situation, everyone laughed at the puddle that Erik and Theron were forming on the patio. It was agreed that they should go into the laundry room off the kitchen where Alice would bring each of them some dry clothes. Seth reached out and squeezed his sister's hand before he wheeled into the house on the heels of the others. Theron was still ensconced securely in Erik's arms.

Kathleen remained in the shadows of the shrubbery surrounding the patio and watched them go.

Hazel, thinking she was alone, straightened her shoulders from the humiliated posture she had assumed and cursed viciously under her breath. She turned around hastily to pick up her belongings from the table. She was about to turn toward the house when she saw Kathleen standing a few feet away, glaring at her. Hazel's hands froze in midair and her breath was sucked in sharply.

"Kathleen, you amaze me. Why aren't you in there taking care of your son?"

Kathleen took two steps forward until she was within inches of her sister-in-law. "And you amaze me, Hazel. Did you think you'd get away with murder?"

Instinctively, Hazel took a step backward, in defense of the threat she saw in Kathleen's dangerous eyes. "I can't imagine what you're talking about," she said, forcing conviction into her voice and standing up to her full height.

"You know exactly what I'm talking about. That was quite an act you put on for them." Kathleen indicated the others, now grouped in the kitchen. "But I think that your tears were caused by frustration over a thwarted plan and not anguish over neglect. You knew exactly where Theron was. His drowning would have been a convenient misfortune for you, wouldn't it?"

Kathleen's arm snaked out and, with surprising strength, grabbed Hazel's wrist in a ruthless clench. "If my son ever runs into an *accident* and you are even remotely near him, I'll ruin you with Seth. Do you understand me, Hazel? I'll open his eyes to you. He'll believe me, too. He loves you, but he loves me more. You'd better think twice before you gamble with Theron's life again. You could lose everything."

Hazel jerked her hand free. She laughed a brittle, harsh laugh directly in Kathleen's face. "Do you think I'm afraid of you?"

"Yes, I think you are," Kathleen replied levelly. "Otherwise, you wouldn't be attacking a baby. On top of the heartless, selfish, manipulative harpy you are, you're a coward. If you want a fight, fight me. I warn you, though, that it would be a senseless battle, because I want nothing of yours. I only want you to let Seth and Theron and me live in peace. Your security isn't threatened by that."

"I don't want a sleazy little slut like you in my house, in my life!" Hazel's face was mottled, congested with fury. "I'll prove to my brother what you are if it's the last thing I do." Her fists were clenched at her sides. Her body was drawn as tight as a bow string. Kathleen thought that the woman was about to have a seizure.

"Just remember what I said and be extremely careful what stakes you gamble with." Kathleen stepped around Hazel, leaving her alone with her impotent rage.

The calm façade that Kathleen presented as she went into the brightly lit kitchen was deceptive. On the inside, she was quaking, first over the terrifying incident itself, and then over the altercation with Hazel, who was obviously deranged. Who would use a helpless child as a pawn in a deadly private game? A desperate, sadistic woman. But why? What could Hazel Kirchoff want that she didn't already have?

Kathleen pasted on a false smile as she greeted Seth. "Kathleen, where have you been?" Without waiting for an answer, he went on, "Erik said that the two of you covered a lot of ground today and picked up some wonderful stuff. He is very pleased with your selections."

She looked up at Erik, who was watching her steadily, worriedly, and said, "He has comparable taste, so my job was easy."

She noted that Erik was wearing some of Seth's casual clothes, which were a trifle small for him. "Where is Theron?" she asked anxiously.

"He's upstairs in his bed taking a quick nap before dinner," Alice answered. "He was tuckered out."

"Why don't you go up and do the same?" Seth suggested, taking her hand and kissing her fingers in turn. "You've just been through a harrowing experience. Take a bath, relax awhile. It'll be some time before dinner's ready. Dress casually. We decided to boil lobsters rather than cook steaks."

"It sounds delicious," Kathleen said, leaning over to caress him softly on the lips. "So does your idea. Will you excuse me?" Then she laughed. "It looks like there are enough cooks in here anyway."

George was dropping cookie dough onto baking sheets. Erik had been assigned to make the salad. Seth was in charge of the lobsters, and Alice was overseeing it all.

"See there?" Seth teased. "You're useless. Get upstairs and rest."

She climbed the steps wearily, allowing her tiredness free rein now that she was out of the others' sight. She crept into Theron's room and leaned over his crib, sweeping her fingers lightly across his soft cheeks and smiling at the dribble that beaded his chin. Her throat constricted painfully and she drew a shuddering breath when she thought of what could have happened.

Her bath was long and luxuriant. She drank the glass of white wine that Seth had insisted she bring up with her. By the time she left the steamy bathroom, her limbs were rubbery and she was relaxed. The bed was too inviting to ignore and she peeled back the spread and collapsed onto the sheets. Drawing the pillow against her in the manner she was accustomed to, she soon fell asleep.

It was a slight bumping noise that awakened her. Instantly, she sat up, drugged by grogginess. The sound had come from Theron's room, setting off maternal alarm bells. She had scorned clothes when she left the bathroom. Now, she slipped on a white eyelet wrapper and hastily tied the sash around her waist just as she flung open the connecting door to her son's bedroom.

Erik was leaning over the crib. She slumped against the doorframe in relief. "What's the matter?" he asked quickly as he looked up and saw her ravaged face.

"Nothing, I . . ."

"I was sent up here to awaken you. When I opened your door, you were sleeping so soundly I didn't have the heart. I thought I'd wake up the captain first." He grinned and her heart melted at the sight of him bending over to examine his sleeping son.

Her bare feet were silent on the thick carpet as she crossed the room to stand beside him. This was the way it should have been for the past two years. They should have been able to enjoy Theron's babyhood together. Erik had been denied that experience. Could she ever make it up to him? It was her own stupidity, her own immature mistake, that had separated them.

"I owe you an apology, Erik."

"You do?" He spoke softly so as not to disturb the sleeping baby.

"If I hadn't been so juvenile, so unsure of myself, I would never have made the mistake I did in thinking that you were married. It was foolish to jump to conclusions and run away like that when I didn't know the facts." She looked up at him then and saw the soft quality in his eyes that he rarely exhibited now. "No matter what would have happened . . . between . . . between us," her voice grew gruff, "you should have known about your son. I'm sorry."

Her head dipped again in remorse, but his hand came up to cup her chin and lift her face. "It's too late for recriminations, Kathleen. I haven't led the most exemplary life these past two years. I've done some things I wouldn't want anyone to know about. I was angry, hurt, disillusioned. I wanted the rest of the world to feel the same hatred I did. I regret some of my decisions, just as you do, but they are done. Let's try to forget them."

He glanced down at the baby once again. His hand was dark against Theron's lighter skin as he stroked the chubby arm and fist. "You did a good job, Kathleen. He's a wonderful boy."

"Yes, he is." As if drawn by some invisible force, she moved next to him and clasped his free hand. He squeezed it tightly.

"Did it . . . hurt much . . . you know, when you had him?"

Kathleen smiled gently. Men usually became as infantile as their offspring when they talked about birth. "Not very much. He was big, but I had a good obstetrician. I wish . . ." She trailed off at the absurdity of her idea.

"What?" he prodded, looking down at her and pulling her closer.

"I was going to say I wish you could meet him—the doctor. He was very kind to me. He was the one who was going to do the abortion before I called it off."

The hand around hers tightened like an iron band. "God! You must have been put through hell."

She leaned her head against his strong arm. "It's one of those things we're better off to forget." Theron made a sucking noise in his sleep and they both laughed softly. "I haven't even thanked you for saving his life today, Erik."

He faced her then. "Do you really think I want to be thanked for that?" She could only shake her head dumbly. She was held by the radiating heat of his blue gaze. "I haven't thanked you for giving him life, either," he said. He took a step closer and leaned down nearer her. "Thank you for my son, Kathleen." He brushed her cheek with his lips. "Did you feed him yourself?"

His gaze fell to her chest, where the fabric over her breast was fluttering with the pounding of her heart. "Yes," she answered hoarsely.

His finger started at the base of her throat and scorched a trail to the first visible swelling of her breasts. "Is it even possible," he asked unevenly, "that I'm jealous of my own son for knowing you so intimately while I didn't even know where you were?"

Kathleen was as intrigued by his mouth as by the words that came from it. She watched the movement of his lips, the silken texture of his mustache, the hint of an elusive dimple, the teeth that lay just beyond his lips. "I'm here now," she whispered.

He raised his eyes to hers in supplication and read the invitation so boldly extended. With deliberate leisure, he tugged on the sash until it came free and the sides of her wrapper fell apart. His hands slipped inside, caressing the smooth, satin skin of her stomach before they settled on her waist and pushed aside the white eyelet. For long, ponderous moments, he stared at her, searing her flesh with eyes that roamed freely and without apology or shame.

His hands moved up slowly to cup her breasts and lift them toward his mouth. He gave each one only a fraction of the praise he felt it deserved for having nurtured his child.

Kathleen swayed unsteadily as he moved away from her slightly to study the rest of her. His hands smoothed over her abdomen. "No stretch marks," he commented in a mere whisper. "Nothing to mar the perfection. Motherhood only made you more beautiful." His fingers glided downward and wound through that tight auburn triangle. Kathleen sighed at the exquisite tenderness of his touch.

His hands went around her and appreciated the fullness

of her hips before settling under the ripe curves and lifting her against him. Their stomachs touched, then her breasts were crushed against his chest. Finally, their mouths melted together in a fusion of spirit as well as of body.

The kiss was thorough and deep. His tongue penetrated her lips slowly, teasing them until Kathleen was pleading with her entire body for him to accept the proffered gift. When he did, his tongue explored her mouth wantonly, seeking the most secret recesses and relishing them.

She pulled away as she placed both hands on his whisker-roughened cheeks. Her mouth came up to his. She teased, tortured, tasted and promised. She gave.

When next he kissed her, his tongue dipped into her mouth again and again, intimating a more profound physical union. Their bodies welded together in a tight embrace that was lenient only in letting them rub against each other.

"Mamma."

The chirping voice caused them to fall apart as nothing else could have. They stared down dazedly at Theron, who had stood up in his crib, hopping up and down. Kathleen clutched the sides of her wrapper together.

"Theron, when did you wake up?" she asked shakily.

The baby was laughing and waving his arms around.

"I think he wants in on the fun."

"Erik," Kathleen gasped, and covered her flaming face with hands suddenly gone cold. "We ought to thank him for waking up. Everyone will wonder . . . We mustn't let this happen again." Indeed, she had almost betrayed her husband under his own roof. God! Guilt swamped her and she put more space between her and Erik. Her eyes were laden with shame when she met his. "We're in Seth's house. I'm his wife."

Erik faced her soberly. "You should have reminded me of that sooner. I'd never want to betray Seth either, but my better judgment deserts me when I'm close to you, Kathleen. It's a fact that is never far from my mind."

She retreated into her bedroom and dressed hurriedly. She

cursed her fumbling fingers and wondered if anyone would notice the high color in her cheeks or the swollen fullness of her well-kissed mouth.

She met Theron and Erik at the top of the stairs as they had planned moments earlier. "Don't look so guilty, Kathleen," Erik said out of the corner of his mouth. "Nothing happened. Believe me, I'm more painfully aware of that than anyone."

The expression on his face was so anguished that Kathleen couldn't help but laugh.

"Sadist," he grumbled. He swung Theron up onto his shoulders. The boy enmeshed his stubby fingers in Erik's hair for a handhold. When Erik whooped in pain, Theron shrieked in delight.

The three of them descended the stairs laughing. Seth wheeled up to meet them. "There you are!" he cried. "We were about to send a search party out, thinking maybe Theron had tied you both to the bedposts." They all laughed, and Seth instructed them to lead the way to the kitchen, where dinner was being served tonight. Hazel was taking a tray in her room, pleading a headache.

In the hall, Seth paused, not following immediately as he watched the trio go toward the kitchen. No one was witness to the pensive expression on his face.

⁕⁀ ⁕⁀

October was always a busy month for the stores, and this season was no exception. Not only was it business as usual, but this year they had Erik's commercials to contend with, too. It was agreed that some should be done in time for the Christmas rush. Erik went into production immediately. All agreed that the ads were good, but nothing as creative as Erik wanted to do for the future. However, the first commercials aired locally generated even more business for Kirchoff's, to say nothing of Erik's new company.

Kathleen saw Erik often, but there wasn't an encore of the

amorous scene that had taken place in Theron's bedroom. Neither trusted himself to be left alone with the other. Other people were always around and she felt that they both contrived to have it that way. When they weren't in business conferences, they were at dinner at the Kirchoffs' house. If anyone noticed the rarity of a single man Erik's age spending an inordinate amount of time with Theron, no one spoke of it.

Hazel had tempered her frequent verbal attacks on Kathleen. The younger woman wasn't naive enough to think that her dire warnings to her sister-in-law had done anything to alter the woman's malicious nature. Perhaps she was only exercising caution by becoming more reticent. To Kathleen's mind, that made Hazel even more deadly, and she was still wary of her.

For that reason, Kathleen was uneasy about leaving Theron for the two weeks she and Eliot would go to New York to do their spring buying.

"Alice." Kathleen approached the woman one day while the housekeeper was working alone in the kitchen. "Are you sure you can handle Theron all by yourself while I'm away? Maybe we should call in some extra help. He's getting so meddlesome."

"That's the tenth time you've asked me that and I've answered the same way each time. I can take care of Theron just fine. Don't you trust me with him?"

Not for the world would Kathleen have Alice think that. "Of course I do! But if you should get busy and someone else should volunteer to watch him . . ." She didn't know how to say what she wanted to. She couldn't say, "Don't leave him alone with his aunt."

Alice eyed the younger woman shrewdly. "I think I understand what you're saying. If you're referring to the day he had his . . . accident . . . in the pool, you should know something. I didn't want to leave him in Hazel's charge. She insisted that I come in here and start dinner and leave him out on the patio to play a little longer. I could hardly refuse her, Kathleen, but I wanted to. I don't know how to tell you this, and you'll think I'm a superstitious old woman, but I had a feeling something bad was going to happen to that baby when I left him with her.''

A silent message passed between them. The housekeeper took both Kathleen's hands between her own. "You go on that trip and do a good job for Seth. He expects it from you. Don't worry about Theron. No one will get close to him unless I'm there. I've even asked George to move his crib into our room while you're gone.''

Kathleen hugged the woman to her, relieved that she hadn't had to spell out her worries but glad that Alice was intuitive enough to catch them.

On the day of departure, Seth went to the airport to see them off. "Buy anything you want,'' he said. "This is going to be a big spring. Don't forget that. Be sure to ask if some of the pieces can be made up early for the commercials that Erik wants to shoot.''

"I will, I won't, I will,'' she promised, laughing and swallowing the hard lump in her throat at the mention of Erik's name. She hadn't seen him in more than a week. "Don't work so hard, Seth,'' she pleaded. He was looking even more fragile recently. His skin seemed to become tighter and more sallow each day, and the fatigue lines around his eyes and mouth had grown more pronounced.

"Don't worry about me. Or Theron. Have a good time. You get away so seldom—''

"Seth,'' she scolded, "will you stop! I don't want to get away from my family.'' Disregarding the naturally curious eyes of the other waiting passengers, she knelt beside his chair and kissed him goodbye.

"I love you, Kathleen,'' he said as she pulled away. His mouth was beautiful when he smiled the way he did now. The generous, loving spirit that characterized him still shone from the depths of his dark eyes though they were pinched and weary.

"I love you, too,'' she said sincerely.

Kathleen adored New York. Each time she traveled to the city, she was imbued with its energy and vitality. Never would she want to live in the concrete canyons, but she looked forward to the five trips she made each year to buy merchandise for Kirchoff's.

She was welcomed with open arms in a city that wasn't particularly known for its geniality. The fashion houses she did business with catered to her every whim. Kirchoff's was an excellent account. At each showroom, she was treated royally.

Yet they all knew that behind Kathleen's feminine exterior was an operating business mind that they dare not try to take advantage of.

"Mr. Gilbert, how nice to see you again," she said to the president of the company who greeted her personally as she and Eliot came into his busy showroom. He was immediately flattered and deceived by her friendly manner, but he was soon to learn that she was not to be trifled with.

"I let you get by with shipping my order two weeks later than you shipped I. Magnin's," she said, still wearing a disarming smile. "If it ever happens again, I'll send the merchandise back without payment. Is that clear?"

Her eyes shone green, almost matching the color of Mr. Gilbert's sickly expression. His manner became effusive. "I can't imagine, Mrs. Kirchoff, what—"

"Do we see your line now or do we not?" she asked levelly.

"Now, of course. Immediately. Just let me . . ." He bustled off to find his most persuasive salesman.

Eliot was invaluable to her on the buying trips. Each night, when they went over the orders they had placed that day, checking them against their budget and the "shopping list" they had made from their inventory at the store, his uncanny memory never ceased to amaze her.

"Those organdy ruffled tops we bought at Valentino's will go with that crepe Anne Klein trouser. What sizes did we order that pant in? Six, eight, ten. Three of each for each store," he mused as he glanced over the orders. "Why don't we go all the way from sizes four to twelve? Pick up the twelves in black only and order three more for each store in the other colors. Except for the blue. It's hideous. I think we can team this pant with different blouses and the customer will probably buy two. What do you think?"

Each night, Kathleen retired to her room while Eliot went out on pursuits of his own to places she didn't want to know about, with people she didn't want to know about, and in the mornings, he was hung over from substances she didn't want to know about. But after three cups of black coffee and half a pack of cigarettes, he was ready to attack Seventh Avenue again and was as sharp as ever.

They were entertained lavishly, for Kirchoff's had a fine and firm reputation as one of the fashion-setting stores in a fashion-conscious city.

One anxious blouse manufacturer could tell by their closed expressions that he was about to lose a sale and began stuttering his spiel. Impatiently, Eliot got up from the table where an empty order form lay and brazenly removed the garment from the man's hand.

"Do you know what's wrong with this blouse?" Eliot asked Kathleen, ignoring the flustered salesman.

"The bow," she said without hesitation.

"Right! This ghastly bow. It's a great blouse without that." He turned to the man and said, "I'll order six dozen in assorted colors and sizes if you can make them without the bow. Otherwise, forget it."

"I . . ." the man stammered.

"And modify the sleeve," Eliot went on imperiously. "It's a great suit blouse, but if customers can't get a full sleeve in a jacket, they won't buy it. I like the graceful style, but take about half the fabric out of the sleeve."

"Yes, Mr. Pate. Of course."

"Can we expect the blouses to be shipped the way we want them?" Eliot demanded politely.

"Certainly," the man said nervously. "I myself was thinking of taking off the bow."

They were still laughing as Eliot hailed a taxi to take them to the Russian Tea Room for a luncheon appointment. They were wined and dined almost each lunch and dinner, being taken only to the best restaurants. Kathleen received no small number of bold, illicit propositions. To her chagrin, Eliot received as many.

After ten days, Kathleen was ready to go home. A day earlier than planned, they rescheduled their flight and returned to San Francisco. She and Eliot parted company at the airport, each glad to be finished with a difficult job and feeling confident that they had accomplished much.

Kathleen surprised everyone when she arrived home just in time for dinner. She had a surprise, too. Erik was there. He was accompanied by a gorgeous, stunning blonde.

Her name was Tamara.

Chapter Sixteen

🌿 🌿

Kathleen!" Seth cried, and wheeled his chair around the end of the dining table, almost running over her with his exuberance.

She laughed as she leaned down to receive his warm kiss. As she drew back, Kathleen was struck by how tired he looked. Had he lost weight? His cheekbones stood out starkly in his gaunt face. His eyes, however, were as radiant as ever, and she didn't doubt that he was glad to see her.

"How was the trip?" he asked as he escorted her to a chair. George and Alice had rushed in when they heard her voice and Theron had been placed in her anxious arms. "What did the spring lines look like? Alice, please bring her a plate. Theron's learned to say car and truck. Darling, was it a fruitful trip?" Seth was so excited to see her that the words tumbled over themselves. She laughed again as she hugged a squirming Theron closer.

"We had a good trip, though we finished early and couldn't wait until tomorrow to come home. We bought some lovely things." Her eyes wandered around the table, including Erik, Hazel and the blonde in her conversation. "Forgive me," she mumbled, "but we haven't been introduced."

"Oh, I'm sorry," Seth said. "I was so delighted to see you that I forgot my manners. Kathleen, this is Tamara. Tamara, my wife and most valued right hand, Kathleen."

"How do you do," Kathleen said politely.

"Hi," was all the girl said.

Erik spoke for the first time. "How are you, Kathleen?" The sound of his voice was her true welcome home. It embraced her. It was rich and deep and masculine, touching her with its timbre.

She longed to go to him and feel his strength, his warmth. But she couldn't. They had an audience and there was a glamorous woman sitting beside him, a woman he had dared to bring to her house. "I'm fine," she answered curtly, not quite meeting his eyes.

"Alice, take Theron back into the kitchen now," Hazel ordered.

"No," countered Kathleen coolly. "I've missed him more than I could have imagined. Tonight he stays in the dining room with us." Kathleen's eyes dared Hazel to challenge her.

"Of course, my dear," Hazel said graciously, though the eyes she turned on Kathleen were as hard as flint.

Kathleen placed a napkin in her lap and her gaze strayed back to the glamorous young woman with Erik. She must be very tall, Kathleen thought. Didn't Tamara have a last name? Was one necessary? Who could forget her once they had seen her? Her hair was the color of moonlight, the palest blonde imaginable, and framed her face in a carefully disordered style that hung to the middle of her back. It was free, untamed. It matched the feline cunning that lurked in her amber eyes. They were cool and calculating, but when they lit on Erik they became slumbrous and warm. Even from across the table, Kathleen could feel the sparks shooting from those eyes.

Once she saw Erik answer Tamara's seductive look with a deep, lazy grin, and the food in Kathleen's mouth could have been dust. She tried to keep her eyes away from them and listen to what Seth was telling her about Theron and the stores, but it was impossible.

Tamara's clinging dress was white, setting off her fabulous tan. From what Kathleen could see, the fabric outlined a perfect, statuesque figure, and left nothing to the imagination.

"If you're finished, Kathleen, we'll go into the living room," Seth suggested. "I don't think you ate enough, though."

Kathleen stared unseeingly at her plate and realized that she hadn't taken more than a dozen bites. "We had a snack on the plane," she said as brightly as she could and reached for Theron.

Erik's hand closed possessively around Tamara's elbow as he led her into the living room. Hazel had engaged Seth in an absorbing private conversation, so Kathleen's only escort was her son.

Tamara practically lay down on the long sofa, pulling Erik with her and threading her slender arm through his. His elbow pressed into her enormous breasts.

Kathleen was finding it hard not to scream at both of them as she sank down into an easy chair with Theron, who was wetly chewing on her string of coral beads. She must look tired, wrinkled and matronly, while the other woman looked young, fresh, alluring and all too willing.

Ritualistically, George brought in the heavy silver tray with the coffee service on it. Everything irritated Kathleen tonight. Why couldn't they all troop into the kitchen and sit on stools and pour coffee out of a percolator into thick, heavy mugs? She longed for those easy talks that she had shared with B. J. and Edna. How she missed the joking, the warmth, that informal way of life!

She was sick of moire-covered walls and brocade sofas and artificial flowers. She was even sicker of a tall, slinky blonde who couldn't seem to keep her hands off Erik.

"You sit with the baby, Kathleen dearest, and let me pour tonight. You must be exhausted after your trip." Hazel's duplicity never ceased. How the woman constantly carried off the act without once dropping character was a source of wonder to Kathleen. She looked away from her sister-in-law in time to see Tamara lean even closer to Erik.

Her thigh rubbed against his in an erotic invitation. Absently, he reached over and patted her knee. Kathleen would have gladly murdered first the girl, then him.

Did she have the right to be jealous? Erik was a virile man. She was married. He had never claimed to love her. She knew that he still had a physical desire for her and that he felt a fondness for her for being the mother of his child. But love her? He had never claimed to in so many words.

What good would it do either of them if he did? She could never leave Seth, and Erik knew that. There was every reason in the world for him to be . . . seeing someone. But why did she have to be so young and beautiful? So sexy? And why did he bring her to Kathleen's house?

That question was answered for her.

"Kathleen, Erik has come up with a great idea for the spring commercials. He wants to go to the tropics to do some location shooting. What do you think? Doesn't that sound great?" Seth's face had lit up with expectation.

"Yes," Kathleen agreed, forcing a smile.

"I think it's a marvelous idea," Hazel said with a sly smile directed at Kathleen.

"He found Tamara through one of the talent agencies in the city," Seth rushed on. "She'll be featured in all the commercials. There will be other models, of course, but most of the scenes will revolve around her." Seth beamed at the model, and she blessed him with a quick wink. "She's beautiful, isn't she? Can't you see her wearing some gauzy summer thing, standing beside the ocean?" He laughed. "Listen to me trying to tell Erik his job!"

Erik laughed, too, and looked at Tamara in appreciation. "Sounds good to me."

Kathleen jumped up abruptly, surprising Theron into dropping the wet beads against her blouse. "I . . . I'm sure that the commercials will all be lovely. It was nice to meet you, Miss . . . uh . . . Tamara. Please excuse me. I'm . . ." She was gasping for breath and there was a stabbing pain in her head. "I'm awfully tired. Goodnight, Hazel, Erik. Goodnight, Seth." She went to him and kissed him hurriedly on the cheek.

"Kathleen—"

"I'll see you in the morning," she cut him off. Before any of them could reply, she retreated with Theron to the sanctuary upstairs, out of sight of Erik and the woman who would go with him on the tropical getaway.

❦ ❦

The day after her arrival home Kathleen spent in her room. The trip had tired her more than she had wanted to admit, and the rude awakening she had been subjected to the night before hadn't helped any.

The day passed slowly. She tried to nap off and on, but each time she drifted to sleep, dreams of Erik, usually with a leggy blonde hanging on his arm, would awaken her, and she would pace the carpet, weep, and then feel guilt and remorse for being unfaithful to Seth, if not in deed, then certainly in mind.

The day after that, she returned to work. Eliot hadn't seemed to be wilted at all by the trip. Indeed, he seemed invigorated, and the enthusiasm he exhibited over the coming season began to grate on Kathleen's nerves—as did everything else.

From the beginning of November until Christmas was every merchant's busiest season and Kirchoff's was no exception. Still, Seth didn't let that stand in the way of the preparations for the commercials. The Caribbean trip was planned for the first week in December.

Kathleen wanted nothing to do with it, but she found that she would be very much involved.

"Do you realize that you're asking the impossible?" she stormed. They were all in Seth's office, having met to discuss the scheduled trip. She flew out of her chair and crossed to the bookshelves, folding her arms over her chest and keeping her back to them. How much more of this could she take?

This was the third such meeting in a week. They kept her in close contact with Erik when she'd just as soon not have to see him.

"Kathleen," Seth said patiently, "we know what a bind we're putting you in. But in order for the commercials to start playing on time, Erik must have them produced shortly after the first of the year. That's why it's necessary to do them so soon."

She turned around and glared at them. Erik was slumped insouciantly in a chair with his feet stretched out in front of him. He was staring at her from under lowered brows. She wished he wouldn't do that. It made her uncomfortable.

"I understand all of that, Seth. I'm not an imbecile," she snapped. "Do *you* understand how difficult it's going to be to have clothes, even samples, delivered by that time? I don't know if I can get even one fashion house to cooperate. They'll laugh in my face."

"We understand the pressure you're working under and know that you'll do the best you can. The commercials will be useless if we have to use last season's fashions. I want only new stuff."

"I know, I know," she repeated tiredly, in her own mean way reminding Seth that he had told her that at least a hundred times. "They're not even cutting next spring's lines yet," she grumbled. "I should know. I just got back from New York, remember?"

"Yes," Seth replied, unperturbed by her sarcastic tone. "And if what Eliot tells me is right, you charmed every manufacturer on Seventh Avenue. Surely you can ask them for one small—no, I'll correct that—one large favor."

She sighed, hitching her shoulders up and then letting them drop theatrically. "What size does the girl wear?"

"Tamara," Erik said. "Her name is Tamara."

"I'm sorry," Kathleen gushed. "What size does *Tamara* wear?"

"An eight. We're using all size-eight models to make it easier on you."

"Thank you ever so much," she said sweetly, and batted

her eyelashes. "I can't tell you how much your consideration is going to help me do the impossible."

There was a heavy silence in the room while the three tried to keep their eyes away from each other. Kathleen was immediately ashamed of her childish sarcasm. What was the matter with her?

"Erik, will you excuse us, please," Seth asked quietly after several long, tense moments.

"Of course." He rolled his length out of the chair and sauntered from the room.

Another silence followed while Kathleen plucked at a loose thread on her sleeve. At last, when she felt that she would burst if Seth didn't yell at her for her abominable behavior, she said, "I'm sorry. I know I embarrassed you in front of your associate and I'm sorry."

He didn't say anything and she was forced to look at him. There was no reproach or anger in his eyes, only worry. "Kathleen, what's wrong?" His voice was like velvet, quiet and soothing. Had he been condemning, she would have fought back, but that compelling voice punctured her haughtiness and she sagged in defeat.

"I don't know."

"Come here," he said. She didn't argue with him. She went to his wheelchair and let him pull her down onto his lap much as he had done the day she had told him she was pregnant. "Are you sure you don't know what's the matter? You haven't been yourself for a while now. If there's something wrong, I want to know about it. Can I help you in any way?"

"Oh, Seth," she groaned into his neck, and welcomed the feel of his arms around her. He was so kind. If she confessed to him now that she loved his friend, that Erik was Theron's father, she knew that he would forgive her. His love was unconditional. But she would never hurt him that way. She adored him too much.

"What's bothering you? Is it Erik?"

Her heart stopped. Did Seth already know? Had she been too careless with the longing looks she gave Erik each time they were in the same room? Did Seth discern the similarity between Theron and Erik, which became more noticeable each day?

She had to say something. "Why would Erik bother me?" She laughed lightly, but it had a brittle sound.

"I don't know. Sometimes I think the two of you really like each other. Other times, I think you're squaring off for combat."

She put her arm around Seth's shoulders and kissed him on the cheek, trying to keep her relief from showing. "The only thing I'm worried about right now is not getting those clothes on time."

He was too intelligent to be put off so easily. "Kathleen." He cupped her face with both his hands and waited until she had raised her eyes to his before he spoke. "I told you once that if you ever wanted anything—*anything*—all you need do is ask. If it's within my limited power to give it to you, I will. I love you. Do you know how much?"

Tears had flooded her eyes now and she read the love that had always been so evident in his glowing brown eyes. She nodded her head slowly. She had an idea of how much he must love her. He was plagued by an unfulfilled, gnawing love that couldn't be nurtured or ignored. She also knew, in this case, that it was an undeserved love and, therefore, that much more precious.

She collapsed against him and cried in racking sobs. Finally, after several minutes, she sat up and accepted his handkerchief. "I think maybe you have too much to do," Seth said. "Tears like that are often the product of extreme exhaustion."

"No. I'm fine now. Maybe all I needed was a good cry." She smiled. "I must get busy now. As you know, I've got to put through several dozen calls to New York and make lifetime enemies of overworked cutters and seamstresses."

He laughed, but was serious when he said, "If anyone can work the miracle, you can. Just don't wear yourself out doing it. Nothing is as important to me as you are."

"I know," she whispered, and kissed him gently on the

mouth. She eased out of his lap and noticed the boniness of his knees through the cloth of his pants.

"Seth," she broached the subject warily, for she knew he was sensitive about it, "are you feeling well? You seem so tired lately. When did you last see your doctor?"

He tossed back his head in feigned exasperation. "What is this? Turn about, fair play? Of course I'm feeling well. George would be offended if he knew you didn't think he was taking proper care of me. He watches me like an old mother hen." He took her hand and pressed it between his own. "Promise me, Kathleen, that you'll never worry unduly about me. I'll be fine. I promise you that."

She wasn't convinced, but she didn't want to nag him with her own concerns. "Then get back to work!" she commanded as she put on a falsely cheerful air and sashayed toward the door. "I'll tell Claire to bring you some coffee." She waved goodbye to him and went out through the secretary's office.

Thankfully, Erik had left.

※＊ ※＊

Late in the morning of Thanksgiving Day, Kathleen came bounding down the stairs with the intention of joining Seth on the driveway. He had already gone out to wait for Erik, who was coming over for one of their basketball-shooting bouts. Since Erik had had the hoop installed, they spent several hours a week at the exercise.

Kathleen had worriedly asked George if he thought it was too strenuous a workout for Seth.

"No," he answered. "Don't discourage it, Kathleen. He enjoys it, more for the competition than for the exercise. Leave him alone. He needs to share something like this with other men his age."

So she said nothing, though she often thought Seth looked completely undone by the time he and Erik finished their games. Now she watched from the patio door as Seth dribbled the ball beside the wheel of his chair. It got beyond his reach and he lost control. The ball bounced and rolled into some bushes. Seth glanced around, apparently looking for George, but he found himself alone.

He wheeled toward the bushes and tried to lean over them to retrieve the ball. Sweat popped out on his forehead as the muscles of his neck and arm strained to reach it. Concerned that he was going to fall out of the chair, Kathleen was just about to go through the door to help him when he doubled up his fists and pounded the arms of his chair.

"Goddammit! I hate being a cripple!" Tears of frustration had mingled with the perspiration that poured down his lean cheeks. His voice was only a hoarse whisper, yet she could hear it from that distance. His face was contorted into an angry mask and he continued to pound on the arms of the chair, cursing it and himself. "Dammit all to hell. Why? Why *me*?"

Kathleen was stunned. Never, since she had known him, had she heard Seth curse his condition. He was always joking about the paralysis. This visible evidence of the anguish he must constantly live with was too pitiable to watch. She momentarily closed her eyes, drawing strength, trying to think of something to say that wouldn't sound patronizing.

When she opened her eyes, the scene had changed. Erik was approaching Seth at a run, his features registering alarm.

"Seth?" He spoke softly, but Seth heard him and immediately ceased his bitter tirade. The dark eyes slammed shut in embarrassment and his head dropped forward as though hinged to his neck until his chin rested on his chest. His fists remained clenched around the arms of the chair. Erik didn't speak. Instead, he crouched down on one knee and stared at the ground, patiently waiting for Seth to initiate any conversation.

Kathleen remained breathless and still behind the drapes at the patio door.

"I'm sorry that you had to witness such a temper tantrum. I don't indulge myself very often, but when I do, I know it's quite a spectacle." Seth spoke with self-deprecating humor.

Erik didn't even smile. He looked up at the other man. "I don't think I've ever told you how much I admire you, Seth. If I were in your condition, if our roles were reversed, I wouldn't handle it with the graciousness you do."

"Ah, Erik, don't pin any medals on my chest. I'm only valorous because I have to be."

"No, you don't. You could be a real bastard about it."

Seth sighed. "Sometimes I feel like being that way. Like now, for instance. I'd like very much to hate you. Don't you think I wish I had your body, your strength? I'm more dependent on other people than Theron is. What do you think such dependence does to a man? I despise being virtually helpless, Erik. I've merely learned to live with it. I confess that I envy you every time I see you."

Erik picked up the basketball from under the bushes and carefully traced the markings on it with his finger. When he spoke, his voice was so low that Kathleen had trouble hearing him. "I confess to envying you. I wish I had your capacity to accept things as they are. For the past couple of years, I've been swimming upstream, battling odds, for something unattainable, wanting something I have no right to want. I can't take no for an answer. I've never been able to. On the other hand, everything you say and do demonstrates a selflessness that I admire because I can't even understand it. It's too foreign to my character."

"Thank you, Erik, but I think you're being far too hard on yourself."

"No, I'm afraid I know myself all too well," he scoffed. He seemed to physically shake off the serious mood and said, "Are you ready to play some basketball?"

"To tell the truth," Seth admitted apologetically, "I don't quite feel up to it today."

"Fine. No problem. How about a beer instead?"

"Sounds good. It's such a sunny day, why don't we just stay out here?"

"Okay, I'll go get the beer." Erik dropped the basketball and loped toward the kitchen door. Kathleen ducked out of sight, not wanting either man to know she had seen him at his most vulnerable.

The Sunday after Thanksgiving found Kathleen working in the freight room of the downtown store. The stores had been closed Thanksgiving Day, and since the following Friday and Saturday were two of the busiest shopping days of the year, she hadn't done some of her own work so she could be on hand if the clerks on the floor needed her assistance.

She and Seth met in the employees' parking lot. They had driven downtown in separate cars, not knowing when the other would be finished. Seth wanted to supervise the hanging of the Christmas decorations. "There's no way I can be an Indian," he joked as he wheeled his chair across the asphalt. "I'm indisputably the chief."

Kathleen had come dressed for hard, dusty work in old, faded jeans and a chambray shirt with the cuffs rolled back. Her hair was gathered into a ponytail. "Is this the fashion plate of San Francisco?" Seth teased.

"This is she," she joked back. "All I'm going to be doing is unpacking boxes and steaming clothes. I dressed for comfort."

"I'm glad you're doing that today. Tomorrow, when the stores open, there'll be fresh merchandise on the shelves. From now till Christmas, we're going to be selling like crazy." His eyes shone avariciously.

"Seth Kirchoff! How very greedy you are. And it isn't even your holiday."

"I give Chanukah presents, don't I?"

They were still bantering back and forth when George helped roll "the chariot" into the service entrance of the store, where workers were assembled with Christmas decorations, awaiting instructions from Seth and Kirchoff's window dresser. Everyone got busy.

"Hey, I like that," Seth said from behind Kathleen several

hours later as she was hanging up a soft yellow suit. "Be sure and keep one of those out for yourself."

"I already have," she said impishly. "I liked it, too."

"You see, two great minds always run on the same course."

The telephone on her desk rang and she reached to pick it up. "Hello."

"Kathleen?"

Her heart jumped crazily as it always did when she recognized the deep rumble of Erik's voice. Since the scene between him and Seth in front of the basketball goal, she had seen little of him. Miraculously, and because manufacturers wanted to stay in good graces with Kirchoff's, the samples Kathleen asked for had been shipped and received. Erik was frantically trying to tie up all the loose ends concerning the trip before his departure date next week.

"Hello, Erik," she said in a casually friendly tone. "How did you know where to find us?"

"I called the house and Alice said you were working today. I had the number of your office telephone."

How had he gotten that? she wondered.

He caught her attention again when he said, "Say, I just got home. I wasn't here last night. Your and Seth's gift was waiting for me on my front porch. Luckily, someone didn't steal it. I wanted to call and say thank you."

"He got the housewarming gift and says 'thank you,' " Kathleen explained to Seth. To Erik, she said, "I ordered it that day we went shopping. You liked it, remember? I . . . we," she amended, "wanted to get you something for your new house."

"It's gonna look great, if I can remember how to hang it. Which end is up?"

"What's he saying?" Seth interrupted.

"He says that he can't figure out how to hang it up." Then, into the receiver, she said, "Don't you remember? The beige part goes on the top—"

"Why don't you go over and show him?" Seth broke in.

"What?" Kathleen exclaimed.

"I didn't say anything," Erik said.

"Not you, Erik," she said in confusion. "I can't," she said to Seth.

"Can't what?" Erik asked.

"Oh, for goodness sake!" she cried. "You two are driving me crazy."

"Give me the phone," Seth said, and grabbed it from her hand. "Erik, what's going on? Did you like the wall hanging? Kathleen described it to me. She liked it, and I trust her judgment." Kathleen chewed on her lip while Seth listened to Erik's reply. She didn't like the direction this was going.

"Well, I think she should go over and help you hang it." There was a silence while he listened and Kathleen held her breath. Erik would probably have plans.

"No, she won't mind. She's finished here. I wanted to hang around until all the decorations were up. I'll send her over." He laughed. "Oh, by the way, you may not recognize her. She looks like a schoolgirl."

He hung up the phone while a dismayed Kathleen listened to his next words with the trepidation of a defendant listening to the decision of the jury. "He would love to have your help. Go on over and I'll see you at home."

"Seth, I don't want to leave you here—"

"Why? Are you afraid I'll get attacked by a giant reindeer?"

"I don't want you to work too hard. You're—"

"Having a ball. I'm all right, Kathleen. Now will you get going? Erik's waiting for you. I'll see you later."

What choice did she have? If she made more of the issue than it warranted, he would wonder why she objected so strenuously to going alone to Erik's house.

She left a few minutes later, pulling on her corduroy jacket against the chill November evening. An ominous fog had rolled in off the Bay and blanketed the city. Her headlights shone on the moisture-slick streets as she drove carefully through the twilight.

Her hands were unaccountably moist on the steering wheel.

She was being silly! Erik no doubt wanted her advice in hanging the artwork, and then she would calmly take her leave. Or maybe he had someone there with him. Tamara? He hadn't spent the night at home last night. He had said so without any explanation as to what or, more appropriately, who had kept him away from home. Had he been with Tamara? Were they warming up for those sun-drenched days in the Caribbean?

By the time she parked her Mercedes—which Seth had given to her soon after their marriage—in front of Erik's condo, she was in a temper. It was with a certain belligerence that Kathleen pressed the button of the doorbell.

Her bad humor wasn't improved when Erik threw open the door and promptly burst out laughing.

"What's so funny?" she demanded, thinking she must have ink on her nose or something even more humiliating.

"I'm sorry, little girl, but I've already bought my Girl Scout cookies. Try me again next year . . . when you're grown up."

"Very funny," she said dryly.

"I thought so," he said cheekily. "Seth warned me that you looked like a schoolgirl. But then, I've seen you this way before. He never saw you at Mountain View." His eyes arrested hers and held them. For a moment, they stared at each other over the space that separated them, each remembering happier days and one moonlit night beside the rapidly flowing river.

To save herself from drowning in those memories, Kathleen tore her eyes away. "No, he never did."

Knowing that the mood was broken, Erik said, "Come in."

She walked past him into the living room. All the furniture they had bought had been delivered. Only the windows remained bare. The room still had the unmistakable sterility of a bachelor's house, but it had improved since the last time she had seen it. There was a cheerful fire burning in the grate, and only one lamp was lit.

"It looks nice," Kathleen commented, thinking that she needed to say something. "You placed the furniture exactly according to my sketch."

"Yeah," Erik said ruefully as he thrust his hands in the back pockets of his tight jeans and surveyed the room with skeptical eyes. "It still needs something."

"A woman's touch," Kathleen said spontaneously, then wished she had weighed that thought before saying it.

If Erik were any kind of gentleman he would ignore the statement. However, he had once told her that he was honorable, not stupid, and apparently that was still his creed. His grin was wolfish as he drawled, "Well, you're a woman. So touch something."

She turned away quickly and slid out of her coat. It was suddenly unbearably hot in the room. "Where is the wall hanging?"

"Right over here. I have it spread out on the floor." She looked on the far side of the sofa where he pointed. "It's really beautiful, Kathleen. I like it even more than when I first saw it. I want to thank you again."

"And Seth," she said quickly. Too quickly. She looked up to catch the pained expression that crossed his face, which was shadowed in the firelight.

"Yes, of course, I meant to include him."

There was an uncomfortable silence as both of them looked at the wall hanging at their feet with the concentration of mystics trying to instill life into an inanimate object. Finally, Kathleen said, "The top of it is here." She knelt down and felt along the rod to which the yarn was attached. "Yes, there are four hooks on the backside of the rod. All we have to do is hammer some nails into the wall." She stood up and brushed off her hands. "Do you have some nails? And a hammer?"

"Out in the van." He was gone only a few seconds when he came back. "I thought you might need this, too," he said, handing her a yardstick.

"How did this suddenly become *my* project?"

"Because you seem to know what you're doing." He smiled. "What can I do?"

"Bring in a ladder."

"Ladder! You don't ask for much, do you?"

She put her hands on her hips, a gesture made provocative by the way it tightened the cloth over her breasts. "Don't tell me you don't have one. How are we supposed to reach up there?" she asked, pointing to the redwood wall that reached a peak in the cathedral ceiling above.

"I see it's back to 'we.' " Erik squinted his eyes as he looked at the wall. "How about a chair? Would that give you enough height to reach the right place?"

She sighed. "I guess so." He went to the kitchen and returned carrying a hardwood chair. "That's nice. Where did you get it?" she asked.

"At the unfinished-furniture store. All I had to do was put a sealer on the chairs and table. They turned out pretty well." He sat the chair down against the wall, then faced her. "Now what?"

She threw him a disparaging look and knelt down with the yardstick to measure the distance between each hook. "Six and three-quarters inches," she murmured. She slipped off her shoes; then, placing her hand on the back of the chair, she gingerly stepped onto it. "Would you say that this seam in the wood marks the center of the wall?"

"Yeah, I think so."

"Okaaay." She drew out the word as she did some mental figuring. She lifted the yardstick over her head until it touched the ceiling and then marked the wall with her fingernail along its side. "That ought to be right," she said. "Hand me the nails and the hammer."

When he had complied, she stuck the nails in her mouth as she drove in the first one. When all were done, she asked, "How are we going to lift it?"

"I'll go get another chair." Erik came back with the chair and, easing his bare feet out of well-worn tennis shoes, lifted the wall hanging as he stepped onto the extra chair.

When all the hooks were secured on the nails, Kathleen said, "Now get down and see if it's straight." Erik obliged and stepped away from her. "How is it?" she asked as she surveyed the artwork.

"It's perfect."

"Do you like it?"

"Very much."

Something in his voice caused Kathleen to turn her head. He wasn't looking at the wall hanging. He was looking at her bottom. "Erik."

"Hmmm?" was his only response as he closed in on her. Before she could react, he had wrapped his arms around her thighs and was rubbing his hands up and down the front of them. "You have the sauciest tush I've ever seen, Kathleen. Why is it that having a baby didn't make you flabby?"

He nuzzled her from the back even as his hands became bolder. He smoothed her hips with his palms and she gasped with shocked delight when she felt the firm clench of his teeth through her jeans on the back of her thigh.

"Erik," she said unsteadily. His hands had worked their way under her shirt and were moving over her ribs. "Erik," she said more forcefully, "I can't stay up on this chair." Indeed, her muscles had been rendered useless by his persistent hands and adventuresome mouth as he continued to nip her through the soft denim.

"Then come down." The words were said simply, but the import of them was unmistakable. With his hands settled on her hips just below her waist, he turned her to face him.

Emerald-green eyes locked with blue and the transmission sizzled with unspoken need. He cupped her hips in each of his hands and drew her abdomen into his chest. Then, his eyes never leaving hers, he undid the bottom button of her shirt and continued upward until all were undone.

"Kathleen." It was a plea. She raised her hands and buried them in his hair, pulling his face into her softness.

He clasped her just under the curve of her bottom and lifted her out of the chair. He didn't set her down until he had carried her to the fireplace. Then, with infinite care, he lowered her to the carpet.

Her own anguished cry of longing echoed his as they came together in a tight embrace. Her mouth opened to receive the plunder of his, welcoming the pain as much as the pleasure. They were a tangle of arms and legs as each sought to bring the other closer, rolling and seesawing on the soft carpet.

Kathleen pulled the bottom of his sweater up over his chest until she felt the hair-roughened skin pressed against her tummy. He helped her as she peeled the garment over his head. Then he eased her out of her blouse and bra. They were flung away without regard.

"No one looks like you," he whispered hoarsely. "No one feels like you, smells like you, tastes like you. God, I want you."

"Touch me, Erik. Let me feel your hands everywhere. Your mouth. It's so good," she cried.

His mouth was hot and urgent as he ravaged her neck, then moved to her ear, aggravating the lobe with his teeth and tickling it with his tongue. His hands celebrated her body, finding without error each curve that he hadn't forgotten and that his memory knew well.

He kissed her breasts with lips on fire. His tongue laved her nipples with the moisture of his mouth. When they were wet and shiny, he brushed them dry with his mustache.

Kathleen made small, imploring noises that sounded like his name. He deftly unsnapped her jeans and worked down the zipper. With her willing assistance, he divested her of the jeans.

His voice was a low rasp as he said, "You're so pretty here." His finger outlined the dark triangle visible through her sheer panties. Kathleen closed her eyes, mesmerized by the pattern his hands were tracing over her. The panties went the way of the jeans. Then there was nothing between them and he was touching her, kissing her, with a familiarity undimmed by the years that had separated them.

"Erik," she groaned. "I haven't forgotten."

"Neither have I, but you're sweeter than I remembered."

Her hands fumbled at the waistband of his jeans and slipped the zipper down. She called his name . . .

The telephone rang.

Chapter Seventeen

❧ ❧

They froze. The telephone rang a second time. A third. Erik eased away from her, cursing expansively and fiercely.

"You . . . you'd better get it," she stammered, rising up to a sitting position. "It may be—"

"Your husband?" he asked bitterly as he jerked the receiver off its cradle.

"Hello," he barked. "No, nothing's wrong, Seth." He looked at Kathleen, who covered her face. "I was standing on a chair and couldn't get to the telephone . . . Yeah, it looks great. Thank you again . . . Yeah, she is a woman of rare talents."

Like a thwarted beast who has been driven beyond his level of tolerance, Erik lashed out viciously at his scapegoat— Kathleen. His anger was unreasonable; it was unjust; but at that point in time, his Scandanavian temper was beyond reason. His face was scornful and mocking as he looked at Kathleen. "Do you want to talk to her? She's available." Everything he said was intended to wound with a double meaning. "Now? . . . Why? . . . Well, I . . ." A heavy sigh. "All right, we'll be right there." He hung up the tele-

248

phone and eyed her with cynical amusement. "You'd better get dressed. Your husband wants to see us."

She had folded her hands across her chest in a gesture of self-protection. It was unfair of him to think the torment was his alone. Instinctively, she reached up and touched his thigh as he stood over her.

At the touch of her hand, he flinched visibly and growled, "Get dressed."

"Erik, I'm sorry. I didn't want it to . . . It's better this way. I couldn't have lived—"

"Lived with yourself if you had been sullied by my love-making?" he finished for her in dulcet tones. Again he cursed viciously, while he paced the room like a caged beast. "Please spare me the guilty conscience. I'm not in a forgiving mood." He glanced down at her and then roared, "Get dressed, god-dammit! Or do you want to be raped? How much do you think I can stand?"

Kathleen scrambled to pick up her underclothes and pulled them on gracelessly. She was shoving her legs into her jeans when she, too, became angry. He was still glaring at her as if she were to blame for the fiasco. She faced him belligerently. "You're the most selfish person I've had the misfortune to know. You don't care about anyone but yourself, Erik!"

"Why should I?" he demanded. "You've taken away my son. I can't have him. Who else should I give a damn for?"

"You . . . you could show a little consideration for me," she said bravely.

He threw back his head and laughed, but there was no humor in it. "Don't tell me. The next question I hear will be 'Do you still respect me?' Right?"

"Oh," she ground out. "You're despicable."

"And what about you, Miss Righteousness? I wasn't using any force down there." He indicated the carpet at their feet. "From now on, I'm not jumping to the bait. I know you for what you are, Kathleen. You derive some perverse pleasure from driving a man to the brink of sanity and then you don't come across. God knows how you must torment poor Seth."

She gasped in mortification and took a step toward him, raising her arm, planning to deliver a stinging slap to his smug face. Her hand was caught in midair.

"At the risk of making my son an orphan, I won't throttle you for trying that. But from now on, you can save yourself the trouble of wagging that sweet little ass in my face, because I'm not interested."

"Go to hell!" she screamed, yanking her arm free.

He laughed. "I've been."

Because she couldn't immediately think of a rejoinder, Kathleen trembled with pent-up rage. Her jaws clamped and she strained each word through grinding teeth. "I don't see how I could ever have let you touch me. You're the most self-centered bastard I've ever known. You think you're God's great gift to women. Let me tell you something." She shook her finger an inch from Erik's nose. "There's more to being a man than virility. Seth is five times the man you'll ever be. He knows what tenderness and compassion and forgiveness are. And I don't think he'd ever try to compromise a friend's wife, either."

The words reverberated in the room like a funeral knell. The silence that followed was ponderous. Erik's head snapped back as though it had been pulled by the sharp tug of a puppet's string. For long moments, neither said anything, only stared at the other.

When Erik finally moved, it was to bring his hands up to cover his face. Kathleen saw his chest rise and fall. He seemed to be starving for air. When he lowered his hands, he said dully, "You are exactly right, Kathleen. My behavior is unforgivable. You may find it hard to accept my apology, but I wish you'd try."

She wanted to rush to assure him that the blame wasn't his alone, but he turned away from her and went to the front door and opened it. Only then did he face her again, his shoulders slumped in dejection.

"It seems I'm not worthy competition for your husband on any level." He didn't wait for her to precede him, but walked out into the night, impervious to the cold. There was nothing to do but follow him.

Each went to his separate car and drove to the Kirchoff residence. When they arrived and walked to the door together, they were less than polite strangers. Tension crackled between them. George met them in the hall and told them Seth was in the den.

"Hello!" Seth called out when they entered. "I'm glad you arrived when you did. George is about to best me in another tournament of chess. I think he cheats, but I'll be damned if I can catch him at it."

George only laughed before he offered to get them all something to drink. Seth declined graciously, Erik and Kathleen with reserved civility.

George retreated, and if Seth noticed the tight, taciturn attitude of his two companions, he didn't show it. He launched directly into why he had asked them to meet with him. When he said what was on his mind, Kathleen fervently prayed that her ears were playing tricks on her.

"I . . . You . . . Seth, have you lost your mind? I can't go to the Caribbean!"

"Why not?"

"Be . . . because I can't, that's why. What would I do there?" She dared not look at Erik to see his reaction to Seth's unthinkable proposal that she accompany the production crew on the trip.

"The modeling agency called me a while ago. The stylist they are sending with the models is frantic. She's afraid that she'll be held responsible if any damage is done to the clothes that will be taken along. More than that, she's sure she won't remember which fashions are supposed to be featured in which commercial and how to coordinate them. She wore me out trying to explain her frustration. Erik, with all your headaches down there, worrying about your cameras, lights, the weather, transportation for twenty people, and so on, you won't have time to think about all of that."

He paused and drew a deep sigh. "Kathleen dearest, you

are the only one I trust, that Erik will trust, to see that every-one has on what they are supposed to have on when he focuses them in his lens."

Kathleen wrung her hands in agitation. She couldn't, she *couldn't*. There was no way she could go on the trip, be in constant contact with Erik after the emotionally wrenching scene in his apartment. Only a glutton for punishment, a masochist, would subject himself to that situation.

"Seth," she laughed lightly, hoping no one heard the un-derlying hysteria, "I can't go on a trip like that at this time of year. You need me here, to help in the stores. Besides, who would take care of Theron? I wouldn't want to leave him for that long. I was miserable without him in New York. He'll think I've deserted him." She hated to use her child as a weapon, but she was engaged in a battle for her sanity, her life.

"I discount each and every argument," Seth said sum-marily. "In the first place, the store has survived decades of holiday seasons, and as valuable as you are, we'll survive this one without you. There will still be almost two weeks before Christmas when you get back. You know as well as I do that Theron is perfectly content to stay under Alice's watchful care. He'll miss you, but he'll get over it the minute you return and won't even remember that you've been gone."

"But, Seth, I don't . . ." She was grasping at straws. *Think!* she commanded herself. "I'm not ready. My passport . . . clothes . . . I couldn't—"

"Your passport is in perfect condition. You had it renewed last year when you and Eliot went to England to buy those woolens. Alice can get your clothes ready in time. When do you leave, Erik? Thursday?" At Erik's nod, he said, "There, you see, you have three days in which to get things together. Eliot can help you pack the clothes and accessories to be used in the commercials."

Kathleen wondered with a detached part of her mind what the two men would do if she started screaming uncontrollably, as she felt she might do at any moment.

"Erik, what do you think? This is your project, after all," Seth said.

Erik's manner was subdued while Seth and Kathleen waited expectantly to hear his answer. "Naturally, she would be a tremendous help. However, I'd never presume to interfere. This is between the two of you. Much as I could use her, Kathleen has to make the decision."

"Kathleen," Seth urged gently, "I need you to do this for me. I'd go myself if I could." He wheeled up close to her chair and took her hands. "I feel that we need a representative from Kirchoff's there. You know the merchandise better than anyone. It'll be hard work, but think of it as a vacation to a tropical climate in December." He smiled and squeezed her hand. "Do this for me."

Put that way, how could she refuse?

The next three days passed in a hazy blur of disjointed recollections. Without Eliot's help, Kathleen could never have coordinated the commercials wardrobe in time and had the clothes packed and ready to board the chartered plane.

Eliot griped petulantly, whining that she couldn't do without him. Why didn't she insist that he go along?

"Because I need you here, Eliot," she answered for the dozenth time. "To look after things."

"It's not fair," he grumbled. "I'd go without salary just for the chance to look at Gudjonsen for a whole week."

"I'm sure Tamara will take care of him."

"That bitch," Eliot scoffed. "I hope he's more discriminating than that. She'd screw anything walking. Four-legged or two."

"Oh, Eliot," Kathleen sighed, and rubbed her forehead wearily. It was a characteristic gesture of hers these days.

Hazel didn't let her go without adding to her anxiety about leaving. One day when everyone else was out to lunch, she slipped into Kathleen's office. Kathleen didn't see her standing in the doorway until she spoke. "So you're winging off to the sunny tropics with the handsome photographer."

Kathleen controlled her suddenly racing heart, schooled her features and answered levelly, "If you're referring to the trip to shoot the commercials, yes, I'm going—at my husband's request."

"Seth is a fool! Doesn't he see how cozy, how easy, he's making it for you and that hulking Gudjonsen? When will you be dropping another bastard on my stupid brother? Hmmm?"

Kathleen had bristled with anger, then quaked with fear. *Could* Hazel know? No. She was only taunting her. Coolly, Kathleen replied, "I don't have to justify to you anything I do, but I have never been unfaithful to Seth. Nor will I be."

"Ha! Given the opportunity, you would. And he's giving you a perfect one. He thinks that by giving you free rein, he'll keep you. He's weak."

"What you regard as weakness is really unselfishness, something totally foreign to you, Hazel. I know where your bitterness comes from. Seth told me about the man who left you standing at the altar. I might be able to sympathize with you if you weren't one of the most hateful people I've ever met. As it is, I can only pity you for the loneliness you bring on yourself."

"Shut up. How dare you pity me! *Me!*" Her face was terrible with hatred. Her whole body quivered with suppressed rage.

Kathleen threw caution aside. She was too wound up, her emotions too raw, to weigh the wisdom of the words she flung at Hazel. "And don't think I don't see through your concern for Seth. It isn't generated by love or even mild affection.

"You resent him because you want to control Kirchoff's. As firstborn, you thought the presidency should have rightfully been passed to you when your father died. He had discounted Seth because of his disability and you because of your sex. When your uncle died and the helm was once again up for grabs, you didn't dare fight Seth for it. It would have been unthinkable for you to engage in a power struggle with your paraplegic brother.

"But perhaps you should have, Hazel. You should have either battled him for it then or learned to live with your decision. You are your own worst enemy, not me. I had nothing to do with your being jilted, or being passed over by your father. Seth loves you. Why, I can't imagine, but I don't intend to interfere with or alter your relationship."

Hazel's eyes narrowed and her nostrils flared when she threatened, "I'll trip you up yet. And the day's coming. When I do, my brother will have to see you for what you are. That will destroy him, and when he's down, I'll get mine. I'll be in control of Kirchoff's." She spun around and stormed from the office, leaving Kathleen more afraid of the woman's mental imbalance than ever before. Hazel was out to win in a contest of wills and would risk anything for victory.

The evening before they were scheduled to leave, Kathleen spent every moment with Theron. Erik had come by earlier and played with him on the living room floor, much to Hazel's disgust and everyone else's delight.

Kathleen watched their tussles with pride in her son and fear that Erik would try to steal Theron from her. It was evident in everything he did that he loved the boy. They were carbon copies of each other. Kathleen only hoped that to everyone else the likeness was less obvious.

Erik left, saying that he would see them in the morning at the airport. Kathleen went up with Alice and tucked Theron into his bed. She would see him again before she left, but there was something special about kissing him goodnight.

"Mamma," he said as she switched off the light.

"Goodnight, my precious," she whispered as she leaned over him one more time and kissed his cheek. She pulled back in dismay. The scent of Erik's cologne still clung to Theron's pajamas. A wave of longing swept over her.

Thoroughly put out with herself for feeling desire for Erik even after having suffered his verbal abuse, she went dispiritedly to her room and began getting ready for bed.

Why must he be so disturbingly, beautifully male? Why was everything he did made to look effortless? He was competent in his work. The first series of commercials he had produced for Kirchoff's were so well done that her heart burst with pride each time she saw one of them.

But he was no knight in shining armor. He had one major flaw. He had admitted it to Seth. He was selfish.

Was that so surprising?

He was a fair-haired child, a golden boy. He had always had things going more or less his way. He had everything he wanted. Now he wanted her, but when she resisted him, he had resorted to contempt. And what would he do about Theron? More than anything, she feared him on that point. He loved his son. To what lengths would he go to have him?

She looked herself squarely in the eye in the mirror over her bathroom sink and asked aloud, "Are you any better than he is?" She wanted him just as much as he obviously wanted her. Unfaithfulness went against everything she believed in and adhered to. Fidelity to one's spouse was an elemental dogma to her. Hadn't that been the one thing that she could never have tolerated from Erik? When she thought he was married, she had run.

It was different with her, though, she thought piously. It wasn't a trivial sexual dalliance she wanted. She loved Erik. Didn't she? Or was she so self-righteous, as he had accused, that she wanted to convince herself that she loved him? Was that only a sanctimonious excuse for the blood that coursed through her veins, looking for an outlet every time she saw Erik, felt his touch?

Did she really love Erik? Or was she only a woman whose natural, healthy sex drive worked overtime whenever a man as attractive as Erik was around?

❧ ❧

She stood in the dimly lit den and tapped timidly on the door. She had never been invited into this room, and her heart was thudding so loudly that she barely heard Seth's "George?"

She swallowed her shyness and answered softly, "No, it's Kathleen."

There was a long, stunned pause, then the soft whisper of bedclothes before he said, "Come in."

She put down her last shred of caution and opened the door, going into Seth's bedroom for the first time. She knew she looked alluring. Her hair was brushed to a silky sheen and hung beguilingly on her bare shoulders. Her diaphanous nightgown of a sea-foam color wafted around her figure as she walked on bare feet toward the wide bed.

All the lights, save the bedside lamp, had been turned out when George quitted the room. Seth's image was diffused in the soft light, or it could have been the blur of tears in Kathleen's eyes that prevented her from seeing him well.

"Kathleen," he whispered, "you look beautiful."

"I hope I'm not disturbing you, Seth." Of course she was disturbing him. Suddenly, she felt rather silly, but was resolved to banish Erik Gudjonsen from her mind once and for all.

"Is something wrong?"

Did she look that upset? "No," she answered softly. By now, she had reached the bed and was looking down at him. Seth was sitting up with a book resting across his lap. He was barechested. She had seen him in swimming trunks when he and George did their therapy in the pool, but she was forever amazed at how well developed the muscles of his arms and chest were. There was a light sprinkling of dark hair, not nearly as much as—

"Seth," she said, and hesitantly sat down on the side of the bed with her hip snugly against the curve of his waist. "Seth," she repeated, not sure where to start. She had never seduced anyone before. Erik didn't count. He had been the seducer "I'm going to miss you while I'm gone."

"I'm going to miss you, too." He smiled, using those beautiful teeth set in his dark, shadowed face, the mouth that curved so magnanimously, the gentle eyes that constantly bespoke contentment in spite of his handicap.

"Are you?" Kathleen laid her hand on his chest. She gently

plucked at the sparse hair, then moved her fingers restlessly, nervously, across the sculpted muscles.

"Yes," he answered.

She leaned over him then and kissed him on the lips. Her breasts, covered only by the sheer nightgown that didn't hide the dusky nipples, brushed against his chest. Sacrificing pride for the sake of her cause, she moved her mouth over his, inviting his lips to open, to kiss her in a way they had never kissed before. When he hesitantly complied, her tongue slipped between his teeth.

His hands were at her shoulders, and he was pushing her away. "Kathleen, Kathleen, why are you doing this?" he asked, pained.

"You love me, Seth," she said desperately.

"Yes. More than my life. You know I do."

"I love you. I want . . . I want to . . . to make love to you." She looked down at her hands still resting on his chest.

The silence was palpable. The two people on the bed were as immovable as statues. Finally, Seth spoke barely above a whisper. "You want the impossible, Kathleen. You know that. Why are you tormenting me?"

"I don't intend to torment you. I want to love you and have you love me."

"Here," he pointed to his temple, "I want to more than I want to live tomorrow. But you know that I can't. If I were able to, do you think I would have abstained for two years?" he asked incredulously.

"Seth," she said urgently before she lost her nerve, "I know that we can't be conventional lovers. That we can't . . . you know . . . There are other ways that I could please you and you me."

"Kathleen—"

She stood up abruptly and whisked the nightgown over her head until she stood before him naked in the soft light. He sucked in his breath sharply, and she saw his fists clench tightly at his sides. "Kathleen," he breathed.

She sat down beside him again and lifted one of his hands,

pressing it to her breast. For long moments, he stared up into her face, wondering if she were indeed a haunting dream. Would he wake up again, discovering, as always, that he could only feel those stirrings in his sleep, but never again in his life? Then his eyes dropped to his hand and her soft breast. He stared at it in awe, not trusting himself to believe that he was actually caressing Kathleen's flesh.

His other hand covered her breast. She leaned over him and kissed him again. This time, Seth's response wasn't as long in coming. His mouth took hers greedily and savored the taste of her. His hands moved, caressingly, lovingly.

Kathleen welcomed his touch and encouraged it as she lay across his chest and made herself accessible to whatever exploration he desired. His hands roamed over her back, around her rib cage and down her stomach. The softness of her belly knew his tender search. Then he dipped lower and touched the hidden femininity he had denied himself even to think about.

"Oh, my God," he ground out as he clasped her to him tightly. Then, just as suddenly, she was released. In alarm, she sat up. Seth's head was pressed back into the pillow, his eyes squeezed shut, his teeth bared in a terrible grimace of pain more agonizing than any he had felt since the fatal night of his accident.

"Seth?" The panic in her voice caused him to open his eyes.

"Kathleen," he gasped. "I'm sorry, but don't ask this of me. Please."

"I'm sorry," she sobbed.

"No, dear heart, *I'm* sorry." He pulled her down to his chest again, but it was in comfort, not passion. "Kathleen, before my accident, I was quite a good lover, I think. At least, several ladies thought so." She could hear the humor in his voice. "I know what I could do for you. I could bring you temporary relief from the desire you're feeling, but I couldn't ever give you what you would ultimately want. And I could never stand to deny you anything. Do you understand?

Please don't ask me to bastardize the way a man and a woman should love.''

"Seth," she mumbled into his chest, and wept. Her tears manifested her deepest despair. She had been wrong to use Seth this way. It was unkind and unfair. He was no witch doctor. He was no magician, and if he were the most powerful exorcist, he couldn't have rid her of Erik. She had known that the moment Seth touched her. Her body still belonged to Erik. It hadn't responded to Seth's gentle touch, and that was a profound grief to her. She owed this man so much.

"Seth, I'm so ashamed. I never meant to hurt you."

"I know, my love. My dearest love."

"We love on a higher plane than others," she said.

His rueful laugh tickled her ear, which was pressed against his chest. "I'm not sure of that. If I could give you a strong, healthy body, I would gladly trade this high plane of love for one more base. But no one could love you more than I, Kathleen."

"I know."

Seth held her for as long as she stayed with him. She cried softly into the curve of his neck. Her murmurings were often incoherent and random. She never knew when she sleepily whispered another's name. But Seth heard it. The shattered expression on his face reflected the heartache he felt inside. For himself and for his beloved.

Chapter Eighteen

Kathleen sat under the thatch-roofed table in a relaxed position and wished she felt as calm on the inside as she looked on the outside. They were taking a break. Everyone in the crew was lounging around the patio at Harry's Bar, which overlooked the Atlantic. Kathleen was covertly watching Erik and Tamara, who had separated themselves from the others and walked down to the rocky beach alone.

Harry's wasn't quite as famous as the Harry's Bar in Venice, but to tourists from the United States it was well known on Grand Bahama Island as a place to buy an American hamburger. Located midway between West End and Freeport, it was a good stopover for a cool tropical drink, beer, or a full lunch or dinner.

One of the lighting crew brought Kathleen a paper cup of goombay punch. She sipped it tentatively. It was fruity and cool, but she knew too many glasses could hit one like a sledge hammer. It was the most dangerous of alcoholic drinks, for there was no alcohol taste.

The drink didn't extinguish the fire that had been smoldering and simmering inside Kathleen for the past few days.

Every time she saw Erik and Tamara together, she boiled with jealous anger. The blonde couldn't keep her hands off him. When he was giving directions to her or any of the other models, she chose to drape herself over him like a vine rather than standing straight and listening as he talked to them in a brisk, professional tone.

He wasn't immune to her attention, though. He was flirtatious with all the models, getting them to do exactly as he asked. Erik's patience with them knew no bounds. But his flirting with Tamara had taken on the attitude of blatant invitation. Each look, each touch that passed between the two of them was rife with innuendo. *They are probably sleeping together already*, Kathleen thought bitterly as she heard Tamara's pealing laughter coming from the direction of the beach. When she couldn't resist looking toward them, she saw the model perched on a high rock. Erik's strong, lean arms were reaching up to lift her down.

Kathleen turned her head away to hide the tears that flooded her eyes. She must get over this. She had no justification for being jealous. She was married and Erik had made it eminently clear how he felt about her. There was no future for them and never had been. He didn't love her.

But she loved him. That was why she was jealous. She couldn't stand to see anyone else touching the body she felt belonged to her. She wanted no one else to know the caress of his eyes or the persuasion of his mouth.

Erik and Tamara were climbing the steps up to the patio now, and he was calling everyone back to work. Harry's had been selected as a taping sight for its stunning view of the surf, its thatched-roofed tables and its convenient location.

Now the serene patio was crawling with active people. The lights, mounted on their stands, had been switched off to cool. Seeming miles of cable ribboned the patio, connecting cameras to recorders and lights to electrical outlets. Heavy metal boxes in which the equipment was hauled from one location to another were positioned in such a way to threaten life or limb should anyone trip over them. It was controlled chaos.

The lighting team was turning on the huge lights again. Erik was adjusting his camera's tripod, spreading his legs wide to reduce his height so he could be eye level with the viewfinder. The stylist was bustling around the models, adjusting a strap here, smoothing a lapel there. Today the girls were arrayed in safari-look clothes in shades of green, khaki and beige. Kathleen had selected accent colors of bright red, yellow and white. The makeup artist, who looked more like a housemother in a sorority, weaved her way among the models, checking for imperfections and imagining them if they weren't there. The hair stylist, whose only masculine attribute was a thin, pointed beard, flitted through the crowd wielding his hairbrushes with the flourish of a matador finessing his cape.

Erik had brought four production assistants with him. Two of them took care of the lighting. The other two did everything. They seemed to anticipate Erik's every need, handing him filters, fetching him extension cords, replacing boxes of tape when one was filled. Kathleen liked them all, and they all seemed to worship Erik. She watched one now as he shimmied up a tree to pluck off a broad leaf that was casting a shadow on one model's face.

"Tamara, this isn't a stag film," Erik was saying.

Tamara was perched on the wall surrounding the patio. She was wearing a pair of army-green shorts and a white blazer. Beneath the blazer, she had on a red halter top. The ocean breeze was catching the light fabric of the top until her left breast was completely exposed. There were good-natured wolf calls from the crew, and the other models guffawed. Tamara was brazenly unaffected.

Kathleen had been appalled by the girl's immodesty. Just the day before, they had all driven to the casino in Freeport, where Erik wanted to feature the formal wear. Unlike its American counterparts in Las Vegas, the croupiers and dealers wore tuxedos and the atmosphere was austere and very British.

Tamara had stormed out of the makeshift dressing room

wearing only a pair of bikini panties and carrying the black satin gown she was to model.

"What in the hell is wrong with this?" she had demanded of a stunned Kathleen. Every eye in the room turned to the two of them.

Kathleen was too astounded at the girl's nakedness to answer at first. "What's wrong with what?" she stammered.

"This goddam dress. It's supposed to fit, but it's too tight in the ass. Who the hell is responsible for that mistake, Mrs. Kirchoff?" She said the name with a slur, and Kathleen had a hard time keeping her hand from connecting with Tamara's carefully made-up cheek.

"Didn't you try the dress on last night as you were supposed to?" Kathleen asked icily. "If there were any alterations to be made, that's when they were to have been done. I didn't bring along a sewing machine just to look at."

"I was busy last night," Tamara had drawled, and winked slyly over Kathleen's shoulder. Kathleen turned around and saw Erik leaning against a crap table, his arms folded, his brows raised in interest at the scene being played out before him. Or was his interest on Tamara's bare breasts, which hung free and in sight of everyone, including the shocked staff of the casino, who were held spellbound and incapable of objecting to the dazzling display?

"What do you suggest I do with it?" Tamara demanded.

Kathleen had an excellent suggestion, but she refrained from saying it. "I suggest," she said calmly, "that you either not be in this commercial, or that you wear the dress, but keep your . . . back . . . from the camera, or that you swap dresses with one of the other girls. A larger dress," Kathleen added cattily.

Tamara's amber eyes narrowed on Kathleen. "It's a faulty garment. I'm a perfect eight."

"More like an imperfect ten," Kathleen shot back.

"You—"

"Ladies," Erik said from behind them, "I suggest that we go on with our work. We've got to be out of here by four o'clock. Tamara, go put something on. As lovely as you are, my dear, this is neither the time nor the place to flaunt that exquisite body. If you can wear the dress at all, put it on. We'll shoot so your derriere doesn't show."

Tamara had flounced off, her breasts and hair bouncing in synchronization. The commercial had been completed, but Tamara was an object of derision for the rest of the day. As one of the crew teased her, "Tamara, you'll be the butt of all the jokes today. No pun intended, of course." Tamara glared at him in a frightening way.

Now, she was again causing a sensation, standing on the wall of the patio, the wind whipping the garment away from her body in a way much more suggestive than her total nudity the day before.

Erik, having been ignored as yet, instructed her patiently, "Do something with the damn blouse." Kathleen heard just the slightest edge of asperity in his voice.

"Well, *I* don't know what to do with it," Tamara pouted.

Erik turned on his heels and scanned the crowd before his eyes lighted on Kathleen. "Kathleen, would you please . . ."

He let his voice trail off, but the implicit request was clear. She was tempted to tell him to do it himself or go to hell, but she didn't. She crossed the patio to the wall. She planted her hands on her hips as she stared up at the model. "Well, I'm not coming up there," she told Tamara, who remained where she was.

Sulkily, Tamara climbed down and presented her chest to Kathleen, who recognized the problem immediately and knew that the whole delay could have been avoided. "You haven't tied the straps tight enough." She walked around Tamara and stood up on tiptoe to reach beneath the blazer to the neck straps of the halter. She loosened the ineffectual knot that Tamara had tied, then made another, pulling the cloth tighter over the model's breasts.

"That's too tight," Tamara objected.

"I agree," Kathleen said. "You're too big to wear a halter, but no one will be able to tell that in the commercial."

"I've about had it with you," Tamara cried, whirling around and bearing down on Kathleen. "No one can be too big! You'd do well with a little more yourself. I—"

"Tamara!" Erik's imperative voice sliced through the air. "Haven't you held us up long enough? Get back up on that damn wall and flash me a smile. Thank God you can't smile and talk at the same time."

There was a twitter of laughter from everyone else as the model resumed her position. "Thank you," Erik said to Kathleen as she passed him.

"You're welcome," was her cool reply.

It had been that way since they left San Francisco. For the week in Ocho Rios, Jamaica, and now on Grand Bahama Island, he had been polite, considerate and detached. They treated each other like strangers who had been brought together to do a professional job, except perhaps with more restraint. Each night, he came to her suite of rooms and went over what he called his shot list for the next day. She checked it against her list of clothes and accessories for each model, making sure that they coincided with what he needed. When they were finished, he would thank her, wish her a goodnight and then leave her alone. They didn't share meals, coffee breaks or unnecessary conversation.

The vacancy in her heart grew until she feared that soon she would be completely empty. The more constrained the relationship became, the more she knew that she loved him. Had she ever doubted it before, it was an undeniable fact now. What she felt for Erik wasn't only a longing for sexual fulfillment. She loved the man.

Yet her love for Erik didn't diminish her love for Seth. What she felt for Seth was real and pure and strong. She loved Seth like a dear brother. He was precious to her; she treasured the love she knew he had for her and Theron.

But she loved Erik more. If Seth had her heart, Erik had her soul. He wasn't aware of it, though.

Each day, he seemed to move further away from her, yet conversely, her love grew. She loved watching him work. He was competent, demanding as much from his subordinates as he gave himself. He worked endlessly, redoing scenes until he was satisfied that the result was the best that could be done. He had an artist's drive for perfection.

His body had been burned to a rich copper by the tropical sun in just the few days he had been exposed to it. As his skin tanned darker, his hair bleached lighter. He rarely wore more than a ragged pair of shorts and a T-shirt that had been cut off to cover only his shoulders and the top part of his chest. By midmorning, it had usually been taken off. It was only at dinner that Kathleen saw him dressed in slacks and a sport shirt.

West End Resort on Grand Bahama Island had been chosen for its complete facilities and its fabulous swimming pool. In the evenings, the crew would congregate around the pool to swim, play cards, converse and drink. It was a congenial group. What few men there were had taken full advantage of the most cooperative of the models and had switched bed partners several times. Kathleen thought she knew who Erik's partner was.

There were no more interruptions that day, and they finished the taping at Harry's Bar just as storm clouds appeared on the western horizon. It had briefly showered on them nearly each afternoon, but these clouds seemed more ominous. Erik hustled to gather his precious equipment, barely breathing until he had safely packed everything.

The caravan was just pulling into the parking lot of the resort when the storm broke. Everyone grabbed what they could out of the cars and dashed for their rooms. Since Kathleen needed space to work and store the clothing, Erik had arranged for her to have a suite of rooms in a group of single-story buildings away from the main hotel. Luckily, she was able to pull the rented station wagon under a covering over the sidewalk. She unloaded the back of it, only getting the clothes slightly damp from the torrential rains before she was inside. Somehow, though, she managed to get soaked.

Gladly, she made a final last trip to the car and carried the last bundle inside. She'd move the illegally parked car later. She shut the room door, but almost immediately there was a knock on it. Her heart somersaulted when she pulled it open and saw Erik standing on the threshold with dripping clothes and wet, clinging hair.

"Hi," he said. "Did you get in okay?"

"Yes," she replied as she moved aside. "Come in."

He squished his way into her room and she shut the door. "Let me turn the air conditioning off, or you're going to freeze." She reached behind him to the wall thermostat.

He felt the brush of her arm against his back. He flinched in reaction. God! When was he going to get over wanting her? Hadn't this purgatory lasted long enough? Or would it go on for eternity? He watched her as she walked to the table and switched on the lamp to relieve the gloom brought on by the rainfall.

When she faced him again, the sheer sight of her was like an assault. She was wearing a pair of green shorts and a green and white striped T-shirt, sleeveless and V-necked. Didn't she know that the shirt was damp from the rain and was conforming to her figure like a second skin? Why in the hell had she chosen today to go without a bra? Did she know her legs were better than any of the models'? Her skin was satin and tanned to the color of ripe apricots. She had kicked off her sandals and stood barefoot. Her toenails were painted a delicate coral.

His eyes came back to her face, studiously avoiding her pouting breasts. Her eyelashes must have been rained on, for they were wet and spikey, and outlined the green luminescence of her eyes. Her lips were partially open, and he thought he could hear small, rapid breaths passing in and out of them. It was the most kissable mouth he had ever encountered, and he almost ached with the desire to close the distance between them and weld his starved lips to it.

Why her? Why, out of all the women he had had in his life, was it she who wouldn't leave his mind? After all that had happened between them, why couldn't he hate her? She had carried his child and bore him in secret. It was only by a quirk of fate that he'd learned of his son's existence.

Erik had been deliberately vicious in his verbal attack on her that evening in his house. He had wanted her to suffer, too. His words had intentionally insulted her, her womanhood. She had dealt him a low blow with her lashing comeback. Painful as the truth was to face, Kathleen had been right. It was wrong for them to betray Seth. It was wrong, and yet . . . Could either of them help the attraction that pulled them together like a magnet?

She had been created to love physically, hard and often. What must her life be like with Seth, whom Erik knew she adored? Was that why her eyes were often sad? He knew her natural disposition was to laugh, to tease. Yet she wasn't the same happy young woman he had met in Arkansas. She was mature, resigned. Had motherhood done that to her? Or was she harboring deep regrets?

However they had each changed, one thing had not. He still wanted her as much as he ever had. His longing for her had changed, though. And that new dimension to it alarmed him. His want had become need. Her approval of him had become tantamount to his peace of mind. Her compliments for his work were far more valuable than the money paid for it. He desired her body, but he wanted her caring, too. Sometimes—often—he longed for the touch of her gentling, comforting hands that soothed Theron. Erik refused to believe he would never know that touch.

She was his. The thought of another man having her enraged him. She was his and so was his son. No one—

"Erik?" she asked tentatively.

He realized then that his face must have shown some of what he was feeling, but he quickly masked it. He wasn't ever going to show her again how much he cared. He had been made a fool of too many times.

"I came to tell you that I've checked with the weather bureau and it looks like we're in for at least twenty-four hours of this typhoon. I've given everyone the day off tomorrow. I was told by a few what they thought of having a rainy day off, but . . .'' he shrugged eloquently and grinned, ''I'm the boss.''

''Are things going well? Do you like what you've done?''

His eyes sparkled with excitement as they always did when he talked about his work. ''Yeah. I started to—'' He broke off suddenly. He was about to tell her that he had wanted to call her to his room to watch the tapes he had shot. At the last minute, he had resisted the temptation. He didn't want to be in the same room with her in the dark and not be able to claim her as his, which brought another question to his mind.

''Have you called home?''

''I called the night before last and everything was fine. I'm going to call again tonight. Theron—'' She stopped suddenly.

''Yes? What?''

''He has a new tooth,'' she told him. ''Right here.'' She pointed to her own teeth.

''No kidding!'' Erik laughed. ''That boy'll be eating steak before long.''

Kathleen laughed, too. ''He already does.''

''Yeah?''

''Ground steak, of course.''

''Oh, of course.'' Erik chuckled. ''I guess I don't know too much about babies.'' The words had been said lightly, but they hung between them.

Kathleen looked away from him as she mumbled, ''No, I guess not.''

Only the sound of the rain alleviated the silence until Erik said, ''I'll park your car if you'll give me the key.''

''Thank you.'' Kathleen dropped her keys into his outstretched hand without touching him.

''Stay close by, with this weather the way it is.''

''I will.''

He nodded and then turned, opened the door and dashed out into the rain.

Kathleen finally got all the clothes and accessories back into their proper boxes just before it was time to go to the dining room for the evening buffet. She thought about having a tray brought to her, but decided that would call more attention to her than if she went to dinner and tried to cover her despondent mood. She didn't think she could stand too many private moments with Erik the way they had been this afternoon. For him to be so close to her physically, but so far away in every other way, was a torture she didn't want to bring on herself if she could help it.

She dressed, went to the dining room and joined a trio of the models at their table. When she was finished eating, Kathleen excused herself and returned to her room, trying to become engrossed in a made-for-television movie being broadcast from a Miami station.

Convincing herself that her despondency was the result of fatigue, she went to bed early, but tossed restlessly for a while before she decided to take a stroll out onto the fishing pier. Maybe that would tire her enough mentally to put her to sleep.

She stepped into a short terry-cloth jump suit and, walking barefoot, skirted the pool area and made her way along the shadowed walkways toward the pier that extended out over the crystal-clear water. The rain had stopped momentarily, but heavy, rolling clouds still scuttled overhead, only letting the moon shine intermittently.

It was during one such moonlit moment, just as she was turning around to go back to her room, that she saw Erik. He was lying on a blanket, very near where the water was lapping the beach with a lacy foam.

There was no mistaking his form. She would have known it on the darkest night. He was wearing only the briefest of bathing trunks and, supporting himself on his elbows, was staring out over the water. A deep chuckle rumbled out of his chest. Kathleen glanced at the sea, searching for something that he could have found so amusing when he was all alone.

But he wasn't. Tamara was rising out of the water, naked and shimmering in the moonlight. Her hair looked like a silver stole thrown over her shoulders and back.

"Aren't you afraid you might step on a sea urchin out there in the dark?" Erik called to her.

"If I do, you'll come save me." Their voices carried across the water and it was apparent they didn't know they had an audience.

"Like hell I will," Erik said. "I'm too relaxed and lazy."

Tamara's tinkling laugh reached Kathleen's ears like the sound of splintering glass. "I know how to get you unrelaxed."

"You can try," Erik challenged. By this time, Tamara was standing over him, dripping water on his torso.

"That's the most fun part," she said.

Kathleen couldn't bear to watch any more after Tamara collapsed onto the blanket beside him. She ran with stumbling footsteps to her suite.

"I ought to fire that bitch!" she screamed to the walls. "After all, I am Mrs. Kirchoff. I'm in charge, aren't I? Don't I represent Seth? And Seth hired Erik. I'll go out there right now and fire her." But even as she turned and put her hand on the doorknob, her resolve evaporated. She wasn't about to return to the beach, knowing what she'd find there. And she wouldn't fire Tamara either. She wouldn't give Erik the satisfaction of knowing she was jealous.

Without thinking of the consequences, she went into the bedroom and pulled one of her suitcases from the rack in the closet and began throwing things into it. When she had taken only what she needed, she left her room and made her way to the resort's lobby. It had started raining hard again.

"I need to leave here tonight. What flights do you have coming into your airport?"

The sleepy night clerk scratched his head. "I don't know, let's see. The weather and all . . ." He trailed off meaningfully. "In the morning, you can get on the plane to San Juan. It leaves at seven. But with the weather—"

"Can someone take me to the airport tonight? I'll wait there."

"I guess he can, but, madam, why don't you—"

"Where is the limousine driver?" she asked imperiously.

"He was in the bar the last time—"

"Thank you. I'm with Mr. Gudjonsen's party. If he needs to get into my room before I return, you may give him a key."

She found the reluctant driver, though he grumbled about having to leave his drink and drive someone to the airstrip when there wasn't even a plane there.

She sat in the deserted building all night. In the morning, she waited patiently for the scheduled flight and was thankful when it was only forty-five minutes late. The rain was still torrential.

The flight to San Juan was extremely uncomfortable, and Kathleen feared that at any moment the aircraft would be plunged into the ocean. Puerto Rico wasn't her final destination, however, for it was too commercial. She wanted seclusion. She asked for information at a booth in the airport.

"You may want to consider Chub Cay. It's a privately owned island," the lady behind the counter informed her. "The resort area is comparatively small. The island is still being developed, but it is lovely and secluded, as you expressed a wish for."

"Yes," said Kathleen. "How do I get there?"

"They're only flying one plane today and it leaves in . . ." she checked a schedule, "twenty minutes."

Kathleen raced to the ticket counter of the island-hopping airline and purchased a ticket. Her heart sank when she saw the airplane. It was about half the size of the one she had just deboarded. Every time she saw a plane now, she remembered watching Erik's jet taxiing down the runway at Fort Smith and the disastrous crash. She had never been comfortable about flying since. Especially in the rain.

What would have happened had that airplane not been involved in an accident? Would Erik have come back that evening? Perhaps over dinner they would have talked about his brother and Sally.

Remorse lay heavy on her heart as she boarded the aircraft.

Blessedly, the flight was brief and she was soon checked into the island resort. For absolute privacy, she had chosen to stay in a cabin away from the main lodge.

Kathleen was driven by a bellman in a golf cart to her door and helped inside the cozy room that overlooked the ocean, then she collapsed onto the bed in exhaustion. The sleep that she had denied herself the night before finally made its claim.

Cacophonous thunder awakened her in the early evening. She walked to the window and pulled the drapes open. The rain was a heavy curtain through which she could barely see. Feeling rested and safe, she went into the tiny bathroom and took a reviving shower. As she brushed through her hair, she thought about calling home, but decided against it. She would call in the morning. Tonight she wanted to be by herself.

She pulled on the terry-cloth jump suit again. The downy yellow color complemented her renewed tan. She curled into the bed and situated the pillow behind her, picking up a paperback book she had quickly purchased at a newsstand in the airport in San Juan.

The storm intensified. The thunder was closer and the crackling of lightning popped in an alarming fashion. She went to the window and reached to pull the draw cord of the drape. Her hand froze as she saw someone running pell-mell through the drenching rain. He staggered against the force of the wind, but still he barreled on.

Her heart lurched to her throat when she realized that the apparition was coming straight for her door. Kathleen barely had time to whirl around in terror before her door crashed open and Erik burst through it.

His jeans and shirt were sodden, and his hair was plastered to his head. He gasped in great, heaving breaths, making his chest rise and fall like a bellows. Raindrops dripped from his earlobes and nose and eyebrows. His hands were balled into fists at his thighs. He glared at Kathleen, who cowered against the windowsill, less afraid of the elements now than of him.

He was a true son of Thor, spawned from the god of thunder during a storm. His eyes were as cold as any North wind. His face was terrible. It was the dark face of vengeance, intent on having revenge on some poor misguided soul who had had the audacity to offend the gods.

"I ought to beat the hell out of you," he growled.

As an ominous refrain, the door slammed behind him.

Chapter Nineteen

er initial fear was replaced by anger, generated by jealousy and frustration. Moving away from the false security of the window, she faced him defiantly, her body straining with suppressed fury. "Get out of here and leave me alone."

"Oh, no, Mrs. Kirchoff. Not after I've risked my life to get here. I'm not about to leave until I've done what I came to do."

Her face paled in spite of her claim to despise him. "You flew out here during *this*?" She indicated the storm outside. "How?"

"I found a pilot with more greed than good sense and bribed him. I left him in the men's room at the airstrip. He's not feeling too well."

"You were crazy to come here. And you've wasted your time and your money and your heroic effort. I don't want to see you. Please leave my room."

He laughed wickedly. "No way."

He took two menacing steps toward her, and to postpone what she now thought to be inevitable, she asked hurriedly, "How did you find me? I didn't tell anyone where I was going."

"You have a bad habit of doing that, Mrs. Kirchoff," he sneered. "This time, you didn't cover your tracks very well. I'll admit when I arrived in San Juan and couldn't find you registered at a hotel, I lost your trail for a while, but it wasn't too hard to get back on it when I started asking around for a . . . never mind what I asked for. I've found you." His mouth narrowed into a hard, bitter line. His drenched clothes had formed a puddle around his feet that squished when he came closer to her. "Why did you run away without leaving word with anyone?" His eyes speared into hers, pinning her against the window.

Kathleen swallowed a lump of fear. He wouldn't hurt her. She knew that. Didn't she? "I . . . I was tired. I needed to get away for a while. I was intending to be back by the time you started taping again. Aren't I entitled to a day off like everyone else?" she asked haughtily.

"Yes, but you were the only one who chose to leave like a sneaking thief in the middle of the night without letting anyone know that you were going. You were the only one who deserted the rest of the crew, leaving the leader of said crew to worry out of his mind. Do you think that's responsible behavior, Mrs. Kirchoff?"

"Stop calling me that as if it were an epithet!" she snapped.

His smile was insolent. "Are you ashamed of your name, Mrs. Kirchoff? Or are you ashamed of how you came to have it? Poor old Seth has never been able to sample your wares, has he? For the life of me, I can't figure out why a decent guy like him bailed you out when you were carrying my baby."

"Shut up!" She shoved away from the window and moved to a small chest of drawers, keeping her back to him. "Someone like you wouldn't understand an honorable man like Seth. All men aren't as spoiled and selfish as you. Nor as base, thinking only of one thing with the single-mindedness of an adolescent boy."

"What makes you an expert on what I'm thinking? Huh?" He was following her around the room. Each time Kathleen moved, he was behind her, trailing her, stalking her, leaving a wet path behind him.

"If I don't know what's on your mind, I'm sure Tamara could tell me. I see she made it back to shore last night without stepping on any sea urchins!" She angrily resumed her original position at the window. The thunder and lightning had stopped, but torrents of rain continued to beat the sand and surf. The wind bent the palm trees to drastic angles.

Erik quirked an inquisitive eyebrow. "You were spying on us?" he asked with amusement.

Kathleen spun around and faced him again, furious. "No! I couldn't sleep, so I took a walk out on the pier. You certainly weren't difficult to spot. You obviously weren't concerned about being observed. Before the scenario became too graphically disgusting, I left."

"Then you don't really know what happened, do you?"

"I can guess."

"Jealous?"

"J— Jealous," she sputtered. "You must be kidding!"

"No, I'm not. You ran away because you couldn't stand to see me with Tamara."

"I couldn't stand to see two adults acting like . . . like naughty children! You must have a *thing* for making love near the water."

The moment the words left her mouth, Kathleen wished she could recall them. Her bosom heaved with emotion and anger as they stared each other down. Now Erik knew that she remembered—cherished—the time he had made love to her near the river.

He stared at her from under lowered brows and his voice was gruff when he said, "So, you remember."

Her heart was pounding and she wanted to drag her eyes away from him, but they refused the commands of her confused brain. "Yes." She ducked her head. "It would have been better if it had never happened."

"Would it?"

Her head came up with a jerk and she said with feeling, "Yes!"

"We wouldn't have Theron."

"Oh," she sobbed, and turned her back on him once again. Weakly, she leaned into the windowsill for support, though she thought nothing was strong enough to hold the heaviness in her heart. He had said "we." He was wrong. He didn't have Theron, she did. She and Seth. Barely above a whisper, she said. "How long are we going to tear at each other this way? Each time we're together, we try our best to bring pain to the other. I surrender. I'm tired of fighting you, Erik."

"I didn't come here to fight." His voice was close behind her, though she hadn't heard his approach.

Blood rushed to Kathleen's head and her eyes closed tightly. "Why did you come after me?"

Erik didn't answer. For the longest time, she stood there, waiting for his answer, but he wouldn't honor her silent plea to hear it. Finally, she turned around to face him, tilting her head back to look up into the face hovering above hers. "Why did you come after me?"

"Because I couldn't let you disappear from my life again. I nearly didn't survive it the first time," he rasped. "I've got to have you in my life, Kathleen."

"I'm married."

"Yes, legally. But that man isn't your true husband." Erik's hands settled lightly but firmly on her shoulders. "Have you and the man you're married to ever had intercourse?"

Then, right then, she should have slapped his face and told him her private life with Seth was none of his business. Instead, Kathleen shook her head. "No."

"Is he the father of your son?" His hands, warm and strong, cupped her cheeks and eased her head backward.

"No," she mouthed as his face descended until his lips rested against hers. He asked huskily, "Who is your husband, Kathleen?"

"You," she groaned softly before his lips claimed hers and she was swept into a captivating embrace. He lifted her off her feet, bringing their bodies as close to each other as clothes would allow.

"Kathleen, kiss me, kiss me," he urged as he raised his lips from hers only long enough to draw breath.

She met his suggestion with abandonment, offering her mouth to the plunder of his and sending her own tongue on wild expeditions. When he finally allowed her feet to touch the floor, he wound his arms around her and pressed her face into his wet shirtfront. "Don't ever leave me again without telling me where you are. I nearly went crazy, Kathleen. God, don't do that to me again." She could feel the expulsion of his breath on each word as he nuzzled her hair.

"No." She shook her head. "I won't." Then her voice changed and she laughed softly. "If you promise me one thing."

He pulled back slightly and looked down at her. "What?"

"That you won't get me all wet the next time you come after me."

He saw that teasing, happy glow in her green eyes, which hadn't been there since he had kissed her and waved goodbye that fateful day more than two years before. The grin he returned was open and carefree, lacking any of the hard cynicism that usually curled his lip into a parody of a smile. "I promise."

He lowered his mouth to hers once again and played upon it. She chased his elusive lips with her own and growled in frustration when they wouldn't be caught. When he raised his head this time, she recognized that devilish gleam in his eyes. "I didn't bring any other clothes. What do you suggest I do?"

"Well," she answered, as if pondering a great problem. "We're probably going to be kissing a lot. And since I don't want to walk around in a wet terry-cloth jumpsuit, I guess the only solution is for you to take off all your clothes."

Erik snapped his fingers and his face brightened. "Now why didn't I think of that?"

She giggled like a young girl. "Why don't you peel them off and I'll get a towel."

He grabbed her arm as she went around him. "One quick kiss before you go."

She obliged him and then went into the bathroom. While she was there, Kathleen quickly sprayed Mitsouko around her shoulders and breasts. It seemed only natural to take off her jump suit. She walked out with the towel in front of her.

Erik was down to his underwear, and then that was no longer a hindrance to his nakedness when he turned around to face her. She caught her breath at the sight of his body. It was magnificent in its strength and hardness.

He came to her slowly, studying her reaction and feeling confident with what he saw in her eyes. When he stood only a breath away from her, Kathleen said, "You are my Danish prince."

"No, that was Hamlet."

She smiled. "He didn't have a thing over you." She lifted the towel to his hair and ruffled through it, though it was almost dried by now. Then she lovingly dabbed the soft cloth to each feature of his face. His shoulders and arms came next, and when the towel was necessarily lowered, she heard him draw in his breath when he saw that she, too, was naked.

She flattened the towel on his chest and rubbed her hands over it to dry him. It was more a caress than a motion of necessity. Her hands moved down over his taut stomach to his abdomen. Kathleen smiled secretly at his disappointment when she removed the towel and draped it across his shoulders. He was compensated by being able to look at her without the screening of the towel.

She took one corner of the towel in each hand and pulled it back and forth across his back, working her way down and at the same time moving closer to him. When she reached the small of his back, Erik held his breath expectantly. His patience was rewarded.

She drew the towel back and forth over his hips as she settled against him. Now it was her turn to open her eyes wide in surprise and gasp in pleasure when she felt the potency of his arousal against her.

"It's your fault," he chided when he sensed her startled reaction. His mustache tickled her ear as he mumbled against it, "You've brought on the ailment, and only you can cure it."

Finished now with games, he put his arms around her and pulled her inexorably against him. His lips covered hers, parting them with his tongue. He nipped her lips gently with his teeth.

Kathleen swayed against him, alive with prickling sensations as every nerve of her body cried out for his touch. The hands that stroked her back and teased her spine were skilled. They cupped her hips and lifted her to meet his passion.

Erik wasted no time. Catching her under the knees and behind her back, he carried her to the waiting bed. He laid her on the pillows and then settled beside her, leaning on one elbow to look down at her.

"Kathleen, don't take me any further if you—"

She placed her fingers against his lips. "Erik, please make love to me. Now."

He reached up and captured the hand caressing the back of his neck and brought its palm to his lips. "I pride myself on my finesse, but I can't wait."

"Neither can I," she whimpered, and moved against him until he had no choice but to stretch his length over her. Her body conformed to his with a silent entreaty, and he filled that aching void deep inside her.

"Sweet . . . !" he grated. "You've always been ready for me, Kathleen. Oh, God, I thought my memory had embellished how good it was with us, but it hadn't. If anything, my love, the memory was diluted." His hands held her face captive as he rained light kisses over it.

She sensed that he was being gentle with her, almost afraid. Staring directly into his cerulean eyes, her lips trembling, she said, "Don't hold anything back, Erik. I want all of you."

"Kathleen, sweetheart . . . precious . . ." His knowledge of her became total. As she arched against each acquainting thrust, they gave their all.

"That's heavenly," she sighed as his strong hands massaged the muscles of her shoulders.

"I thought you'd like this."

"How do you know how to do it so well?"

"Practice." He laughed.

"Oh, you!" she cried, and turned her head to look up at him.

He swatted her playfully on the bottom. "Lie back down or I'm going to stop." The massage had been his idea after they had showered and returned to the bed.

"No, you're not. You like touching me too well."

"Don't get sassy, or I'll have to punish you."

She lifted one curious eyelid while the other was buried in the pillow. "How?" Kathleen asked in an unconcerned drawl.

"Oh, I can think of a lot of diabolical ways. For instance," he said as he moved his hands down her back to her hips, "I may have to get meaner and do this." He was kneeling between her thighs now and kneading the backs of them with competent hands. His fingers teased her mercilessly, not quite touching what she longed to be touched.

"Erik . . ."

"Has the lady learned her lesson?" Erik asked as he lay on top of her and slipped his hands under her to caress the breasts she made available by raising up slightly.

"Yes," she answered languidly. His breath was hot on her skin as he moved her hair aside with his nose and began to nibble her ear.

His hips settled more solidly on hers and she felt the tentative probings of his manhood. "Erik, please."

He kissed her cheek smackingly. "No. I've waited a long time for you, Kathleen." He placed a hand on her shoulder and turned her over. He brushed back the hair from her forehead and smiled at the look of dismay on her face. "Is this the same woman who accused *me* of being naughty? Hm?"

"The very same," she said mischievously, reaching for him.

He dodged her hands. "Behave yourself. Last time we got a little carried away. It went by too fast. I want to take my time. I want to adore you first."

He kissed her. It was a sweet kiss that bloomed into passion and encompassed their entire mouths. It was a kiss of giving and receiving, of teasing and fulfilling, of promising and pledging.

"You always smell so good," Erik whispered as he worried the area under her ear and worked his way around her throat and down her chest.

He raised up and looked in awe at her breasts. His hand settled on one and rubbed it gently in a circular motion. "Raise your arms over your head," he instructed. Kathleen complied and he stared down at the lovely picture she made.

Her hair formed a dark auburn cloud on the white pillow. The perfection of her face was set in that lovely frame. Her skin, the tanned areas contrasting with the paler flesh blocked by her bikini, glowed warmly. Her nipples were proud and inviting crowns.

"You're perfect," he murmured. "Just the right size. Not too large, not too small. Infinitely female." He lowered his head and flicked his tongue over the taut nipples, watching as they enlarged under his attention. "Beautiful," he whispered. Then he closed his mouth around one eager bud and it was cherished in a most gratifying way. His lips trailed to the other breast as he said, "I wish you still had milk. I would have loved to taste it."

Her hands lowered and she wrapped them behind his neck. "I'm sorry you find me lacking."

"I find you lacking in nothing."

His hands wandered over her rib cage and onto her stomach and abdomen. Sensitive fingers fluttered over the auburn delta, fanning it gently, then moved lower to separate, find and please.

A small, satisfied moan issued out of her throat as his lips followed the course charted by his hands. When he knelt between her thighs and lifted her to receive the tribute of his mouth, she offered no resistance. He kissed her into sweet oblivion, deeper and more wonderful than any she had known. With the heat of his mouth, he branded her as his.

Before she was swept away by a floodtide of passion, she clasped his head with her hands and cried, "Erik, not that way. With you."

He raised himself over her and melded his body with hers. He plunged deeply and she closed around him. He stirred, expanded, touched her womb. Withdrawing, he nudged the secret spot with the smooth, glistening tip of his manhood. Then he was within her again, stroking her. The cycle was repeated until Kathleen thought she would dissolve. She heeded his words and didn't hurry it. They had time. Eternity. For surely this was rebirth.

When they finally allowed themselves to succumb, they did so together and became one in body and in spirit.

"I'm starving," Kathleen said from the bed. She was sitting up against the headboard with the sheet pulled up to her chin. Erik was standing at the window watching the clouds as they rolled east over the ocean. The storm was spent and only a remnant of soft rain was left in its wake.

Erik turned and grinned boyishly at her. "It's no wonder. I think we burned up about ten thousand calories since last night."

She blushed prettily. "Well, if one needs to lose a couple of pounds, I can't think of a better way to diet."

"You don't need to lose any. You're too skinny as it is."

"Skinny!" She dropped the sheet as she sat up in indignation. "I'm not skinny."

He looked at her breasts unabashedly. "I'll concede that some parts are more filled out than others."

Kathleen threw a pillow at him, but he deftly caught it before it could do any damage. "I guess you're hoping that I'll chivalrously volunteer to go get us something to eat."

"I think that's the least a gentleman could do. You didn't even buy my dinner."

"My clothes will get wet again," he whined.

"So you'll just have to take them off again. And I couldn't possibly wear clothes and make you feel self-conscious, so I'll just leave mine off, too. But, of course, if you'd rather not . . ."

"I'm going, I'm going," Erik said as he pulled on his semidry jeans and shirt. "I'll be right back. Don't move." He winked as he shut the door behind him.

She moved only enough to rest her forehead on her raised knees. "I won't think about it," she averred to herself. "I won't think about the consequences of this, or anything right now but being with Erik. I love him. Surely I deserve this small time out of my whole life. Don't I? *Don't* I? I won't think about responsibility or loyalty or duty or morality. Tomorrow doesn't exist. Today he's with me, loving me. I refuse to think beyond that. I love him. I love him."

When he returned carrying a sack of groceries, she welcomed him with open arms.

He laughed as he shook water out of his hair and onto her naked skin. "See, you've already broken your promise never to get me wet again."

"I broke it when we got in the shower last night," he teased as he bent to kiss her on the nose. "You weren't complaining then."

"I was being polite," Kathleen said righteously.

"Polite! I've heard of southern hospitality, but, baby—"
She stuck a sweet roll in his mouth to shut him up.

He had bought them doughnuts, fruit, crackers, cheese, potato chips, chocolate bars and a can of tuna—which was useless, since they had no way to open the can. Nevertheless, it was one of the happiest, if one of the most unbalanced, meals that either of them had eaten. They ate it picnic-style on the floor. Erik had changed out of his wet clothes, but they decided to uphold a semblance of civilization and wrap towels around themselves. Erik insisted that it was only fair that hers come no higher than his, so they compromised on the waist-line as the line of demarcation. He did allow her, however, to drop her string of coral beads around her neck. "They hang in such a naughty place," he remarked, tracing the line of beads.

When they had eaten all they wanted, deciding to save the leftovers for later, she reached for a hairbrush. Rising to her knees, she faced him and started raking the brush through his hair.

"I'm glad your hair grew back around your scar," she said as she found the faintly pink line marking the head wound he had suffered in the airplane wreck.

"Yeah. It only took a few weeks once the bandage came off. My hair grows fast."

"It's beautiful," she said musingly.

"You're beautiful."

Kathleen looked down to see that her breasts were directly in front of his face and swaying beguilingly as she used the hairbrush.

"Put that thing down." He captured her wrist, shaking it gently until the brush was dropped to the floor. He placed her arms around his neck, then leaned his head into her chest. She made a low, contented sound in her throat when she felt him blowing on her skin, bringing her nipples to erect attention with his warm breath.

"Touch me," he commanded. "Take me between your hands and feel how much I want you." His breath hissed through his teeth when she did as he asked. "No one else, Kathleen. No one is like you," he vowed. "You've be-witched me, and under your spell, I become stronger than I've ever been and at the same time I tremble with weakness."

She caressed him, and as she did, he felt more of a man than ever before in his life. "Now," he pleaded.

His hands lifted her toward him until he was supporting her on the strength of his thighs. Then he was sheathed in liquid velvet.

"Kathleen." Her name was almost a sob as he clasped her

to him. Gently, almost without passion but with something much stronger, he rocked her against him. Each time she came closer, he went deeper, until only the universe was more secure in itself than they were with each other.

A new feeling welled up inside Kathleen. This was different. She felt a completion that went beyond orgasmic fulfillment. She was Erik; he was her.

When the full impact of the tumult came, she chanted his name. His own hoarse cry was, "You're mine!"

※ ※

"Is there really a dimple under there?" she asked lazily, trailing a finger along his mustache. They lay on the bed facing each other, replete. Only their hands weren't idle as they explored, languishing in the privilege of touching.

"Maybe I should shave that side of it, so you'll know for sure." He captured her finger in his mouth and sucked it gently.

"Don't you dare!" she exclaimed.

A deep laugh rumbled in his chest. "Why not?"

"Two reasons. First, I might think you were extremely ugly without it."

"Thank you. What's the second reason?"

"It feels good," she cooed.

"Oh, yeah?" He raised up on one elbow, his eyebrow cocked suggestively. "Where? Here?" He touched the corner of her mouth with his finger.

"Un-huh." He leaned down and kissed where he had touched.

"Here?" he asked, capturing an impudent nipple between his fingers.

"Un-huh." Like a weapon designed strictly for seduction, the mustache brushed across the tip of her breast.

"Here?"

Her back arched reflexively, lifting her hips off the bed, as he touched her again. "Yes, Erik," she breathed.

He lowered his head. Before the game was over, her body knew well his mastery.

፨ ፨

The rain finally abated late in the afternoon and they walked on the beach hand in hand.

"I understand that on a normal day, when the tide goes out, there is a sandbar several hundred yards from shore," Erik told her. "You can walk out to it. When the tide comes in, it's completely covered up and no one could ever guess it's there."

"It's a lovely island," Kathleen remarked needlessly. Any place would look beautiful to them now.

All day they talked. He told her about quitting his job in St. Louis and going to Europe. He went into more detail about Jaimie's being adopted by Bob and Sally.

"He's like a different kid from the one you knew. He's opened up so much, it's amazing. No one can shut him up. Of course, my mother adores him. Until little Jennifer was born last summer, he was her only grandchild."

Silently, both of them amended that. Theron was her grandchild, too.

"Is she still in Seattle?" Kathleen asked to cover up the uneasy lull in their conversation.

"Yes."

"And Bob and Sally?"

"They live in Tulsa. That's why they were able to get to Fort Smith within hours of the accident. Bob's name was on my identification card as next of kin to notify in case of an emergency. They drove straight to Fort Smith after the doctor called them. Bob is an engineer for an oil company."

They talked about everything but studiously stayed away from the subject of Seth and her marriage. For that day, it didn't exist.

"I've never slept with Tamara," he said when they were sitting in the sand still wet from the rain.

"What?" Kathleen acted as if she hadn't heard him. Then she looked back out to sea. "I never said you had."

He laughed and draped an arm around her shoulders. "But that's what you thought. Give me some credit, Kathleen. Did you really think I'd want a slut like that?" He seemed genuinely dismayed. "Every man from here to Timbuktu has been invited between her legs. I went alone to the beach. She followed me."

"But I saw her come out of the water naked and fall on top of you. She—"

"She got promptly thrown off, too. Only you didn't wait to see that part." When he saw Kathleen's skeptical look, he said, "Oh, I admit, she was after me from the word go, but I never accepted the invitation. In fact, I discouraged it. Subtlety escapes Tamara, and she doesn't take rejection well."

"I wanted to kill her every time she put her hands on you." The green eyes shone with a fierce light.

"You're a little tigress, Kathleen Haley," Erik teased, and neither of them noticed that he hadn't used her married name. "What about all the times you've had your hands on me? Hm?"

"That's different," she defended.

"I'll say it is."

They returned to the bungalow, not trusting the privacy of the beach now that the rain had stopped.

※ ※

"I just called the airstrip. No planes will be flying out tonight, but there'll be one here first thing in the morning." Erik spoke the words mechanically, not allowing his despair to show. He sat on the edge of the bed, staring at the telephone as though he hated it.

"All right," Kathleen said as she came out of the bathroom.

He raised his eyes to hers, then took both her hands and

drew her down on the bed beside him. He memorized each nuance of her face, breathed in the fragrance that belonged only to her. "We have to go home, Kathleen," he said quietly.

She touched his hair, his shaggy brows, his mustache and the lips beneath it. "I know. But not tonight. Tomorrow."

He lay back and pulled her into the curve of his shoulder. His expression was pensive. Strands of her hair were sifted slowly through his fingers.

"What?"

"Hm?"

"What are you thinking?"

He drew a deep breath. "I was thinking a most distressing thought."

She raised up and leaned over him. She had never seen him so introspective, except perhaps the time he had told her about his Ethiopian experience. "What, Erik?"

"It has occurred to me that every time I've been with you, I've come on like a rampaging bull. I've taken advantage of this explosive attraction we have for each other and used it without any tenderness."

"Erik, that attraction is reciprocal. You've never taken more than I've been willing to give."

"Haven't I?" he asked, swinging his legs to the floor and crossing to the window. Kathleen sat up in the middle of the bed, perplexed by this new side of the man she thought she knew well.

"Erik, what is it? What's bothering you?" she asked gently.

He leaned against the windowsill and stared out over the water. "It bothers me to think that you might not know how I feel about you. It bothers me to think that you might justifiably believe that all I care about is your sexuality. I've never told you that there are so many other things . . . Kathleen—" He gestured helplessly, struggling for words. "I find it difficult to convey tender emotions."

"That's not true. You're affectionate with Theron. I remember how you handled the children at the camp. You were—''

"Yes," he cut in impatiently. "Yes, but with you, more often than not, I'm abusive. You, more than anyone, provoke my temper, which I admit is dangerously short. And I don't understand that, because I do care a great deal for you, Kathleen. Some of the things I've said to you, done to you, are . . . there's no word strong enough. Why do I continually wound you the way I do? Almost as if I'm punishing you."

She sat silently, pleating the covers of the bed between trembling fingers. She cleared her throat of the knot suddenly grown there. "Why . . . why do you suppose you can't express your feelings, Erik?"

He pushed away from the window and went to a chair. Falling into it heavily, he stared at the floor between his widespread knees. "My father was a kind man. He never did anything to intentionally hurt anyone. But he never displayed affection either. Never once do I remember him hugging Bob or me. I know he loved Mother, but I never heard him tell her he did. He scoffed at overt shows of affection. He equated tenderness with weakness. I guess I take after him that way. I don't want to. I try to be as physically affectionate with Theron as possible. I don't want him to miss that . . . that fondling." Erik looked up at her then. "I want you to know that, as much as I'm capable, I love you. I'm sorry I can't express it any better than I do. And I need to know that you care at least a little for me," he added gruffly.

"Erik," she whispered. "Erik." Being married to Seth prevented her from verbalizing the love that flooded her whole being, but she could show it to him. Kathleen opened her arms and he came to lie beside her on the bed.

All through the night, she held him.

Chapter Twenty

※ ※

Where the hell have you been?'' Eliot demanded angrily.

Kathleen had just turned the key in the doorknob of her room at West End. She and Erik had made the flight from Chub Cay. Erik was standing behind her and she could feel the scowl forming on his face when he saw Eliot.

"What are you doing here, Eliot?" she asked, stupefied. She hadn't quite assimilated the fact that her idyll with Erik had come to an end. By slow degrees, they had withdrawn from each other as they got closer to Grand Bahama Island. First by not touching, then by not speaking, then by not looking, they had ceased to be that one unit they had formed in the small room on Chub Cay and became two individuals again. Each felt an inevitable wedge being driven between them that neither wanted to accept or cope with. Now Eliot was glaring at her accusingly and looking at Erik as if he would like to kill him.

"I hope you've had a good time, Kathleen," Eliot dripped with sarcasm. "I've been here since yesterday afternoon waiting for you."

"I . . . took some time off. I went to another island. The storm came up. Erik was anxious about me, and when he came—"

"Spare me the titillating details." Eliot shot a venomous look at Erik.

"What was so important that you had to come here without even calling?" Kathleen asked hurriedly.

"Seth's in the hospital," he said succinctly. "He's in ICU. He didn't want you to come rushing home on his account, but George called and told me he thought you should come home right away. Your husband's dying," he said brutally.

Kathleen clamped her hands over her mouth. All the blood drained from her face as she stared at Eliot over the tops of her hands.

"Eliot, you can stop throwing daggers at us. Kathleen didn't know," Erik said with exceptional calm. "Please tell us what's happened."

Eliot stared at them sulkily. For the first time, Kathleen noticed how haggard he looked. His clothes were rumpled and his hair was mussed. He hadn't shaved. She'd never seen Eliot with one thread out of place. "Seth was taken to the hospital three days ago. George told me that when Seth had his accident, his kidneys were irreparably damaged and have been degenerating ever since. He's apparently fought it, but his system is now poisoning itself. He didn't want us to call you, Kathleen. George and I decided otherwise."

She took two steps toward him, her hands extended in a pleading gesture. "Eliot, were you exaggerating? He's not really . . ."

Her voice trailed off and she searched his face for traces of characteristic cynicism. There were none. He looked at Erik, then back to her, and she knew that what he had said was true.

"No," she wailed. "Please, God, no!" She covered her face with her hands and crumpled onto the bed.

"Kathleen." It was Erik's voice. "You haven't got time for that now."

"He's right, Kathleen," Eliot said. "I came down in a chartered jet. We've been waiting for you to come back. We need to return to San Francisco immediately."

"Yes. Okay," she mumbled, and began roaming sightlessly around the room. What was she supposed to do? She couldn't think.

"Leave all this stuff here. I'll have it packed up and sent home," Erik offered. He placed his hands on her shoulders and turned her to face him. "Don't worry about anything. I'll wind things up here and then join you in San Francisco tomorrow morning."

"No!" She jerked away from him. His face registered mute surprise. "I . . . I think it would be best if you stayed here and finished what you were doing. Seth would want that, and I don't think you should be . . . close to . . . at the hospital."

The implication was clear. She didn't want him with her. Her wandering eyes, which refused to look at him, irritated him. He pinched her chin with his thumb and forefinger and turned her face toward him. With steely blue eyes, he looked into the guilt-ridden depths of hers. His mouth went thin with anger. Over her head, he spoke to Eliot. "Take care of her. If there's anything I can do, let me know. We'll cut this short and I'll be back by the day after tomorrow."

"Okay," said Eliot as Erik closed the door behind him. Kathleen sat on the bed again, staring at her hands, her shoulders slumped. She had neither the mental nor physical fortitude to do more than that. She was moving only by commands.

Eliot walked over to her and said, "Kathleen, let's go."

Without carrying more than her purse, she left the room with him. The trip back to San Francisco she never remembered. Kathleen did as she was told, but thought of nothing except her husband lying in a hospital bed in critical condition while she had been loving another man on a tropical island. She deserved to be punished, but why had God selected Seth instead of her? Hadn't Seth suffered enough? Why was he the recipient of the retribution she deserved?

She wanted to go straight from the airport to the hospital, but Eliot refused. "You look like something out of a monster movie, Kathleen. Seth's gravely ill, and your appearance will do nothing to make him feel better. When you go in to see him, you should be looking like the goddess he believes you to be." By his words, Kathleen knew that Eliot didn't think of her as such, but she was too concerned about Seth to care at that moment what Eliot thought of her.

She was glad she had consented to go home first when she looked at herself in the mirror. She did indeed look like something out of a nightmare. Hurriedly, she bathed, washed her hair and twisted it up neatly, and applied a minimum amount of makeup.

Theron, of course, was elated to see her. She hugged him fiercely but played with him only a few minutes. He began to wail mournfully when she gave him back to Alice and left with Eliot. Her son's crying broke her heart, but her first priority now was her husband.

Hazel was standing sentinel outside Seth's ICU. Her expression was venomous as she watched Kathleen approach. "You took your time," she hissed. "Personally, I had hoped never to see you again, but Seth will be delighted that you have arrived in time to watch him die."

"Where is the doctor who's treating him?" Kathleen asked, ignoring Hazel's cruel words.

"He's in there with Seth." She turned her back to Kathleen and moved away.

Kathleen leaned against the wall weakly. Eliot, who hadn't left her side except for the time she was dressing at home, took her hand and squeezed it between his. "I'm sorry," he said. "I acted like a real sonofabitch."

Kathleen smiled up at him. "You acted like the true friend you are." She shut her eyes briefly and said quietly, "Besides, I deserved no lighter judgment."

"Don't be too hard on yourself, Kathleen. You couldn't have known."

"I should have. I sensed something, but when I asked him

about it, he wouldn't tell me.'' She sighed. ''I should have insisted. I should have been here.''

''You're here now. That's the important thing.'' He hesitated a moment before he asked bluntly, ''You're in love with Gudjonsen, aren't you?''

Quickly, she looked up at Eliot. ''How . . . how did you know?''

He smiled. ''When two people conveniently disappear for two days and come back looking as guilty as you two did, it's rather obvious what they've been doing. And as pure of spirit as you are, you couldn't screw . . . pardon me . . . you couldn't make love to someone you weren't in love with. Am I right?''

''Yes, I love him,'' she said softly. ''But I love Seth, too. Only differently, you know?''

Eliot hugged her to him. ''Yeah, I know. Ain't life grand?'' All the bitterness in the world was concentrated into his words.

The door beside them opened and George came out followed by a balding man whom Kathleen assumed was the doctor.

''Hello, Kathleen,'' George said kindly, and took her hand. She wished everyone would stop treating her with such kindness. She didn't feel that her recent behavior warranted it.

''Hello, George.'' She found when she tried to speak that her lips quivered uncontrollably.

''I wanted to tell you months ago,'' George said. ''I urged him to tell you, but he didn't want to worry you. He's been very sick.''

''I know. I thank God he had you to take care of him. He wouldn't let me,'' she said.

''Mrs. Kirchoff, I'm Dr. Alexander. We've spoken on the telephone, but never met. How do you do?'' He made no effort to shake her hand and she didn't offer hers to him.

''Hello, Dr. Alexander. How bad is my husband's condition?'' Where had she acquired that calmness of voice? She didn't feel it inside.

The doctor's eyebrows lowered over his nondescript eyes and he studied his shoes. "I won't pretend that it's anything but critical. He's known for some time that his illness is terminal, but he refused to let me do anything about it."

"*Why?*" she cried. "If there's something—"

"You should discuss this with your husband, Mrs. Kirchoff."

"May I?"

"Only for a short while."

"You said I could go in when you came out," Hazel interrupted from behind the men standing protectively around Kathleen.

Dr. Alexander seemed at a loss for words. "Surely, Ms. Kirchoff, you wouldn't deny your brother a visit with his wife."

"She should have been here instead of lolling around in the Bahamas. Who has been here night and day, waiting, caring . . ." Her voice trailed off into a torrent of sobs that Kathleen knew were affected. To the bitter end, Hazel was going to keep up her act of being the hovering, loving sister. In other circumstances, Kathleen would have gladly scratched out the woman's eyes for being so duplicitous.

The doctor, convinced that Hazel was inconsolable, led her away. Kathleen pushed open the door of the room. To her, it resembled a torture chamber. Machines she could only guess the functions of were beeping with each of Seth's vital signs. It was a macabre decoupage of tubes and needles and bottles.

Only Seth's eyes were familiar as they opened when he heard her approach.

"Kathleen," he croaked, and raised his hand to catch hers. "You're back early. You shouldn't have come back to witness this." His face softened and his mouth worked emotionally before he said, "I'm glad you did, though."

Tears ran unchecked down her cheeks no matter how desperately she tried to stop them. "Seth, Seth, why? Why didn't you tell me?"

"What could you have done? You would have worried and fretted and not done your job at the stores, which are so much more important than I."

"No!" she cried softly. "Nothing is as important."

"Oh, yes, my love. Many things are." He rubbed the back of her hand with his thumb. "You, for instance. And the television commercials. How are things going with them? How is Erik? Is he satisfied with his work down there in the Bahamas?"

She nodded her head impatiently. "Yes, yes, the commercials are going to be beautiful. Just what you wanted. E— Erik is well." She swallowed convulsively. "Seth, I don't want to talk about that. I want to talk about your letting Dr. Alexander help you."

"Kathleen, I don't want to be a burden to anyone any longer. I'm tired of being crippled. If I had a transplant, I might rob a child, or an otherwise healthy person, of a needed kidney. Why should I be that selfish? Even with a new kidney, I'd still be paralyzed. I don't want to go through dialysis for years, because in the long run, the results would be the same." He pressed her hand to his chest and looked deeply into her streaming eyes when he said, "I'm going to be well and whole again very soon, Kathleen. Do you understand what I'm saying? I look forward to it. I want to be well again."

"Seth . . ." She sobbed and fell across him, burying her face in his neck and weeping out her grief and shame and guilt while he comforted her.

🌿❦ 🌿❦

The sun rose and set on another day, but Kathleen was unaware of it. She went home only when forced to eat and bathe and change her clothes. She didn't cry any more during her short visits with Seth. She smiled and looked as pretty as she could, for this was the way he wanted her to be.

Hazel dropped her sweet veneer and acted the harridan

she was. Eliot deemed her a "bloody bitch," and Kathleen concurred. Seth had asked to see his sister only once since Kathleen's arrival, using the time he was allowed visitors to see his wife. The doctor had cut Hazel's visit short, saying, "Good God, woman, now is not the time to discuss business." Kathleen could only guess at what Hazel had been saying to Seth before the doctor interrupted.

George and Eliot were with her constantly. They called the store managers and were assured that the Christmas business was bustling. Kathleen related that to Seth and he smiled, his ravaged face lighting up to some of its former radiance. "Terrific! But I'm not surprised. I've always hired good people."

It was close to midnight when the doctor came out of the room and shut the door softly behind him. Hastily, he stuffed something into his pocket. He stared at the floor before looking up at the young woman who had jumped off the waiting room couch and was approaching him.

"He'd like to see you, Kathleen. He's taken a sedative so he can sleep." The doctor met her eyes levelly. "I think this may be it."

Kathleen sobbed and reached out to grasp George's supportive hand. "No," she whispered.

"She's not going to see him unless I do!" Hazel said shrilly. "I want to see him first and tell him what a whore she is." She turned on Kathleen viciously. "You don't fool me..I know why you wanted to go off to the Bahamas. You wanted to go down there with that photographer. You were probably sleeping with him the whole time. Why did it take that queer," she pointed a finger at Eliot, "who guards you like you were a princess, two days to bring you back? Were you off somewhere with that muscle-bound, yellow-haired ape? My brother's not going to die without my telling him what a tramp he's married to."

"Shut up," Dr. Alexander commanded, finally losing his composure. "If you open your mouth one more time, Ms. Kirchoff, I'll have you evicted from this hospital. I don't give a damn how much money you have. Your brother wants to see his wife and he's going to. You're going to sit down and be quiet or I'll personally throw you out. Do I make myself clear?''

"You sonofabitch! How dare—''

"Yes, I dare,'' said Dr. Alexander as he took her upper arm in an iron grip and began dragging her down the hall.

"You're a whore!'' Hazel screamed as the doctor pulled her after him. "He knew it. Even when he married you, he knew you were a whore. He's weak! Spineless!''

Kathleen covered her ears and turned away.

"Kathleen,'' George said softly, and placed his hand on her shoulder to turn her around. "That is a crazy woman talking and everyone knows it. Seth loves you. Now, dry your eyes and get in there to him where you belong.''

"We'll be right here,'' Eliot said.

She nodded dumbly and dried her eyes on the handkerchief George offered. When she was composed, she went into the dim room. The machines were still beeping. Tiny green and red lights flashed. All else was still.

"Kathleen,'' Seth said weakly.

"Yes, darling.'' She went to him quickly and sat on the edge of his bed, taking his hand in hers.

"Did I hear some commotion outside?''

"S— Someone dropped a tray, I think, and everyone got excited.''

"Are you sure it wasn't a bedpan?'' He laughed pitifully.

She smiled. "Maybe it was.''

"You look beautiful tonight. I always liked you in that color of green.''

"That's why I wore it. I knew you liked it.''

His hand came up to stroke her cheek and then rub a strand of her hair through his fingers. "You're so beautiful.''

"No,'' she said, shaking her head. "No, I'm not.'' She longed to rid her heart of its guilt and tell him just how ugly she was, but she knew that would only add to his torment.

She was helpless to keep the physical pain away, but she wouldn't be responsible for his emotional death as well.

"Yes, you are. You're the most beautiful woman I've ever

seen.'' His eyes closed and he drew a deep, shuddering breath that terrified her. Then he opened his eyes again. ''Kathleen, take care of Hazel for me. She won't have anyone but you and Theron. She'll need you. Help her. She's not strong like you are.''

Kathleen would promise him anything. It was a promise she would never have to keep. Her help would be the last thing Hazel would want. Seth would die still blind to his sister's hatefulness, but Kathleen wouldn't destroy any of his illusions about anyone. ''I will,'' she said. ''I promise.''

He sighed in relief. ''How is Theron?''

''He's wonderful. He said 'puppy' today. Alice told me.''

''He's a wonderful son. I wish I could have seen him one more time.'' He took her hand in his and held it as tightly as his reduced strength would allow. ''He was mine, wasn't he? For the short time I had with him, he was my son.''

''Yes,'' she said on a sob. ''Yes, my beloved, he was yours.''

''I can't tell you how happy the two of you have made me. For the past two years, I've felt like a man again, with a wife and a son. Thank you, Kathleen.''

''Darling, it's you who should be thanked.'' A tear rolled down her face and he caught it on the tip of his finger. ''Seth,'' she pleaded, ''don't leave me. I'll be so alone without you.''

He smiled gently. ''You won't be alone for long.'' Before she could question him on that, he continued. ''If I were whole and strong, I'd fight anything or anyone for you, Kathleen. But I'm not. I'm very tired. Love me enough to let me leave.''

''I do love you, Seth.''

''Stay with me tonight.'' He clutched her hand.

''I will. I'll be right here for as long as you want me.''

''I want you for eternity,'' he whispered, and the beautiful mouth curved into his gentle smile. Once more, he found the strength to touch her cheek. ''Kathleen, you are my dearest, dearest love.'' Then he closed his eyes.

For once, fate favored Seth. He died just as he wanted to—painlessly, in his sleep, taking the vision of Kathleen's face with him.

Erik watched the petite figure as she walked toward the flower-banked casket. She walked unassisted, though George and Eliot were close behind her. Hazel walked beside her, but at a distance.

Chairs had been provided at the gravesite for members of the family. Others stood clustered around, as Erik did, watching the survivors of Seth Kirchoff as they took their seats to listen to the brief words the rabbi would deliver.

She looked thin and pale, Erik thought. Her dress was a simple black sheath, unrelieved by any jewelry. Her hair had been pulled back into a bun at the nape of her neck. She had scorned a hat and veil like the one that swathed Hazel's head.

Kathleen sat down primly, tugged on the bottom of her skirt and straightened her back. Her head was held at a proud angle. Despite the Christmas season, all Kirchoff department stores had been closed today so that Seth's employees could attend his funeral. Kathleen was setting an example for them, Erik knew. Seth would have wanted them to conduct themselves bravely and with dignity.

Theron wasn't with her, of course. Nor was Alice there, which explained who was watching the boy. The eulogy was short and poignant. Immediately, when it was over, Kathleen stood up and greeted those who had converged upon her. With serenity and grace, she shook hands, received kisses on the cheek, comforted those who were reduced to tears. Claire Larchmont, Seth's faithful secretary and friend, was inconsolable.

God, what a woman, Erik thought as he watched Kathleen speaking gently to Claire. What a courageous little soldier. She was so beautiful. She had left a mark on him as permanent as a birthmark. He would never be rid of her. It would take time, he knew. But now there was no reason they couldn't be together. Her, himself and their son. He wanted that more than anything.

For the rest of his life, he would be grateful to Seth for taking care of them for him. Few men would have done that so lovingly and unselfishly. Above all, and in spite of everything, Seth Kirchoff had been an admirable man. Erik regretted not getting back from his trip in time to tell Seth how much he thought of him. Brief though their friendship had been, he would miss Seth.

The crowd was beginning to thin. Unnoticed, Erik moved closer. Only a few stragglers were speaking to her now. He watched Hazel as she walked up to her sister-in-law. Something about that woman had always disturbed him. From beneath the heavy veil, he heard her speak to Kathleen.

"You play the grieving widow very well, Kathleen. Wouldn't people be surprised to know what you're really like?"

Erik's eyebrows drew together in puzzlement. He hadn't known the other woman was openly hostile to Kathleen.

Kathleen sighed resignedly. "Hazel, can't we please bury the hatchet along with Seth?"

"Shut up and listen to me. My brother was a simpleminded idiot to ever bring you into our lives, but I've tolerated you for as long as I intend to. I want you and your bastard out of my house and out of my life. Do you understand?"

Erik saw Kathleen stiffen defensively. "You tried to threaten me once before. Remember the swimming pool?" Kathleen asked. "What I told you then still holds. I want no part of your life, Hazel. And as soon as the will is probated, I'll arrange to live elsewhere. In the meantime, you stay away from me and from my son. If you so much as come near him, you'll pay the consequences."

The older woman was quaking with rage. The veil covering her face trembled. She turned on her heels and stamped toward the waiting limousine.

Kathleen's chest expanded as she drew in great gulps of air. She shook her head when George tried to take hold of her arm. "Are you all right, Kathleen?" Erik heard him ask her.

"Yes, I'm fine."

Erik couldn't believe what he'd just heard. The swimming pool and Theron. Hazel had been . . . God! His musing pinpointed to one chilling conclusion. Hazel was obviously deranged.

Kathleen was at her mercy. And Theron. He moved from his place under the temporary canopy and came up behind her. She seemed so small, frail and helpless. He wanted to take her in his arms, lend her his strength and comfort, tell her that everything would be all right. They would be together soon.

Instead, he only spoke her name.

She pulled herself up abruptly. That voice. The one that she loved. He spoke her name like no one else. She was ready to fall into his arms and beg never to be released.

She steeled herself against the emotion that engulfed her. She was Seth Kirchoff's widow and she would act accordingly. More than anything in the world, she wanted Erik, wanted to be with him, but she couldn't have him after all that had happened.

At first she had felt that Seth's death was her punishment for her adultery. That, she realized, was ridiculous. Seth had been sick long before Erik had come to San Francisco. Seth would have understood and condoned their loving. He would have forgiven her the most unforgivable transgression, but she could never forgive herself.

She loved Erik. She always would. But she wouldn't allow herself the luxury of having him. She wanted his love, but his only claim to loving her had been qualified. She wanted security with him and Theron, but she didn't feel that it was their destiny. Why had so many roadblocks been thrown in their path if they were meant to be together? Too much anguish, too much pain, had been suffered for her loving Erik. The price it exacted was too high. She could no longer pay it.

Hard as it was to do, she turned around to face him, ordering her control not to slip. "Hello, Erik. Thank you for coming," she said by rote. She didn't meet his eyes, but talked to the knot of his necktie.

"I wanted to be here, with you," he said, and she caught the hidden emphasis on the last two words. "What can I do to help you?" he asked softly.

"Nothing," she said waspishly. Immediately, she saw the stark realization enter his eyes. He knew she was shutting him out. His mustache twitched with a grimace of internal pain. She couldn't afford to spare him. She had to be merciless. "Everything has been seen to. I have George and Alice to help me. Eliot will take care of things at the store until I decide what to do."

"Kathleen . . ."

His voice had an undercurrent of pleading in it, and she rushed on. "As soon as you've produced the commercials, Eliot will view them."

"I'm not here to discuss the goddam commercials," he said with ominous softness. "I'm here to talk about you. And me. About what happened between us a long time ago and most recently on Chub Cay."

She shot an embarrassed look toward George and Eliot, but they were engaged in their own quiet conversation.

"There is nothing to discuss, Erik," she said casually. "I doubt that I'll be seeing much of you. I plan to take an extended rest. Goodbye."

She turned away from him and took half a step before he brought her around. "Okay, Kathleen, deny us a life together, which I know you want as much as I do, but you won't keep my son from me. For months, I've been looking for a good excuse to take him from you. Now I have one." He glanced meaningfully toward the limousine where Hazel was ensconced, and Kathleen knew he had heard the threats. "I don't think I need to elaborate."

She clutched at his arm. Her lips were bloodless as she choked, "No, Erik, you wouldn't."

"Wouldn't I? What have I got to lose by trying?"

He fairly spat the words as he shoved her away from him and then strode toward his car. The trio stood looking after him, stunned. Erik didn't look back, or he would have seen the young woman in black slump to the ground in a faint.

Chapter Twenty-one
꙰ ꙰

Kathleen watched as Theron forsook the toy train for the brightly colored box it had come in. He sat amid the paper and ribbons of his opened Christmas packages at the foot of the decorated tree. Alice and George had insisted that the boy celebrate a real Christmas despite Seth's death.

The two weeks since his funeral had been painful ones for Kathleen, but she had survived them. She had been insulated from some of the grim chores. George handled everything. Hazel refused to even go near her brother's rooms.

Hazel. She was a constant source of antipathy to Kathleen. The woman so burned with hatred that it consumed her, decaying her from within. She went to her office every day, wreaking havoc where she could. The distressed store managers called Kathleen asking for guidance on how to deal with her unreasonable directives. Kathleen soothed them as well as she could, telling them that Hazel was pressured by grief and persuading them to treat her with forebearance. She knew they weren't convinced, but they were too polite to contradict her in deference to her husband's recent death.

Kathleen didn't return to work. She spent her days with

Theron, whom she felt she had neglected for the past month. He didn't seem to have suffered unduly. He was as sturdy and energetic as ever.

She smiled as Alice opened the cashmere sweater Kathleen had given her. Alice's face lit up with surprise and delight. George was equally excited over the tweed hat that was found in his package. They hadn't given Kathleen anything and she hadn't expected it. Alice came to her now and kissed her lightly on the cheek.

"I'm cooking you a traditional Christmas dinner, Kathleen. And I'm going to see to it personally that you eat every bite. George has picked out a fine wine we can drink with it."

Kathleen patted Alice's hand. "Thank you. That sounds lovely. Can I help?"

"No, ma'am. You sit right here and play with Theron." She hedged before she said softly, "He has another present that was delivered yesterday. Aren't you going to let him open it?"

"Yes," Kathleen sighed. "I suppose so."

The box stood under the tree against the wall, and try as she might, she couldn't ignore it. He was Theron's father, after all. It was only natural that he'd send his son a Christmas gift.

That she knew. It was what she didn't know that bothered her. What did Erik intend to do about his son? The angry, resolute set on his features and that last dire warning he had slung at her at the cemetery had haunted her day and night. He had refrained from claiming his son for Seth's sake. Now that Seth was gone, nothing stood in his way. Since he knew of Hazel's overt hatred for the boy, he might well convince himself that he was acting in the child's interest by getting him out of harm's way.

"Theron," Kathleen called to her son, who was now chewing on a ribbon. "Come here. You have another present." She took his hand and he toddled after her to the large, gift-wrapped box. "Do you want me to help you?" she asked. "Apparently not," she replied wryly when he began ripping off the paper with maniacal zeal. He had exhibited an amazing acumen for opening presents.

"Oh, my goodness!" Kathleen laughed in spite of herself when she read the printing on the box. "He's crazy."

The box did indeed contain a bright red tricycle, complete with bells, police decals, shiny lights and a siren that wailed at one push of a button. Kathleen tried it and the sound shattered the relative peace. Alice and George came running.

Both of them clapped their hands and started laughing at Theron's perplexed look. George lifted the boy onto the black vinyl seat. His chubby legs weren't quite long enough for his feet to reach the pedals, but he grinned proudly. Only recently had another physical trait he had inherited from Erik been made manifest. He had a dimple in the exact spot as his father's.

"Erik must be out of his mind," Kathleen said, laughing. The older couple looked at her quickly. Did she realize that she had mentioned the man's name? She did, and flushed hotly. The name that was never far from her mind had finally been vocalized. She often wondered if they suspected the nature of her relationship with Erik. George had heard Hazel's tirade in the hospital corridor. Surely he had told his wife about that scene. Theron looked like Erik more and more. Did they know? From their attitude, she couldn't tell. They treated her with the respect and friendliness that they always had.

"Theron'll grow into this in no time," George said. "Maybe Erik will come over and teach him how to ride it."

"Ric, Ric," Theron crowed as he pushed the button for the siren.

"Maybe so," Kathleen mumbled, then busily began gathering up the discarded paper.

After the huge turkey dinner she shared with George, Alice and Theron in the breakfast room, Kathleen retired to the living room to look at the Christmas tree and nurse a second glass of wine. Hazel had taken her dinner in the dining room all alone. What a pitiable woman she was, Kathleen thought.

The lights on the tree blurred through her tears as a wave of homesickness worse than any she had known before swept over her. Where was her home? She had Theron, but this wasn't their home. This house was Hazel's and always would be. As soon as the will was probated, Kathleen intended to take Theron away from here, even if Hazel hadn't issued the ultimatum. But where would she go? Where was home? Who was home? Erik . . .

I wonder whom he's spending Christmas with, she thought with a stab of pain. Is he sharing wine in front of his fireplace with a woman? Cuddling her? Kissing her? Saying—?

Stop! She couldn't think of that. If she thought about Erik, she would go mad. And if she didn't think about him, she would die.

She had to talk to someone. She picked up the telephone and called the only family she had. "Edna, Merry Christmas!"

"Kathleen! Dear, it's so good to hear from you. B. J., turn off that ball game and pick up the extension. It's Kathleen."

"Hi there, sweetheart," B. J. boomed into her ear as he picked up the second phone.

Their voices sounded so good to her, a balm to her wounds. It was the best Christmas present she could have asked for. "First of all, thank you for the flowers you sent to Seth's funeral. I've written you a note, but they're not all mailed yet."

"Honey, you know we don't want any thanks. If we could have, we would have come out there to be with you."

"I know. I understand. It's so good to hear your voices."

"Kathleen," Edna said. "How are you? How's the baby? Are you all right?"

Their love reached through the wires and touched her, opening a floodgate of emotion that she had kept safely dammed. She poured out the entire story, starting with the day she had taken Erik to the airport in Fort Smith. "Theron is Erik's baby," she admitted softly.

"Kathleen, do you think we're so old and feeble that we

couldn't figure that out?'' B. J. asked. "We've known all along who that baby's daddy is. Does *Erik* know it?''

"Yes,'' she said calmly, then launched into the other half of her story, telling them of his reappearance in her life, their subsequent antagonism and then the days in Chub Cay. "I can't stop loving him. I slept with him, and when I came back, Seth was dying.'' She broke off with heartrending sobs that anguished the two people listening to them.

"Kathleen, you poor baby,'' Edna said, and Kathleen heard the tears cracking the older woman's voice.

"You and that young man have been fighting tooth and nail since you first laid eyes on each other. Why don't you just tell him how you feel?'' B. J. asked.

"Because I'm not sure he loves me. All he wants is Theron, and I'm afraid he's going to take him away from me. Not that I'll let him without a fight, but he could make life miserable for a long time.''

"That's a pile of crap if I ever heard one,'' B. J. said.

"Kathleen, that's nonsense. You didn't see him when he came looking for you after his accident. I've never seen a man so in love, sick with it.''

Kathleen shook her head sadly. "No. He was only angry that I'd run out on him.''

"He won't do anything to hurt you or that boy,'' B. J. said. "I'm too good a judge of human nature not to know that.''

"You don't know him now. He's different from the way he was at Mountain View. He's . . . callous . . . hard.''

"I wonder what would turn a man like that?'' Edna asked, her meaning implicitly clear.

Kathleen changed the subject and told them about Theron's latest exploits. "I hope you can come out and see him soon. You'll love him.''

"We already do,'' B. J. said.

Just before hanging up, Edna said, "Why don't you and Theron fly down here to see us? He could play in the woods. It would do you good.''

"I'd like to, but I don't know when I can. Things are rather unsettled just now. Let me see what's going to happen."

She didn't have long to wait. Two weeks into the new year, the Kirchoffs' lawyer called Kathleen and Hazel to his office and read them Seth's will. Its contents surprised them both.

Unknown to everyone except himself, his attorney, and the purchaser, Seth had sold the Kirchoff stores to a larger department store chain. Conditions of the sale were that his sister hold a position on their board of directors for as long as she wanted and that the name of the stores remain Kirchoff's for the rest of her life. Kathleen was to remain in her present position for as long as she wished. She didn't interrupt the lawyer's sonorous voice to reveal her plans in that area of her life.

The house was also left to Hazel, as was the majority of Seth's estate. Kathleen was bequeathed an amount which seemed immense to her, but was actually modest when one measured Seth's wealth. He had also left her a country house in the Napa Valley north of San Francisco. He had never even mentioned the property to her, although the attorney told her Seth had purchased it over a year ago.

Hazel was enraged to find that her brother had sold the stores out from under her, but was victorious, she felt, over Kathleen. There had been no mention of Theron in Seth's will, a surprise to Kathleen, a source of celebration for Hazel. Her share of Seth's estate outweighed Kathleen's many times over.

"You and your brat will be out of my house within a week," Hazel said as they left the attorney's office. "I never want to see you again if at all possible."

Kathleen didn't honor her with a comment, though Hazel's eviction was a welcome relief. She didn't want to spend one unnecessary night in that house. What would Hazel's reaction be should Kathleen tell her who Theron's father was? As

cunning as she was, why had Hazel never guessed? Kathleen
had often feared that her sister-in-law would recognize one
of Erik's traits in the boy. But she wasn't searching for clues
to his parentage. It was his and Kathleen's mere existence
that was the bane of her life, not where they had come from.
Had Hazel been less intent on sabotaging Kathleen's work
and causing friction between her and Seth, Hazel's eyes might
have been opened to the one trump card that could have truly
beaten her nemesis. She had been holding an ace and hadn't
realized it. Now it was too late. The game was over.

Kathleen looked into Hazel's pinched, triumphant, gloating
face and was almost tempted to tell her everything. But what
purpose would that serve? Hazel had no bearing on her future
now.

George drove Kathleen to the Napa Valley house Seth had
willed her, and she was delighted with it. One look at the old
brick house, fashioned after the chateaux of France, convinced her that this is where she wanted to live with Theron.

The realtor from whom Seth had bought the property
met her there to show her around. The house had been
modernized only a few years before, but still retained old-
world charm, having interesting nooks and crannies hidden
in its intricate maze of rooms. Furnishings had been purchased with the house. It would only require a thorough
cleaning and some of Kathleen's personal touches to get it
ready for occupancy.

The attached winery had been deserted years ago, and the
vines had been neglected, but she wasn't worried about that
for the present. With the money left her by Seth and the salary
she had saved over the past two years, she had enough money
for her and Theron to live quite well for several years. She
would worry about what to do with the rest of her life later.
Right now, she just wanted to live in peace.

As George was helping her back into the Mercedes, he
remarked casually, "I think Alice is going to love it here.
That little apartment on the far side of the kitchen has a nice
view of the vineyards."

"George!" She whirled around in surprise. "You mean that you and Alice want to come out here to live with me?"

"If you'll have us."

"Of course, I'll have you." She laughed. "It's just that I thought you'd stay with Hazel."

He shook his head. "Kathleen, it was Seth who hired us. We worked for him. Since he's gone, we work for you. I'll maintain the house, the grounds, the cars, and do anything else you want me to, but I don't want you to pay me. Two or three mornings a week, I'd like to go into the city and work as a volunteer at a rehabilitation center for the paraplegic."

"That's wonderful."

"I was wondering what you planned to do with Seth's van. I—"

"You may have it to use or give away as you see fit."

"Thank you. With your permission, I'd like to work on the vines. I've always had a hankering for wine, you know, and I've been reading up on it for years. I think with a little luck, I could make a go of a small vineyard and winery."

"Yes, yes. Thank you, George." Impulsively, she threw her arms around him and hugged him. "I need you and Alice now more than ever. I'll pay her a housekeeper's salary. I insist," Kathleen said when she saw he was about to object. "And I demand the right to sample every bottle of wine."

"You've got it," he said, and offered her his hand to shake, sealing their agreement.

A few days later, Kathleen met with the new owner of Kirchoff's and politely resigned her job.

"You don't have to," he told her. "We know your capabilities. Your husband credited you with the turnaround Kirchoff's made a couple of years ago. We'd like very much for you to stay on."

"Thank you, but I feel that I must do this." She knew that the heart of Kirchoff's had been Seth. When he died, the heart went out of it, and she didn't want to pretend otherwise.

"I would, however, like to recommend my assistant for the position. Eliot Pate is a gifted young man who knows as much about my job as I do."

"Kathleen, thank you, my darling! I just got a call from our new owner and they want me to assume the job you so stupidly resigned." Eliot sounded as if he were on cloud nine.

"It wasn't stupid. I have a little boy to raise, you know. You deserve the job, Eliot. I envy you the exciting things that will happen to you over the next few years."

"You can always come back and help me," he offered.

"I may drop in to look over your shoulder sometime."

"You have an open invitation. There's one job I hope you won't dump in my lap."

"What?"

"Those goddam fashion shows. Kathleen, I have no patience with those bullies who run lights and the bitches who arrange for flowers. Would you please do those for me? At least for a year? *Please?*"

She laughed. "Okay, okay. How could I refuse?"

"Wonderful!" He paused a moment, then said, "Kathleen, I think Gudjonsen is tops. Have you seen those commercials? The new owners are turning handsprings. Erik's not only talented, he's a helluva guy. He's been working like hell . . ." He cleared his throat and Kathleen smiled. She'd never known Eliot to be at a loss for words. "What I'm saying is that if the two of you have a . . . thing . . . you should tell the rest of the world to go—"

"Thank you, Eliot," she said quickly. "I'll keep that in mind, but Erik and I don't have a 'thing.' "

"I wouldn't stake tomorrow's martini lunch on that, but you've always been so goddam closed-mouthed about your private affairs."

"And you've always been outrageous, but I love you. Call me."

"I will, probably screaming for you to come back and relieve me of all this." They laughed together, and then he said in a rare serious tone, "Be happy, Kathleen."

She was happy. Or at least content. She, Theron, George and Alice were settled into their new home, and she barely missed the bustle of the store. She was entranced with the house and her plans to fully decorate it.

February was well upon them. When it snowed in the mountains of Oregon and Washington, it rained a cold rain in the valley. On one such day, Kathleen was sitting alone in the homey living room. A bright fire crackled in the hearth. Theron was upstairs asleep. He had had a cold for the last few days and was now, under medication from the pediatrician, sleeping it away. The Martins had gone into San Francisco for the day to do some extensive shopping for the country kitchen.

When Kathleen heard the car motor, she didn't think they could already be back, so she got up to look out the window.

Her heart danced and then jumped to her throat as she saw the battered blue Dodge van chugging up the pothole-riddled driveway. She mouthed his name, but no sound came out. Instinctively, she clutched her chest in an effort to still the pounding of her heart.

By now, he was on the porch and pulling the old-fashioned bell. Kathleen went to the door and opened it without hesitation.

For a small eternity, they stared at each other, hungry eyes combating to gain the most ground. Without speaking, he walked in. He shook off his rain-dampened coat and hung it on the halltree beside the door. With his back to her, he surveyed the room. His head nodded in silent approval.

"Hello, Kathleen." He turned around to face her.

"Hello, Erik," she grated hoarsely. Why couldn't she

speak? She was a bundle of nerves. Was he here to make some threat about Theron? Would he overpower her and take him by force?

"Where's Theron?" he asked, as if reading her mind.

"Upstairs asleep," she said guardedly.

Erik only nodded absently. "The house is nice, very nice. Do you like it?"

Was it her imagination, or was he as nervous as she? "Yes, I love it. It's quiet here."

Without invitation, he sat on the sofa in front of the fire and stared into it for a moment. Then he looked up as though surprised to find her still standing. "Sit down."

She didn't move. "What are you doing here, Erik?"

He continued to look up at her as he withdrew an envelope from the breast pocket of his shirt. Handing it to her, he said, "I received that in the mail three days ago. It's from Seth's attorney. He was instructed to mail it to me on a specified day. Dr. Alexander had gotten it from Seth the night he died."

Kathleen wanted to ask him what all of that meant, but he was staring moodily into the fire again. She looked down at the envelope. It was innocuous enough, having as its letterhead the name and address of the law firm. She opened it and pulled out two sheets of paper. One was a contract for the loan Seth had made to Erik's new company. It had been rubber-stamped "Paid in Full" in red ink.

The other sheet of paper was filled with Seth's handwriting, not as legible or firm as it usually was, but identifiable just the same. It was dated the night before he had died.

Dear Erik,

My attorney will confirm that there is a secret trust fund in the Bank of America for Theron. You will find that it is a sizable amount and, hopefully, will grow even greater with accrued interest, so that by the time he's ready to enter whatever field he chooses, he will be well equipped financially. The contingency of his receiving said funds on his twenty-fifth birthday are somewhat odd. It is my last wish that you will see they are met.

By his second birthday, April fifteenth of this year, I ask that his name be legally changed to Gudjonsen. It is my belief that a son should bear his father's name. Thank you for loaning him to me for a short while. My gratitude is exceeded only by the love I have for him and his mother. I would also hope that she be included in that name change. It should have been hers long ago.

I considered you a friend in life. So do I still.

Seth

Kathleen lowered the paper before her tears could blur the ink. "He knew."

Erik stirred, though he didn't look at her. "It would seem so."

She dropped down onto the couch beside him. "I should have known that he would. Seth was so perceptive, so attuned to emotions. He would have seen, would have guessed." They were silent again. She looked up at Erik timidly. "What are you going to do?"

He raked a hand through his hair and stood up, crossing to the fireplace. His booted toe moved a log closer to the flames, and sparks shot up the chimney. "Hell, I don't know," he said on a deep sigh. "I've spent these past two days deliberating what to do. I started to ignore it, but the attorney called to verify that I had received the letter and to inform me that he had a copy of it." He braced his arms wide on the mantel and hung his head between them in an attitude of abject despair. "We could contest the will, but . . ." He spoke without conviction. He wanted that hassle no more than she did. "How can I deny my son that kind of opportunity, Kathleen?"

"I don't suppose you can," she answered quietly, not wanting any part of the decision only he could make.

"Of course," he reasoned aloud, "his receiving the money is contingent only on his name being changed, not yours."

Pain ripped through her and tore at her heart. How could he be so cruel? He didn't want to be stuck with her as his wife, but he wanted to change his son's name. He had to wrestle with his conscience and go against Seth's request, and hope that she wasn't going to make things difficult for him.

"Yes," she strangled out.

"I had hoped that one day your name would be the same as mine." He turned around. "But I want you to marry me because you love me as much as I love you, and not for the sake of our son."

Kathleen continued to stare at her hands lying in her lap, disbelieving what she had just heard. Her reflex was to snap her head up and look at him, but she was afraid she was mistaken. Instead, she squeezed her eyes shut and prayed that Erik had said what she thought he had.

"Kathleen," he said unevenly. Now she did raise her eyes, and saw two eloquent, glistening tears rolling down his lean, rough cheeks. "Don't run away from me again. You've always accused me of being selfish, and God knows I am. But I'm going to make the most selfish request of my life now." He swallowed hard. "If you must, marry me only because of Theron and in accordance with Seth's letter, but please marry me. You don't . . . it can be . . . we don't even have to sleep together, just, please, marry me."

"Erik!" She bounded off the couch and threw herself into his arms. At first he was too incredulous at her reaction to respond, but her warmth and softness against him soon overcame his stupefaction. His arms wrapped around her as he buried his tear-dampened face in the hollow of her neck.

"Erik, didn't you know I loved you? Couldn't you tell how much I loved you?"

"No, no," he said as he dried his tears with her hair. "Every time I was near you, with you, you ran from me afterward."

"Because of my feelings for you. They were so much a part of me that I thought they were visible to everyone. Darling, I have loved you since Mountain View. Seth knew when I married him that I was still in love with my baby's father. I never kept that a secret from him."

Erik straightened so he could look down into her face. He brushed back her hair. "I have loved you for so long. There was always something in the way, something between us. I can't believe that you're here now telling me you love me."

"I am and I do."

"Why did I fight loving you? And that's what I've done, Kathleen. I've fought it. You evoked emotions in me no one else ever had, and they frightened me, left me stripped bare and vulnerable. I was terrified I'd be left empty again like I was after the accident."

She shuddered and closed her arms tighter around him. "I'm so sorry for the anguish I caused you then."

"Darling, if we start itemizing the times we've hurt each other, my list will be much longer than yours. That part of our life is over. I love you. Perhaps because of the example I was set, I grew up thinking that loving was a sign of weakness. I know now it's a sign of strength. But I'm not strong enough yet to contain it all. I need you, Kathleen. Love me."

"My love," she sobbed. Together they collapsed onto the couch, holding, touching, cherishing, assuring each other with precious words and gestures.

Each gave what the other needed . . . and more.

❧ ❧

"I like this house," Erik said. They were lying in her bed. Eventually, they had quitted the sofa, dressed and shared supper with Theron, who was ecstatic over seeing "Ric." They had bathed the baby together, marveling over him, and played with him until he grew sleepy and had to be put to bed. Now Kathleen lay cuddled against the hard, vibrant body that she loved.

"Thank you," she said softly, contemplatively. She teased the underside of his arm with wandering fingers. "But, you know, it's inconvenient to the city. I mean," she rushed on, "it would be a great place to come to on weekends, but I'd rather live closer in. Like in that condo you have," she said tentatively.

Erik reached down and lifted her chin until he could see her face. He studied it for a while, and then he said gently, "You're something. Do you know that? I could never ask you to give this up and come to my much more modest house."

"I know you couldn't, but I want to live there. This can be a retreat for us, but I want to finish decorating your house and live there with you and Theron." She looked up at him alluringly. "I can't wait to get you in that hot tub."

He grinned responsively, but was serious when he said, "I'm still struggling to get my business off the ground. Every cent I've got is invested in it. I won't be able to keep you in the lifestyle to which you've become accustomed."

"I never cared for that. I wondered why Seth didn't bequeath me the majority of his estate. Now I know. He knew I'd be uncomfortable with it."

"He knew *I* would be." He kissed her forehead and played his fingers across her lips. "I love you, Kathleen."

She raised up on her elbows and said, "I love you, Erik. More than any house. More than an inheritance. More than anything. I'll never run away from you again. You're my security, my home, my life. Believe me, I've learned that running away never solves anything. It only prolongs it. Had I not been orphaned at the age I was, maybe I wouldn't have been so afraid of life's consequences. Intelligently, I knew better than to duck the issues, but sometimes emotions override intelligence."

"Did you ever wonder why we were put through this? Why we couldn't have met at Mountain View, fallen in love and *admitted* it, gotten married, started our family without having fought so damn hard for it all?"

Kathleen pondered his question at length before she attempted an answer. "I don't think either of us was mature enough to accept the responsibility of that kind of relationship when we met. We weren't capable of making the commitment, because we were each so wrapped up with ourselves. The life, the happiness, we'll know now has more value, because it was so hard to come by. And we wouldn't have known Seth. I think we both learned what it really means to love from him."

Erik was quiet for a full minute before he said, "You're too young to be that wise."

"That's just what a woman who is lying naked with her lover wants to hear—how wise she is."

He laughed. "Let's bring Theron in here to sleep with us tonight."

"Okay, but later. I'm selfish and want you all to myself for a while longer."

"I think I can suffer through that."

She kissed him, and as with all their kisses, what had been intended as a brief caress became one of passion. Finally, she dragged her mouth from his. "When will you marry me? Tomorrow?"

He stretched lazily and said, "Gee, I don't know." His eyes rested on her breasts as he drawled, "I may not respect you in the morning."

Kathleen's green eyes narrowed and she slipped her hand down his body. "It's not your respect I want right now." His breath was sucked in quickly as she found her target.

"Perhaps we . . . Perhaps we should set the date after all . . . ah, Kathleen."

"Do you know what I'd like?"

"No, but it's yours," he said breathlessly. "Anything, darling, anything."

She chuckled and continued her sweet torture. "I'd like for all of us to go to Arkansas and get married in the chapel at Mountain View. I want B. J. and Edna to be included. We could invite your mother, Bob and Sally, Jaimie and Jennifer,

George and Alice, maybe even Eliot would come. And, of course, Theron will be there."

"Right now," Erik ground out, "I'd agree to . . . to anything."

She draped his chest with her hair and leaned over him, brushing her lips across the flat brown nipples as she asked, "Do you love me?"

"Yes. God, yes."

Her tongue flicked over him and he moaned in ecstasy.

"Tell me," Kathleen insisted, her mouth now teasing his lips.

He caught her hand with his and pressed it against him. His blue eyes pierced through the darkness like a beacon and captured her in their magnetic light. "Yes. With my heart, with my life, I love you, Kathleen." He lay atop her, gathering her to him and relishing her nakedness. His lips kissed her while his hands stroked the silkiness beneath them.

"See how right we are, Kathleen." Her eyes followed his down the length of their bodies lying entwined. He straightened his arms, levering himself up so they could see his virility nestled in her receiving warmth. Lifting his eyes to hers, he nudged her provocatively. "Touch me. Please."

She lowered her hand between them and closed her fingers around him. The smooth, love-bathed tip knew the brush of her thumb. "I love you, Erik."

"I love you."

As they watched, his body was fused with hers. Their loving knew no bounds, but it was far more than physical. This time, it was made complete by the knowledge of the other's commitment. Not only their bodies, but their spirits as well, were forged by a conflagration that burned in a timeless sphere.

George opened the door quietly and peered around it. "They're all in there, all right," he told a curious Alice who was trying to see over her husband's shoulder. "Snug as three bugs in a rug, all in the same bed and apparently naked as jaybirds." He chuckled. That earned him a slap on his arm.

The three people lying in the bed were unaware of their audience. They all slept facing the same direction. Erik's arm was stretched across Kathleen and his hand rested on the shoulder of his son, who was curled up against his mother.

"They belong together like that," Alice whispered as George shut the door.

"Yes, they do. Indeed."

By the year 2000, 2 out of 3 Americans could be illiterate.

It's true.

Today, 75 million adults... about one American in three, can't read adequately. And by the year 2000, U.S. News & World Report envisions an America with a literacy rate of only 30%.

Before that America comes to be, you can stop it... by joining the fight against illiteracy today.

Call the Coalition for Literacy at toll-free **1-800-228-8813** and volunteer.

Volunteer Against Illiteracy. The only degree you need is a degree of caring.

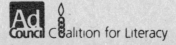

Ad Council Coalition for Literacy